RIVEN

**Center Point
Large Print**

**This Large Print Book carries the
Seal of Approval of N.A.V.H.**

RIVEN

JERRY B. JENKINS

CENTER POINT PUBLISHING
THORNDIKE, MAINE

This Center Point Large Print edition is published in the year 2008 by arrangement with Tyndale House Publishers, Inc.

The text of this Large Print edition is unabridged. In other aspects, this book may vary from the original edition. Printed in the United States of America. Set in 16-point Times New Roman type.

ISBN: 978-1-60285-282-2

Library of Congress Cataloging-in-Publication Data

Jenkins, Jerry B.
    Riven / Jerry B. Jenkins.--Center Point large print ed.
    p. cm.
    ISBN: 978-1-60285-282-2 (lib. bdg. : alk. paper)
    1. Large type books. I. Title.

PS3560.E485R57 2008b
813'.54--dc22

2008025431

To Steve Musick

Let the water and the blood,
From Your riven side which flowed,
Be of sin the double cure,
Save from wrath and make me pure.
—FROM "ROCK OF AGES"

AUTHOR'S NOTE

This is the novel I have always wanted to write.

I determine whether a novel idea has merit by how long it stays with me. Do I find myself telling the story to my wife and other confidants? Is it the type of tale that will draw me back to the keyboard every day?

Two-thirds of my published books have been novels, and only three have had that effect on me. Oh, I give my all to every one, but special joy and anticipation attend those that genuinely feel like the best ideas.

In your hands lies my fourth such labor of love.

The two main characters have remained in my memory since high school forty years ago. The story idea is perhaps twenty years old. And those mystical, interweaving elements I hope make it all work have been tugging at me for more than a decade.

If a novelist has a life's work, this is mine. I hope in the end you agree and that *Riven* stays with you long after the final page.

JERRY B. JENKINS
COLORADO

RIVEN

CHRISTUS
Heri, Hodie, Semper

Heinous as any murder can be, the crime is not the story here.

Rather, along with many other elements—seemingly unrelated at first blush—the crime serves as mere impetus to what really happened. And that proved unforgettable to any old enough to remember.

The unnamed state in which these events occurred had for nearly two centuries flaunted its renegade spirit, thumbing its nose at Washington. A succession of maverick governors, including one who engineered the state's four-year secession during the Civil War, had served to fashion the commonwealth into a virtual landlocked island unto itself. Only Louisiana rivaled its no-nonsense prisons, only Texas its record on capital punishment.

The state's leaders and citizens were as proud of their tough-on-crime reputation as they were of the state's highway system, constructed and maintained wholly apart from federal funds and linking to the interstates only at the borders. The governor was as proud of the state's decades-old reputation for budget surpluses as the legislature was of its historic capitol building.

Our two main characters, however, had never before given a thought to matters of state and could not have imagined how such would so thoroughly determine their fates.

1

With the man's first step, the others on the Row began a slow tapping on their cell doors.

The tiny procession reached the end of the pod, and the rest of the way through security and all the way to the death chamber was lined on either side with corrections officers shoulder to shoulder, feet spread, hands clasped behind their backs, heads lowered. As the condemned reached them, each raised his head, snapped to attention, arms at his sides, feet together.

What a tribute, he thought. Who would ever have predicted this for one who had, for so much of his life, been such a bad, bad man?

October, seventeen years earlier | Touhy Trailer Park

Brady Wayne Darby clapped his little brother on the rear. "Petey, time to get up, bud. We got no water pressure, so . . ."

"Again?"

"There's a trickle, so give yourself a sponge bath."

"Ma already gone?"

"Yeah. Now come on. Don't be late."

At sixteen, Brady was twice Peter's age and hated

13

being the man of the house—or at least of the trailer. But if no one else was going to keep an eye on his little brother, he had to. It was bad enough Brady's bus came twenty minutes before Peter's and the kid had to be home alone.

Brady poured the boy a bowl of cereal and called through the bathroom door, "No dressing like a hoodlum today, hear?"

"Why's it all right for you and not for me?"

Brady closed his eyes and shook his head. "Just do what I say, okay?"

"Whatever."

"Straight home after school. I got practice, so I'll see ya for dinner."

"Ma gonna be here?"

"She doesn't report to me. Just keep your distance till I get home."

Brady rummaged for cigarettes, finally finding five usable butts in one of the ashtrays. He quickly smoked two down to their filters, tearing open the remaining three and dumping the tobacco in his shirt pocket. Desperately trying to quit so he could stay on the football team, Brady couldn't be seen with the other smokers across the road from the school, so he had resorted to sniffing his pocket throughout the day. If he couldn't cop a smoke from a friend after last class and find a secluded place to light up, he was so jittery at practice he could hardly stand still.

Brady grabbed his books and slung his black leather jacket over his shoulder as he left the trailer, finding the asphalt already steaming in the sun. Others from the trailer park waiting for the bus made him feel as if he were seeing his own reflection. Guys and girls dressed virtually the same, black from head to toe except for white shirts and blouses. Guys had their hair slicked back, sideburns grown retro, high-collared shirts tucked into skintight pants over pointy-toed shoes. Oversize wallets, most likely as empty as Brady's, protruded from back pockets and were attached to belt loops by imitation silver or gold chains.

So they were decades behind the times, even for rebels. Brady—an obsessive movie watcher—was a James Dean fan and dressed how he wanted, and the rest copied him. One snob called them rebels without a clue.

Brady scowled and narrowed his eyes, nodding a greeting.

The fat girl with the bad face, whom Brady had unceremoniously dumped more than a year ago after he had gotten to know her better than he should have in the backseat of a friend's car, sneered as she cradled her gigantic purse to her chest. "Still trying to play jock?"

Brady looked away. "Leave it alone, Agatha."

"More like a preppy," one of the guys said, reaching to flick Brady's schoolbooks.

"*You* definitely don't want to start with me," Brady said, glaring and calling him the foulest name he could think of. The kid quickly backed off.

Brady knew he looked strange carrying school-books. But the coach kept track.

The trailer park was the last stop on the route, and the yellow barge soon drifted in, crammed with suburbia's finest: jocks, preppies, and nerds—every last one younger than Brady. No other self-respecting kid with a driver's license rode the bus.

In a life of endless days of open-fly humiliation, this boarding ritual was the most painful. Brady took it upon himself to lead the group. They could hide behind him and each other, avoiding the squints and stares and held noses as they slowly made their way down the aisle looking, usually in vain, for someone to slide over far enough to allow one cheek on the seat for the ride to school.

"Phew!"

". . . brewery . . ."

". . . smokehouse . . ."

". . . B.O. . . ."

Brady neither looked nor waited. His daily goal was to find the most resolute rich kid and make him move. Today he stared down at the short-cropped blond hair of a boy who had been trying to hide a smile while pretending to study. Brady pressed his knee against him and growled, "Move in, frosh."

"I'm a sophomore," the kid huffed as he made room.

On the way home, Brady would ride the activities bus. There he would for sure be the only one of his type, but football earned him his place among the jocks, cheerleaders, thespians, and assorted club members. Wide-eyed at first, they seemed to have grudgingly accepted him, though they still clearly saw the trailer park as a novelty. One evening as he trudged from the bus, Brady had been sure everyone was watching. He turned quickly, only to be proven right, and felt face-slapped. At least the trailer park was the first stop at the end of the day.

11 a.m. | First Community Church | Vidalia, Georgia

Reverend Thomas Carey knew he would not be getting the job when the head of the pastoral search committee—a youngish man with thick, dark hair—dismissed the others and asked Grace Carey if she wouldn't mind waiting for her husband in the car.

"Oh, not at all," she said, but Thomas interrupted.

"Anything you say to me, you can say to her."

The man put a hand on Thomas's shoulder and spoke softly. "Of course, you're free to share anything you wish with your spouse, Reverend, but why don't you decide after you hear me out?"

Grace assured Thomas it was all right and retreated from the sanctuary.

"You tell her everything?" the man said.

"Of course. She's my—"

"She knows we saw you at your request, not ours, and that we didn't feel you warranted a visit to hear you preach?"

Thomas Carey pressed his lips together. Then, "I appreciate your meeting with us today."

17

The committee chairman pointed to a pew and leaned against another as Thomas sat. "I need to do you a favor and be frank with you, Reverend. I can tell you right now this is not going to go your way. In fact, we're not going to bother with a vote."

"That doesn't sound fair."

"Please," Dark Hair said. "I know these people, and if I may be blunt, you rank last on the list of six we've already interviewed."

"Shouldn't you poll the others on their—?"

"I'm sorry, but you have a three-year Bible college diploma, no real degree, no seminary training. You're, what, in your mid-forties?"

"I'm forty-six, yes."

"Sir, I've got to tell you, I'm not surprised that your résumé consists of eight churches in twenty-two years—the largest fewer than 150 members. Have you ever asked yourself why?"

"Why what?"

"Why you've never been successful, never advanced, never landed a church like ours . . ."

"Surely you don't equate success with numbers."

"Reverend Carey, I'm just trying to help. You and your sweet wife come in here, I assume trying to put your best foot forward, yet you look and dress ten years older than you are, and your hair is styled like a 1940s matinee idol."

Dark Hair extended his hand. "I want to sincerely thank you for your time today. Please pass along my best wishes to your wife. And be assured I meant no disrespect. If it's of any help, I'm aware of several small churches looking for pastors."

Thomas stood slowly and buttoned his sport jacket. "I appreciate your frankness; I really do. Any idea how I might qualify for a bigger work? I don't want to leave the ministry, but our only child is in her second year of law school at Emory, and—"

"When there are many Christian colleges that would give a minister huge discounts?"

"I'm afraid she would be neither interested in nor qualified for a Christian school just now."

"I see. Well, I'm sorry. But the fact is, you are what you are. None of your references called you a gifted preacher, despite assuring us you're a wonderful man of God. If you cannot abide your current station, perhaps the secular marketplace is an option."

5 p.m. | Head Football Coach's Office | Forest View High School

Brady hadn't even thoroughly dried after his shower. Now he sat in Coach Roberts's cramped space with his stuff on his lap, waiting for the beefy man. Every player was listed on a poster on the wall, his place on the depth chart and his grade in every class there for all to see. Brady knew what was coming. He should have just skulked out to the bus and, by ignoring the coach's summons, announced his quitting before being cut.

But he knew the drill. Never give up. Never say die. Keep your head up. Look eager, willing.

Finally Roberts barreled in, dropping heavily into a

squeaky chair. "I gotta ask you, Darby: what're you doing here?"

"You asked me to come see you—"

"I mean what're you doing trying to play football? You're a shop kid, ain't ya? You didn't come out as a frosh or a soph. I smell smoke all over you."

"I quit, Coach! I know the rules."

"We're barely a month into the year, and you're makin' Ds in every class. You're fourth-string quarterback, and entertaining as it is for everybody else to watch you racing all over the practice field on every play, we both know you're never gonna see game time. Now, really, what're you doing?"

"Just trying to learn, to make it."

Brady couldn't tell him he was looking for something, anything, to get him out of the trailer park and closer to the kids he had despised for so long. They seemed to have everything handed to them: clothes, cars, girls, college, futures. No, he wasn't ready to dress differently; he took enough heat from his friends just for carrying books and playing football.

"Listen, your teachers, even the ones outside of industrial arts, tell me you're not stupid. You're a good reader, sometimes have something to say. But you don't test well, rarely do your homework. What's the deal?"

Brady shrugged. "It's just my ma and my brother and me."

"Hey, we've all got problems, Darby."

Do we? Really? "Like I said, I quit smoking, and I'm trying to get my grades up."

"Look, I want to see you succeed, but frankly you're a distraction here. I rarely cut anybody willing to practice and ride the bench—"

"Which I am."

"Yeah, but this isn't working, and I don't want to waste any more of your time."

"Don't worry about wasting my—"

"Or mine. Or my coaches'. If you're determined to get involved in some extracurricular stuff, there's all kinds of other—"

"Like what?"

Coach Roberts looked at his watch. "Well, what do you like to do?"

"Watch movies."

"Don't we all? But is it a passion for you?"

"You have no idea."

"You want to be an actor someday? study theater?"

Brady hesitated. "Never thought of that, but yeah, that would be too good to be true."

"Now see, with that attitude, you'll never get anywhere. If you want to try that, try it! Talk to Nabertowitz, the theater guy. See if there's a club or a play or something."

"There's rumors about him."

"Do yourself a favor and keep your mouth shut about that. Those artsy people can be a little flamboyant, but the guy's got a wife and kids, so don't be jumping to conclusions, and you'll stay out of trouble."

Brady shrugged. "I'd be as new there as I was here."

"Oh, I expect you'd be a sight among that crowd,

though there's all kinds of behind-the-scenes stuff I'll bet you could do. But I need to tell you, football is not your thing."

2

Ravinia Carey, named after a beautiful suburban Chicago park her parents had enjoyed while in Bible college, had sounded none too thrilled that they would be "dropping by" that evening.

"We're on our way through Atlanta to look into ministry opportunities," Thomas had told her from a pay phone, as cheerily as he could muster.

"You're leaving Foley? What happened?"

"We'll talk about it when we see you."

"Oh, Dad . . ."

"Listen, hon, is there anywhere we can stay on campus? In a dorm, or—"

"Dad, this isn't some church camp. No. The Emory Inn is within walking distance, and you'll find the campus too complicated for parking anyway. Just have someone point you to Gambrell Hall, and I'll meet you there."

"All right," he had said slowly, writing it down. "Any idea how much a room might—?"

"It's owned by the university; just tell them you're a parent."

And so there Thomas stood after slowly pulling a U-

22

Haul trailer more than 150 miles behind the eight-year-old Impala. Gas mileage was abominable with the extra weight, so he had tried to offset an expensive fill-up against a cheap fast-food meal. Grace hadn't complained. She never did.

Even with the discount, the room rate made him blanch. "Might you know of any place more reasonably priced?"

The young black girl behind the counter leaned close and whispered with a smile, "Nowhere you'd want to stay, sir, really."

He and Grace carted in a few items, and she stretched out on the bed. "This feels so good after sitting all day."

"What are we going to tell Rav?" he said.

"That the Lord will provide."

Thomas sighed. "You know how she hates clichés."

"That cliché is true, sweetheart."

Thomas found a hand towel and gave his black oxfords a once-over, tucking away a tiny hole that had appeared in one of his socks. He ran a comb through his hair and massaged his chin, debating getting rid of his late afternoon shadow.

Soon Grace rose and smoothed her dress. "We'd better go. I can't wait to see her."

6:30 p.m. | Touhy Trailer Park

Brady arrived home to find a familiar car on the apron next to the single-wide. He smelled dinner before he opened the door.

"Hey, Aunt Lois," he said, tossing his stuff.

The short, freckled dishwater blonde rushed from the stove to hug him tight. "Oh, Brady!" she said. "Where's your mama?"

"Probably stopped off somewhere," he said. "You'll be able to tell where from her breath."

"You ought to speak of her with more respect."

"Yeah, she deserves it. Petey here?"

She nodded toward the back. "Tell him ten minutes before corn bread, beans, and rice."

"He'll want iced tea, too."

" 'Course."

Brady picked through the ashtray.

His aunt poked her head around the corner. "Oh, Brady! No!"

He shrugged. "I just quit football, so give me a break."

"Football or not, those things'll kill you."

"I can only hope. What're you doing here, anyway?"

"You're not happy to see me?"

"Sure I am. I always am. But—"

"I come with bad news, if you must know, but I can't tell you without tellin' your mom and Petey, so don't ask."

Brady found his brother in the back, riveted to a video game.

"Wanna play?" Peter said without looking up.

"It's rude to be back here when Aunt Lois is visiting."

Peter sighed and paused the game. "She's just gonna tell us about Jesus again."

"Just nod and smile and tell her you'll get to church again sometime soon."

Gambrell Hall | Emory University

Ravinia looked stiff when her mother embraced her, and she barely seemed to return the touch. Thomas shook her hand, and they sat in the student lounge.

"You look well," Grace said. "I wish you'd let your hair grow out a little."

"I wish I had time to take care of more hair, Mom. Regardless, I'm straight, if that's what you're worried about."

Grace squinted at Thomas.

"She's not a lesbian," he said.

"Oh, my, Ravinia! I wasn't even suggesting—"

"To prove it, one of these days I'll introduce you to Dirk."

"Dirk?"

"Dirk Blanc. Works at MacMillan next door, the law library."

"He's a librarian?" Grace said.

Ravinia laughed. "He's a student too, but most of us work, you know."

"I know," Grace said, "and we're sorry you have to."

"Even most students with normal parents have to work, Mom."

"Normal parents?"

"Those not dependent on congregations for their income."

25

"Well, one doesn't go into the ministry for the money, sweetheart. But God's people have been good to us over the years."

"Oh, please. *No*-body's been good to you, and you know it. You give and give and give, and what do you get? Ushered out. So, what happened at Foley?"

"I'd rather talk about what you're doing, Rav," Thomas said.

"You promised to tell me."

"Well, I said I'd rather talk about it in person, yes, but there's time. . . ."

"No, there isn't. I have no time, Dad. I study and I work and, if I'm lucky, I eat and sleep. And if you're telling me that once again—surprise, surprise—you're between churches, sleep may have to go too. So just tell me."

"Where are you attending services, honey?" Grace said.

"Can we stop this, Mom? Even if I had the time, I don't have the interest right now. And I have the feeling that whatever it is you're about to tell me about the faithful at Foley just might close the church chapter of my life."

"Oh, don't say that, Ravinia," Grace said. "We're certainly not going to blame this on the people. The Lord just made it clear to us that it was time—"

"To move on, sure. I've heard that before. So what was it this time, Dad? You pick the wrong color carpet for the sanctuary? Spend too much time preaching through the Old Testament? What?"

"Actually, we're pretty proud of what your dad brought to that little lighthouse. Sorry, cliché. But he got a visitation program going and even replaced their old children's night with one that had updated curriculum. The kids loved it."

Ravinia stood and rubbed her eyes. She moved to a window and gazed out. Appearing resolute, she returned. "All right, you're not driving all the way up through here looking for 'opportunities' if everything's peachy in Foley. Now out with it."

"You're going to make a fine lawyer," Thomas said, forcing a smile.

"I'm going to start by suing those people if they did to you what the previous bunch did."

"Oh, no; you know we don't solve church problems in court."

"Maybe you should. You certainly have grounds. Honestly, Dad, I know as well as anybody that you're no Billy Graham. And, Mom, your piano playing and puppet thing are never going to make you famous. But how can people watch you work yourselves to death— on *their* behalf—and still treat you like garbage?"

Thomas chuckled too loudly. "Thought you hated clichés."

"Don't change the subject, Dad. You know I'm not letting you go until you tell me what happened."

"Can't we take you to dinner?" Grace said.

"C'mon! We both know you can't afford it. Follow me through the cafeteria line, and you can share my meal."

"That wouldn't be right," Grace said. "It'd be like stealing."

"The place is full of lawyers! I'd find you counsel."

Thomas was warmed to see even Grace smile at that. "Rav," he said, "we just wanted to see you because we were passing through. And we thought it only fair to tell you that we won't be able to help with your schooling anymore. At least for a while."

"It's all right, Dad. I'm grateful for what you've done already, and I know you couldn't really afford that and certainly didn't owe me anything after the way I've disappointed you."

"I wouldn't say you've disappointed us."

"Well, I hope I have, Mom! I've tried to!"

Ravinia said it with a smile, but Grace looked pained.

"I'm just saying, I appreciate knowing, and I will make this work somehow. I'll start my career the way everyone else does: in debt. I'm not aiming for some high-paying corporate job, but I'll be able to dig out eventually."

"You know you could go to our denominational school and—"

"Mom! I'm way past that. Anyway, if I was honest on the admissions forms, they wouldn't take me. Now I need to go eat within the next half hour, and then I'm studying till midnight. But I'm not leaving you until you tell me what happened, so unless you want me to starve . . ."

"I'll keep your mom's plate warm," Aunt Lois said as she and Peter and Brady crowded around the tiny kitchen table. "Brady, you want to pray for us?"

"No, ma'am. You, please."

"Petey?"

Peter shook his head. "All I know is, 'God is great, God is good, now we thank Thee for our food.'"

"Well," Aunt Lois said, "that's not half bad, but let me. Dear Lord, thank You for these precious boys and for my sister-in-law, wherever she is. Protect her and bring her back to Yourself. Give her strength when she finally hears what I have to tell her.

"Now, Lord, never let these boys forget all that I've taught them about You, that You died on the cross for their sins so they don't have to go to hell but can live in heaven with You. And thanks for our food. In Jesus' name, amen."

Peter was smirking when Brady opened his eyes, so Brady shot him a scowl before Aunt Lois noticed.

The woman had good intentions, Brady knew. It was hard not to love Aunt Lois.

A minute later Brady noticed a tear running down his aunt's cheek. "What's wrong?" he said.

"I'm just thinking about your mama and the news I have for her."

3

Ravinia Carey sat with her arms folded, shaking her head. "That's it? They just 'felt it was time'?"

"Well," her mother said, "maybe it *was* time. We'd been there nearly four years, and perhaps your father had done all he could."

"I didn't do it alone, Grace. You worked as hard as I did."

"They didn't use the old ready-for-a-younger-man line?"

Thomas had always found his daughter's direct stare disconcerting. He shrugged. "Actually they did."

She huffed and looked away.

"Well, attendance *was* down a bit."

Grace jumped in. "But that was as much because of the plant closing and several families having to leave."

Ravinia waved her off. "Just tell me they did right by you, other than kicking you to the curb."

"I got severance, yes."

"How much?"

"Well, that's confidential, Rav. I felt it was fair. . . ."

"It's not confidential from your own daughter! Tell me they gave you a month for every year you served."

"Oh," Grace said, "they wouldn't have been able to afford that. With core families leaving—"

"How much, Dad?"

"A week for each year."

"Unbelievable."

"But you know they had provided a parsonage at no cost," Grace said.

"Like you would have been able to afford rent on that salary. And I'm sure it was a castle. Anyway, all that means is that you have zero equity. Honestly, Dad."

"Rav, listen to me," he said. "I don't know what the future holds, but—"

"Please don't tell me you know who holds the future!"

"—but I know this: I made a commitment a long time ago, and I'm not about to stray from it now. I told the Lord I would obey Him and follow wherever He leads."

Ravinia looked away. "I'm trying to find something in that to admire. You're consistent; I'll give you that. But how long will you keep banging your head against a wall?"

"Oh, honey," Grace said, "we're happy to serve. You know that."

"But why isn't anyone else happy with it? You wonder why I've 'lost the blessing,' as you've always so eloquently put it? I know you're not in this for personal gain, but do you think this is fair? You devote your entire lives to the church, and what do you have to show for it?"

Ravinia looked past Thomas and broke into a beatific smile. "Dirk!" she said, rising.

Thomas turned and stood as a tall, bald young man

embraced his daughter. "Excuse me," Dirk said, shaking first Grace's hand, then Thomas's. "I've heard so much about you."

Dirk said he and Ravinia had to hurry to the cafeteria and insisted her parents join them. "My treat," he said.

"Oh, you don't have to do that," Thomas said.

"Sure I do! Come on."

The Darby Trailer

"You and Petey clear your own table, don't you?" Aunt Lois said.

"We hardly ever eat at the table," Brady said.

"Honestly. . . . Well, at my house, everybody buses his own dishes."

"What's that mean?" Peter said.

"Clear your place and at least put the dishes in the sink. I'll wash 'em tonight. And we'll flip to see who dries."

"Let Petey dry."

"Hey!"

"I got a job," Brady said. "I don't need to be doin' housework, too."

"What's your job?" Aunt Lois said as they maneuvered around each other in the tiny kitchen.

"When the park Laundromat closes each night, I go clean it. Dust the machines, mop the floor, fill the detergent dispensers, collect the money from the coin boxes."

"How long's that take?"

"About an hour, but it's every night, so I make a few bucks a week. That's how I pay for my movies and could afford the fees for football. Ma sure wasn't gonna spring for it."

"And now you've quit? What kind of sense does that make?"

"I wanna do something else, that's all."

"Can I play my video game until it's time to dry?" Peter said.

"You got homework, young man?"

Peter laughed. "In third grade?"

"Go on, then," she said.

Brady sat back down as his aunt did the dishes.

"You know what I got to ask you, don't you?" she said.

He shrugged. Of course he knew.

"She touch him again since you threatened her?"

"You kiddin'? I told her I'd kill her, and I meant it."

"You wouldn't kill your own mama."

Brady swore. "You know I would."

"Don't talk like that. You know better. And you know it's the booze that makes Erlene—"

"It's more than booze now, ma'am. I don't know what else she's doing, but trust me, when she's not drunk, she's high."

Cafeteria | Emory University

It didn't take long for Thomas to determine that Dirk Blanc's budget was hardly stretched by paying for a couple of visitors' meals. It turned out he was the offspring of two lawyers and worked at the library only because he felt it was the right thing to do.

"Dad and Mom do a lot of pro bono work, so it didn't seem fair to make them foot the whole bill for my degree."

"They sound wonderful," Grace said. "Are you people of faith?"

Thomas noticed Ravinia blink slowly as if mortified, but Dirk didn't miss a beat. "Not really, no. But we certainly admire religious people and applaud what you do. Don't misunderstand. We're not atheists by any means. I'd say we're more spiritual than religious."

"'Religious' doesn't really describe us, either," Grace said, but Thomas surreptitiously pressed his knee against hers and she fell silent. This wasn't the time or place. If Ravinia was as enamored of this man as she seemed, there would be more opportunities to get into this.

Dirk shot Grace a double take and smiled pleasantly. "Not religious? A pastor and a pastor's wife?"

Ravinia rose. "Let's get some dessert."

The Darby Trailer

Aunt Lois looked at her watch. "What time's your mama get off work?"

"Hours ago."

"But she parties?"

Brady snorted. "That's one way to say it. I think sometimes she and her boss party alone."

"Is she often this late? What time do you have to clean up the Laundromat?"

"Half hour or so. It closes at ten."

"And you leave Petey here alone?"

"Have to. Can't wake him up and drag him along."

"You poor boys."

"Don't worry about us. Worry about him when I finally get out of here. I wish you'd take him."

"Don't think I haven't thought of it. But she'd never stand for it."

"What does she care? He's just in her way."

"But she'd at least see him as personal property, and no way she'd let me raise him."

"You might be surprised," Brady said.

"I should have started home an hour ago. I told Carl I'd be back by midnight."

"No way now. You wanna go with me when I go to work?"

"I'm not leaving your brother alone, even if you think you have to. But you hurry back. Your mama's gonna demand to know why I'm here, and I want to tell you all together."

"Even Petey?"

"'Fraid so."

"So it's about Daddy, eh?"

"Hush."

The Emory Inn

Thomas knelt by the bed next to Grace, as he had done every night since their wedding.

"Rav's in love," she said. "We either need to get that

35

boy saved or pray it doesn't work out. The last thing I want is to see her unequally yoked."

"Hmm."

"What are you thinking, Thomas?"

"I don't know. Just that I'm not so sure they'd be unequally yoked."

She turned to face him, and he knew he shouldn't be surprised. "What are you saying? I led that girl to Jesus myself."

"Well, it's clear she's left Him somewhere along the way, wouldn't you say? How old was she, Grace?"

"Very young, of course, but so were you and I when we came to faith. I believe she meant it and knew what she was doing."

Thomas felt himself welling up, and he did not want to break down in front of Grace. She had always been so strong for him, through every struggling pastorate and every dismissal.

"I'm praying Rav was sincere, honey," he said. "But do you realize how long it's been since she even pretended to be a believer?"

Grace lowered her forehead to the mattress. "I know I wouldn't want to relive her teen years for anything."

Touhy Trailer Park

As Brady finished tidying the Laundromat, he wished his mother would stay out all night, forcing Aunt Lois to wait. It was nice to have her there. But of course he was curious, too. What had his father gotten himself into now?

Brady used a special key to open the coin boxes and dumped all the change into a bucket he took into a back room to sort. Besides the envelope of cash the owner tucked into a ceiling joist for him each week, Brady also absconded with the equivalent of three washes and three dries from each of the ten washers and ten dryers. Truth was, he made more skimming than he did in pay. That was something he would not tell his aunt. She was already praying overtime to keep him out of hell, he knew.

Another benefit of Brady's job was getting his choice of the magazines stocked for people waiting for their wash and dry cycles. He believed his lifting of his favorites was less obvious because he made sure to leave *Time*, *Newsweek*, *Sports Illustrated*, and of course all the women's magazines. He waited until the new *People* and *Movie News* and *Entertainment Weekly* came in, then took the previous week's editions.

If his aunt asked about the magazines, he would tell her the boss had said he could have them. He would not be able to explain his jacket pockets bulging with quarters, so he would just move slowly and find a reason to head back to his and Peter's bedroom, where he could unload.

But as he came within sight of their trailer, he saw his mother's rattletrap car parked next to Aunt Lois's.

4

The Darby Trailer

Erlene Darby was just emerging from her car, sensible shoes incongruous with a too-revealing black waitress's dress that matched her dyed hair.

"Hey, Ma."

She whirled and swore. "Don't do that, Brady! Like to scare me half to death."

Have to be twice as loud next time, then.

Erlene nodded toward Aunt Lois's car. "What's she doing here?"

"Won't say. Some news about Dad."

"Hope it's bad."

"Likely is. She's fixing to wake up Petey so we can all hear it together. You're a little late. Later than usual."

"I'll thank you to mind your own business."

Lois had apparently heard the car and was waiting at the door. She embraced Erlene tight.

"All right, all right, Lois. Let me sit down. Then out with it."

"Nice to see you, too. I didn't know you worked nights."

"Well, if you'd called before just showing up, maybe I could have saved you some put-out." Erlene dropped her sweater and purse and settled into the nearest chair. "What a day."

"What'd you do, Erlene," Lois said, "drink your dinner?"

Erlene flipped her an obscene gesture.

"No cause for that. I'm just asking."

"Yeah, you're just asking like you always do. I didn't invite you here, and I don't guess you want to stay long, so can we get on with this?"

Lois nodded at Brady. "Wake your brother, please."

"Is that really necessary?" Erlene said.

"What, you're worried about him now?" Lois said.

"Yeah, Ma. You weren't worried about him wh—"

"Don't start with me, either of you! You act like that kid's a saint!"

"He's eight years old!" Brady shouted. "How bad can he be?"

"Just get him, please," Lois said.

His mother lit a cigarette as Brady moved down the hall.

"You shouldn't be smoking inside with these kids here, Erlene," Aunt Lois said.

"I'll do what I please in my own house."

"And your kids be hanged."

"Brady smokes too."

"But you know better."

Peter came padding out wrapped in a blanket and squinting. Brady thought the little boy and his mother locked eyes, but both quickly looked away without even a greeting.

Erlene said, "All right, Lois, the gang's all here."

Brady's aunt drew a quavery breath. "Kids, you

know your dad hasn't been well for a long time."

"Your brother hasn't been their dad for a long time either, Lois."

Lois glared at her. "He'll always be their dad."

"You kidding me? Peter barely remembers Eddie, and Brady was Peter's age when he left. And how many times you boys seen him since?"

Peter shrugged.

"Couple," Brady said.

"And what'sa matter with him?" Peter said. "The d-thing?"

"Diabetes, yes," Lois said. She pressed a hand to her mouth, then to her chest. "He's never been good about taking care of himself and following doctors' orders."

"When he even went," Erlene spat. "Like he can afford that. He wouldn't have insulin except for welfare. And he only uses that to make up for eating whatever he wants."

Lois held up a hand. "Eddie fell into a diabetic coma this morning and—"

"A what?" Peter said. "What's that?"

"Just something that happens with that disease if you're not careful. Anyway, he died this afternoon."

"Died?" Erlene said, her voice thin.

Brady had half expected this, but it was clear his mother hadn't. She stubbed out her cigarette, and he hoped she would leave it like that. It would be almost like having a whole one later.

He had long despised the man who had abandoned

them, though he thought he might have left a wife like his mother too. And he resented that his dad hardly ever communicated with him or Peter. Still, Brady felt an emptiness deep in his gut.

Peter looked puzzled. "So I don't have a dad anymore?"

"When did you ever?" Brady's mother said, her voice still reedy and hollow. Brady figured even she had to feel this somewhere inside.

That his aunt had lost her brother suddenly hit Brady, and he said, "I'm sorry for your loss, Aunt Lois."

"I hadn't allowed myself to cry yet," she said, tears flowing now. "Thank you, Brady. And I'm sorry for you all too."

"Sorry for me, too, Lois?" Erlene said, her edge back.

"'Course I am. You loved him once."

"That was a long time ago. I don't guess there's anything at all in the way of an estate."

Lois narrowed her eyes and shook her head. "Just debts."

"And I guess that's the end of my piece of his monthly check."

Lois stood and grabbed her coat. "Honestly, Erlene, don't you care that this is my brother we're talking about, once your husband and the father of your children?"

"That never meant anything to him either, so spare me."

"Eddie was a good boy once, Erlene, raised in the church."

"Yeah, and now you're going to tell me again how I ought to have these boys in church so they can, what, turn out like their father?"

"That's enough, Ma!" Brady said. "Either thank Aunt Lois for coming all this way or shut up."

"I oughta knock you silly, talking to me that way!"

"Oh, how I wish you'd try," Brady said.

"Please!" Lois said, her hand on the door now. "I just thought you deserved to hear it in person, and I wanted to tell you the funeral will be Saturday."

"Not in a million years," Erlene said.

"Do what you want," Lois said, "but I intend to come get the boys early that morning. You can ride along or not, but they ought to be at their own father's funeral."

Friday | Association of Rural Bible Churches

Thomas and Grace Carey held hands and beamed across the desk at ARBC Executive Director Jimmie Johnson.

"This is an answer to prayer," Grace said. "A direct answer."

"The Lord works in mysterious ways," Johnson said. "Thomas, I've known of you and your work for years, and your references are exemplary. Let me show you just what we need and how this might work."

He led them to a map on the wall of the adjoining conference room and pointed out five stick pins in an irregular circle that encompassed about 100 square miles. "We have a small work in each of these areas—the largest in Oldenburg comprising about ninety regular attendees; the smallest, right there in Colfax, down to about thirty now but with real potential. My thought is this: The larger work has its own building and even a parsonage, though I want to be frank. It's old. It's dilapidated. And it's not much. But with the help of the congregation, I'm assured it can be made livable, and of course, it's free."

"We don't require much," Grace said.

"That would be your base of operations. From there I see you serving this and the other four churches. I know that's spreading you mighty thin, and you're going to have to be creative about scheduling a worship service for each church each week. Only one other of the congregations has its own building. Two others meet in homes and the fifth in a school."

"Frankly," Thomas said, "I'm eager to get started."

Grace nodded. "He's so good about meeting new people and getting them taught and motivated."

"You understand you're not going to get rich with this," Mr. Johnson said, laughing. "Not one of these bodies can afford their own shepherd, so they know they'll have to kick in and share. We can provide a small stipend, probably enough to cover your mileage is all, but you'll have to work out with the individual congregations their share of your salary. We'll help mediate if necessary, but that's the best we can do.

"Now, would you like to pray about it?"

Thomas looked at Grace, wondering whether she would suggest they take a moment alone, maybe in the car. But she looked radiant, joyous. He could tell she truly believed this was of God, and he had a hard time doubting it himself. There was certainly nothing else on the horizon. Not one of the other churches he'd contacted had shown an iota of interest. And there was nothing he would rather do than invest his life in such work.

Thomas shrugged at her and cocked his head. She raised her brows and nodded.

"Sir," he said, "we're in."

"That's wonderful! Let's go back to my office and turn on the speakerphone so I can inform someone at each church. And you can meet them by phone."

Saturday | Lily of the Valley Church of the Holy Spirit

Brady wore a borrowed bolo tie and left his leather jacket in his aunt's car. And he had found an old white shirt for Peter, though he seemed to swim in it. Even without a tie, he looked dressed up enough for Brady's taste.

Brady felt the sea of eyes as he and his brother followed Aunt Lois and Uncle Carl to the front row. In some ways, this was just a bigger school bus, but open seats were waiting.

The boys had been in this church before, had even

sat through a few Sunday school classes. Their uncle had pleaded with them to stay overnight and come again the next morning, but Brady had begged off. "I have to work tonight."

Brady had never felt he really had a father. When his dad had lived with the family, he was worse than their mother was now. Brady had feared him, dreaded seeing him. And while it seemed strange when his father disappeared nearly eight years before, Brady was relieved. Sure, it was embarrassing when other kids talked about their dads and asked about his, and he learned from his mother to hate that his dad hardly ever contacted him, even on special days. But all in all, Brady Wayne Darby found life better without his dad in the picture.

So he was surprised that emotion eventually caught up with him when the funeral people wheeled in a plain casket and positioned it not six feet from him in front of the pulpit. They opened the lid, and the man who lay there looked gaunt and pale, as if he had aged thirty years since Brady had seen him.

Peter leaned over. "Is *that* Dad?"

Brady nodded.

"When did I see him last?"

"I don't remember."

"I think I was five. He rubbed my head, and I didn't like it."

Aunt Lois sat next to Brady, weeping loudly and dabbing her eyes through all the songs and the simple eulogy that mostly just told the dates and details of her brother's life and death and surviving family. Brady was embarrassed when she threw an arm around his shoulder and pulled him close.

Brady found himself intrigued by the pastor's message.

"One thing we don't do in this church—never have and won't start now—is pretend. I'm not going to try to persuade you that Edward Wayne Darby was a devout man of God. I'm not even going to try to tell you that anybody here knows for sure whether the man is in heaven.

"He had his good points and he had his bad, and for most of the years I knew him, he wanted nothing to do with this church or the faith. But I can tell you this: he knew better. He was raised here, was taught the Scriptures, and at one time claimed to know the Lord.

"Truth is, most of the rest of his life he didn't act like it, so only he and God know if he was ever sincere about it and truly saved. It is appointed unto man once to die, and after that, the judgment. But to as many as received Him—that's Jesus—to them He gave the power to become sons of God, even to them that believe on His name.

"Do you believe on His name today, beloved? Regardless who we are or where we stand with God, unless Jesus comes back first, Eddie Darby's fate faces each one of us. . . ."

5

Oldenburg

Thomas Carey had always enjoyed the honeymoon period in any new work. The people aimed to please, treating the new pastor and his wife like royalty, and all seemed right with the world. But Thomas had also learned the hard way the truth of the ancient adage "Beware the wagon that meets the train."

At the end of the long, white-stone driveway that led to the ramshackle parsonage sat a monstrous black SUV. A well-dressed couple in their late fifties immediately clambered out. He was big and red-faced with thinning white hair and a meaty handshake. She was reed thin with short hair and glasses and carried a pie covered with a blue and white checkered cloth.

"Paul Pierce," the man said, pumping Thomas's hand. "Chairman of the elders and the deacons and the now-defunct search committee. And this here's Patricia."

"Oh, my," Grace said, accepting the pie. "This is still warm! Thank you so much, Pat."

"Patricia."

"Sorry. Patricia."

"Well, come on," Paul said, pulling Thomas toward the house. "We'll get your stuff unloaded, but you're staying with us tonight until we can find you some furniture."

47

"Are you sure?" Thomas said. "We've got air mattresses and can make do here if—"

"Oh, don't be silly. If I'd had a little more warning, I'd have had the youth group clean this place up and even paint it, get the ladies to hang some curtains, make it nice for ya. But all in good time."

Paul opened the torn screen door that had a hanging spring. He thrust a key into a sticky lock, and when the bolt finally gave way, he pressed his shoulder against the door, then kicked at the bottom until it broke free. He flipped on a light, and Thomas knew Grace had to have seen—or at least heard—creatures scattering. The must and dust assaulted him, but he tried to imagine the place with a little work. Okay, a lot of work.

Thomas found himself wondering about the pie. If Patricia knew he and Grace were staying with them, why bring it? But, of course, Grace was already exulting about their new home.

"It's just the right size, and it will soon be perfect."

Patricia laughed. "Aren't you the most precious little thing?"

The Pierces proved industrious, pitching in to unload the trailer in less than thirty minutes. Paul locked the place and handed Thomas the key. "Now let's get that trailer dropped off; then you follow me to our place. Bet you're starvin'."

"Guess your mama works weekends, hey?" Aunt Lois said as Uncle Carl pulled up to the trailer.

"Every day except Monday," Brady said, eager to get inside and raid her carton for a pack of cigarettes. It had been so long since he'd enjoyed a whole one.

"You want me to come in and straighten the place a little?"

"Nah, it's all right. Petey and I can do it."

"I don't want to clean house," Peter said, but Brady gave him a look.

"Let me," Aunt Lois said.

"No, really. We're good."

"Take your brother to church tomorrow, hear?"

"Okay."

"I don't want to!" Peter said.

"We're going, and that's that," Brady said, sliding out of the car.

"Where do you go?" his aunt said.

"That little Baptist church on the other side of the park."

"Good."

Brady tried to look as solemn as possible and thanked his aunt and uncle as Peter bounded into the trailer.

"That boy needs you, Brady," Carl said. "I worry about him."

"I got his back," Brady said. "Believe me."

By the time Brady got inside, Peter had already changed and was playing a video game.

"We don't really have to clean up this place, do we?"

"'Course not."

"And we aren't going to church either, right?"

Brady snorted. "Like that'll happen."

Peter paused the game and looked up. "So you lied."

Brady pulled off the bolo tie and sat. "White lies. Telling people what they want to hear so you don't hurt their feelings. That's why you got to not say out loud everything you do and don't want to do. Just say, 'Yeah, sure.' It's not like they're gonna check."

"What if they do?"

"What? Ask us? We just tell 'em some Bible story we learned in Sunday school and say the sermon was boring. What're they going to do, call the church to see if we were really there?"

Peter shrugged and turned back to the game.

"But *you* shouldn't lie, Petey."

"Except to not hurt people's feelings?"

"Right."

Brady found his mother's stash of smokes—two whole cartons, one still unopened. He hid it outside, under the trailer, and took a pack from the other. Tearing off the cellophane, ripping the tinfoil, tapping the pack against his palm, sliding one out, lighting up—all of it relaxed him.

Petey came from the back. "Let me try one."

"No."

"Mom'll never know."

"No, but I will. You got to promise me you'll never smoke."

"Everybody smokes."

"Not everybody."

"Why do you?"

"Got started and can't stop. Costs money and kills you."

"Doesn't cost *you* money."

"It will. Now promise me."

"Okay."

"I'm going to a movie and you're going with me."

"Yeah!" Peter said.

"We've got to hitchhike."

Oldenburg

"Do you think this is all theirs?" Grace said as Thomas followed the SUV through a gate and down a half-mile drive through acres and acres enclosed by seemingly endless white fences.

The sign above the entryway had read, "Pierce Dairy."

"Likely. Pretty nice."

The sprawling house and adjacent garage looked like a hotel. Once inside, Patricia took the pie back from Grace and served them in the dining room. Paul launched into a history of the church, "if you can call it that anymore. Used to have almost 250 people. Less than 100 now, but I guess you know that. We've

51

already spread the word you'll be preaching tomorrow, so we might have a few more. The curious, you know."

"You want me to preach tomorrow already?"

"Why not? Surely you've got a chestnut or two you're fond of."

"He does," Grace said, delicately dabbing her lips. "Thomas, you could preach 'Down to Joppa,' the Jonah message."

"If I can find my notes, I suppose I could," Thomas said.

Grace laughed. "If you can't find them, you could preach it by heart. *I* could preach it by heart!"

Had he really preached that same sermon that many times? Thomas supposed he had. "Who's been handling the pulpit work?"

"Paul has," Patricia said, brightening. "And he's good."

Paul smiled and looked down, obviously pleased. But he said, "Now, no I'm not, or we wouldn't have lost so many people."

"That wasn't your fault."

"But I'm not trained. Just a well-read retiree. Been a Sunday school teacher, superintendent, that kind of thing, for years. But the people are ready for a real preacher. If you're up to it, Pastor Carey."

It sounded so good to be called that again. Things had been so bad in Foley for so long that the people had quit calling Thomas "Pastor." They had gone to "Reverend" and then finally to just "Thomas." Now he felt emotion welling as he recalled that Grace often referred to him as "Pastor" in front of others.

"I'll consider it an honor to address the flock tomorrow. And then I suppose I'd better start making the rounds of the other congregations and formulating some sort of a plan of attack."

"Well, they aren't really congregations per se, Pastor. Barely hanging on as I understand it. You know what you ought to do? Start a little committee to oversee the rest, make them satellite churches or sister churches, something like that. Strength in numbers, you know? I'd be happy to head that up for you."

"And I'd be happy to serve on that committee too," Patricia said.

9 p.m. | The Darby Trailer

Brady knew enough to hide his pilfered cigarette pack in the inside pocket of his jacket, which hung in his tiny closet. It didn't help.

As he sat there smoking, his mother said, "You better be buyin' your own."

"I wish," he said. "Beer store's still carding, you know. I been making do with your leftover butts."

She rummaged in the cabinet above the sink. "I thought I had six packs left."

"You keep track now?"

"With a thief like you in the house, 'course I do—hey! I had another whole carton! Brady!"

"What? Don't look at me! Like I'd steal a whole

53

carton from you! That'd be a little obvious, wouldn't it?"

"It *is* obvious! Now where is it?"

"I swear, Ma, I know nothing about it."

"You're a liar."

"Okay, I'm a liar. I stole 'em and sold 'em to Petey and his friends."

"I'm sick of you being smart with me, Brady. I ought to—"

"What're you gonna do, smack me? I wish you would."

"Just tell me where my other carton is."

"I told you—"

"Yeah, you even swore, like that's gonna make me believe you. Now come on, those aren't cheap."

"I didn't take 'em, Ma. But I will tell you this: I forgot to lock up before we left this morning, so . . ."

"So someone came in and stole my cigarettes and nothing else? And they didn't take them all, just one carton? What do you take me for?"

"You don't want to know."

Oldenburg

While Grace stayed with Patricia Pierce and settled into one of their guest rooms, Thomas rode with Paul to the Oldenburg Rural Chapel a couple of miles away.

"I'm embarrassed by how it looks," Paul said. "But with so few people, we just don't have the funds to keep it up. Truth is, most of what *is* done I've had to pay for. The others haven't been blessed like Patricia and me, but on the other hand, I can't finance everything. Wouldn't be right. And wouldn't teach these people how to do for themselves."

A teenage boy was mowing the grass in front of a plain, redbrick building with a Norman Rockwell steeple. In the sanctuary, several women were dusting and vacuuming, and they looked embarrassed to have to greet the new pastor in their work clothes.

Thomas was impressed by the sanctuary; he'd never seen anything like it. Old burgundy drapes and a wood-stained cross provided the only contrast to white pews, white walls, white doors, white trim, white ceiling, white platform furniture—including the pulpit—even white light fixtures.

"It's really quite beautiful," Thomas said. "I can't wait till Grace sees it. Clearly someone designed it this way on purpose."

Paul grimaced and nodded toward the pastor's study, and Thomas followed him in. "You can camp out here any time you want, even if you're planning messages for the other churches."

Thomas assumed he would preach the same sermon several times each week but didn't feel obligated to explain that.

Paul pointed to a side chair and then sat behind the desk himself. "You want the truth about that sanctuary? That was my doing."

"You're an interior decorator too? Well, it sure is—"

Paul held up a hand. "Fact is, redoing that space was the cause of our second-to-last split. There was so much bickering over colors and schemes that I just put my foot down, said I wasn't going to give another dime if people couldn't grow up. We picked the color of the drapes out of an offering plate, had a contest— won by the women's missionary society—to see who got to pick the color of the cross, and made the rest of it white."

"You don't say. Who would have guessed it would have turned out so—"

"Well, I like it too, but it dredges up bad memories. We lost more'n a hundred people that time. Tell you the truth, most of them said it wasn't how the sanctuary turned out that bothered them. It was how much power they thought I had."

Thomas nodded. "That is often an issue with people."

"Lost the pastor, too, though I was in favor of that. The new guy wasn't much better and didn't last long, and we've been without ever since. You're going to be a breath of fresh air."

"I'll trust the Lord to help me do my best."

"You do that, and I'll be behind you a thousand percent. I'm going to suggest that each of the five churches contribute exactly one-fifth of your support. Executive Director Johnson says the denomination will throw in a little for expenses. Um, you look dubious, Reverend."

"Oh, I generally prefer to stay out of such things, Paul. But I've never been 'shared' like this before, so I'm in new territory. I just wonder if the smaller bodies will feel it's fair."

"Well, you tell me, Pastor Tom. Do you plan to give us more time, more of your week, more of your work?"

Thomas hadn't been called Tom for thirty years. "No, actually Grace and I feel it would be best if I really tried to give each body the equivalent of a full day a week, then have one study day, and one off day."

Paul stood and moved to the window, his back to Thomas. "You know, that actually sounds like a fine plan. 'Course, you know what it does, though, don't you? It supports my idea that everybody pays equally."

Thomas wasn't so sure, but it was certainly too early to start rocking the boat.

Paul turned to face him. "Now, what did you think of Patricia's idea of an oversight committee consisting of us two couples?"

Patricia's idea? And just the two couples?

Thomas cleared his throat. "Frankly, Paul, I'd wait on that. Let me meet the leaders from each body and—"

"Fair enough. Put it on the back burner for now. But at least let me take you to each church and introduce you."

"I guess that would be okay, as long as they know I

come under the auspices of the denomination and that they aren't, you know, under the authority of this church."

Paul headed for the door, and Thomas rose. Paul threw an arm around him and pulled him close. "That's some good thinking, Tom. We're going to work well together, you and me."

That evening the two couples enjoyed dinner; then Paul insisted they watch baseball on television. Neither Thomas nor Grace—certainly not Grace—followed baseball, and Thomas was antsy to get a little time alone before Sunday morning.

When the hour grew late, he finally begged off, though it was clear this befuddled the Pierces. "You know the game is tied and will likely go into extra innings."

"Yes, I'll be eager to hear in the morning how it ended."

6

Monday | Backstage, Little Theater | Forest View High School

Brady had seen Clancy Nabertowitz only from a distance. He was thick and seemed robust for a short man, sporting a full shock of curly hair and a loud bow tie.

"Auditions begin in twenty minutes, young man. I can give you exactly half of that."

They sat in dim light on either side of a folding table

amid the ropes and pulleys. Brady explained that Coach Roberts had suggested he look into drama.

"Well, he ought to know," Mr. Nabertowitz chirped. "Have you ever seen anyone so animated on the sidelines? I'd love to see what he could do onstage. But regardless, why you? Wait, don't tell me. Omigosh, I hope you can act. We'll find out soon, won't we?"

"I don't know. I—"

"Of course we will. Unless you're just wasting my time. You're here to audition, right?"

"I didn't even know today was—"

"Well, you're here. Listen, you have to know I don't get—don't take this wrong—'your kind' here often. Ever, actually. Is it a look, just for today? You trying out for the role of Conrad Birdie, or—?"

"Like I said, I didn't know. But I'd rather try drama than football, so . . ."

"Experience?"

"You mean in drama?"

"What else? You're, what, a senior?"

"Junior."

"You look so old, and you have that ethnic thing happening, almost Italian. *Are* you Italian?"

"Not that I know of."

"Dark skin. Fast beard growth, am I right?"

Brady nodded.

Nabertowitz seemed to study him. His delivery slowed. "You know what I'd do with you? I'd lose the 'burns, and you could play much older. You could be the dad. I mean, you look like Birdie, but

I'm pretty sure I've got the guy for that. Unless you have experience. What did you say about experience?"

"I didn't. I don't."

"But you love drama. Live theater."

"Well, I love movies, and I mean *love* 'em."

Nabertowitz looked crestfallen. "So, like, what, *Terminator 2, Naked Gun*?"

"Nah. I'm goin' down the list of the best hundred ever and trying to see them all. My favorites? Of all time? *The Verdict* and, um, *Deer Hunter*."

The drama teacher nodded and smiled with his mouth closed, then slapped both palms on the table and roared. "I get it! This is priceless! It's a gag, right? Someone put you up to this! Who was it?"

Brady shook his head. "You've lost me."

"C'mon! You come in here looking all retro—and, pardon me, but like a burnout—yet your two favorite movies just happen to be mine, too, and you expect me to believe . . . ?"

"You pulling my chain?" Brady said.

"No! You're pulling mine! I love it! Okay, quiz time. Tell me your favorite picture this year."

"I'd have to think about it."

"Of course you would. Until you remember what someone told you mine was. Come on, there's lots to choose from. Crystal and Martin have comedies out. Costner as a really bad Robin Hood. The Jodie Foster–Anthony Hopkins vehicle that'll probably win it all."

60

"*Fried Green Tomatoes* actually."

Nabertowitz leaped from his chair. "I love it! You're good! Now who?"

"Who?"

"Who set me up? This is priceless."

"Listen, I don't know what you're talking about. I don't know you or anybody who knows you, and I feel like you're laughing at me."

"What're you, serious?" Nabertowitz said, sitting back down.

"Dog-dyin' serious."

"I like that line. Now, are you swearing on a stack of Bibles no one told you that the three pictures you just mentioned include two of my all-time favorites and my favorite from this year?"

"How many times do I have to say it?"

The teacher finally fell silent and just stared. "All right," he said at last, "pop quiz. Tell me what you liked best about each of those pictures."

Brady leaned back and looked at the ceiling. "Can't pick just one thing about *Deer Hunter*. The acting was dead-on. The torture scenes were like you were right there. Everybody was good. Streep was fantastic. But, okay, favorite? Christopher Walken when he was, you know, shell-shocked."

In Brady's peripheral vision, Clancy Nabertowitz sat nodding. "Where have you been all my life?"

"The other two? I just think Newman was at his best in *The Verdict*. But mostly I like movies that aren't afraid to be quiet."

The teacher cursed in a whisper. "You're going to make me cry. Tell me one more time this isn't a put-on."

"Ask me that again and I'll punch you in your face."

Nabertowitz held up both hands. "I believe you. It's just . . . I work with a lot of great kids. But what do *they* love this year? *City Slickers*, *Addams Family*, *Sleeping with the Enemy*, *Father of the Bride*."

"Those were okay."

"But you know what I mean."

"'Course I do," Brady said. "There's good, and there's great."

"What'd you say your name was again?"

Brady told him.

"Your last name's an anagram of your first. How quaint. Was that on purpose?"

"I don't even know what that means, so I doubt it."

"You must audition today, Brady. Tell me you will."

"If you think I should. Like I said, I got no experience."

The teacher tossed him a script. "Speed-read. Everyone else knows what they want to try out for. And as I said, the role of Birdie is set."

Oldenburg

Thomas Carey found himself relieved that Paul Pierce had not joined the swarm from the church that was busy transforming the parsonage from a

62

hovel to a cottage. He was twenty-sixth-mile exhausted, and Grace looked the same, but it had to warm her heart as it did his to have so many people determined to make them feel welcome and comfortable.

The Jonah sermon had seemed to go over well, and the crowd was the biggest in a long time, according to Paul. People were already taking turns committing the Careys to meal invitations. Grace said, "Thomas, I may not have to cook for weeks."

Paul finally showed up late in the afternoon, dressed in a suit.

"I thought you were retired," Thomas teased.

"And I thought you'd be ready," Paul said.

"For . . . ?"

"The ride to Colfax. You've got just enough time to jump in the shower."

"We're meeting them tonight?"

"They're having church tonight, Tom. And don't worry, Jonah will suit 'em just fine, though you might want to shorten it a tick. We'll meet with their board after the service."

"Paul, I wasn't even aware—"

"Come on, Pastor. You put me in charge of overseeing all these churches; you got to know I'm on the job."

Thomas stole a glance at Grace. "Why, I haven't even eaten, and I'm bushed."

"We'll grab something on the way," Paul said. "And your wife ought to be there too."

"I've got to run, Brady," Mr. Nabertowitz said, looking at his watch, "but here's how this works: Everybody who wants to audition sits in the house, and I talk about the play—in this case, the musical—from the stage. Then we switch places. I sit in the middle of the house, and everyone gathers backstage and picks a number. They audition in that order. Got it?"

"I don't even know what to try out for."

"Well, read fast. Look at the part of the father, like I said."

"I need more time. Is today the only day?"

"Today and tomorrow, but there might not be much left by then."

"I'll see you tomorrow."

7

There was no getting around it. The tiny flock of the faithful that met in the rec room of one of the parishioners' homes seemed more than pleased to welcome the new circuit pastor and his wife, but the iciness between many of them and the Pierces chilled the room, not to mention the service.

Thomas didn't want to probe that history. He also decided that using the little music stand for a pulpit or even standing to preach seemed too much in the small space before so few people. So he remained seated and joined heartily in the singing; then he and Grace answered a few questions about themselves before he launched into Jonah going down to Joppa.

Someone called out, "I hope you don't see Colfax as Joppa!"

Thomas laughed. "Anything but," he said. "I've heard so much about you all. You know, the Lord's not interested in numbers. He's interested in souls."

"But the more the merrier," Paul said.

Thomas endured the awkward silence before continuing.

Addison

"Thought you got cut, Darby," someone said on the activities bus.

"You thought wrong. I quit."

"So now you're in the chess club?"

The laughter made Brady flush. "You lookin' to get hurt?"

That stopped the chuckling. The smart mouth, who would abandon the bus as soon as he was old enough to drive whatever car his parents gave him for his sixteenth birthday, held up both hands. "Relax, big boy. Just teasing."

Brady turned and stared out the window, trying to shut out the whispers. At times like this an ache washed over him for something new, something different, something better. Everybody else sat with a buddy or a cluster of friends. He was empty-train-depot lonely, and he hated everything about his life. Hated everybody.

Except Aunt Lois and Uncle Carl. They were embarrassing and weird but hard to hate. And of course Brady didn't hate Petey.

Petey.

What kind of a brother was Brady being to him? The kid was smart, that was clear, already starting to question everything. Used to be Brady could tell him anything, and Peter would buy it. Now the kid could see through Brady when he didn't make sense. Peter wanted to know why he couldn't do what Brady did.

If he was to be any kind of a role model and wanted anything good for Peter, Brady knew he ought to quit smoking, stealing, lying, being a bum. He ought to study, change his look, get a real job. But it was too late. He wasn't sure his grades would qualify him for a role in the musical even if he somehow landed one.

Brady dug the script out of his bag. Was Nabertowitz right? Should he entirely change his look and avoid what Hollywood called being typecast? That would shake up the school, wouldn't it? Not that he was known by more than a few, but it would be noisy if a guy like him suddenly became normal, an actor with a whole new look.

When the bus rolled into the trailer park, Brady was deep into the script of *Bye Bye Birdie*. He had heard of the old movie with Dick Van Dyke and Ann-Margaret, but he had never seen it. Musicals were hardly his thing. But now he was reading fast, imagining himself in the role of the father.

As he reached the front of the bus, still reading, the kid in the back hollered, "Checkmate!"

Brady spun and glared, and the kid and his friends looked away, snickering. Brady considered charging back there and drilling the kid with his fist, but the bus driver—an older version of himself—growled, "Don't do it. Not worth it."

Brady was still fuming as he trudged along the asphalt. It was unlikely his mother was home yet, and he hated the idea of Peter being there alone, but something in the script drew him, and he wanted to get through it. The sun was fading, so he stopped under a streetlamp and read fast.

By the time he was three-fourths of the way through the pages, he knew. Typecast or not, Conrad Birdie was his part. Nabertowitz said he had already cast it, but that probably meant he had some preppy trying to affect a look. Brady already had the look, the attitude, the swagger. The father's role was fun and grumpy and maybe had a little more meat, and even the manager had way more to offer. But Brady knew he wasn't ready for a lead like that. Maybe someday.

If Nabertowitz could be believed, all that would be left the next day would be bit parts. Even the father would likely have been cast, unless the director was saving it for him. Well, Clancy Nabertowitz was in for a surprise. Brady headed for the trailer with a spring in his gait that hadn't been there for months. Soon he was actually jogging.

Glad to see his mother was not there yet, he burst inside, lit a cigarette, and hollered for Peter. "Get your jacket! We're going shopping!"

"For what?"

"You'll see. Now hurry."

While Peter was shutting down his video game and getting his coat on, Brady went to his car-fund stash and pulled out two hundred dollars.

"Hitchhiking again?" Peter said.

"Yeah, but just into Arlington."

Oldenburg

By the time Thomas and Grace finally returned to the parsonage and sat sipping tea, he was exhausted. "Amazing what they've done here," he said.

"Most of these people seem wonderful, Thomas."

"Most?"

"I'm not blind or deaf, dear," she said, "and neither are you. Paul Pierce is going to wear you out. You'd better start setting your boundaries now."

Thomas nodded. "This is unusual, though. I'm like the old circuit-riding preachers. I wonder what they did about church politics. Someone had to run the places while they were away."

"Paul doesn't just want to run this place. He wants to run the whole circuit. Maybe you ought to get

Jimmie Johnson in your corner before Paul makes a mess of everything."

"How would that look? All of a sudden Paul hears from headquarters? No, I've got to face this—and him—myself. It may not be pretty, but you're right; I have to do it soon."

They sat in silence.

Grace smiled at him. "Kind of nice not to have a telephone ringing all the time, isn't it?"

He nodded. "But we'll need one before long."

"Tomorrow soon enough?"

"Really, Grace? That's faster than in town."

"It was my first order of business. I can't wait to bring Ravinia up to date without having to stand at some pay phone."

Euclid Street Haberdashery | Arlington

"That's a funny name," Peter said. "What's it mean?"

"Just clothes, I guess," Brady said.

It was an unusual place, one of few outlets where kids like Brady could get the kind of clothes they liked. The store had all the traditional men's fashions—suits, slacks, sport coats, ties, socks, shoes, belts, hats—but it also had a section that catered to, well, Brady's type. Leather jackets, big wallets with chains, tight pants, and best of all, just the right kind of shoes. It all seemed out of place in a suburban store, but apparently the owner knew a revenue stream when he saw one.

Brady, his curled script still in his hands, told the salesman exactly what he wanted and why.

"You're in luck, sir," the man said. "I have just the thing. Follow me, and may I make a suggestion?"

"Sure."

"Do you have an electric guitar?"

"No."

"Can you borrow one?"

"I don't play."

"You don't have to play. It's just a prop. I did a little musical theater myself, so trust me. You audition in this suit carrying an electric guitar, and you'd have to be the worst actor in the world to not get the part. I mean, come on, you look like Birdie in street clothes. Imagine yourself in this."

With a flourish, the man pulled a suit off the rack and squared it up so Brady and Peter could get the full effect.

"Oh, man!" Peter said. "Brady, you've *got* to get that!"

Brady stared and shook his head. "That's gonna be way out of my price range."

"It's on sale!"

"Of course it is."

"I'm serious. And we have it in your size. It would have to be tailored, but—"

"I have to take it with me tonight, man."

"Hmm. We usually like a few days. Tell you what, I'll do it myself, while you wait."

Brady showed him how much money he had.

"Hmm. You're a little short, but given the circumstances, we'll make it work. But you have to tell me how everything goes tomorrow. And if you know anybody with an electric guitar . . . the louder the better."

"I told you, I don't play."

"I'm not talking volume, sir. I'm talking color. Just be sure it doesn't clash with the suit."

Brady and Peter got home with just minutes to spare before Brady had to clean the Laundromat. Worse, his mother's car was there. And she was on his case from the minute he opened the door. *Where have you been; why didn't you leave a note; what have you gone and wasted your money on now; what's the idea keeping a kid out this late?*—the whole bit.

Brady hurried Peter off to bed. "Just mind your own business, Ma, and don't try to tell me Petey *is* your business. You're the one who's supposed to be here with him, not me. I do more with him than you do. I had an errand to run; what was I going to do, leave him here alone? Now I gotta go to work, and then I'm stopping over at Stevie Ray's."

She was still screaming at him as he left.

Brady had never worked so hard and fast. He had the Laundromat tidied in no time, and that night he didn't skim even a quarter.

At 10:30 he knocked at Stevie Ray's trailer. A thirtyish man with a long ponytail and wearing workout shorts and a wife-beater undershirt answered the door.

"Hey, dude," he whispered. "C'mon in. Gotta be quiet. The baby just went down."

"You busy?" Brady said, stepping in.

"Nah. Just watchin' the end of the news. Have a brew."

Stevie Ray pulled a couple of Buds from the fridge. Brady knew he shouldn't, because he planned to be up all night memorizing lines. But, hey.

Stevie Ray muted the TV as they sat. "So what's up? Haven't seen you in a while. Heard your dad passed."

"Yeah. Listen, I was wonderin' if I could borrow your Stratocaster."

Stevie Ray took a long pull and studied Brady. "You kidding? That's my life, man. Cost more'n my car. And you don't play anyway, do you?"

Brady explained why he needed it. "I mean, unless you have a gig tomorrow. I could have it back by seven or so."

"We only play weekends now; you know that. Doing the Ramada Friday and Saturday and some kid's birthday party Sunday."

"Cool."

"So you don't need the amp? You're not gonna plug it in?"

"I'm just going to hold it and pretend."

"You'll keep it in the case at all times otherwise?"

"Promise."

"And you're not gonna let anybody else so much as touch it."

"I swear. Man, I really appreciate this."

72

"You're a nut, Brady. You know that, right?"

"Yeah."

Stevie Ray went to get the guitar, and Brady could hear him talking with his wife. Then he laid the case on the couch and opened it. "I'm just an old rocker," he said, "but I learned something from the pros. You treat your ax like a gem. None of that trashin' your equipment for me. Maybe those dudes can afford a new one every week, but not me."

The gleaming instrument was metallic blue with white trim. Perfect.

"Stevie, you're as good a picker as I've ever heard—Clapton, Harrison, all of 'em included."

"Yeah, yeah," Stevie Ray said, smiling. "And those guys don't work on cars between gigs. Listen, so much as a scratch on this thing and you're dead."

"I'll protect it with my life."

8

Oldenburg

Thomas Carey had never considered himself handy, but things around the new house needed attention. So he was up at dawn, dressed in work clothes, and unshaven. He never, ever, missed his morning Bible reading and prayer ritual—even on his days off. Today, as usual, Ravinia was at the top of his prayer list. How he agonized over her, pleading with God to draw her back to Himself.

Normally Grace was fixing breakfast by the time Thomas had finished his devotions, but he heard no stirring and decided to tackle a few small projects in the bathroom while waiting. He was under the sink with tools and caulk when hunger overtook him and he wandered out to see about Grace. He found her still in bed.

"A little punky this morning," she slurred.

"Big day yesterday," he said. "I'm exhausted too. Hungry? Let me bring you something."

"Not really, but that'd be nice. Something light and easy."

He laughed. Toast would tax Thomas's kitchen abilities.

He put water on to boil for tea, poured a small glass of orange juice, and soon delivered both with lightly buttered toast and marmalade. But Grace was asleep again, her breathing even and deep.

Her graying hair was pulled back into a bun, and yet even without makeup she still looked like the sweet young thing he had met at Bible college. Thomas sat on the edge of the bed and laid a hand on her shoulder, but she did not stir. He idly munched toast and sipped the juice, finally leaving the room to finish his chores.

Loud banging at the door startled Thomas, and he leaped to his feet, catching a glimpse of himself in the mirror. He hoped he could find a cap between the bathroom and the front door. Visitors on his day off was a pet peeve, but worse was being seen out of uniform. Any other day, by now he would be shaved, showered, combed, and in at least a shirt and tie.

He splashed a little water on both hands and ran them through his hair, reminded by the sound of splashing on the floor that he had not yet resecured the drain. If only Grace were up and could save him the embarrassment of appearing at the door with stubble on his chin. . . .

The phone installer was expected that day. Thomas supposed he could abide being seen this way by a workingman or woman. But no such luck. It was Paul and Patricia Pierce in full shrillness.

"Got a little worried about ya not being in the office this morning," Paul said as they entered and sat. "It'll be handier when you've got a phone. What's up?"

Thomas hesitated. Did he really have to explain himself to Paul? It seemed too soon to put his foot down, stand his ground, all those things Grace had urged him to consider. "I generally like to take Monday off," he said.

"And you did, right? Tuesday starts the church week here, as a rule."

"Well, I was pretty busy here all day yesterday, and then last night was the—"

"You were on your own time putzing around here yesterday, and last night was hardly working, was it?"

In fact, Thomas had met a third congregation and conducted a service the night before, but Paul had been there and knew that.

"I have a lot to finish here today, so I'll be back in the saddle tomorrow."

"With the week half gone and five churches to worry about?" Paul said. "Well, you're younger'n I am, so I guess you can cram it all in. Where's the missus?"

"A little under the weather this morning actually. I'll pass along your greetings."

It was as if Patricia Pierce had heard the news about Grace as a signal to rise. She began tidying the room, opening curtains, adjusting this and that.

Thomas was suddenly overcome with anger and had to bite his tongue. He imagined himself demanding that these people leave and give him and his wife room to breathe.

But he would not do that. Never had. God would give him grace, he decided, and it would all seem minor once they were gone.

"Hey!" Paul said. "Here's the phone company now."

Within minutes a young man was drilling and wiring and installing a phone jack near the counter that separated the tiny kitchen from the living room. Both Paul and Patricia had ideas where it should go, but Grace had lightly penciled the spot on the wall.

"I wish she was up," Patricia said, "because I believe she'd agree that here would be less conspicuous."

The installer said, "You've got plenty of wire to put the phone where you want. The jack can go anywhere."

"Sure," Patricia said, "if you don't care a thing about decor."

The installer checked his paperwork. "You also wanted an extension phone in the bedroom?"

Thomas explained that his wife was still asleep and asked if that could be installed another time.

"Probably be another week, and I'd have to charge for a separate visit."

"He won't bother her, Tom," Paul said. "And you don't want to pay twice. That would have to be a personal charge. You wouldn't expect the church to—"

"Next week will be fine," Thomas said. "And of course I'll cover it. Now I should see about Grace."

"And I'll see you at the office later?"

"No, Paul. I'm taking today off. Next week I'll get into the routine of taking Mondays off. I'll be in tomorrow."

"I've got a meeting with two of my sons tomorrow, Thomas."

"Do you need to be there when I am?"

"Well, no, I guess not. But being your first week and all, and with me overseeing the other congregations for you—"

"Will you be around Thursday, Paul?"

"Sure."

"Then let's talk about the other congregations at that time."

"Talk about them?" Paul said.

"Thursday."

Addison

Brady Darby had not considered how conspicuous he'd feel with a garment bag over one shoulder and carrying a guitar case onto the school bus. At least it gave him a reason to leave his books at home.

"You in a band now?" fat Agatha whined. What had he ever seen in her? Well, he guessed he knew that well enough.

"Yeah," he said. "The Beatles are gettin' back together and want me to play lead. Shut up."

Oldenburg

When Thomas again checked on Grace, he noticed that while the tea had clearly been sipped, nothing else on the tray had been touched, and she was asleep again. She was rarely ill and hardly ever lost her appetite. He was just glad she had been spared the Pierces' drop-in. They had taken down the Careys' new number and would likely be the first callers.

Thomas knew whom Grace would call first. He could only hope Ravinia would be encouraged by their new situation. His wife would know better than to tell her all about the Pierces.

Forest View High School

Brady ducked into Mr. Nabertowitz's office just before first bell and asked if he could stash his stuff somewhere. "It doesn't fit in my locker, and I don't want to lug it around all day."

"What in the world is it?"

"You'll see."

"How interesting! You have props?"

"I guess."

"What's with the guitar?"

"Like I said, you'll see."

"I love that you're coming prepared, but as I told you, we've cast most of the leads. We have a guy who would be perfect for the father, but he can't carry a tune. Can you?"

"I think I can, but I'm not trying out for the father."

"There's nothing left, son. Just town kids, bit parts."

"I'm auditioning for Birdie."

Nabertowitz sighed and shook his head. "I told you I had someone for that."

"Is it a done deal? 'Cause I don't think I'm interested in anything else."

"You're going to have to thrill me, and I'm going to have a real problem if I change now."

"Sorry."

"Truth is, I wouldn't mind the problem. My Birdie hardly has the bad-boy look I want. He'd be much better as the jealous boyfriend. But he wants the part, and he's earned it. He's going to Northwestern next year, and his parents are supportive of me and the program here and are thrilled to death he has the lead."

"Birdie's not the lead."

Nabertowitz cocked his head. "I thought only I understood that."

"Anybody who's read the script ought to know Birdie is just the title character. The lead is the manager. Give hotshot that part. Can he sing and dance?"

"He sure can."

"Then there you go."

"I have an older-looking kid for that. Real promising."

"Make him the father, hotshot the manager, me Birdie."

Nabertowitz led Brady to the door. "You'd better get to class. And we're way, way ahead of ourselves here. I'll let you audition for Birdie, but you must know it's a long shot. It's not a terribly demanding part, as you know. The look is paramount, and you have that. But it's also crucial you can sing and dance, and not even you know that yet."

The rest of the day, Brady went over and over in his mind his plan for the audition. He sat in the backs of classes and assumed his bored, defiant look, so teachers didn't bother with him. He carried no books, took no notes, just sat and thought. He'd never sung in front of anybody but Petey, but he always sang along to the radio—classic rock, oldies, and hard rock. Who knew whether he was any good? He sure didn't.

Dancing was another matter. He had been to a few and there were those who seemed to appreciate a James Brown thing he could do. Birdie was, of course, more of an Elvis figure with a hip shake Brady would have to learn. But for today, he'd stick with what he knew.

Problem was, every time Brady really thought about the prospect of standing alone on stage, in costume, singing and dancing for Nabertowitz along with who knew how many kids, he seriously doubted whether he could go through with it. Part of him had a feeling this might be his ticket from trailer trash to respectability, something that would allow him to rescue Petey from the same horrid existence. But another part of him was certain this was a pipe dream, the ridiculous notion of a nobody from nowhere.

He sat watching the clock during his last class, weighing the prospect of just gathering up his suit and guitar and heading home.

Oldenburg

Grace had finally roused around lunchtime, complaining of fatigue and a lack of appetite. But Thomas persuaded her to try half a cheese sandwich—again testing his culinary skills—with a little more tea.

"Anything specific, hon?" he said. "You need to see a doctor?"

"I don't think so. I'm just wiped out. We've been through a lot in just a few days."

"Tell me about it."

Thomas was stunned to learn that she had been wholly unaware the Pierces had been there. "You slept through all that? Paul's not a quiet guy."

She nodded. "How long were they here?"

"Long enough to try to supervise the phone installation."

"What? You didn't tell me! I want to call Ravinia!"

Thomas pointed her to the phone, encouraged that she suddenly seemed perkier. He cleared away the dishes as she dialed.

"Yes, thank you, just a minute," she said, then covered the receiver. "Thomas, write this down. Rav's suitemate says she has a new number. She's moved."

"Moved? What—go ahead, I'm ready."

Grace recited the number and hung up. "She's not in the dorm anymore. The girl says she found a roommate off campus to save money."

"That's prudent, but it sure happened fast."

"She's always been good with money," Grace said as Thomas slid the new number to her. "But I wish she didn't have to do this."

Thomas sat, waiting his turn to talk to his daughter.

"No answer," Grace whispered, then, "Oh, wait." She squinted, then opened her mouth as if to speak before quickly hanging up. "Oh no."

"What?"

She stood and moved toward the bedroom.

"Grace! What?"

"You don't want to know."

"Of course I do; now what?"

"Call her yourself," she said, shutting the bedroom door.

Thomas dialed, his fingers shaking. The number

rang four times; then came his daughter's cheerfully recorded voice: "You've reached Dirk and Rav. Leave a message after the beep and . . ."

Thomas found Grace curled on the bed, sobbing. "It may not be as bad as it sounds," he said.

"Oh, Thomas, it's one thing for us to be old-fashioned, but let's not be naive."

9

Forest View High School

Brady seemed to move in slow motion, such was his dread on the way to the Little Theater. All around him fresh-scrubbed preppies bustled, laughing, gossiping, seeming eager to get to the sheets taped to the door, listing parts already cast. A few girls glanced at Brady, clearly wondering what he was doing there. Another held her nose and leaned to whisper something to a friend, but she quickly straightened when Brady glared.

He recognized none of the names on the sheet and again considered forgetting the whole crazy idea, until he noticed "Alex North*" on the Conrad Birdie line. At the bottom he found "*Pending." So Nabertowitz was withholding his final decision until he'd seen Brady onstage.

No pressure there. As Brady headed toward his suit and guitar, kids were saying, "Did you see that? North's not in for sure."

"No way."

"Why?"

"C'mon—he's automatic."

A small wicker basket lay on a table in the music room adjoining the stage. Kids were drawing numbers from it. Brady hesitated. He could just grab his stuff and still make the bus. This was crazy. Nobody would look at him straight on, but he felt everyone's eyes. He had as much business here as a linebacker in an antique store.

Brady made up his mind to go home. He marched to the closet and grabbed the garment bag and guitar case.

"Hey!" a girl squealed. "Is he stealing something?"

Brady whirled. "Who, me?" Everyone froze. "These yours?"

"No, I just—"

"Then shut your mouth!"

Nabertowitz entered and seemed to quickly detect the awkwardness. "Hi, Brady," he said. "Did you get a number?"

"No."

"Grab one."

If Brady hadn't been stopped, he'd have been out of there by now. With everyone staring, he put his stuff back in the closet and grabbed a slip from the basket: 38. *Oh, great.* If he didn't get this over soon, he was going to explode.

His eyes found the girl again, a cheerleader type.

"I'm sorry," she whispered, flushed. "I just thought—"

"I know what you thought," he said and moved to the wing of the stage, where he could watch.

"I'm really sorry," she said, grabbing a sheaf of papers off a table and moving past him. "That was stupid of me."

Brady wasn't sure why, but she had somehow made him feel sorry for her. She had assumed a guy like him could only be up to no good in the music room, and worse, she must have considered him stupid enough to try to steal something in front of dozens of people. Well, he wouldn't berate her anymore, but he'd show her.

To Brady's surprise, the girl strode directly to a spinet piano just offstage and arranged her music. From the darkened seats, where Clancy Nabertowitz sat surrounded by kids who had apparently been cast the day before, the director called out, "First sixteen girls, town chorus!"

From both sides of the stage they came, some looking eager, others petrified. Brady could identify. He knew that by now he was the talk of the place. But these girls had a job to do, and within minutes, Cheerleader was whaling away on the piano as the others cavorted all over the stage.

A girl stepped up behind Brady. "Is it true you're trying out for Birdie?"

He turned. "What's it to you?"

"Nothing to me. Might mean something to my boyfriend, though. That's him right in front of Mr. N."

Brady squinted. A short, good-looking kid sat

staring at the stage, arms folded, scowling. "Doesn't seem as impressed with the dancers as everyone else is."

"He'd better not be," the girl said, laughing. "'Course, he's worried about you."

"He doesn't even know me."

"He knows of you. He and Mr. N. are tight. He always gets the leads."

"He shouldn't have any trouble beating me out."

"You ride a motorcycle?"

Brady grimaced and faced her. "What makes you ask that?"

"You look the type, that's all."

"I can't afford a motorcycle."

"Well, you'd look good on one."

Brady turned back to the stage, feeling himself redden. Had he just been hit on by a popular girl? Impossible.

During the hubbub of kids taking and leaving the stage, Brady noticed the girl at the piano sneaking a peek at him. What was this? Never seen his type before?

She mouthed, "Forgive me?"

He cocked his head and shrugged, nodding. She beckoned him over.

"I'm really not usually like that," she said.

"Forget it."

"Thanks."

Again confused and tongue-tied, he moved away, only to stop and spin. "You want to make it up to me?"

She looked wary. "How?"

"You know 'Blue Suede Shoes,' the Carl—"

"—Perkins classic? Of course. I don't have the music, but I could figure it out. It's not in this play, you know."

He shot her a look.

"Sorry. Guess you knew that."

"Yeah, I knew. And do you know the lighting guys?"

She nodded.

"Okay, here's what I need. . . ."

An hour later Brady was as antsy as he had ever been. These kids all seemed to know each other, to know what they were doing, and to be doing it well. Nabertowitz hollered, "Thirty-seven! Hi there! What're you auditioning for?"

"Bartender!"

"Very good. When you're ready."

Brady hurried to the closet, grabbed the garment bag, and ducked into the bathroom. It frustrated him to find a few other guys in there. The conversation quickly stopped. He hadn't wanted to change in a stall, but that was his only choice now.

Brady got the door shut and opened the bag, kicking off his shoes and trying to maneuver in the tiny chamber. He heard a snicker. What must they be thinking?

He swore when he realized his belt didn't fit the tiny loops in the suit slacks. It still wasn't too late to back out. If he didn't answer when the director called his number, end of story.

But as he pulled his shoes back on, Brady could think only of the trailer, his wasted mother, and Peter. Maybe this wasn't the only way out, but it could be a start, and he owed that much to Petey. Somehow he knew that if he could keep his brother at the forefront of his mind, he could do this. He had no idea whether he was any good or if he would wind up humiliated, but he could at least try.

Brady emerged relieved to see the bathroom empty, but when he got into the music room, the same guys were bending over the now open guitar case. "Sweet!"

"A Strat!"

"Touch that and I break your face," Brady said.

The boys recoiled. "Just looking, pal. Chill."

"Yeah, well, it isn't mine and I'm not supposed to let anyone—"

"Great threads, by the way."

From the theater Brady heard, "Thirty-eight!"

He lifted the guitar, heavier than he expected, and slung the black leather strap over his shoulder. He should have practiced this. He just missed the door-jamb with the neck, and as he moved to the side of the stage, still out of sight, the houselights went black.

Maybe this wasn't such a good idea after all. Brady padded carefully toward the single mike at center stage as murmurs faded to silence, but he could see nothing. What if he plunged into the orchestra pit? He treaded gingerly, feeling carefully for solid ground. Finally Brady nudged the mike, pulled it close to his mouth, and took a deep breath.

Forcing his fear somewhere deep inside, he belted, "Well, it's one for the money!" and the girl at the piano banged a loud chord. "Two for the show!" and she came in again. "Three to get ready, now go, cat, go!" and the spotlight hit him.

Somehow Brady had begun on pitch, and now that he was into it, he just let loose. Air-picking the gleaming blue Stratocaster, he could see the spotlight dancing off his suit, gold lamé from head to toe.

During a piano interlude, Brady danced all over the stage to the squeals and cheers of the crowd, and the light followed him. No one was going to believe this hadn't been choreographed and rehearsed. How could he ever thank the piano girl and the lighting guys?

When he finished, Brady took a sweeping bow and ran from the stage, holding up his pants with his free hand.

"Get back out here, Brady Darby!" Mr. Nabertowitz squealed. "Encore! Encore!"

Brady stopped, panting.

"Go back," someone said. "Curtain call."

Hands from everywhere pushed him back out. He visored his eyes with his hand but couldn't see Mr. N. in the darkness.

"Kill the spot!" the teacher said, and the houselights came up. "Ladies and gentlemen, may I introduce Mr. Conrad Birdie!"

More cheering and clapping, but it was not lost on Brady that Alex North rose and stormed out.

Well, Alex was Nabertowitz's problem. For now,

Brady was Christmas-morning happy. He imagined himself on the cover of the program, but he also knew there would be a lot of hard work between now and opening night.

By the time he got back to the music room, Nabertowitz was there. "You are something special, my young friend!" he said. "You can sing. I hope you have a little range in your dancing, but we can work on that."

"You gonna have trouble with North?"

"Of course." The teacher leaned close. "Between you and me, I'm worried more about Mom and Dad, but I can handle it. You just worry about learning your part."

Brady carefully reboxed the guitar, and this time he kept it with him when he returned to the bathroom. But his clothes were not hanging in the stall. Had he forgotten which one he'd changed in? As he moved from door to door, he noticed two sinks were full of water.

One also held his shirt.

The other his pants.

10

Thursday | Oldenburg Rural Chapel

Paul Pierce was away for more meetings with his sons, so Thomas Carey felt productive all morning, talking by phone with contacts at each of the other four churches in his circuit, getting a little studying and sermon preparation done, and even somewhat organizing the modest office. At the back of his mind was Grace, who had again been slow to rise and exhibited a strange bruise on one wrist. She attributed it to the heavy work around the house but couldn't remember a specific injury.

The puzzle of Ravinia was always with him. What had he and Grace done wrong? How had they failed her? How would God bring her back? Thomas had always believed and taught that God wooed unbelievers but chastised His own when they strayed. He dreaded that for his daughter.

And then there was also the coming confrontation with Paul.

Thomas hated the word *confrontation* almost as much as he hated the activity itself. He imagined himself straightforward and firm when he knew he was right, but the truth was, Grace was better at these things. She was slow to anger and usually diplomatic, but she was not afraid to speak her mind when she felt it important. Thomas had good intentions, but he always seemed to think of a better way to have said something long after it might have been effective.

There was no getting around it though. If he didn't start standing up to Paul, his life would quickly become miserable. Such long-term grief would be much worse than the sharp pain of a brief encounter where he stood his ground. Thomas jotted a few notes on what he wanted to say and how to say it. Paul was expected at 2 p.m.

Brady Darby felt like a Connecticut Yankee in King Arthur's court. He had never read the Mark Twain novel, assigned in English the year before, but the title had amused him, and the class discussion had given him an idea what it was about. Now he could really identify. In a matter of forty-eight brief hours, he had become the talk of the drama department.

He still looked the same, smelled the same, dressed the same. But suddenly he was no longer invisible to the larger culture. Usually, except for the occasional peek or sneer, aside from the negative attention on the bus every morning, normal kids looked right through his type—if they looked at all. Of course they were afraid of him, and that suited Brady fine. He scowled and snapped and blustered enough to keep them at bay.

But now it seemed a lot more kids knew his name. He was no longer able to trudge through the halls with his eyes cast down, because everywhere he went someone was sure to call out, "Hey, Brady! Go, dude! Birdie, man! Way to go!"

Brady was fully aware of glances from girls who used to turn up their noses at him. This he didn't get. Were they really interested or just curious? Had he become a novelty, some sort of a mascot? Brady wasn't sure what to make of it all.

Most bizarre was that Agatha had stepped in front of him while boarding the bus that morning and forced her big body down the narrow aisle to where a young girl sat alone. "You," Agatha said, pointing, "move back there. Brady and me are sittin' here." And the girl had moved.

Brady found himself strangely grateful to have enough room to sit, though Agatha took most of the bench. But he also felt conspicuous. He had long since lost any interest in her—which had been private and solely carnal anyway. She leaned against him and whispered, "You gotta tell me if it's true you wore the gold suit home on the activities bus."

"So what?"

"Why didn't you change?"

"None ya."

"Say what?"

"None ya business."

She turned and stared out the window. Finally she turned back. "Whatever became of us, Brady?"

"There was never any *us*," he said.

"You could have fooled me."

"Then I fooled you, Agatha."

"I hate you."

"Grow up."

Just after lunch Brady was summoned to Clancy Nabertowitz's office and enjoyed the stares as he headed that way.

"You seem really into this," the teacher said.

"I am. Still learning, but it's fun."

"Where are your books, Brady?"

"My books?"

"Your textbooks."

"Oh, uh, in my locker."

"I saw you come in this morning empty-handed."

"Yeah, I didn't have homework, so I left 'em here."

"You need to know, son, that your landing this role has become noisy. Everybody seems excited about it."

"I know."

"We're already selling tickets six weeks before we open, and we're going to be sold out. I'm talking with the principal about doubling our performances over two weekends."

"No kidding? Cool."

"Well, it won't be cool if my Birdie disqualifies himself. You think I don't know that you didn't quit football? that your grades were as bad as your athletic ability? Don't say anything; just listen. I've known you a few days, and I recognize unusual talent when I see it. But if you're not careful, you're going to screw up a wonderful opportunity. You have the potential to make something of yourself. Already I see you mouthing other characters' lines, like you're memorizing the entire musical."

"I'm trying."

"Do you know how rare that is?"

Brady shook his head. "Seems important to me. Makes everything easier."

"Well, of course it does, but not even many pros have the energy and the interest to do that—though they should. I see you really giving yourself to this,

94

and I'm convinced this could be the best production we've ever had here."

"Wow."

"Wow nothing. You had better swear to me you won't become academically ineligible. I mean, Alex can play Birdie in a pinch, but I don't know if anyone else can play Albert. You let me down, this goes from something really special to one big mess."

"I hear you."

"Do you?"

"Yeah, I do. I'll get after my grades."

"It won't be easy with rehearsal every night. And you have a job?"

"Just an hour every night."

"Just an hour. When will you study?"

"Study hall."

"That never works."

"It'll have to."

"Yes, it will. Now are you promising me?"

"I'll do my best."

Nabertowitz leaned back and stared at the ceiling. "You're not overwhelming me with confidence."

"What do you want to hear?"

"I want to hear that you recognize what an incredible opportunity this is, that it means as much to you as it does to me. You think I do high school drama because I wouldn't rather be on Broadway? Like most everyone, I had to finally admit my limitations. Now nothing thrills me more than to discover talent and get kids on their way to at least a fun avocation."

The teacher shook his head and leaned toward Brady, whispering, "I'll deny I ever said this, but you're better than my star pupil. Alex is going places, and he'll have some fun. But he's limited by his frame, his voice. His type is a dime a dozen. But a big Travolta type like you? The sky's the limit, Brady. And don't be tempted to think then that education isn't important. You and I both know that if you drop out of school, you'll never really pursue this. I don't expect you to be a scholar, but please, please, for me but mostly for you, do what you have to to stay eligible."

Brady didn't know what to say. He just nodded.

"And I need a favor," Mr. Nabertowitz said. "Alex's parents are coming this afternoon to 'talk,' and I want them to meet you. I frankly think that if they can put a face to the name, it'll be harder for them to demonize you, know what I mean?"

"Not really, but I'll meet them, sure."

"Be on your best behavior. Watch your temper. Maybe you could even say something nice about Alex."

"Like what? The kid's an—"

"Come, come. Surely you can tell he's got talent. You don't have to say anything about his personality or character. You want to be an actor? Muster something."

"Whatever. Doesn't it kill him that Mommy and Daddy are coming to fight for him?"

"Oh, it's not being represented that way at all. They're just coming to watch rehearsal. They want to talk to me after, of course, and only an imbecile would wonder why, but let's play along."

"They can't talk you into him replacing me, can they?"

"Oh, heavens no! Don't worry about that."

Oldenburg

Thomas took a call from Grace and worried that she still sounded weary. "You doing okay?" he said.

"I'm fine, hon. Just wanted you to know I would be praying during your meeting."

"And have you talked with Rav?"

"I can't yet, Thomas. There's nothing I could say that she doesn't already know. We'll have to talk with her together, let her know we still love her, love her unconditionally. We do, don't we?"

"Of course."

At five minutes before two, Paul Pierce burst in without knocking. "Well, look who's working!" he said, smiling and reaching across the desk to shake hands. "Tom, Tom, the preacher man!"

"Good afternoon, Paul."

"Come take a walk with me, Tom. Stuffy in here."

"Well, there are matters we need to discuss."

"I know that. That's why I'm here! C'mon."

Thomas followed him out and they strolled the property. "I thought we should talk about the supervision of the other church bodies," Thomas said.

"All in good time. I've got a couple of sheets I want to show you about how I plan to supervise 'em, and I've got a plan for a—what do you call it?—installation service for you."

"For me?"

"And for Grace. Get all the churches to come here, since we've got a big enough building to hold 'em, and we'll do up a nice deal—music, tributes, eats. What do you think?"

"Oh, well, Paul, I'm not sure that's necessary. This work is not about—"

"Now just let us do it, Tom. Give honor where honor is due and all that. Patricia and I will handle everything. You and your bride just show up, okay?"

"I'll talk to Grace about—"

"Just be a man, Tom, and tell her when it is. She'll love it, believe me. We'll do it next Sunday night."

"I suppose that would be fine, and I appreciate it, Paul, but—"

"And you don't have to even prepare a message. I mean, say a few words, sure, but don't go to any trouble. In fact, if I can be frank with you, Tom, we need to talk a little about your preaching."

Thomas wished he'd brought a jacket. The fall breeze was as irrepressible as Paul. "My preaching?"

"If you can call it that." Paul laughed a little too loudly. "I'm joshin' ya, Tom, but seriously. I know I've only heard you the two times, and both times it was the same sermon. But I specifically instructed you to shorten it some for the folks at Colfax, and if I'm not mistaken, it was almost word for word what you did here."

Instructed? "Oh, not word for word, but—"

"But you said yourself it was an old chestnut you've delivered lots of times. I got to tell you, Tom, it has a little age on it. You refer to lots of commentary writers, when people want to hear your own thoughts."

"Well, that's how most preachers form their thoughts, Paul. We read, we study, we compare passages, we compare and contrast commentators and decide which we agree with, then share that with—"

"I'm just sayin', okay? Work at being original and tighten up your delivery. We don't want people's eyes glazing over, now do we?"

"I know I'm no great orator, Paul. . . ."

"Now there's an understatement! Ha! I'm glad you have a sense of humor about it, Tom. It'll work out as you settle in and get to know us."

Thomas stopped and rubbed his eyes. "Paul, we really need to talk about the oversight of the other congregations."

"I know we do. Come on in and I'll show you my plans."

Forest View High School

Just before rehearsal that afternoon, Alex North finally locked eyes with Brady. "Don't worry," Alex said, "I'll be ready when you crash and burn."

"What's that supposed to mean?"

"Just that besides playing the lead, I'm under-studying for you. Mr. N. says you're flunking out of the play, so I'll be ready. Who knows? I may have to play both parts."

Flunking out? Nabertowitz actually told him that?

"What're you, nuts? Most of your scenes are *with* Birdie, you idiot."

"I'm just saying I could do both, and it's unlikely you can do one."

"How about we go outside so I can kick—"

"Gentlemen!" Mr. Nabertowitz said, breezing in. "I'm not even praying for chemistry, but you two are going to have to work together, so . . ."

Brady approached the director and whispered, "You told him I was flunking out?"

"I said no such thing, Brady. I merely told him you had some academic issues and that we had to be pre-pared for any eventuality. Now, I'll talk to him about what he thinks he heard. You just concentrate on what *you* need to do. And by the way, his parents are in the front row."

11

Oldenburg Rural Chapel

Thomas had not expected his discussion with Paul Pierce to go smoothly, but this was absurd. The man was still sitting there, in the pastor's office, arguing point by point why his plan to supervise the other churches made more sense than Thomas's doing it himself.

"I'll explain myself one more time, Paul, if I must. I'll be at each location every week. They don't want to feel like sister churches or daughter churches of this one, and frankly, I'm sensing you have personally alienated some of them."

"*I* have? *Me?* Tell me one person who's said that, and I'll tell you why."

Thomas shook his head. "Now, Paul, I'm going to have to ask that you defer to me as your pastor on this. I deeply appreciate all your help, and Grace and I cannot deny that you and Patricia have gone the extra mile in getting us settled in and making us feel welcome. . . ."

"But you don't need me anymore."

Oh, for the love . . .

Thomas had run into this type before—perhaps not as stage-mom brash as Paul Pierce, but the kind that resorted to cheap tactics when not getting his way. Paul sat there looking and sounding like a big baby. He had summarized Thomas's position by exaggerating it to the ridiculous. And he wasn't finished.

"If you'd rather Patricia and I just show up for services and sit in the back and don't even attempt to come alongside and help, fine."

Thomas almost fell for the trick, nearly jumping in to reassure Paul that that wasn't what he wished at all. But fortunately, perhaps because of Grace's praying, he kept his senses.

"Here's what I want, Paul, if you really want to help. I want you to not take this personally—"

"How can I not?"

"—and I want you to be willing to agree to disagree but defer to me as your shepherd."

"I've been here for decades, Tom! I—"

"And I want you to continue in your leadership role in this church, teaching me the ropes, handling the logistics . . ."

Forest View High School

The Norths were hard to miss. Besides looking too young to be the parents of a high school senior, they looked like they belonged on the cover of some fashion magazine. Alex's dad actually had a cashmere sweater slung over his back, the sleeves tied in front.

A little girl was distracting Alex's mom by running all over the place, and more than once the woman had to retrieve her and make her sit. A few minutes later she was gone again, apparently as soon as her mother became engrossed in Alex's performance.

And Alex was good, playing perfectly the whiny musical agent beset by an overbearing mother. Brady had to admit that Alex rose to the occasion and actually exhibited some urgent compassion for his own Conrad Birdie character. Maybe they could pull this off after all, despite all that was already between them offstage.

Brady felt good about his own performance too, though he knew Mr. N. would notice how many times he peeked out at the house. He was just trying to get a read on the family dynamic, dreading the staged meeting.

Interestingly, Mr. Nabertowitz found some errand for Alex when that time came, then made it appear he had just thought of the introduction. "Oh, Mr. and Mrs. North, I want you to meet our Conrad Birdie. This is Brady Darby."

Mr. North thrust out his hand, seeming to measure the boy with his eyes. Without a smile, he said, "Jordan North, Alex's father. And this is my wife, Carole. Alex's sister, Katie, is running around here somewhere."

"She's right behind me, actually," Mrs. North said, turning to try to pull the girl into view.

Katie peeked at Brady and smiled. "He's cool!"

Brady felt himself redden, and ignoring that Mrs. North had not offered her hand, he reached for it anyway, resulting in an awkward pause. He realized his mistake and was pulling away when she seemed to reluctantly reach for his hand. He laughed and shook her hand, but it was limp as a soggy newspaper, and Brady could see he repulsed her.

"Alex says you live in a trailer," Katie said from behind her mother's leg.

"Katie, hush," Mrs. North said quickly as Brady's smile disappeared.

"Well, do you?" Katie insisted.

"A *trailer?* Yeah, right! Do *you?*"

Mr. Nabertowitz jumped in. "I just thought you all

should meet, since Alex and Brady will be working together, and—"

"We live in a mansion!" little Katie said.

"I'll bet you do," Brady said, somehow gathering himself. "Anyway, nice to meet you all. Alex is really good."

"Thank you," Mr. North said. Mrs. North was looking elsewhere.

When they moved away, Katie was still standing there smiling shyly at Brady. "I'm nine," she said. "You date younger women?"

Not rich little wenches like you. "You kidding?"

"Of course, silly. I bet you do live in a trailer."

"No costume tonight, Conrad?" someone trilled on the activities bus.

Brady had been furious to have to carry his sopping clothes home in a plastic bag after his audition, wearing his leather jacket over the suit. It may have been dramatic and won him the part, but it made him look like an idiot offstage.

Brady had learned not to even turn to see who needed a beating. He just kept reading his script, knowing he should be studying. He amazed himself with how much he had already memorized, and he couldn't argue with Mr. Nabertowitz that if he applied that same skill to schoolwork, he wouldn't have anything to worry about.

Soon, however, he found himself unable to concentrate as he ran over and over in his mind the meeting with the Norths and their bratty daughter.

Brady was surprised to see his mother home from work already. It bothered him that she was usually out at all hours of the night with her boss-slash-boyfriend, but at least that way he didn't have to worry she'd be putting her hands on Petey when Brady wasn't there. He sure hoped Peter would tell him if she did, but the boy knew Brady had threatened her, so who knew if he was hiding something?

She was yelling at Peter when Brady entered.

"Zip it, Ma!" Brady said.

"I'm tired of him sitting around playing video games all the time!" she said. "He ought to be doing something productive!"

"Like you?"

"Don't start with me, Brady."

"He's eight, Ma. Get off his case. It's almost his bedtime anyway—as if you'd know."

"You're gonna stop being smart with me, Brady."

"Don't count on it."

"By the way, you must be in trouble."

"What're you talking about?"

"Mr. Tatlock called. Wants to see you at the Laundromat right away."

"I'm not due there till ten."

"He said now. What'd you do?"

"Tried to burn the place down, what do you think? C'mon, would I do something wrong at the only place I get any money?"

"Just get over there."

"I'm proud of you, Thomas," Grace said, sounding as tired as she looked. "It sounds as if the Lord gave you the words and the courage to say them."

"Oh, I don't know," he said. "I don't think Paul is happy."

"Men like Paul are used to getting their own way."

"Yes, and when they don't . . ."

"Let's let tomorrow take care of tomorrow."

"You think I should let them have the installation service?"

"Of course! You deserve it."

"You know better than that."

"Well, I think you do, but even if you don't, just give the Lord the glory and let the people welcome you."

He shrugged. "Paul may have lost his enthusiasm for the idea by now."

"Drop one of his own brainstorms? Somehow I doubt it."

"Well, I'm certainly not going to ask about it," Thomas said. "If it happens, it happens."

"Like I said, let tomorrow take care of tomorrow. Now, you know what I'd like to do tonight?"

"Tell me."

"I'd like to sing."

Thomas had to smile, despite the tough day and his worry over Rav and his wife. Grace had the sweetest demeanor and a voice to go with it. He could carry a tune, but Grace sang like an angel.

"What do you want to sing, ma'am?" he said with a twinkle.

And Grace began softly, "On a hill far away stood an old rugged cross. . . ."

The Laundromat

A short man in his midthirties with dark curls, Tatlock had spoken personally with Brady only twice since the day he hired him. He had spent half a day training Brady and had checked in on him just one other time, when customers complained that Brady was speeding through his cleaning routine and leaving the place a mess. They were right, and Brady had straightened up.

"I've been doing better with the dusting and sweeping, sir," Brady said as they sat across from each other at a small table in the back room. "Hope you've noticed."

"I have, and I appreciate that, son. What I don't appreciate is that while we have clearly seen an increase in business, I'm making less profit than ever. How do you account for that?"

"Oh . . . well . . . I'm never here during the day, so you couldn't prove it by me that we have any more or less customers than before."

"Are you this stupid, Darby? Do you really not suspect that I inventory the wash and dry cycles I sell here every day? You think I don't keep track of how many boxes of detergent and softener I put in the dispensers each week? This is a low-maintenance but also very low-margin, high-risk business. It's all about volume."

"You keep track of the washings and dryings?"

"Of course! The machines have built-in counters. And the boxed goods? That's easy. I know exactly how many I buy and how much I make on each one. Last month I barely made a profit. There's only one explanation."

"You accusing me of something?"

"There's nobody else here."

Brady rose quickly, towering over the man.

Tatlock slowly stood. "You're going to pay me back, Brady."

"I'm gonna tear you up."

The man held up a hand and spoke softly. "Before you even try, do you recall my telling you my other business?"

"What do I care?"

"It matters. Do you need me to remind you?"

"You teach kids or something."

"I teach, all right. I run a karate school. You think I learned that from a book? My glory days are long past, but I could kill you with one hand. Look at my hands. Go on, look."

They looked meaty enough. Maybe he was telling the truth.

"Shake my hand, son, like you did the day I hired you and you promised to treat this place like your own. Problem is, you really did. But it's not your own, is it? Now shake my hand."

Brady felt like a fool, but he reached out. Tatlock's hand seemed twice as thick as his, and it was calloused. The man gripped firmly.

"I won't hurt you, but you can tell I could, can't you?"

Brady shrugged and nodded. There was no future in challenging this guy. "Well, I'm innocent. I don't know where your money is, and since you obviously don't believe me, I quit."

"It's not that easy. You owe me at least two hundred dollars. It's probably a lot more, but that's what I'll settle for. And that's the only thing that's going to keep me from calling the cops. Now give me your keys. You've got three days to get me the money."

Two hundred was all Brady had left in his car fund, but he didn't want to risk actually answering to the police. Not when the musical was in rehearsal and he had to do something about his schoolwork.

"What'd he want?" his mother said.

"He wants me to work more hours; you believe that? I can't with schoolwork and the play and all."

"You could use the money."

"Forget it! I quit."

"Tell me you didn't!"

"I did. He's an idiot. Thinks I can work an extra hour each night. No way."

"You'd double your money, Brady! Don't be a fool. Tell him you'll do it."

"Too late. I already quit."

"*You're* an idiot. What're you gonna do for money?"

"I'll find something when the play's over."

"And you're gonna mooch off me till then? No way."

"Don't worry about me."

Brady knew he should study, but even his script wasn't inviting as he undressed for bed. He was jittery, and a cigarette didn't help. He wanted to sneak over to Stevie Ray's for a beer, but when he had returned the guitar the other night, they had wound up drinking till dawn and he'd suffered a hangover the next day. No more of that.

He dug around in the closet for his stash and found less than five dollars.

"Ma! Where's my money?"

"Be quiet or you'll wake up your brother!"

"I don't care! Now where is it?"

"Don't ask me! I didn't even know you had money."

"Yeah, right. You didn't take my car fund?"

"I don't need your money!"

"Well, somebody took it! What am I supposed to live on till I find a job?"

"That's your problem. You're the one who quit."

"If I find out you took it, I swear—"

"Oh, please. Stop threatening me, Brady. It's getting old."

He slammed the door in her face and flopped onto the bed. Something made him grab his long, greasy hair and pull as hard as he could. He screamed into his pillow, but nothing could lessen the rage. He wanted to hurt someone. He didn't know who, and he didn't care. The kids who soaked his clothes? The girl who had accused him of stealing? Alex? He could take that kid's head off without a second thought. North's snotty family? Tatlock? Funny thing about him: he was right. Brady was ashamed, humiliated, caught.

Problem was, where was he going to get two hundred now?

12

Sunday Night | Oldenburg Rural Chapel

To Thomas's great surprise, Paul and Patricia Pierce followed through on the installation service, and even Jimmie Johnson, the denomination's executive director, showed up to make it official. It seemed as if every member of the five bodies had made it, and 230 filled the pews.

A makeshift kids' choir sang, as did an adult ensemble. Two soloists performed, and an old farmer played "I've Got a Mansion Just Over the Hilltop" on, of all things, a handsaw.

Mr. Johnson read a couple of kind letters from parishioners in two of Thomas's former churches, then had to excuse himself for a trip that required him in Illinois by the next morning. Thomas assumed no one else gave that more thought than he did, but it would prove portentous.

Grace gave her testimony, telling how she was led to Christ by her father—also a pastor, now in heaven—when she was a little girl. "And I've never looked back. I used to wish I had a dramatic story like some who were saved out of lives of sin and degradation. But I've learned over the years that it's just as much a miracle of God to have been born into a wonderful family and never really stray. Oh, I was a sinner in need of God, but now I'm thankful I didn't have to suffer through deep pain or cause my parents heartache."

Thomas detected a strange silence at that last comment, a stillness even in the body language of the crowd. People had been attentive enough anyway—Grace was easy to admire. But perhaps many had wayward children. He couldn't put a finger on the response. Maybe he had imagined it.

Grace finished by telling how she and Thomas had met on a blind date at Bible college and how their life of service to God had been all and more than she ever could have hoped for. "We believe being here is a divine appointment, and we look forward to worshiping with all of you."

Thomas breathed a sigh at the applause, grateful she had changed her mind about publicly asking for prayer for their daughter. He admired Grace's transparency and agreed that often it was good to show that pastors' families were normal too. But when she had raised the subject that afternoon, he had counseled her to let the people get to know them a little better before revealing that their own daughter was going through a rough patch of searching.

When finally it was Thomas's turn, he ran through Paul's counsel on his way to the pulpit. Boorish as the man was, and wrong as he may have been about Thomas shortening his sermons, he was likely right that tonight was not the time for a message. He simply said "a few words," as the euphemism went, thanking one and all, briefly giving a testimony remarkably similar to Grace's, and finishing with an anecdote that people always seemed to appreciate.

"When I was in grade school," he said, "I came down with rheumatic fever and spent three weeks in the hospital and the rest of the summer and a month or so into the fall in bed. I never felt that ill, and frankly I enjoyed the attention, but I believe something during that time made me a pastor. My mother sang with me, prayed with me, and read the Bible with me and to me. But more, she urged me to begin memorizing not just verses but also chapters and even books of the Bible. I continue that practice to this day. After first learning the entirety of John chapter 3, I memorized all four Gospels, most of Paul's epistles, and all of the so-called postcard books of the New Testament.

"I recommend memorizing, believing that the Word will never return void. Psalm 119:11 says, 'I have hidden Your word in my heart, that I might not sin against You.'"

Nearly everyone stayed for pie and coffee downstairs, and while Thomas enjoyed standing with Grace and shaking hands and trading pleasantries, he hoped she didn't notice that Patricia was keeping her distance. Paul was nowhere to be seen.

"I hope it doesn't appear rude, Thomas," Grace said, "but I'm going to need to sit down." He quickly found her a chair. "I haven't seen any of the elders," she whispered as the receiving line continued.

"I'm sure they're around somewhere," he said, noticing that occasionally one of the leaders of the other congregations was summoned to slip away too.

When the crowd finally thinned, Thomas looked forward to getting Grace home. She looked pale and exhausted. But finally Patricia Pierce approached, all business. "Paul asked if you both could meet with the elders before you left."

Touhy Trailer Park

"You're moping around here like you lost your best friend, Brady," his mother said. "What's the matter?"

"Nothin'."

Truth was, he was dreading a call. And when it came, he rushed to beat his mother to the phone. Tatlock.

"Time's up, Brady. I'm waiting at the Laundromat."

Brady dumped his last four dollars and thirty-eight cents into his jacket pocket. He had begged and tried to borrow and even thought of stealing, but he'd had no luck. He had interviewed at Leon Dennis Asphalt & Paving, which bordered the trailer park to the east, and was waiting for word on a job. But the Hispanic foreman had laughed when Brady asked if the job—provided he got it—could be worked around his school activities and maybe include a $200 advance.

"Weekday evening hours only, eh?" Alejandro had said. "Come back at seven on Monday and I'll let you know. It won't be much. Maybe just cleaning up around here."

"I'll take anything."

The only source Brady hadn't tried for the $200 was Stevie Ray, so he stopped there on his way to the Laundromat.

"What're you, kidding me?" Stevie said. "If I had two hundred bucks I'd throw a party. We live paycheck to paycheck, and the band barely breaks even. If I had it, I'd loan it to ya, but I don't."

Brady trudged to the Laundromat with a tingle up his spine as if he'd been summoned to the principal's office.

Oldenburg Rural Chapel

"I've asked my wife to take the minutes," Paul said as Patricia followed Thomas and Grace into a small classroom. Paul sat behind a table, flanked by other Oldenburg elders and a representative from each of

115

the other congregations. No one would look him in the eye but Paul, and the outside elders didn't look happy.

"This joint meeting of the circuit elders shall come to order," Paul said.

"Excuse me, Pierce," a man from Colfax said, "but I need to say again that there is no official circuit, thus there can't be a joint meeting of our elders. This meeting was not announced, and there was no published agenda, so this is nothing but some personal vendetta."

"Duly noted," Paul said. "Thank you, Mr. *Robert's Rules of Order*. Patricia, please put that in the minutes."

"If there can't be a meeting, there can't be minutes," the protester said, rising. "I'm not going to be part of this, and, Reverend Carey, if I were you, I'd not subject myself to it either."

The man stormed out.

"We still have a quorum," Paul said.

"What's going on, Paul?" Thomas said.

"All in due time."

"I'm out of here too," another said, and he and the two other outsiders left.

"All right, no problem," Paul said. "Patricia, this is now solely a meeting of the Oldenburg elders, all present and accounted for."

"Well," Thomas said, "I am as curious as I can be, but must I remind you that I also am an elder here, and this is the first I've known of this meeting?"

"Excuse me, sir," Paul said, "but you are out of

order. For the purposes of this meeting, you are here as the pastor and not as an elder."

"Um, pardon *me*, Paul," a younger elder said, "but officially I'm the secretary. As your wife is not an elder—no offense—shouldn't I be taking the minutes?"

"Fine," Paul and Patricia said in unison, and she made a show of slapping her notebook shut and putting away her pencil. But she did not leave.

The other elders looked as if they would rather have been anywhere else.

"Okay," Paul said, "meeting's called to order and all that." He bowed his head and closed his eyes. "Lord, lead us in these difficult talks, and may we do Your will. Amen." He looked up. "Pastor Tom, we got us a problem."

The Laundromat

"You bring my money?" Tatlock said.

"No, but I brought a down payment."

"How much?"

Brady emptied his pocket onto the top of a washing machine and had to catch a stray rolling penny.

Tatlock laughed. "Four bucks and change? You've got to be kidding."

"Listen, Mr. Tatlock, and just hear me out. You're right, I did steal from you, but I know it was wrong and I'm sorry and I owe you the money. I'll get it—I swear I will. Thing is, I didn't even spend it all. I had your money, but now it's missing."

"Someone stole the stolen money?"

"That's right. But I'll do anything to keep you from calling the cops, because I'm watching out for my little brother, trying to get my grades up so I can stay in the school play, and I've already applied for another job. If I get it, the first two hundred is yours, and I mean it."

"You're in a school play?"

Tatlock sounded both skeptical and curious, so Brady told him all about it.

"Now you see, Brady, this is the kid I thought I was hiring. You seemed thoughtful and industrious enough. I like that you care about your little brother. And I appreciate your admitting you did wrong. But actions have consequences. I'm not giving you your job back, and I'm not going to recommend you for any other job. But I will do this: as long as you bring me at least forty dollars a week, every Sunday night, same time, right here, until your debt's paid, I won't report you."

"Thanks, man. I appreciate it. I really do."

"I want you to learn from this, Brady. You don't get away with stuff in life. You can make something of yourself. I'll never forgive myself if going easy on you makes you think you can pull something else like this."

"Believe me, it'll never happen again."

Brady left, seething. Oh, it would happen again all right. He just wouldn't allow himself to be found out next time.

Silence hung in the tiny classroom before Paul Pierce suddenly became parental, his voice low and calm. "Pastor Tom, I know you're a man of the Word, that you care about the Scriptures and doctrine. I've noticed from day one your well-worn Bible and that you can quote from it by memory. I wonder if, as we get into the matter at hand, you would favor us by reading aloud 1 Timothy 3:1-5."

Oh no . . .

"First Timothy happens to be one of the books I have memorized. The passage says, 'This is a trustworthy saying: "If someone aspires to be an elder, he desires an honorable position." So an elder must be a man whose life is above reproach. He must be faithful to his wife. He must exercise self-control, live wisely, and have a good reputation. He must enjoy having guests in his home, and he must be able to teach. He must not be a heavy drinker or be violent. He must be gentle, not quarrelsome, and not love money. He must manage his own family well, having children who respect and obey him. For if a man cannot manage his own household, how can he take care of God's church?' "

Paul cleared his throat. "Now, Tom, would you agree that if a man is not qualified to be an elder, he's sure not qualified to be a pastor?"

"I would agree."

"And that if a pastor kept it a secret that he was not qualified, that should cost him his job?"

Grace gasped, and Thomas put a hand on her knee.

"Of course," Thomas said. "But I'd appreciate it if you would just get to your point, Paul."

"Oh, I figure you know where this is going. As I told the leaders of the five congregations, Patricia and I truly wanted to welcome you and your lovely wife and throw an installation service that would honor you."

"It did, and we appreciate it."

"But we had hoped to surprise you. You see, we wanted to do more than just read a couple of letters from old friends and have the denomination chief make an appearance. So we—or I should say Patricia, because she's thoughtful this way— thought it would be nice if your daughter could be here too. Patricia took what little she had learned of Ravinia—" he pronounced it with a long first *I*, and Thomas corrected him—"Fine. My apologies. Patricia took the trouble of tracking her down at the law school there at Emory and was ready to pay for her to come and surprise you tonight. You know what she found?"

Thomas fought to hide that his whole body was quaking. "You're aware, Paul, that my daughter is no child. She's twenty-four years ol—"

"Do you know what Patricia found, Tom? Your daughter, the daughter of an elder and the pastor of this church, is living with a man who is not her husband!"

"And you lay that at my feet?"

"You're her father! How does having a daughter like that fit with the last verse you just quoted?"

Grace put a hand firmly over Thomas's, and he set his jaw.

"No answer?"

Grace pressed Thomas's hand harder. She spoke just above a whisper. "If you are men of God, we would ask that you pray for our daughter."

"Oh, we have and we will. You may rest assured of that. And we will pray for you, too. But until your husband can 'manage his own household,' as he just quoted, he will not be taking care of our church."

"God's church," Grace said.

"Same thing."

"Frankly, sir, it doesn't sound like it."

"You disagree with God's Word?" Paul turned to a skinny, bald man on his right. "Ernie, I believe you have a motion?"

Ernie looked pained and his fingers fluttered as he straightened a small sheet of notebook paper before him. "Uh, yes. Yes, I do. I make a motion that—"

"You move," Paul said.

"Pardon?"

"You don't 'make a motion,' Ernie. Let's get this right. You *move*."

"Okay. I move that the Reverend Thomas Carey be removed from the office of pastor of the Oldenburg Rural Bible Church Circuit until such time—"

"Excuse me, Paul," Patricia whispered. "Without

the other elders, we'd better just say 'of the Olden-burg Rural Bible Chapel' for now."

"Well, he can't pastor the others if he's not pastoring here."

"That's up to them."

"But I'm—we're in charge of them."

"Let's just do it this way for now."

"Fine. Let the minutes show the motion is that Carey be removed from being pastor of just this church. Go on, Ernie."

"—until such time as he has proven he can manage his own household."

"And in the meantime?" Paul said.

"Oh yeah." Ernie looked back at his sheet. "And in the meantime he will be subject to discipline by the board of elders for failure to reveal that he was not managing his own household. Such discipline shall include a confession before the congregations—"

"Singular for now," Patricia said.

"—*congregation* and weekly meetings with the chairman of the elders for instruction and correction."

Thomas leaned back and stared at the ceiling. Then he focused on Paul. "If you think for one second that I am going to—"

"Excuse me, Tom, but there's more."

Ernie turned his sheet over. "Be it understood by these present that during the term of said discipline—man, this really reads funny—Reverend Carey's salary shall be suspended and he shall be required to pay rent on the parsonage."

"Did you discuss this with Jimmie Johnson?" Thomas said.

"All in favor?" Paul said.

But Thomas and Grace were on their way out.

As Thomas slowly drove back to the parsonage, Grace buried her face in her hands.

"I'm worried about you, sweetheart," he said.

She straightened. "Don't worry about me, Thomas. Hatred has a way of clarifying things."

"Surely you don't hate anyone."

"I'm praying about that, but no, I was referring to the Pierces' hatred of us."

"This can't stand," Thomas said. "I'll get hold of Mr. Johnson in the morning, and—"

"He's out of town."

"But I'm sure he's reachable by phone."

"This is beyond him, Thomas. You know the hall-mark of the association is the autonomy of the local bodies. These people have to stand up to Paul. That's all there is to it."

"The rank and file probably know nothing about this."

"You've worked in small churches all your life; you don't think the phone lines are melting by now?"

"Well, hon," he said, "I'm not about to turn and run."

"And I don't have the energy to stay and fight. I won't allow you to be put through this. If there is not immediate opposition to this craziness, we're leaving."

13

Brady Darby felt strangely flat as he made his way home from the Laundromat. His mother was dozing before the television, a freshly lit cigarette in the ashtray. Brady took the smoke and turned down the TV, but as he undressed in the bedroom, he had second thoughts about smoking where Peter was sleeping.

He quickly finished and stubbed out the butt, then sat on the edge of his bed, just a few feet from his brother. He felt an urge to talk to Peter, to admit what he had done and say he had learned from it and wanted to be sure Peter never made the same mistake. Might things actually start to turn for the better for Brady if he somehow protected his brother this way?

But no. He could never admit that to Peter. And Brady had no intention of changing his own ways. He just had to be more careful, that's all. He felt like a wimp for confessing to Tatlock, but he had at least bought himself a little time to pay back the money.

Brady stretched out on his back in the darkness, his hands behind his head. Even with everything he had been going through and worrying about, still he had succeeded in memorizing pages and pages of the *Birdie* script. He enjoyed impressing Nabertowitz, and knowing everyone else's lines really helped his own performance. Maybe by pulling this acting thing off he could hide the person he really was, at least enough to pave the way for Peter not to follow his example.

Brady felt comfortable in his skin, comfortable with his look. Some said there was no future in it, that everybody in the park lived for Friday nights when they could start a hard weekend of partying and booze and dope and then try to recover in time to keep financing that life on an hourly wage somewhere. How did people like the Norths do it? It couldn't be that they had just been born into better lives. Brady was determined to create the same kind of existence for himself, doing whatever he had to do, short of going to college and getting a so-called good job.

As he drifted toward sleep, Brady shook off the shame of having been caught. He looked forward to the next day—well, not to school, but to rehearsal. And after that he would visit Alejandro at Dennis Asphalt again.

Oldenburg

"I've been wanting to talk to Ravinia," Grace said, slumped on the couch next to Thomas. "I've wanted us both to talk to her. But what do we say? She knows how we would feel about her and Dirk. And by now she has to know we know. If she thinks these people are treating us shamefully because of her, she won't feel responsible. She'll just be angry and want to strike out at them."

"It would be hard to blame her. Now, Grace, please

rest. It's clear you're not well, and I need you to be strong."

"Oh, I'm strong enough, and I won't sleep anyway—not until we know what's going to happen here."

"Nothing's going to happen here. You know I won't agree to discipline in this case, especially under Paul Pierce."

"You don't have to tell me that. You'd do that over my dead—"

"Don't even say that, sweetheart."

"You know what I mean. I need to know, and I mean tonight, whether the people are going to let this stand."

"How do we do that?"

"Call someone. Call Ernie."

Thomas rummaged in a kitchen drawer for the church directory, but as he reached for the phone, it rang. It was Jimmie Johnson.

"So you've had your meeting?"

"Yes, sir," Thomas said. "You knew about this?"

"Yes. I wish I could have stayed for it, but my trip couldn't be avoided. Is it true you told Pierce you wanted him and his wife out of the way, out of leadership?"

"Just the opposite, Jimmie. Do you have time to hear my side of it?"

"Sure, but let me tell you why you're not going to win this one, Thomas."

"No chance?"

126

"None, and here's why. We get these squabbles all the time, and it's always an old pillar's word against the new guy. The denomination used to investigate and hold hearings, but with our local autonomy policy, our findings and our decisions have no teeth. We went through this with the previous two guys there, and Pierce skated through both of them. Too many people in that church are on his payroll—or I should say his sons', given that Paul is so-called retired—so no one stands up to him. It's a losing proposition. Best I can do is give you a letter that says we believe you are without fault here, which might help in your next slot."

Thomas sighed. "I can't believe it's all fallen apart so quickly. We really thought we'd found the right fit here." He outlined for Johnson the decision of the elders.

Jimmie was silent for a moment. Then, "Suspension, discipline, and rent. All right, Thomas, I'm going to tell you up front that this is pure gossip and that I have no business passing it along. I do it only to encourage you, but you are not free to quote me or use it."

"There's no need," Thomas said. "I imagine Paul has a few skeletons."

"It's worse than that. It goes to hypocrisy. He has three grown sons, not a one of them living for the Lord. They don't even attend church. Six, seven marriages between 'em. There, I've said it, and that's all I'm going to say."

"What's your counsel, Jimmie?"

"Pack up. Get out. Fold your tent and steal away."

"And he wins."

"Yeah, he wins."

"And where am I supposed to go? I can't keep doing this, sir. Grace is under the weather, and—"

"Listen, have you ever thought of getting out of the pastorate?"

"Jimmie, I was called to this. It's all I know. What would I do with myself? Teach Bible college? I don't have enough education. Missionary work? I'm too old."

"Actually I heard about something just the other day. Let me look into it and get back to you. Wherever you land, leave a phone number at headquarters, and I'll find you."

"I have no idea where that will be."

"You've got friends, don't you? Someone who'll take you in until you land on your feet?"

"I'll think about it," Thomas said. "And thanks for hearing me out."

"I'm awfully sorry, Thomas. I should have given you more warning, but I guess I just naively hoped you'd be the guy who could work with Paul."

When Thomas hung up, Grace was at his elbow. And when he had filled her in, she reached for the phone.

"Who are you calling?"

"Do you trust me, Thomas?"

"You know I do."

"Then let me do this." She called the moving trailer

rental place and left a message that she would be there when they opened in the morning and wanted the same size unit they had dropped off not long before.

"You don't want to take a few days?" Thomas said. "Say our good-byes?"

"I don't want to be here a minute longer than I have to be. And the last thing I want is Paul or Patricia showing up to try to talk you into submitting to his authority."

"Oh, I reckon Mrs. Carey would drive him off her land with a shotgun."

"Don't tempt me," she said. "I know we're supposed to love our enemies and pray for those who despitefully use us. Only God can do that for me. Keeping from broomsticking that man would be the hardest work I'd ever have to do."

The rest of the night, Grace busied herself packing. Thomas handled the big stuff and pleaded with her every half hour or so to take a break, get some sleep, start again in the morning. But she kept working.

Monday evening | Dennis Asphalt & Paving | Addison

Alejandro was stocky with smooth dark skin, a moon-shaped face, gleaming teeth, and a full head of black hair that hung over his forehead. He leaned back in a cheap chair before a desk covered with a mountain of papers.

"Okay, Mr. Brady Darby, you might be in luck. I got a guy hurt his back and is gonna be out awhile. Can

129

you give me two hours a night, Monday through Friday?"

"Two?"

"Needs to be two, man."

"Okay. But I can't get here till seven."

"You mind workin' alone?"

Brady shook his head. "What do I do?"

"I'll teach you, and right now. You ever drive a fork-lift?"

"No."

"It's easy. I mean, you gotta learn, but you'll get it. Follow me."

Alejandro led him to an outbuilding where row upon row of steel forms had been filled with cement or concrete—Brady didn't know which, so he asked.

Alejandro looked surprised at the question. "Cement is *in* concrete, man. Concrete is the cheapest way to make car stops. Some people call them blocks. There are some plastics and composites coming that might eventually run us out of the business, but for now, we're the biggest. Our crew spends most of the day pouring these and letting them harden. They're six feet long, four inches high, and six inches wide. Once they set, our guys knock off the holds and free the blocks from the forms. You see how each one has two slots underneath? That's where the lift forks go, and that's where you come in."

Alejandro motioned for Brady to follow, and the foreman scampered up into the seat of a forklift truck, proving more agile than he looked. He fired up the machine and deftly handled the controls, expertly lifting each finished car stop and setting it in place on a thick wooden skid.

"Once you have a load that's as high as it is wide," he hollered over the engine noise, "you're ready to load it onto the truck!"

The six-foot square load of car stops appeared to tax the forklift, and Alejandro slowed now as he pivoted the machine and proceeded to the back of a flatbed truck with a winch built onto it.

"Just ignore the winch, unless you set them on there wrong and have to straighten 'em!" Alejandro shouted. "That's for off-loading at the job sites otherwise!"

In a few minutes he had loaded three pallets onto the truck. "It'll hold twelve total, three more on the bottom, six on top. You wanna try it?"

"Sure!"

Alejandro showed Brady the controls and had him drive the forklift around the yard, around a pile of raw goods, between a couple of paving trucks. Brady was tentative and overcorrected at first, but soon he began to get the hang of it. Then Alejandro had him feather the controls until he had a feel for lifting and tilting the forks. When he had to maneuver inside the outbuilding, however, things got dicey. Once he slammed on the brake just before hitting the metal doorframe.

"You can see that's been hit a lot of times, even by experienced guys," Alejandro said. "But it's good to not do that."

When Brady tried lifting the first car stop, he drove the forks into the stop above the slots, pushing the entire form into the next and breaking the first stop.

Brady swore.

"That's all right. Everybody's got to learn. You got a week to quit doing that. Then we start taking it out of your pay. Each of these stops costs about what we pay you per hour, so you don't want to break any. Break two on a shift and you make no money."

"I'll learn!"

"Of course you will."

It took Brady an hour to load two pallets and get them onto the truck.

"You'll get better and faster each time," the foreman said. "Just remember, we have to dock you for broken or even cracked ones, because they become scrap. Can't sell 'em."

In two hours each night, provided Brady could manage this, he would make three times what he made in an hour at the Laundromat. The first two hundred would go to Tatlock, of course, but soon enough he'd be back on track with his car fund. That day couldn't come soon enough.

Peebles, Ohio

Thomas Carey felt fortunate that old Bible college friends had proven hospitable without even having to be present. Thomas had caught them by phone just as they were leaving for vacation, and his old buddy insisted that the Careys "camp out at our place for as much of the next two weeks as you need." He told Thomas where to find the key and was adamant that he and Grace wholly make themselves at home.

"He didn't even ask why we needed a place, Grace."

She had been dozing next to him in the front seat. "That's wonderful. True friends. Maybe he knows of an opening somewhere."

It was nice not to have to unload much. Their stuff filled the trailer, but all they needed were their toiletries and a few changes of clothes. Thomas immediately phoned the denomination headquarters and left his temporary phone number for Jimmie Johnson. When he found Grace hanging their clothes in the guest room closet, he said, "You need to get to bed. You look terrible."

"Why, thank you, Dale Carnegie."

"You seriously don't look well. And that bruise has grown."

"Can't figure that one out. Age, I guess."

"It's more than that. Once we get settled somewhere, you're seeing a doctor."

"Yes, I suppose I should," she said, which startled Thomas. Grace was the most doctor-averse person he had ever met. He'd had to force her to get an annual physical once she turned forty. Not once had she gone willingly, let alone volunteered. And now she was saying that she supposed she should? He prayed she would take it easy in the meantime. Fat chance.

To his relief, once Grace had dropped into bed, despite

that it was a small and strange one, she slept soundly.

The next morning, as Grace continued to sleep, Thomas began calling everyone he knew, briefly explaining that their most recent assignment had simply not worked out and they were now eagerly looking into new opportunities.

Thomas meticulously kept track of every phone call, determined to reimburse his hosts for the use of their phone. He enjoyed several long conversations with old friends, reminiscing and updating, but no one was aware of openings anywhere.

When hunger pangs hit midmorning, Thomas realized he had not heard Grace stirring. On the one hand, she needed her rest. On the other, she also needed to get moving and eat. He found her awake but still. He told her of many of his phone calls and passed along greetings from old friends.

"I've just been praying and thinking and singing."

"You can sing at a time like this?"

"Sometimes it's all I can do. I'm dreading the next conversation with Ravinia. I want to scold her, to advise her, to be the parent I should be to a prodigal. But you know she'll come out with guns blazing when she realizes what's happened. They'll wish they'd never tangled with her."

Thomas had to smile.

"What?" she said.

"Imagine Paul Pierce trying to deal with her."

Grace chuckled. "Imagine Patricia. I'd tell Rav to keep calling her Pat."

Alejandro was closing the office when Brady showed up with Peter and introduced him.

"Nice to meet you, *muchacho Pedro*. You are welcome to watch your brother break my car stops, but you must stay far from the machinery and the work area, *comprende*?"

"He talks funny," Peter said.

"He wants to know if you understand, Petey."

"Oh yeah, I do!"

"Call me if you need anything, Brady. And don't worry about doing too much tonight. It would be good if you can load the whole truck, but keeping from breaking any is more important. And you know I'm only paying you for two hours, even if it takes more time."

"I'll fill that truck, sir."

14

Peebles, Ohio

The call from Jimmie Johnson came late that night. "Thomas, your daughter is frantically trying to reach you. All she had was the number in Oldenburg, and when she finally reached someone at the church, they told her you were no longer there."

"Thanks, Jimmie. We'll call her. And you mentioned a potential opening for me."

"I did, and there's a real possibility here, but I want to talk with you in person first."

"Why?"

"Really, Thomas, I don't want to talk about it by phone. It's not a pastorate, but it's still full-time ministry. It would require a move to Adamsville. I'd like to meet you there on my way back to headquarters. Could you be there for lunch tomorrow? I would not advise bringing Grace."

"Grace is always with me."

"I know. But I'd like to chat with you in private, and then I want you to decide whether to pursue this before exposing Grace to it."

"You make it sound like the city dump."

"No, no. It's really quite interesting, but you need to check it out for yourself. You said she was under the weather anyway."

"That's why I'd rather not leave her."

"She's that bad off?"

"It's just that we aren't sure what the problem is. But I'll let her decide."

Dennis Asphalt & Paving

"Boring!" Peter called from atop the cab of the flatbed truck. "And I'm tired!"

"I gotta finish this," Brady hollered back from the forklift. "And I don't want you walking home alone."

"Ma's gonna be worried about us and probably mad."

"I left her a note. Now just hang on."

Brady had broken only one car stop, which he left in plain sight for Alejandro. But being so careful had cost him time, and it was already after ten. He was determined to fully load the delivery truck. He wanted to prove himself quickly and lock in this job. He liked the idea of being so close to the office—and, he assumed, petty cash or even a safe—with no one else around.

Peebles

"Seems to me if there's one person we can trust," Grace said, "it's Mr. Johnson. I'll be fine. You go tomorrow and hurry back because I'll be dying to hear."

Thomas got on the extension phone in the guest bedroom while Grace dialed Ravinia from the living room.

Their daughter had never been one to ease into a conversation.

"All right," Ravinia said, "I know we've got some hard talking to do, but tell me why I should forgive you for worrying me to death. For all I knew you could be lying somewhere dead by the side of the road. What happened?"

"Now, dear," Grace said, "we knew how you'd react, and obviously you know how we feel about your new living arrangement."

"Does that make me an untouchable, Mom? You were never going to speak to me again?"

"You know better than that."

"Do I?"

"Yes, now stop being ridiculous. Your father will tell you what happened in Oldenburg after you tell us about your conversation with Patricia Pierce."

A long pause.

Finally, "Well, first of all, I liked the idea. She sounded nice enough, and I was actually encouraged that a church had finally figured out how to welcome a new pastor. But then she said she hadn't realized that I was married, that my parents hadn't mentioned that for some reason—and believe me, I caught her tone—but that my husband was certainly welcome too, and wouldn't it be a wonderful surprise.

"Of course I told her right away that Dirk and I were not married, and you could have cut the silence with the sword of the Lord. She said, 'Yeah, well, I'm going to have to get back to you on that.'

"I said, 'So, we're uninvited; is that it?'

"She said, 'Are you telling me that you and this Dirk are roommates?'

"I said, 'More than that, ma'am; we're lovers.'"

"Oh, Ravinia," Grace said.

"C'mon, Mom. This is not news to you. I figured you had called. I hadn't wanted you to hear it that way, but you know I wasn't going to hide anything."

"I almost wish you had."

"No, you don't. I'm a lot of things, but I'm not a liar. You have to give me that."

"That *is* commendable, Rav," Thomas said. "But

there is the matter of considering our feelings."

"Your reputation, you mean. So you got run out of there because you've got a daughter living in sin; is that it? You don't have to answer. I know. I grew up with people like that."

"We're not like that, Rav."

"I'm not talking about you, Dad. You're surprisingly nonjudgmental, considering the people you associate with. But what do you call it when they judge you unqualified because a grown woman doesn't still obey your wishes?"

Thomas spoke haltingly, telling Ravinia about the suggested course of action by the elders.

Ravinia responded with a hint of tears in her voice. "Dad, I'm about as livid as I can be. I'm sorry you and Mom are on the lam again, but I couldn't be more proud that you did the right thing. All you have to do is say the word and I'll find somebody to make these people wish they'd never even dreamed of this."

"You know we'd never allow that," Grace said.

"Of course I know that. But it's a crime that they hide behind their religious status, their . . . their . . . I'd just love to teach them a lesson."

"Leave that to the Lord," Grace said.

"Dad, please get out of the ministry. I know you believe in it and think you're serving God and all that—"

"I *am* serving God, Rav!"

"So where is He in this? Why does He let you get bludgeoned every time?"

"We don't blame this on God, honey," Grace said. "It's His people who are imperfect, and—"

"You consider Patricia and her husband and their cohorts *God's* people?"

"They're just human, Ravinia."

"They're evil."

"Now don't—"

"I know. I'm evil too. But I have to tell you again, most of the people I've met since I left home have zero interest in God or church and certainly Jesus, but—with a few exceptions—none of them would ever do to another person what your so-called fellow Christians have done to you your whole career."

Thomas rubbed his forehead and forced back a sob. "Rav, we would be remiss if we didn't express how we feel about where you are right now."

"I know, Dad. I know, I know, I know, okay? Spare us both the lecture. I don't mean to hurt you. I hope you know I still care about you or I wouldn't have even tried to find you."

Thomas fought the urge to say she was showing her concern in a strange way. "And we want you to know that we love you unconditionally and that we're praying for you."

"And for Dirk?"

"Of course."

"Mm-hm. Dad, please find something else to do. I mean for work. You're smart and you're kind. There must be something less stressful, more fair."

"Well, I'm looking. I'll keep you posted."

Peter was yawning as they moseyed home. "I don't have to come with you every night, do I?"

"'Course not. But you got a chance to see what I do."

"Yeah, and it was cool. But it's just the same thing over and over. And it looks harder than cleaning the laundry place, but at least you get to drive that thing."

"It's more money, and that's important. I don't want to live here all my life. Do you?"

"No way. But I don't know what I want to do."

"Just get out, I hope."

"Long as I can live with you."

"Yeah, that's not going to be easy. Soon as I get out of school or get a car, I'm gone. I'd have to fight Ma to let you live with me, and how would that work anyway? I couldn't watch you, be home when you get out of school, all that. Maybe I can still talk Uncle Carl and Aunt Lois into taking you till you get out of school."

"Ma'll never let that happen."

"Let me worry about that. She touched you since I warned her?"

Peter shook his head.

"You tellin' me the truth?"

"Yeah. She hollers at me a lot. Threatens me."

"Just one more time . . ."

"I know. And she knows. But when she's drunk, I get scared because I think she forgets."

"That I warned her? She'd better not."

"Why does she hate me, Brady?"

Brady shrugged. "She hates everybody. She's had a hard life, but you'd think she'd want to keep us close. I hate her."

"Families on TV look like they have fun sticking together."

"That's just made up, Petey. You know anybody but Carl and Lois whose family is still together and seems to get along?"

Peter shook his head.

When they got home, Erlene Darby stood in the doorway, staring at them.

"What are you thinking, keeping Petey out this late? Give me one reason I shouldn't whip your tail."

Brady pushed Peter past her and told him to get to bed. "Because I'd kill you, Ma, that's why. You think I'm gonna leave him here with you when you come home drunk and mad?"

"I'm not mad at him, Brady! I'm mad at you!"

"Just don't worry about me. If Petey's with me, you know he's okay. If he's with you, I never know."

"He deserved that beating, and you know it."

"Nobody deserved that."

She flipped him an obscene gesture.

"Yeah, that's nice. I'm so glad I've got a classy mom."

She swore. "Get out of my sight."

"Gladly."

Brady stomped back to his and Peter's bedroom and undressed, banging doors and drawers and dropping onto the bed.

"Sorry, Brady."

Brady fought his rage. He didn't want to break down in front of Peter.

"Oh, it's not your fault, little man. I shoulda known she'd be ticked. I can't take you with me every night, so just get along with her any way you can. Stay out of her way. Do what you're told. And if you ever feel scared, like she's gonna do something to you, you know where I am, and you come running."

15

Noon, Wednesday | Denny's Restaurant | Adamsville

Thomas didn't have much of an appetite, and he wished Jimmie Johnson would get to the subject: the Careys' future.

But Jimmie was eating ravenously, sometimes talking with his mouth full and about only inconsequential matters. Finally he wiped his mouth and pushed his plate forward and his chair back. "Ever done prison ministry, Thomas?"

"Cook County Jail when I was a student in Chicago. Jail stuff in small towns. A prison in Alabama. Nothing extensive."

"How'd it go?"

Thomas shrugged. "I always felt terribly for the

prisoners. But I could never tell if I was getting through. Just preached Christ, you know. Never got into teaching or discipling, anything like that."

"But you could."

"Sure."

"Ever thought about becoming a prison chaplain?"

"Can't say I have. You have no more churches that need an old expository preacher?"

"You're not that old, Thomas, but you do carry yourself that way. Ever been told that?"

"I have. I don't guess I care that much about appearances."

"Sure you do. You're well groomed, clean, neat. A little dated, but more than presentable."

Thomas sipped his coffee. "Now there's high praise."

Jimmie laughed. "I'm just trying to encourage you, because I've got to tell you, if I'd been through what you've been through, I'd have thrown in the towel a long time ago. All I hear about you is that you're a wonderful servant, but people tend to walk all over you. If I have to be honest, and I know no other way to help, your preaching doesn't get high marks. Nobody says you don't know your Bible, but you're no—"

"—Billy Graham. Yeah, I know. I should put that on my résumé. But I'm not a quitter, Jimmie. And if it's true I get bullied now and again, are you sure a prison chaplaincy is the right move? I'm not sure I could handle the endless jokes about a captive audience and all that."

"You'd get your share of those. I don't know, Thomas. My fear is you're out of options. But I'm not going to try to talk you into anything."

Thomas turned and stared out the window, exhaling loudly. "Well, where's the opening?"

"The state penitentiary."

"Right here? It's a supermax, isn't it?"

"State-of-the-art for the worst of the worst, they tell me. There are something like twenty-two thousand inmates in this state, and the worst nine hundred or so are here at Adamsville."

"Quite a mission field."

"Now you're talking."

"That would be a baptism of fire, Jimmie, when the worst place I've been is Cook County and that more than twenty-five years ago. How'd this position come open anyway?"

"Our guy's retiring. Been in the system forty years. Lots of rules and law changes make it almost impossible to get a chaplain in there, but because we had one for so long, and the administration loved him, we can grandfather in someone new if we act fast."

"Who would the new guy work for? You or the state?"

"The state, but while it includes benefits, they don't pay much, so we subsidize. It's still not much, Thomas, but it'd be regular and you wouldn't have to worry about congregations coming up with your salary."

"That would be nice."

"You're open to this?"

"Grace and I will pray about it."

"See why I didn't want her to come? She couldn't visit the prison anyway, and if she did, she might be against it."

"Can I visit?"

"We can see. But Chaplain Russ is happy to talk to you, provided you're at least curious."

"Oh, I'm at least that."

"Then you'll forgive me if I wave him over?"

"Excuse me?"

"He's here, just in case. That's him in the corner."

A large, ruddy, robust man in his late sixties smiled shyly and raised his brows. Thomas offered a subdued salute, and Jimmie beckoned him. He brought his sandwich and coffee with him.

After quick introductions and a laugh when Thomas said he felt conspired against, Ross said, "Reverend Carey, I'm not gonna try to sell you on this. Fact, I might try to talk you out of it. It's not for a weak man, not for someone looking to take a break."

"Oh, I assure you—"

" 'Cause let me tell you what ASP consists of, bein' a security-level-five institution. First off, it's got a death row. There's nine in that pod right now. Then you've got your real baddies, lifers who have murdered, raped, abused, whatnot. Then you've got your attempted escapees from other facilities. There's none of that here, understand, because this place was built in what's called an envelope design. Other words, say a guy somehow escapes his cell—which hasn't even happened since this place opened ten years ago. These guys are in their houses—that's what we call their cells—twenty-three hours a day. They get an hour alone in the exercise unit, which is just a few feet away from their cellblock, and every three days they get to go to the shower. That's the only chance they'd get to try to pull something. But let's just say they did. From the exercise area or the shower, they subdue a corrections officer—don't ever demean those professionals by callin' 'em guards, by the way, or worse, turnkeys or screws—and somehow get out of the cellblock. That's just the first of eleven envelopes they'd have to open to even get out to the yard, which is surrounded by walls, guarded by sharpshooters in the towers, and covered by razor wire. And every one of those envelopes is constantly watched, live and on monitors, and every door can be unlocked only with the cooperation of an officer in a control unit."

"So, like you say, it's not going to happen."

"Exactly. And you can imagine what that kind of living does to a man, especially a convict."

"If these guys are in their cells, their houses, all that time, when do you have chapel services?"

"Oh, you don't. You gotta understand, these guys are not allowed any physical contact with each other. Zero. The only time they're in the proximity of *any*body is when they're cuffed and shackled and searched and escorted by officers either to the shower or to exercise."

Thomas stole a glance at Jimmie, who looked curious and also seemed to gather that Thomas was intrigued.

"So you're not teaching or preaching or counseling. What are you doing? Going cell to cell?"

"Oh, no preaching, that's true. And no, I can't visit any inmate without his filing an official request. The only contact is through the front door of his house, though if he goes through proper protocol, we can meet maybe once every two or three weeks in what's called a separation unit. That's a secure room with a Plexiglas shield between the inmate and the visitor, and it's usually used by lawyers. A tiny slit allows single sheets of paper to be passed back and forth. Other than that, I have no contact with inmates except through the front door of their houses. I can't be there unless they've invited me, and I'm not allowed to proselytize."

"Sounds pretty restrictive," Thomas said. "How do they even know to ask for you?"

"Oh, they all know. Everything gets around, and new inmates are given a packet that tells them all of the regulations, services, and restrictions. That tells them a chaplain is available."

"Sounds like really hard, depressing work."

"It is. Let me tell you, you don't do this job for the warm fuzzies or the thank-yous. If you get any of those, it's a sure bet someone is running a con on you, pardon the pun.

"Inmates work on the softies, the ones they call

148

'chocolate hearts,' because they're always melting for a sob story. You'll have to learn that the hard way, because I figure as a pastor you feel for people."

"And you can't feel for these lost souls?"

Russ seemed to consider that. "Well, you can try, but here it's different. You can't let 'em see your soft side or you've already lost. You've been a pastor, so you've had people trying to act spiritual around you, more spiritual than they are. But you can usually tell, can't you, by the look in their eyes?"

"Yes, it is easier to tell real transformation that way."

"Well, I've seen that look two, maybe three times since I've been on this job. And only once since being at the supermax. And that time? I was wrong."

Thomas looked at his watch, worried about Grace. "I don't know, Jimmie. I appreciate this, but I don't know."

"Hey," Russ said, "then don't do it. You got to be called to this, my friend. But here's the upside if the Lord is in it: You may never know this side of heaven when you've made an impact. But these are the saddest, neediest souls on the planet. I've prayed with guys on their way to their executions. Who knows what happened with them? I'll know someday."

"Can I see the place, take a little tour?"

"Actually, you can't. See, the warden is the caesar, okay? And it just so happens that he reports to the state's executive director of the Department of Corrections, who is handpicked by the governor. Here's

149

the deal. The executive director himself replaced the warden here three years ago, loves it, and runs his DOC shop right out of the prison. So our warden reports to himself! Ha! Name's Frank LeRoy—we call him Yanno—and he and the gov are like this." Chaplain Russ held up two fingers, drawn together.

"You call him what?"

"Yanno. Comes from his favorite expression. You make a request, he says, 'Yeah,' not meaning he's gonna grant it but that he hears you and understands what you want. Then, in the same breath, he gives you his answer."

"No."

"Exactly. You talk to Director LeRoy, you're gonna hear 'Yeah, no' more than once, guaranteed. 'Course we know better'n to call him that to his face."

"Yeah, no," Thomas said.

Russ roared. "I like this guy! Anyway, Yanno is not big on outsiders coming in for a look. In fact, there's no way."

"I can't see the place before deciding whether I want to consider this?"

Russ shook his head. "Works the other way round. You pray about it, talk with your wife, decide whether you're called to it; then I go to Yanno and get you in for an interview with NCIC. That's the National Compliance Integrity Commission. They run about a ten-day background check, and if you're clean, Yanno is the last hurdle."

Thomas smiled. "Oh, I'm clean."

"Squeaky," Jimmie said. "Trust me."

"Well, that may be," Russ said, "but if you've forgotten a speeding ticket, even a double parking rap, they'll know."

6 p.m. | Forest View High School

Brady had had a particularly good day on the boards, as Mr. Nabertowitz had instructed him to call the stage. Not only had he nailed all his lines, hit all his notes, and even shown more flair in his dancing, but he had also prompted more than one coactor on his or her lines. That drew a smirk from Alex North, despite that he was one Brady had helped, but it brought heaps of praise throughout rehearsal from the director.

"I need to talk to you before you go," Mr. N. said as he dismissed the cast and crew.

"Okay, but I can't miss my bus. I get home just in time to have dinner with my brother and get to my job."

"Your job? You're working *now?*"

"They let me do it on my own schedule, so it's all right."

"No, it's not all right, Brady. I told you I was going to keep track of how you're doing in class, and I'm not getting good reports."

"I'm working as hard as I can, sir. I don't think I'm failing anything."

"You don't think? You have to know, son. You can't

151

afford one F, or your GPA dips to where I can't use you."

"Man, I can't let that happen!"

"No, you can't. Because it's not just you, Brady. It's every other kid involved in this thing. And it's me. I risked a lot going with you in this role, and I've told you and told you that if we have to make a late change, the whole thing becomes a mess. Now don't let me down."

"I won't. I promise."

"What's your plan?"

"My plan?"

"See, that's your problem, Brady. You don't think ahead. You're on the brink of failing three courses. What are you going to do about that to ensure it doesn't happen?"

"I don't know. Get all my homework done. Study harder, more, for tests and stuff."

"You've got to be proactive, son. You know what that means?"

"I'm not stupid!"

"I wasn't implying you were. I just mean you need to get to those teachers, tell them you know you're in trouble and that you want help. They can assign tutors to help you during study hall. They'll help you themselves. Believe me, almost any teacher would love to be asked for help. They *want* to see you succeed. Now will you do that?"

"Sure."

Not a chance. I'm not playing preppy for anybody.

16

Grace had sounded okay on the phone before Thomas pulled out of Adamsville, but he insisted on bringing home dinner. "You rest until I get there. We have a lot to talk about."

"Give me a hint."

"I'd rather not."

"Please, Thomas."

"Well, maybe you can think and pray about it before I get there. It's a prison chaplaincy."

"Oh, my."

He chuckled. "My response exactly."

Thomas spent the entire drive ticking off the pros and cons and soon began to weary under a burden of guilt. The situation, strange and exotic as it was, would clearly be a nine-to-five weekday job. He supposed he might be called in some evening for the occasional emergency, but otherwise, he would have a routine he had not enjoyed as an adult.

What kind of a man was he to long for that? Rising every morning at the same time, being able to have devotions and breakfast with Grace, getting home at a decent hour, not having to worry about the phone ringing, the endless committee meetings, the people problems he'd had to endure for so many years.

As he drove, Thomas found himself daydreaming

about the structured existence he had always yearned for. He had felt called to preach and teach and pastor, but everything that went with it had proved a distraction. And his daughter was right; it wasn't in him to fight all the forces that wanted to use and abuse him.

Could he make a difference in prisoners' lives? He certainly couldn't hurt, couldn't make things worse for them. He imagined, and Chaplain Russ had confirmed, that real results would be scarce and hard to evaluate. But that was God's work, wasn't it? Wasn't Thomas's role simply to be faithful and diligent?

By the time he reached a Chinese carryout place a few blocks from the borrowed home, Thomas realized he had allowed the glamour—yes, it seemed that way to him—of a new life, an ordered day, to outweigh all his misgivings. He realized he had been beaten down, wearied, wounded by all the shots he'd taken so recently. From being summarily dismissed by the folks in Foley, to the condescension of the search committee chair in Vidalia, to the tough discussions with Ravinia and then her blatant rebellion against all she had been taught . . . from the mess with the Pierces at Oldenburg, to even the kind but stabbing assessment of Jimmie Johnson, all the while worried about what was happening with Grace—well, he was just weary.

Inside Thomas felt stooped and old and depressed, yet as he waited for his order, he caught a glimpse of himself in the ornate mirror behind the counter. He stood ramrod straight, shoulders back, head high, and smiling. Genuinely, warmly smiling.

A young family with a noisy toddler amused him, and the girl at the cash register had a refreshing countenance. But Thomas knew his renewed vigor was from the Lord and that the prospect of the new job—despite its sobering environment—was making him his old self again.

Addison

It was clear when Brady stepped in the door that his mother was payday drunk. Trouble was, he never knew what kind of a drunk she'd be. Sometimes she was sullen and quiet and sad and just sat dozing or smoking as she watched TV. She might weep and complain about life and plead for someone to tell her they loved her. Brady was long past succumbing to that temptation.

It was the other times that bothered him, when she'd had just enough booze or little enough food—who knew what combination might set her off—to make her angry. Then no one could do anything right. Nothing pleased her.

For now she was sitting, but she was clearly out of it. And as the time came for Brady to head to the work site, he debated taking Peter with him. Of course Peter didn't want to go, and he kept assuring Brady he would keep his distance and that, yes, he would escape if he had to.

But then, all the while Brady was on the forklift truck, improving his dexterity with the machine (and thus hopefully his elapsed time), he was listening and watching for his brother. Would Petey come running? And if he did, would he have eluded her in time? If he showed up with so much as a mark, Brady was prepared to make his mother pay. He didn't even know what that meant. Would he beat her? threaten her with the old sawed-off his late father had stored somewhere in the back? Would he kill her?

He honestly didn't know, but he had a feeling most people would be sympathetic to him if they knew he was protecting an eight-year-old boy. Part of Brady hoped it wouldn't come to that. Another part of him hoped it would.

He had spent enough time on the machine that he should have been more accurate, but his state of mind caused him to break two car stops. For a few minutes he drove in anger and once had to hit the brake so hard to avoid hitting the metal building that he nearly pitched out of the seat.

Just as he was loading the last pallet under a black sky by the light of the security lamps in the company yard, he heard a noise and jerked to see if it was Peter. It wasn't, but his action caused the load to shift, and one stop slid halfway off the pallet. It hung there, and Brady could feel the weight pulling on the truck.

He slowly lowered the forks, but it was clear the hanging stop would touch the ground before the flat bottom of the pallet. If he was careful, perhaps it would push itself back into position without breaking. When it was just inches from the ground, he toyed with the levers that controlled the hydraulics, but at the last instant he held one too long, and the hanging stop hit the ground and cracked, held together only by a thin strip of rebar.

He swore. Three broken stops in two hours of work! Alejandro was a good guy and had predicted this learning curve. But with that third break, Brady knew he had actually cost the company money for that shift. He would not be docked, but what would the foreman think?

Alejandro had said such was the price of his training, but with everything else going on in Brady's life, he suddenly couldn't abide this. It was embarrassing, humiliating. Worse, what if the former guy's back got better and Alejandro got tired of waiting for Brady to be productive? Maybe he would get switched to sweeping floors for just pennies or, worse, lose his job.

Brady carefully snagged the broken stop with one fork and slung it out of the way, then grabbed another good one, completed the pallet, and loaded it onto the delivery truck.

He knew the right thing was to move the broken stop onto the pile with the other two so Alejandro would see the true picture in the morning. But forty feet past the delivery truck was a steep drop into a ditch. Did anyone ever look down there?

Brady hopped off the truck and crept to the edge. He

squinted in the darkness where it appeared a trickle of water ran through some gravel. Hurrying back, he fired up the machine, grabbed the third stop, and drove it to the edge. He raised the lift and angled the forks so the cracked slab slid off. But he didn't hear it roll to the bottom.

Furious, Brady scampered off to find that the thing had stuck to the muddy side of the gulley, midway down. Maybe that was good. Someone would have to look hard to see it. But it would be even better if he could cover it. There would be no getting the truck down there without it flipping, so Brady ventured down, quickly ankle deep in the soggy incline. It took him twenty minutes to dig and spread more mud over the block.

As he parked the forklift and went to turn off the lights in the outbuilding, Brady saw how mud-caked he was. His shoes were covered, his pants filthy to the knees. He'd have to leave early the next night and wash them at the Laundromat, but the shoes were another matter. He hosed them down before walking home, squeaking and leaking as he went.

At the trailer he sat on the steps and removed shoes and socks, setting the shoes where the morning sun might dry them before he left for school. He wrung out his socks, making enough noise to rouse his mother. She moved to the doorway and blocked the light.

"So what'd you do, fall in? Thought you were driving a forklift."

He turned and pushed past her.

"Answer me, you oaf! You too uncoordinated to even stay in a truck?"

There was so much he wanted to say, to do. But if he could just settle into this job, get them comfortable enough with him that he would never be suspected if he raided the office, he would be out of the trailer soon enough.

Nabertowitz was still on his case about his grades, but Brady had an image to protect. What would it look like, him meeting with a teacher, especially more than one, and having a tutor assigned? Some kid, maybe even younger, sitting with him in study hall and working with him?

Like that would happen.

Peebles

"You're going to be surprised at how this hits me, Thomas," Grace said, dishing out their meals as if moving in slow motion. "While it doesn't sound like there'll be a role for me, at least that I know of—perhaps I can write letters or send in baked goods or something—I can at least pray for you and for the men you'd minister to. But two things about it are really attractive to me. Can you guess?"

He smiled, chewing, and shook his head.

"First, we will be able to find a church to just attend and enjoy. Can you imagine simply drinking in some teaching and not having responsibilities? How I'd love that. Oh, I'm sure we'd both get busy soon

159

enough, teaching Sunday school and whatnot, but we'd just be members. Lord, forgive me, but it sounds delicious. I could organize the ladies to somehow minister to prisoners."

"You said two things."

She nodded and sat back, setting down her chopsticks after only two bites. "I did, but I'm feeling a little selfish about it. I believe I'd have more time with you. You wouldn't be there all hours, would you, like you've had to be at the churches?"

Thomas laughed. "We're feeling guilty together. Nothing sounds better to me. I also like the idea that you can take a break for a while. Whatever's wrong with you, whether it's just a bug or something serious, we'll have time to find out before you have to dive into anything."

"And that can wait. I feel wasted, I confess. But I don't think it's anything dire. Why don't you pursue this, and if it happens, once you get settled in and we find a place to live, if I still feel I need to, I'll see a doctor."

17

Thursday | Forest View High School

Brady Darby's last class of the day was metal shop in the industrial arts wing, and much as he liked working with his hands, he found himself more distracted there each day, looking forward to rehearsal. Metal shop had been the only class in which he'd been able to maintain higher than a D, but a big test was coming. Unfortunately, it was a book exam, not a project one. If he was only assigned to fashion something, he thought he was as good as anyone in the class. But if he had to come up with the whys and wherefores and melting temperatures and stress calculations, he'd be lost.

Worse, while his instructor was discussing the test, Brady's mind was elsewhere. Until he saw Mr. Nabertowitz at the door. The drama teacher apologized for the interruption and huddled with the shop instructor. Then both turned and nodded at Brady. Mr. N. motioned for him to come, and Brady quickly gathered his stuff.

"We have a meeting with the dean," Nabertowitz said as they headed down the hall. "Be on your best behavior."

"Hosey?" Brady said.

"Dr. Robert Hose to you. And you know what'll happen if you give him an ounce of attitude."

"Believe me, I know. Hauled me in for spit wads freshman year. Thought he was gonna expel me. Worse than terrorizing Mr. Peepers—you know who I'm talking about—in study hall was slouching in the chair in Hosey's office."

"Yes, no slouching."

"So, what'd I do now?"

"That's another question not to ask, at least that way. If you really don't know, say so, but you know he'll ask if you know why he wanted to see you. And we both do, don't we?"

Brady shrugged.

"Well, don't we?"

" 'Course."

"I'm going to bat for you, Brady. You do your part."

Dr. Hose was a short, compact man with close-cropped black hair. He did not rise from behind his desk when Brady and Nabertowitz entered, and Brady wondered where a guy bought a three-piece suit he could keep buttoned while sitting without looking like he was going to burst.

The dean narrowed his eyes at Brady as he pointed to chairs facing his desk. "Still smoking, I smell, huh, Darby?"

"Trying to quit, sir. You were right. You said it would become almost impossible."

"Almost. I quit, cold turkey, when I got out of the service. You can do it. I suppose you know why I asked to see you."

"I sure do, sir. My grades."

"It's not my practice to allow a teacher in here when I'm delivering bad news, but Nabertowitz thinks you're worth fighting for. Are you?"

"I'd like to think so."

Hose made a show of lifting a sheet and studying it. "If you were in sports, you wouldn't be allowed to compete. Why should I let you be in a play?"

"A musical," Nabertowitz said, falling silent when Hose flashed him a look.

"Whatever it is, you'd be up there acting like you belong with kids who do their homework, pass their classes . . . are, in short, good citizens."

"I'm really working on turning things around, Mr. Hose."

"Dr. Hose," Nabertowitz said.

"Right."

"Your turn, Nabertowitz," Hose said. "Sell me on this kid. He's about a tenth of a grade point from probation, and you know what that means."

"Well, Bob—uh, Dr. Hose—Brady comes from a difficult home."

"Don't we all?"

"Sure, but some worse than others. His father died recently; his mother is working but has some issues."

"What issues?"

"It's fair to say she struggles with addiction, and—"

"She's a drunk," Brady said. "And I got a little brother, eight, I'm watching out for. Plus I work. Part-time."

"Well, that's admirable," Hose said. "I lost my father too. It's a reason but not an excuse, you follow me?"

"Yes, sir."

"Let me just leave it this way, Darby. All the rest is interesting but doesn't matter to me. My priority is your academic performance, which means it has to become your priority too. Nothing less. Mr. N. tells me you have talent, maybe even a future. But I'm telling you, you're going to lose it all if you don't wise up and get after this. Your midterms are just before the play—the musical—opens. You can't afford one F. Even one, and you're out of the musical. Got it?"

Brady nodded.

Mr. Nabertowitz said, "Bob, we have an important rehearsal tomorrow afternoon. I'd love it if you could make it."

Hose looked amused, as if he couldn't imagine anything he'd less rather do. "I'll check my schedule," he said. "I gotta tell ya, I've never seen a burnout in a play before."

Friday Morning | Adamsville

Outgoing chaplain Russ met Thomas Carey at the same Denny's where they had been introduced, then drove him toward Adamsville State Penitentiary, less than a mile away.

"I'm going to tell you the truth, Reverend," Russ said. "I'm not sure you're right for this. Don't get me wrong—I'm grateful you're interested, and it gives me a real sense of relief that we're going to get somebody in my chair without maybe losing the chance forever. I just sense you're too nice a guy."

"I appreciate your candor. And I suppose I'll have a lot to learn. I don't know about changing my character or personality, though."

"That's what I'm worried about. I wouldn't ask you to change who you are, but these guys'll chew you up and spit you out, given half the chance. I daresay

164

you're going to be pushed and pulled and stretched and tested like never before, and unless you can adapt to a really hostile, alien environment, you're going to find it hard going."

"Well, if the Lord's not in it, I won't get the job, will I?"

"Oh, I believe you'll get it. I just want to see you keep it."

"May I call you when I need advice?"

"I'm going to be a long way away, Reverend. And my advice is always going to be the same. Trust no one. Believe no one. Be tough."

"Doesn't sound like pastoring to me."

"You're not going to be their pastor, man. You're going to be their chaplain. You represent God to them, and while, yes, He loves them, He also knows everything about them. He can't be conned. You dare not be."

"You're scaring me, Russ."

"I hope so."

Russ pulled off the road, and the car crunched through gravel leading to the checkpoint at the edge of the expansive property. Before reaching the guardhouse, he pulled off to the side. "Your first day," he said. "My last. I want to drink in the sight one more time, and you need to never forget this first glance. I'm used to it after ten years here and a lifetime in the system. But just check it out. You land this job, you'll be working in one of the most secure penal institutions in the world."

A strange coldness swept over Thomas as he gazed at the fifteen-foot cyclone fence that enveloped the entire acreage. Its top was adorned with spiraling bales of razor wire five feet high and five feet thick. A quarter mile inside the fence was a twelve-foot solid wall of concrete, no windows, one massive two-door iron gate in the center. Watchtowers were spaced evenly from the corners along the top of the wall, and while Thomas could see no one in them from that distance, Russ assured him that each had two veteran marksmen with enough firepower to eliminate any threat.

"Not a detail is left to chance here, my friend. Nobody's playing. The cons call this place the Real Deal. Ready?"

Thomas wasn't so sure. But he nodded anyway, and Russ pulled slowly to the guardhouse. A uniformed man emerged, clipboard in hand.

"I assume you know this guard," Thomas said.

"I know them all," Russ said, "but don't forget what I told you. Let that be the last time you use the word *guard* here, unless you're referring to the guardhouse. This man, and most of the staff here, are highly trained professionals and deserve to be called corrections officers. Got it?"

"Mornin', Russ," the man said, leaning in and glancing at the laminated ID card hanging around the chaplain's neck. "This Carey?"

"The Reverend Thomas Carey," Russ said. "Yes, sir."

"Good morning, officer," Thomas said.

The man nodded. "Bring the pastries for the warden, Russ?"

"That's tomorrow."

"Right."

The officer moved around to Thomas's side of the car and motioned for him to lower the window. "Full ID, please, including Social Security number."

Thomas produced the documents and the officer clipped them onto his board, studying them and leaning close to compare Thomas's face with his photo. "Still live in Alabama, Reverend Carey?"

"No. Settling here soon, I hope."

"You've been instructed regarding contraband and are carrying nothing that would violate our policy or give the admittance officers any reason to detain you?"

"Correct."

"Thank you, sir, and have a good day."

The officer returned Thomas's documents and waved Russ through.

"That pastry business was a code, you know," Russ said.

"Code?"

"He knew you were coming, of course. But on the off chance that someone else knew that, incapacitated you, and forced me to drive him into the facility, I'd have one chance to let the officer know. All I had to do was say I forgot the pastries, and there's no way this car would have moved another inch."

"Interesting."

"And you'd have had a nine-millimeter Glock pressed against your temple until backup arrived to disarm and subdue you."

Thomas shook his head. "So, similar to Sunday school."

Russ pulled into a parking lot a hundred yards from the front gate. Most of the forty spaces were already filled. Each had a name painted on a reserved sign. "If all goes well, your name will be here by the time you start. Down there's the warden's spot and those of his staff."

"And you say the warden is also the executive director of the state's Department of Corrections?"

Russ nodded. "Which makes him the dictator here."

"That's not all bad."

"Not at all. Streamlines everything. Less paperwork. He reports directly to the governor, and like I told you, they're tight."

Russ led Thomas to the great iron gate, wide enough to allow vehicles through, where they were met by another officer and run through the same routine as at the guardhouse. "What could have changed between there and here?" Thomas said. "I'm not challenging procedures. Just wondering."

Russ shrugged. "Nothing is left to chance; that's all."

Both emptied their pockets and took off shoes and belts before passing through a metal detector. They were admitted through a narrow single door cut into the gates. When the door was shut and locked behind them, Thomas finally saw the main complex, which dwarfed several smaller buildings.

"All the inmates are housed in the main unit. The outbuildings are only for staff. The warden's office, the administrative offices, and your office are in the main building."

Stark sidewalks took them from the gate to the big building about fifty yards inside. The ground was bare dirt, and there were no trees, shrubs, or landscaping of any kind. Russ's ID tag worked as a passkey for the lock on the entrance, and they were soon inside.

"We're buffered from the cells by this wing of offices," Russ said. "But you'll see the rest soon enough. And then you'll know why all prisons are clichés. I've been in lots of 'em, and regardless the level of security, the size, the location, anything, they're all the same. Slamming, swearing, smells, sights, sounds—all of it. Welcome to hell, Thomas."

18

Forest View High School

Brady sat in English late in the morning, knowing he should speak to Mrs. Stevens at the end of class and also knowing he wouldn't. Diagramming sentences and parts of speech would make up more than half the next exam, the diminutive lady told the class, "so don't say you didn't know. You have ample time to master this material."

Maybe if I had a clue. Brady hadn't been so lost since studying all the organizations within the United Nations in Current History the year before. What was current about something founded so many decades ago?

No amount of help from Mrs. Stevens, and certainly no snot-nosed student tutor, could give Brady a handle on this stuff. And for the life of him, he couldn't imagine when he would ever need to know any of it. Sure, the UN stuff, if he were to become president of the United States, but even then, would he need to know so much English?

On his way out of class, Mrs. Stevens called out, "Going to be prepared, Mr. Conrad Birdie?"

"You bet," he said.

"I hope so, son," she said. "I'm looking forward to seeing your performance."

That was the most she had ever said to him, and he found himself wondering if she meant in the musical or on the exam.

Brady found a note from the office taped to his locker. "Call Alejandro."

Terrific.

Adamsville State Penitentiary

Thomas Carey felt the furtive stares from the staff as Russ led him through the maze of glassed-in offices

170

and cubicles, finally to the short corridor that housed the warden, his aides, clerical staff, and a tiny, windowless corner office stuffed with institutional gray metal furniture.

"Gotta go out in the hall to change your mind," Russ said. "It's not mahogany row, but it's empty. I've cleared out. You get the job, you get the digs. Guy from NCIC isn't here yet, but lemme see if I can introduce you to Yanno."

At the other end of the hall, Russ chatted with Warden Frank LeRoy's secretary, a short, stocky black woman he introduced as Gladys, wearing a loud purple muumuu. She knocked softly on the warden's door and ushered Russ and Thomas in.

LeRoy, a big man in ill-fitting clothes—shirt too tight around the belly, trousers too short—was hanging up the phone. His office was bigger than the others and painted nicely, but the furniture was as modest as the chaplain's. Plaques and pictures hung everywhere, and the desk was messy.

"So, you're gonna be the new chaplain?" LeRoy said as he shook Thomas's hand.

"Well, I hope so, sir."

"Got to do the NCIC thing first, you know," Russ said.

"Oh, so you're just starting the process. Once they waive all the restrictions over your sordid past, we'll welcome you to the team."

Thomas was puzzled until Russ burst out laughing. "The warden says that to all newbies. I think he's aware you're a man of the cloth without a criminal record."

Thomas smiled.

"Well," LeRoy said, "we all have records. Some just served more semesters than others. Ever served time, Carey?"

"Oh no."

"Russ has. Did he tell ya?"

"No," Thomas said, sure this was another joke.

"Seriously," LeRoy said. "A little county time, wasn't it, Russ? NCIC cleared him, though. Probably wouldn't happen today."

"Long time ago," Russ said. "Listen, Frank, I was wondering. You know that little office down there hasn't seen a coat of paint in years. I've got everything off the walls and out of the desk and cabinets. Might be a good time to spruce it up, you know, before Thomas moves in."

"Yeah, no," LeRoy said, and it was all Thomas could do to keep a straight face. "I mean, if you get the job, Carey, and you want to do a little spackling and throw a can of paint on the wall, feel free. But with budgets and all, that's on you. Proud as this state is of its prisons, money will always be an issue."

Gladys poked her head in. "NCIC is here for Reverend Carey, waiting in the chaplain's office."

The "guy" from the National Compliance Integrity Commission turned out to be June Byrne, a tall, handsome woman in her midfifties with red hair and freckles. She wore large pieces of jewelry and carried a bulging soft leather satchel. From it she produced a three-inch-thick sheaf of computer printouts and set them on the desk in front of her.

After shaking Thomas's hand and introducing herself as a former police chief, she said, "If this turns out to be your office soon, thanks for letting me use it." As they sat, she said, "What makes a man want to become a prison chaplain?"

Thomas briefly told her of his faith, his education, and his pastorates. He was more nervous than he expected and found himself wishing he had some water. "I just care about people and their souls and hope I can offer something to the men here."

"Uh-huh. Well, you realize I'm not interviewing you for the position. My job is to assure the state Department of Corrections and the federal government that you comply with all requirements for personal and professional integrity. Ever been convicted of a crime?"

"No."

"Ever been arrested?"

"No."

"Should you have been?"

"Pardon?"

"Ever done anything that should have got you arrested, but you got away with it?"

Thomas chuckled. "No."

"Cheat on a test, steal from your mother's purse, shoplift a piece of candy from the store?"

"Believe it or not, no."

"I don't believe it, but I can't prove it, and such are

not worthy of a polygraph, so I'll have to take you at your word."

Thomas wondered why he felt guilty. He really wanted this woman to believe him. "I lied to my mother once," he said. "Told her something was mine when it actually belonged to my brother."

She looked amused. "You devil you. So what happened?"

"Conscience got the better of me and I wound up confessing."

"Get punished?"

"Oh yeah. Big-time spanking."

"You don't say. That's the way I was raised too. How old were you, Thomas?"

"Eight."

Ms. Byrne erupted in laughter. "Better put that in your file, hadn't I? FBI may want to look into it."

"I just wanted you to know I'm not perfect, but I really haven't ever done any of those other things you suggested."

June Byrne was suddenly all business, flipping through her printouts, brow furrowed. "You once got a refund from the Bible college you attended, but it was twice what you were owed."

"That's right. You people are certainly thorough. I noticed they had overcharged me for some extracurricular stuff I never took advantage of, so I was owed something like a hundred and fifty dollars."

"One hundred sixty-eight dollars and seventy-three cents."

"Right, okay."

"It was a choir bus tour that you never went on."

"Right. I had paid for it but then couldn't go."

"But they reimbursed you twice."

"Yes, they did. And of course I returned the extra."

"How long did that take?"

"Well, let's see; it's been years. Seems to me it came on a Thursday, I had to work the next day, then came the weekend, then I mailed it Monday, so they got it probably the next Wednesday."

"You held it almost a week?"

"Not really. I mean, I didn't deposit it or anything. I returned the same check they sent me. The school never mentioned a problem."

"It's not a problem, Reverend Carey. It's just a question, and interesting. Unlikely to become an issue. And then there's the matter of four speeding tickets in the last twenty years, one citation for excessive lane changing, and one for double-parking. You're aware that last is a federal offense?"

"Excuse me?"

Ms. Byrne grinned. "A little NCIC humor, Reverend. Lighten up."

"Oh! Sorry."

"Your credit reports look clean—a little heavy on credit card debt, not unusual for those in your line of work. Late on one card payment, late on your mortgage twice, but—"

"Oh, I'm sorry, but that's incorrect, ma'am."

"I'm listening."

"Grace and I have never owned a home, never had a mortgage. And to my knowledge, we've never been late on a rent check either."

"The mortgage part was a test, Reverend Carey. Making sure you're paying attention."

"Believe me, I am."

"Is it not true that you are currently overdue on your rent for the parsonage to the Rural Bible Chapel in Oldenburg?"

"Oh, for the love of all things sacred! If you have the time, I'll gladly tell you that story, and trust me, I won't leave out one detail."

"Do tell."

Forest View High School

Brady's mind raced as he dialed Dennis Asphalt & Paving. Of course he knew what this was about. It amazed him that in seconds he could concoct more than one elaborate tale, never even considering just gushing the truth and begging Alejandro's forgiveness.

As soon as Alejandro came on the line, he said, "Hey, Brady, sorry to bother you at school, but I got a problem."

"A problem?"

"I think you know, son."

"No, sir. No idea."

After a long pause, Alejandro said, "You think I'm blind? There's a stop missing, but we both know where it is, don't we?"

"I don't. I mean, I saw one was missing, but I don't know who took it."

"Listen, Brady, I told you there'd be a learning curve, didn't I? You didn't have to try to hide the damage."

"I didn't. I swear."

"Uh-huh. How'd it get down the ravine, then? You think you're the first to think of that? We take inventory, you know."

"Yeah, I know."

Alejandro chuckled, and for the first time, Brady thought he might skate. "That's where all the broken ones go eventually, man. Why try to hide it? C'mon, Brady. I gotta be able to trust you. I'm not gonna take it out of your pay, but just tell me next time, okay?"

"Well, it wasn't me, so . . ."

"Fine, but you're responsible."

Brady spent the rest of the day berating himself. Why did he bring this stuff on himself? And how hard could this homework be? If he just tried, his teachers would notice. But it was too late. There was no way he'd be ready for the exams, regardless. He would have to be so good at rehearsal that afternoon that everyone would see he was irreplaceable.

19

Thomas Carey's best suit had been out of fashion for a decade, but Grace had matched the navy with a light blue shirt and medium blue tie. As he pulled up to the guardhouse at the state penitentiary, Thomas felt he looked as professional as he was able. He had splurged on new socks, and he always kept his oxfords spit shined. His big Bible was on the seat, and despite his discomfort at entering the facility alone for the first time—and wishing Chaplain Russ wasn't already a full-time retiree hundreds of miles to the south—Thomas could barely contain his excitement.

The job was his. June Byrne had been amused, then enraged, by his account of the travesty in Oldenburg. He had passed her scrutiny without a hitch. In a few minutes he would be welcomed by the warden and his staff with a coffee and pastry break; then the warden himself would debrief him and lead him on a tour.

"Let me just study your face and your car for a second," the officer at the guardhouse said, double-checking Thomas's documents. "We're careful, but we like to make this as quick and easy as we can on our full-timers. Every day I'll peek in your backseat, and I'll watch your eyes in case you need to tell me anything—like if someone's stowed away in your trunk—but otherwise, like I say, we won't detain you."

"Pardon me," Thomas said. "That sounds great. But if someone forced me to bring him here in my trunk, couldn't I just—?"

"Leave him in there? Sure. But what if he had an accomplice at your house and was holding a loved one hostage who might be imperiled if you didn't get the bad guy inside here?"

"I see."

"It's rare, Reverend. But we try not to miss a thing. Welcome aboard."

Forest View High School

Mr. Nabertowitz had broken his own long-standing rule and begun to allow spectators at the daily rehearsals, and the Little Theater was usually at least half full. "Normally I worry that letting people in early will spoil sales," he said. "But we're already sold out for all six performances, and I want all the buzz I can get."

News of the first dress rehearsal had traveled farther and wider than anyone expected, and the place was jammed. Parents came. Friends came. Even the local press showed up.

If Brady thought he'd gotten a taste of popularity by simply landing the Conrad Birdie role, he was soon to know what it was like to be a bona fide center of attention. The cast looked great, Brady shone in his gold lamé suit, and while the staging and timing were understandably still in process, it was quickly becoming clear that this show was going to be something special.

The highlight of the afternoon for Brady had been standing next to Mr. Nabertowitz when the father character was singing his big number about what was the matter with kids these days. The actor could barely carry a tune, and when he went for the high dramatic notes, he failed miserably and disgustedly shook his head.

Mr. N. had warned the cast that he would not hold back during dress rehearsal, even when outsiders were there. "You screw up, I'm going to tell you, so be prepared."

Not unkindly, he urgently told the boy, "You have got to get this. This is a showstopping song. You're getting better on most of it, but you need to find those notes and nail them. Otherwise the show is stopped for the wrong reason."

They ran through the scene a couple more times, and the actor got no closer. Finally Brady asked if he could talk to Mr. Nabertowitz privately.

"Make it quick."

"I have an idea, if you want to hear it."

"I'm desperate, son."

"He's not going to hit those notes. That's not something you can learn. The problem is when he breaks character and acts disgusted with himself. Tell him to play it straight and belt it out at the top of his lungs, like he's proud of himself for hitting the notes he's missing. People love a buffoon."

Nabertowitz studied Brady. "You might be on to something. He's perfect in the speaking parts, and he knows all the lyrics. But we're going to bog down waiting for him to do something he seems incapable of."

The director called the boy over and briefed him. The actor looked dubious but said he'd give it a try. "Kids!" Nabertowitz shouted. "From the top!"

This time, when the actor got to the difficult parts, he spread his feet, squared his shoulders, planted his fists at his waist, threw his head back, and belted it out for all he was worth. He missed the notes by a mile but sang with a sneer of confidence, as if performing an aria at the Met. The audience erupted in cheers and laughter, and Forest View's *Bye Bye Birdie* had its singular moment.

Brady's performance was stellar. He hit every line and note and step with just enough charm and swagger and danger for the role, and Mr. N. crowed to everyone that he was also like an assistant director. He let it be known to all that the idea that made the father's performance work was Brady's alone.

All the success served to make Brady Darby the most popular, talked-about, sought-after kid in the school. He even had attention from girls—real women, cheerleader types—like he had rarely experienced before. He wasn't stupid. He knew the type. They loved the attention of getting next to the bad boy.

They weren't really going to date him or fall for him, and while he daydreamed about several of them, no preppy girl and he were going to become an item.

But this was sure fun.

As opening night approached, so did midterm exams. Brady hoped everyone in authority—though he had been warned otherwise—was prepared to make an exception in his case. Because while he was as ready for opening night as he had been for anything else in his life, he was not ready for midterms.

Adamsville State Penitentiary

Thomas had never worked for the state before, and he was pleasantly surprised to find how nice bureaucrats were to newcomers. He was treated the same at the main gate as he had been at the guardhouse, with two officers assuring him they would recognize him from now on and telling him they hoped he'd work out the way Chaplain Russ had and stay at least as long.

That was Thomas's dream too. He couldn't help himself. He was an optimist. He had seen every new church and ministry opportunity as something unique from God, and while each in its own way had gone south on him over the years, nothing had ever fully taken the wind from his sails. He was committed. He would remain true. He would stay in the Word, as he and people like him were wont to say about studying the Bible every day. He would rise at dawn and kneel and pray and read and memorize. He and Grace would sing together each evening. And he would look for opportunities to introduce people to Jesus. Adamsville State Penitentiary sure seemed the ideal place for that.

He had to admit that there were parts of ministry he wasn't that good at. The preaching thing, for one. Oh, he had tried, had given it all he had. He had seen and heard the best of the best at Bible college and at the occasional conference over the years. He'd been inspired and taken notes and even tried copying the techniques and mannerisms of the most engaging preachers. But he knew he had never riveted a crowd, never persuaded anyone just from the strength of his own passion and delivery.

He was better at the one-on-one: teaching, discipling, encouraging. That was why this new role seemed a perfect fit. Thomas had taken Russ's misgivings to heart and knew he would have to be wise as a serpent and gentle as a dove, as the Scripture said. That would all come in time. For now, he had a lot to learn.

Gladys, decked out in orange, including her eyeshadow, was remarkably cheery for a woman in her role. She couldn't have been much older than he, but Thomas felt mothered by her—in a good way. She escorted him to Human Resources, where he was initiated with keys, a packet of brochures and pamphlets, and an employee manual. He signed more documents than he and Grace had had to sign to rent the tiny four-room ranch three miles from the prison.

Thomas had just arrived for his first day on the job, and already he was eager to get back home to help Grace unpack and set up housekeeping. Her health seemed to have rallied with the new opportunity and a home to call her own. He just hoped she didn't overdo things.

Thomas worried about his wife. Soon, he feared, he would have to press Grace to see a doctor. Not only was she not herself physically, but her demeanor had also been affected by whatever was ailing her. He knew better, but Thomas had long seen her as perfect, almost too good to be true. He wasn't complaining, but there were days he would have loved to see her as more human. Nothing ever seemed to get to her, and part of him even suspected that her equanimity had been partly to blame for Ravinia's revulsion of them.

He'd never dared raise this with Grace, and he knew his own bland consistency in all things spiritual had to be frustrating for a young woman too. But he could identify with Rav's complaint that she had been raised in the house of a matron saint.

Several days before, however, a bit of Grace's sheen had worn off, and she had tearfully confessed to him what she considered a sin that had eroded her conscience.

"I wrote a letter to the Pierces," she said.

"You didn't."

"I did. And I even used a bad word in it."

"Whatever you called them, they deserved it," Thomas said before he could catch himself.

"I need to apologize," she said.

Thomas knew she was right, but he wished she wouldn't. Few people stood up to Paul Pierce. He could only imagine the man fuming at the brass of the former circuit pastor's tiny wife.

"I want to send a note of apology even before I hear back from them."

"You think they'll write back?"

"Of course."

Grace had fired off the follow-up letter, but she never heard from the Pierces.

Thomas had pestered her for days to tell him what she had called the Pierces, and when she finally admitted she had regrettably referred to them anatomically, it was all he could do to hide his glee. Even now he chortled aloud when he thought of it.

Loaded with all the stuff from the personnel director, Thomas found his way back to his office. He would have to bring in a box of personal photos to adorn the walls and make it homey, but for now he just set the furniture the way he wanted it and jotted a list for Gladys—as she had instructed—of the office supplies he needed.

When he delivered it to her, she rang a tiny hand bell on her desk, and people seemed to appear from nowhere. Offices and cubicles emptied, and men and women of all ages and races—though they all seemed to dress in the same plain, cheap business wear—moseyed into the central area and lined up for a pastry and a cup of coffee.

Frank LeRoy was the last to appear. "Okay!" he said. "Thanks for coming. Get yourself something to eat and drink and introduce yourself to our new chaplain. Then let's get back to work."

"Yeah, no," someone whispered, and several laughed.

"What's that?" the warden said.

"Thank you!"

"Oh, well, thank Gladys. She arranged all this like she does everything else."

Gladys bustled here and there, making sure everyone was taken care of, while Thomas stood awkwardly, wondering if he should try to eat and drink while greeting all these new associates. He decided against it, but Gladys brought him a plate with a doughnut on it and a cup of coffee.

"I'd better go easy on the sweets," he said.

"Oh, go on and have one," she said. "It's a party."

"Lot of calories, I'll bet."

"Tell me about it," she said, beaming. "I say, 'Get thee behind me,' and then I eat 'em, and they do!"

Maybe it was first-day jitters, but the unexpected humor caused a snort when he laughed. He would have to engage with the warden's secretary more when occasions arose. It was a joke, but she had quoted Scripture. He wondered where she was spiritually.

Thomas managed to hold both his plate and his cup in one hand as he shook hands with nearly everyone and quickly recited for each where he was from, that he was eager to introduce his wife someday, and how glad he was to be there.

"You seen the unit yet?" someone said.

"That's next, I believe, after my meeting with Warden LeRoy."

"You'd better decide after that how glad you are to be here."

20

Forest View High School

Dean Hose called Brady out of a morning class. Brady had no advocate along this time.

"Against my better judgment, I slipped into that dress rehearsal."

"No kiddin'? Did Mr. N. know?"

Hose shook his head. "Thing is, live theater is not my deal, especially musicals. But I loved it. I'll be bringing my family and even another couple."

"Cool."

"You're really good, Darby. Who would have guessed?"

"Not me. Thanks."

"Anybody who can do what you do on that stage is no dummy. So what are you doing about your grades?"

"I told you. I'm trying harder, gonna get my homework done, study for these tests, look into getting some help."

"C'mon, Darby. Who do you think you're talking to? That's a load, and you know it."

"Sorry?"

Dr. Hose pointed to the brass plate on the edge of his desk. "You see my title, 'academic dean'? *Academic, son.* You think I'm not in daily touch with every teacher in this school and don't know who is and who isn't in trouble? You haven't talked to one of your teachers about your situation, haven't asked for help, haven't asked for a tutor, and worse, you're *not* keeping up with your homework. That one I can't figure at all. At least do that!"

Brady hung his head. "You wouldn't understand."

"Oh, believe me, I understand. You're not the first smart kid who's more concerned about his image than his grades. It's one thing to be the hip tough guy who crashes the preppies' party and lands the sweetest role in the musical. But to do your daily assignments, carry your books, take notes, get help—no, that's beneath you. Am I right or am I right? Huh?"

Brady felt exposed. "Let's be real. I'm going to be a workingman all my life. I just can't get myself worked up over these classes."

Hose stood and thrust his hands into his pockets. He peered out the tiny window in his door, then turned to face Brady. "That's something else that's always puzzled me. Most of your friends are in work-release programs where they take shop classes in the morning and head for a job in the afternoon. Why not you? You get to start that as a junior."

Brady shrugged. "Can't afford a car yet, so I haven't gotten a job like that. Anyway, I wanted to play football, and when that didn't work out, I tried out for the musical."

"You know, don't you, that if you don't do something drastic, you're going to be out of the musical? Past that, how will you ever graduate? While there's nothing wrong with being a workingman, as you say, you're never going to get to be a foreman if you don't have a sheepskin. It's all right to punch a clock, but wouldn't you like to at least be on salary someday, get some benefits, have a little job security? You're going to want a wife and a family, aren't you?"

Now Hosey had hit Brady where he lived. He had no crazy notion that he could find the right woman, have the right job, find a decent place to live, and make the family thing work the way his aunt and uncle had. Desperate as he was to be a good example to Peter, he was already failing miserably at that and could only hope against hope that Peter had no idea.

Brady nodded. "You think I could try that work-release thing when the play is over?"

"I do. But, listen, you can't just let everything slide until then. It happens that your midterms end the Friday night the play opens, so your grades won't be recorded until Monday. But if your GPA slips an iota, you'll disqualify yourself from the three performances the following weekend. And the work-release thing would be out the window too."

The warden waved Thomas in while still on the phone and pointed to a chair. "All right, then, George. I'll be back to ya."

He hung up and studied Thomas. "There's still time to turn tail and run, Reverend," he said, smiling.

"I don't guess I'll be doing that. I'm excited about this."

"It'll be no picnic. That was Andreason on the phone. The gov and I go way back, you know. College. He's not happy about me trying to run the DOC from here, but for now I've got him convinced it's cheaper. We're saving a salary, for one thing, and I have a good team. But I do have to travel a fair amount to the other facilities, so you won't be seeing me a lot. Our work doesn't overlap much anyway. Gladys can answer most of your questions. I'm glad we've got ya, because I know the spiritual health of the population here is important. It's not very good, of course, but it's important."

"You believe that?"

"I sure do. I'm a churchman myself, ya know."

"Really?" Thomas wondered why Chaplain Russ had never mentioned that.

"Yeah, saved when I was a little kid, the whole bit. Now saying I'm a churchman is a little overstated, 'cause I admit I find more reasons to stay home than go anymore. But I get out when I can."

Thomas was tempted to ask about the man's personal devotional life but feared it would be too forward this early in their relationship. He also wanted to urge the warden to become regular again in his church attendance for the sake of the survival of his spiritual life. But he wasn't the warden's chaplain. Russ had reminded him of that. "The people in the office might come to you with a question, but they don't want to be approached. Your constituency is the men in the cells, not the staff."

LeRoy looked at his watch. "I got to be heading out in a couple of hours, but that leaves plenty of time to give you the lay of the land. You've never been in a place like this, so prepare yourself. You may hear things you've never heard before, smell things, see things. You show the least bit alarm, they'll be on you like wounded prey."

"But they can't get to me."

"Not physically, no. And they might be more likely to behave because I'm with you. But there's an incredible rumor mill inside any penal institution. Everybody knows Russ is gone and the new guy is coming in. It won't surprise anyone who you are."

"I was thinking of carrying my Bible, you know, just to make plain who I am and what I'm about."

"Yeah, no," Frank LeRoy said. "Word to the wise: I think they'd see that as a little pious, a little holier-than-thou."

"I see. If someone greets me . . . ?"

"In a civil way? It's okay to respond, but keep it noncommittal. Tell them you look forward to getting to know them eventually, something like that. As you know, they have to ask for you to visit, so it's on them. And then you've got to watch all the religious games they'll play, trying to get next to you, get favors, get you to get them a free phone call—usually for some made-up crisis. And then when you don't, they'll try to lay a big guilt trip on you, questioning whether you care, challenging your faith, your interest, your love, everything. Russ used to get guys whining about how he never came around, when they knew as well as he did that they had to officially request a visit. Now, you ready for a look?"

Forest View High School

Brady knew exactly what he should do, yet he also knew he would not do it. He should swallow his pride and enlist all the help he could in order to succeed on the midterms, believing that even if he failed, his teachers and Dean Hose would recognize that he was giving it his all. They would be able to make concessions for him, keep him in the play, keep him in school, and transition him into the work-release program.

But that crazy part of his brain, that lazy, hope-things-will-work-out part of him, heard the timing issue—that his midterms could all be Fs and still not affect his first three performances—as a license to coast. He knew there was no way he could pass even one test with that attitude. He would be flunking himself out of of the play, even out of the work-release program.

But what if a talent scout saw him that first weekend? Then Brady wouldn't need school. He wouldn't need anything but his dream and his passion and his talent. And maybe, just maybe, he would be so impressive that the school would let him try the work-release program on probation.

Hose had been crystal clear on that score, though. It wasn't going to happen. The second weekend of the musical was in no way guaranteed—unless Brady failed, and then it was guaranteed he would be on the outside looking in.

Yet still Brady mentally shut the door on his midterms. He wouldn't be cracking another book, taking another note, talking to any teacher, employing any tutor. He would do his best on the tests, excel on the boards, and hope for a miracle.

Stupid, stupid, stupid, he knew. But he had never played the game before, and he wasn't about to start now.

Adamsville State Penitentiary

"Eight percent of the state budget goes to incarcerating criminals," Warden Frank "Yanno" LeRoy said as he led Thomas Carey out of the office wing and down a long, sterile corridor. When they turned right, Thomas's senses were assaulted. The tang of industrial cleaners hit his nostrils, and as they approached the first envelope, as Chaplain Russ had called it, he heard all the clanging and yelling.

"These men cost us over three hundred dollars a week each," Yanno said. "It's no surprise some wonder why we don't just execute 'em all and save money."

Thomas couldn't imagine anything worse. Sure, some no doubt deserved to die. But to kill them all just for economic reasons? How, then, could any of them be reached for Christ?

He was quickly processed through the double entry into the main unit, surely because the warden was with him. The corrections officers greeted the warden, and they were friendly, though businesslike, with Thomas.

As they moved into the corner of the massive first floor, Yanno stopped to point out things and explain. And from all over the unit came shouts and cries.

"Padre!"

"Father!"

"Reverend!"

"God squad in the house!"

Thomas tried to take in everything at once. In some ways, this reminded him of a zoo. Cement floors, concrete block walls, tiny slits of windows, and cages everywhere. He was surprised to notice that each cell had a solid steel door with an opening for a food tray, the rest of the front wall made up of two-inch square openings, almost as if metal strips had been woven. There were no bars, per se, except between corridors and envelopes. Each man's "house" was identical.

"Each cell is seven feet by ten feet with a built-in bunk, a concrete stool, a metal table, and a sink-toilet unit."

"I'll never complain about the size of my office," Thomas said.

"I hear that. But this is the price for bein' a bad citizen. They carp and complain and write letters and cry to the public, but we're not trying to be mean. They're not in here for chewing gum in class, know what I mean?"

Closer to the cells, the industrial cleaner smell was overwhelmed by a stench that seemed to be a combination of sewage, garbage, and body odor. "Each man is responsible for cleaning his own house, and we give 'em what they need for that once a week. They tend to misuse good cleaning products, so they get watered-down stuff that can't be turned into anything dangerous. And some of them just don't care to clean their places. Again, that's on them. If they want to live in filth, that's their problem. Once a week someone is let out, by himself—shackled and cuffed, of course—to mop the area around the pods. The banks of cells are the pods."

The cells were arranged five side by side, with another five directly above them, a single shower stall at one end, and the exercise area at the other. The ten-cell units were arranged in a circle of six, clustered around a two-story watchtower. From the tower,

195

which Yanno called the observation unit, corrections officers could see into all sixty cells.

"The locks are controlled from within the tower, but each man's house also has a manual locking device, so we're talking triple security. When an officer is extracting a prisoner for a shower, a meeting, the work assignment, or his daily one-hour visit to the exercise kennel, he signals the tower first. The electronic lock is disengaged for that one cell; then the officer must remove the manual lock before using his key for the main lock."

"Did you call the exercise area a kennel?"

Yanno nodded. "I probably shouldn't, because the bleeding hearts would just love to quote me that way. But it's a ten-by-twenty-foot, two-story, fenced-in area with fresh-air grates in the ceiling. Certain times of the day a man can catch a glimpse of the sun through there, but usually, no way. As you can see, it looks like a big kennel."

As they strolled, Thomas was struck that so many of the inmates—all wearing white T-shirts, khaki pants, and soft slippers—were living in the dark. Many had clothing draped over their lights, and paper hung even over some of the four-inch-wide windows cut vertically near the top of each cell.

"I don't get it," he said. "You'd think with the lack of a view of the outside, they'd want all the light they can have."

"Isn't there something in the Bible about that, Reverend? Something about men living in darkness because their deeds are evil? Russ tells me you've got the whole Bible memorized, or something like that."

"Well, not the whole thing. But, yes, I know that verse. And the ones around it. 'There is no judgment against anyone who believes in Him. But anyone who does not believe in Him has already been judged for not believing in God's one and only Son. And the judgment is based on this fact: God's light came into the world, but people loved the darkness more than the light, for their actions were evil. All who do evil hate the light and refuse to go near it for fear their sins will be exposed. But those who do what is right come to the light so others can see that they are doing what God wants.'"

"Wow," Yanno said. "That's impressive."

"If you'll indulge me, Warden, there's another passage that speaks to this."

"Fire away."

"Zechariah, the father of John the Baptist, said, 'And you, my little son, will be called the prophet of the Most High, because you will prepare the way for the Lord. You will tell his people how to find salvation through forgiveness of their sins. Because of God's tender mercy, the morning light from heaven is about to break upon us, to give light to those who sit in darkness and in the shadow of death, and to guide us to the path of peace.'"

Yanno cleared his throat. "Was your voice breaking there?"

Thomas nodded but could not respond. He had been

197

warned about being soft, yet now he found himself on the edge of tears, praying his lips wouldn't quiver and give him away. All these men—these sad, lonely, desperate men—caged, hapless, hopeless, lost. His heart broke over them, and he hadn't met a single one.

"I'm gonna tell you one more time, Carey. You can't let 'em see your soft side. Now I know that goes against all they teach you in seminary and stuff, but just by the nature of your job, these guys already assume you're an easy mark. Don't prove 'em right, whatever you do, or we'll be looking for another chaplain before the end of the month."

21

Adamsville State Penitentiary

To Thomas Carey, the difference between the ASP supermax and, say, Cook County Jail in Chicago was like the difference between *War and Peace* and *Love Story*.

Cook County was a chaotic, depressing place, and the evil there was exacerbated by the relative freedom of the inmates to congregate. It was overcrowded, dangerous, and appeared nearly unmanageable because gang members still associated with one another, guards were compromised, and sometimes even escape attempts were successful.

ASP, though, was an entirely different kettle of felons. Warden LeRoy admitted that many on the outside considered his zero-tolerance policies overkill. "But they simply don't understand my constituency. These guys have proven over and over that they understand only one language, and that is maximum force, complete deprivation of freedom, and punishment rather than reform. They have lost the opportunity to redeem themselves, because every time they've been offered that chance, they've violated the state's trust. Their previous hitches were in *correctional* facilities. This is a *penitentiary*. We allow them to be as penitent as they want, but clearly they don't want to be reformed, or they wouldn't have wound up here."

Thomas considered himself a man of justice. Actions had consequences. People needed to be punished. He even allowed that some were worthy of capital punishment, though that notion had fallen into disrepute among many within his own profession. It was hard to argue for something so final and brutal in light of the Bible's teaching on love and respect and forgiveness. And yet the Scriptures were also clear that one who sheds another's blood should have his own blood shed. Thomas acknowledged that a death sentence was no trifle and that all the checks and balances and safeguards—fair trials, appeals, and all the rest—were a crucial part of the process. But still, he believed, justice mandated the ultimate punishment in extreme cases.

Yet now, as he tried to absorb all that his senses were trying to communicate, Thomas found himself overwhelmed with pity for this massive population of men. Did they deserve this? Apparently they did. Why could they not have learned at some earlier, more copacetic level of incarceration that changing their ways would spare them this inhumanity? Had they not heard the stories from inside this place?

Yanno told him that even here the cons tried every scheme to manipulate the system, "but at the end of the day, they lose. Every time. They are in their cells twenty-three hours of every twenty-four. They are allowed out only when no other inmate is, and they are strip-searched, manacled, cuffed, and led about by corrections officers. When they return to their cells, they go through the same procedure in reverse. They dare not ask an inch of leeway. They don't deserve it, and they won't get it."

Yanno led Thomas to the far end of the unit, within a hundred yards of the main gate. Already Thomas had learned not to turn at the shouts and jeers of the inmates. He was intrigued, however, by a man about his age who stood quietly next to his solid door, peeking out through the squares in the front wall. The man was balding and paunchy.

"You the new chaplain?" he said.

Thomas looked at the warden, who nodded. "Just stay back about two feet," he whispered.

Thomas approached. "Yes, sir, I am. Thomas Carey is my name. And yours?"

The man reached his fingers through the opening. "Call me Zach."

Thomas looked to the warden for permission to touch the man's fingers. Yanno shook his head.

"Nice to meet you, Zach. I look forward to getting to know you."

"Yeah, me too. I'd like you to stop by as soon as you can."

"I think that can be arranged."

"Yeah, no!" LeRoy said. "Zach, you know the protocol. You know how to go about requesting a visit."

Zach pressed his lips together and shook his head, then cursed both men. Thomas wanted to assure him he would be happy to come back if the proper request was submitted, but Yanno pulled him away. "You're tempted to make nice, but he's just pulling your chain. You'd be falling right into his trap."

"But I'm here to minister to him if he wants."

"Exactly. If he wants. We'll both know how much he wants that if we see the paperwork, won't we? What else has he got to do? He asks for the form, fills it out, turns it in. We call that a kite, because he's sending it into the wind, hoping it'll fly. If it's all in order, you schedule it. But let me tell you something: you won't be hearing from Zach."

"You're sure?"

"People will do what people have done, Reverend. Zach never once in ten years requested a visit from Russ."

Thomas shook his head. The guy had sounded so sincere. "Tell me, why is he so out of shape? Does he not take advantage of the exercise room?"

Yanno shook his head. "Just goes and hangs around. No one turns down the exercise time, but few exercise or jog or even stretch. They like the change of scenery and the space, but not many are motivated to stay fit. There's no smoking in here, so everyone has been through withdrawal, and they're healthier that way. And naturally they don't have access to booze. But the food is what it is—high fat, high starch, low on nutrients. It's hard to overeat because they don't get huge quantities, but if all you do is sit and stand all day, you soon go to seed."

Most of the inmates—with a few bodybuilder and youthful exceptions—were as soft as Zach looked. The population was largely minority, though it seemed the entire globe was represented. Thomas couldn't shake a dark, heavy feeling that saddened him to his soul.

"We're just processing a new inmate," Yanno said, leading Thomas to the intake cell. A young Hispanic man wearing only his underpants sat in the five-by-five-foot windowless chamber away from the sight and even the sounds of the rest of the population. The room had neither bunk nor stool. The front wall was Plexiglas, but the only view from the cell was the cement blocks on the other side of the corridor.

The man looked both petrified and defiant.

"Got as far as the wall in one of our other facilities but surrendered rather than be shot. A lot of times they don't give up, you know. That's known as suicide by cop. They make you kill 'em. Some even get themselves hopelessly tangled in the razor wire, but they don't quit struggling till they're dead. This guy wasn't that stupid, but he had to know he'd wind up here."

"Why no clothes?"

"Policy. You come here, you get stripped of everything but your underbritches. You're body-cavity searched, hosed down, dried off, and put in this cell until your house is ready. Then you get your slippers, khakis, and tee. He'll be shackled and cuffed and led to his house, and he won't be allowed out for anything but a fifteen-minute shower once a week for the first ninety days. In fact, he won't have any privileges. No TV, no radio, nothing to read, nothing to write with. We don't apologize for it. We're tryin' to break 'em, and they have to prove they're worthy of privileges."

"So he behaves for ninety days, and then what?"

"He gets paper and pencil, electricity, a tiny black-and-white TV, and a radio. He gets his daily hour in the exercise kennel."

"I noticed the TVs. They have cable? Movie channels and all?"

"Yeah, but no porno. Watchin' TV is the closest these guys come to community."

"How so?"

"Guys in the same pod will all watch the same show and then discuss it, argue about it. It's like they're watching together, despite that they're in their own houses."

"So it behooves this guy to keep his nose clean the first three months."

"And that's not easy, Carey. The newcomers get both barrels from everybody. They scream at 'em, challenge 'em, mock 'em, taunt 'em. They try to get them to be belligerent to the officers, get them in trouble. And that rumor mill I told you about? Everybody watches TV all day. They see the news; they know as much about a guy's case as he does, and they push him till he breaks, if they can. 'What'd you do? Is it true what the prosecutor said? Did you enjoy making the victim suffer?' That kind of thing. The best plan for a newbie is to not answer, ever. They'll demand to know if he's gay, if he's a rapist, a child molester. They'll predict when he'll crack. Worst part is, it's hard enough to sleep in here. For one thing, they're not often tired at night, so there's racket all the time. But when the hollering is directed at you, it's impossible."

A commotion led them back into the unit, where a naked inmate, standing in the tiny shower stall, was hollering. "C'mon, man! I been here more'n an hour and I'm cold!"

From the watchtower a staticky voice came over the intercom. "He's coming. Just hold on."

"Then turn the shower back on, man!"

Silence.

The con recited a litany of vile curses.

"The shower runs for ten minutes," Yanno told Thomas. "Then it's off for three; then it runs for two more. The guys have to learn to wash up, then rinse off. Sometimes the water's cold. We try to keep it hot, but sometimes there are other priorities. Once it's run through both cycles, hot or cold, the inmate has to wait there until his officer comes back to chain him up and get him back to his house.

"The guys get issued a razor when they get in there, but they have to return it when they're done, and it has to be totally intact. These guys'll make a weapon out of anything."

"Where would they be able to use it?"

"You'd be surprised. That's why they're searched every time they're removed from or returned to their houses. And often we search the houses when they're out for a shower or exercise. The worst problem is feces bombs."

"Oh, my. Do I want to know?"

"Probably not, but you need to. This ain't grade school. Yes, these guys will collect their own feces, wrap it in paper, and when an officer tries to deliver their food through the slot in the door—during which the inmate is supposed to stay at the back of his cell—the con will race forward and fire the mess at the officer, sometimes hitting him in the face. Regardless, as you can imagine, that's a horrible, disgusting attack and can be dangerous. The officers wear rubber gloves and sometimes face masks, but we've had personnel injured. That is a felony and carries dire consequences."

"Such as?"

"He's forcefully extracted from his cell by our goon squad. That name was made up by the population, but it fits, so we use it too. A group of at least six officers, wearing full body armor and one of them carrying a Plexiglas shield, approaches the cell and orders the inmate to back up to the food slot and extend his hands behind him to be cuffed. If he cooperates, they shackle him and take him back to the intake cell for what we call Administrative Segregation, or Ad Seg. Depending on how long you're assigned to stay, it's the worst experience a man can have here. He's in his underwear for days, no shower, no exercise, no place to sit or lie except the bare floor. No pillow or even a blanket. Eats sack lunches of thin lunchmeat sandwiches. No contact with anyone."

"What if they refuse to allow themselves to be cuffed?"

"We inject noxious gas into their house. Sometimes it takes two canisters, but not even the toughest can stand that for long. Either they back up to the slot and get cuffed, or we burst in and subdue them. Some of these guys have a high pain threshold. They'll camp out at the back of their cell, coughing, wheezing, crying, but they won't surrender. And when the squad comes in with pepper spray and Tasers and all, they kick and punch and pinch and scratch and bite until the team forces them flat on the floor. It's a game to them. They have nothing to lose. We videotape every extraction to cover ourselves legally."

"But they have to know they're going to Ad Seg, right?"

"Sure. Some of 'em do it just to be obstinate, some

for the attention—any is better than none, they figure—and some do it just for the change of pace and scenery. Listen, some guys eat pieces of their cell. Anything small enough to fit in their mouths, they try to ingest it. Plastic around the light fixture. Wire mesh. Anything that will get them in trouble, give them a health issue—which we're required to treat. These guys are the most innovative on earth.

"There's all kinds of ways for a guy to break the rules. Refuse to return his tray to the slot. Refuse to return every utensil and dish. Disobey a direct command. Spit at an officer—that's a felony. Refuse to stand during what we call the live count. There are three counts every twenty-four hours, but the one just before dinner demands that each man is standing by his bunk so we know he's alive and well.

"Any contraband that turns up during cell searches is grounds for discipline. Like I said, these guys'll make weapons of anything they get their hands on. I'll show you our samples room last. You won't believe it. But first death row and the execution area. Ever seen one?"

Thomas shook his head. He was curious, but he already had more to consider than he had ever dreamed. No TV show or movie came close to this reality. It would have been all right with him to put off this part of the tour for another day, but he was getting the picture that this may be his only extended time with the warden, and he dare not exhibit any weakness.

"Death row looks just like any other pod, but it's in the very bowels of the place. As you can see, no one's getting out of here. It simply isn't possible, and we overdo it to make doubly sure. The condemned are as far from any ultimate exit as they can be. Eleven envelopes, then the main gate, then the guardhouse, then the fence.

"Nine of the cells on the row are filled right now, and none of these guys has ever been more'n twenty feet from this pod, unless it's for meetings with their lawyers, and that's all within this envelope too. Well, come to think of it, we got us a Native American back here who gets access to the sweat lodge every so often."

"The what?"

"Your brochures will tell you about that. There's a handbook on 'religion behind bars.' Bottom line, if a guy can prove he holds a sincere belief, we have to accommodate him, short of a compelling governmental interest, such as security. And I hope you know that even though you're a Christian and a Protestant and all that, you work for the state, and you have to try to get things to any of these guys, regardless of their religion. Wicca, Islam, you name it; if they want a book or a pamphlet, you can't deny 'em unless the publication promotes violence or crime. Anything you end up stocking for their spiritual health has your stamp on it. It's lent to them for the length of their stay. They're only borrowing it, but they can have it until their release or execution."

208

"I have to accommodate even satanists?"

"So far we've dodged that one, because the very nature of satanism seems to violate our compelling interests. It helps that the governor and I agree on that, and George doesn't cater to Washington. But you're going to hafta get familiar with the RLUIPA. That's the Religious Land Use Institutional Persons Act, and it's the one that makes us provide wood and fire in an area where American Indians can build a sweat lodge, if that's their sincerely held belief."

The two-tiered death row was noisy, but not as much as the other pods Thomas had seen. Some of the men glanced at him; others just sat looking nowhere. Two were busy writing. Three others were watching TV. It was not lost on Thomas that two had open Bibles in their cells.

"That one's doing it just for your benefit," Yanno whispered, "but this one over here might be for real. Henry Trenton. Calls himself the Deacon, and he had a regular meeting with Russ every week."

"Here, or in the—"

"Here, which is unusual. Typically a guy will ask for a visit in the separation room, just for something different to do, but mostly because he wants to talk confidentially. It's considered a bad thing to have the chaplain visiting your house all the time. Makes you look soft. Being what they call chaplain-friendly is not a good thing. What you do for one guy, you've got to do for all. If the chaplain goes with a con to his parole board hearing, believe it or not, it looks bad to the board—for the con *and* the chaplain."

"You don't say."

Yanno nodded. "The con looks desperate. You look like a pushover. I've never seen a chaplain change a board's mind."

The Deacon, gray-haired and looking late sixties, sat gazing at the two men. "You wanna meet the new chaplain, Deke?"

The old man shrugged.

"It's up to you," the warden said.

The Deacon stood, and the two approached. Thomas took his cue from the warden and stayed back from the door.

"Child murderer," the Deacon said, as casually as if calling himself a member of the local Jaycees.

"Sorry?" Thomas said.

"Murdered three kids so they wouldn't rat me out. But here I am."

Thomas introduced himself.

"You can't replace Russ, I hope you know."

"I wouldn't even try. I'll just be myself. But if you'd like to continue your weekly meetings—"

"That will be totally up to you," the warden said.

"Yeah, well, not likely," the Deacon said. "But I'll think about it." He sat back down and looked away.

"Did I offend him?" Thomas said.

LeRoy chuckled. "Did *you* offend *him?* He offended society and God and children and every rational human being. Don't you worry about offending him.

His execution is scheduled before the end of the year, and all his appeals have been exhausted."

"How awful."

"Yeah, no. It's long past due. Now, come on, I'll show you the contraband sample room. The execution chambers are on the way."

"Chambers, plural?"

"Oh, yeah. We're the only facility in the United States that's a full-service death provider."

Yanno's attempt at humor made Thomas shudder.

"Yep, we let the condemned decide. Hardly any place has a gallows anymore, but we do. And even fewer have electric chairs. Barbaric, they say. Ours sits in a gas chamber—another dying breed. Guy can sit strapped in that chair and take the juice or the gas. Then there's the hospital room, as our guys call it. That's supposedly the humane way to go, you know. They paralyze you, then pump you with poison."

They came into view of three glassed-in rooms that looked out onto a bank of two dozen chairs for viewers. The warden flipped a switch, and the blinds raised in all three rooms. The first was about double the size of a phone booth, with an ancient wooden stairway leading to a platform with a four-by-four beam extended horizontally above it. "Just enough room for an officer, an executioner, and a chaplain, besides the condemned. Noose goes around the beam. Spring-loaded trapdoor gives way. Bingo."

The next room bore the ugly chair with its metal skullcap, leather straps, and cords running everywhere. "Our multipurpose room," Yanno said. "You get your choice, but you have to pick one. And then there's the fancy room, with the gurney and all the comforts of a hospital. This is the one Washington wants us to use, if any at all, though you know even this has come under fire as inhumane. What do they think murder is? The press hates that we offer the menu of four options. Other states are jealous. We agree some of these methods are more gruesome than others, but as the result is the same, and justice is the game, we don't much care which a guy chooses."

"Has the Deacon chosen?"

"He's old-school. Wants the noose. I think it sounds glamorous to him. Maybe you're lucky he doesn't seem to take to you. Maybe he won't ask you to stand up there when he drops."

Lord, spare me.

"Hey, you wanna sit in the chair, get your picture taken?"

"Are you serious?"

"Absolutely! Lots of people have done that. Just say the word."

"Warden LeRoy, I need to ask you a serious question. Your answer will not change my mind—and I might as well tell you up front that there is nothing I'd less rather do. . . ."

"There's no danger! Power's off. We strap you in, even put the cap on you, put a mask on—"

"No, sir. Thank you."

"But you had a question."

"I'm just wondering if it makes me look soft for not wanting to."

The warden studied him. "No. No, it doesn't. Makes you look mature. Sensible even. I don't show off the picture of me, though my family gets a kick out of it. You can imagine what the press would do with it. If it makes you feel any better, Russ was just as dead set against it as you."

"That does make me feel better."

"I respected him for it. You too."

Subdued—shaken was more like it—Thomas followed Yanno to the sample room. It was a macabre museum, exhibiting the endless creativity of the criminal mind. Here he saw bars of soap in a sock, meant to be used as a club that could render an officer unconscious. Plastic toothbrushes had been filed to points so sharp they could pierce a man's chest to his heart. Electrical wire, removed from the wall and woven, then sharpened, was as deadly as a razor. Knives formed from the tiny blades inside disposable razors. Hardware from a bunk had been fashioned into a supersharp shank.

"What's this?" Thomas said, lifting what appeared to be a papier-mâché knife. It looked brittle but felt solid as steel.

"Believe it or not, that is made of toilet paper, toothpaste, fruit juice, syrup, and sugar. All that, mixed and tightly wound and left to dry for several days, results in the weapon in your hands. This particular one found its way into the forearm of one of our biggest and toughest officers. He required forty stitches and was out of work nearly a month."

"And what did the perpetrator suffer for that?"

"Three months in Ad Seg and another twenty years added on to a life sentence, which means nothing to him. He gained a rep with the rest of the population that he felt was worth the time in the hole."

Thomas had taken only one bite of the party doughnut and one sip of coffee, so he should have been hungry by the time Yanno walked him back to his office. But with the sights and smells and sounds colliding in his brain—slamming doors, turning locks, alarms, two-way radios, intercoms, TVs, shouting, swearing—food was the furthest thing from his mind.

After thanking the warden for his time and assuring him that, yes, he believed he could learn to adapt and to handle this, Thomas slumped at his desk. His plan that first day had been to not bring a lunch but rather follow the crowd to the staff cafeteria. He'd wanted to get to know his colleagues informally and get a taste of institutional food, which Gladys had assured him was much better than what the inmates were rationed.

But Thomas could not bring himself to rise from his chair.

"Oh, Lord, I've been so sheltered. I had no idea. I feel empty, worthless, without any resource to reach these men. Help me. Give me something. Show me what I can do."

Suddenly he wanted more than anything to be with

214

Grace. He wasn't sure how much he should tell her. She would want to help somehow, to come alongside and aid him in this ministry. But he would never allow her into that pit. Nothing would be served by so offending her sensibilities. Anyway, he had five hours before he would see her. Much as he wanted to be anywhere but right there right then, how would it look, his leaving early the first day on the job?

This was hardly the only crisis in his life. He reminded himself that the regular hours, the ability to attend church rather than lead it, the extra time he'd get with Grace—all those were on the positive side of this ledger.

But he worried about Grace's health. She was better, that was certain, but clearly not back to her old self.

And then there was Ravinia. How he ached for her! Ironically, she would be encouraged by this new career path of his. But he could not call her without Grace on the other line. It just wouldn't be right.

They had decided not to hound Ravinia, and they had even chosen not tell her of this chaplaincy until it was a done deal. Well, now it was. They could call her that night.

22

Dennis Asphalt & Paving

Brady was startled when a figure appeared in the fading light and leaned against the metal outbuilding. Brady had been with the company just long enough to start feeling comfortable, but he wasn't sure he felt enough ownership yet to hop down off the forklift and ask if he could help the man.

Brady kept an eye on him as he finished loading a pallet and deftly positioned it on the delivery truck. Now his path to the finished forms in the building would take him directly past the onlooker and Brady would have to acknowledge him.

The man offered a polite salute and stepped back as the forklift rumbled near.

"Mr. Tatlock!"

Brady shut down the machine and climbed down to shake the Laundromat owner's hand. He was reminded of the man's beefy firmness. "What brings you here?"

"You do. I'm impressed that you're keeping up with your payments. Shows me something. But I need a favor. I tried to get a ticket to your musical there at the high school and was told they were sold out, all six shows."

"True. How'd you hear about it?"

"There are posters in every store window, but don't

you know it's all over the trailer park? You're a celebrity, Brady. Now don't you kids in the show get some tickets for your friends and family?"

"Yep."

"Yours already all spoken for, or would I be able to buy a couple off of you?"

"We're not supposed to sell 'em, but I've got a couple to spare if you could take the value off my balance."

"I could live with that."

"Really?"

"I'd love to take the wife. Be able to say I knew you when you were nobody."

"I've been giving mine to other cast members because I don't have that many people who want to come. But I have a few left."

"Any for the second Saturday show, first weekend?"

Brady nodded, thinking. "You could do me a favor too, sir, if you don't mind."

"Name it."

"Think you could bring my little brother? He's dying to see it, but I wasn't sure how I'd get him there."

They worked out where and when Peter should meet the Tatlocks. Brady felt giddy the rest of his shift; he found himself maneuvering the forklift like an old pro, finished ahead of time, and didn't break a single stop. And for a time he had been able to push to the back of his mind even his impending midterms. The

217

last one came on Friday just hours before the curtain for opening night, which would make it the toughest chore he could imagine. Even if he had studied. Which he hadn't.

Adamsville

It still amazed Thomas that the emotional drain was as taxing as physical labor at this stage of his life. He should have learned it many times over in the pastorate. He had never been one for working out and was not an athlete, not even a weekend warrior. The most exercise he got was mowing the lawn. His job was sedentary, and except for getting in and out of the car and walking the halls for the occasional hospital call, he'd done nothing in decades that should have physically taxed him.

But when criticism came, contentious meetings or aspersions on his abilities, he had often returned home desperate to just lie down. That was how he felt now, and what had he done that day? Stood around at a short party. Walked a few hundred yards with the warden inside the prison.

He knew what was weighing on him—the stark reality of the Adamsville State Pen. That and having lost his appetite until he pulled into the driveway.

Just as he had feared, Grace had done too much. She looked the way he felt, but the cozy little house was almost entirely set up the way she wanted it. There were empty boxes all over that he would have to break down and store. And she had left a few wall hangings for him that were too high for her.

But it was clear she had busied herself all day. He felt whipped because of the assault on his sensibilities, but she had truly earned her exhaustion. She proudly led him to the tiny spare room at the back of the house, which was bright because of windows on three walls and sat next to a half bath. Grace had moved in all of Thomas's boxes of books and his files.

"Oh, hon, you could have made this a sewing room or your own reading room."

"You've always wanted a home office," she said. "And now that you don't really need one, you have it! We ought to be able to find a desk at a garage sale or somewhere."

He smiled. "If you're sure, I'd love that. I can read and pray in here. It'll be perfect."

Grace fixed a light supper, which Thomas devoured, even eating her leftovers. "I could have made more," she said. "And we have dessert in the fridge."

"I'll get it," he said.

"I'll pass."

He helped her clear the table and do the dishes. "You need to get off your feet," he said.

Grace insisted she felt fine and said she didn't even think she'd need to see a doctor after all. Thomas wasn't so sure, but she had never been easy to persuade.

Finally they sat in their new living room and she quizzed him about his day.

Thomas didn't hide that it had been as harrowing a day as he could remember, but he refused to go into any detail that might upset her. "It's just going to be a tough, tough mission field," he said.

"How can I help?"

"By praying. And getting others to pray."

"That should be easy. As soon as we find a church, I'll rally some ladies."

He told her of all the rules and regulations that would keep her from visiting or sending in gifts of any kind, including food.

"That sounds awfully strict."

He forced a smile. She had no idea.

"Well," he said with a sigh, "we should call Ravinia now."

Dirk answered the phone, which flustered Thomas. The young man was chipper and friendly, as if oblivious to the fact that his lover's parents could not possibly be happy with their daughter's living situation. "How're you both doing?" he said. "Rav and I have been curious to death about where you've landed and whether you're well."

Grace was silent.

"That's why I called, Dirk," Thomas said. "I do have a new situation I'm excited about. Is Rav handy?"

"I'll get her. Unfortunately this isn't the best timing, because we have a thing we're going to in about fifteen minutes, but—"

"Oh, we can call back."

"No, no! Ravinia has really been quite anxious to hear. Here she is."

"Hey," she said, sounding rushed and distracted. "Tell me everything."

"Hello to you, too," Grace said flatly.

"Hi, Mom. Sorry. Like Dirk said, we're on the run in a few minutes, but talk to me."

"Believe it or not," Thomas said, "your old man is no longer a pastor."

"You're kidding."

"Don't refer to yourself as her old man, Thomas."

"Yeah, Dad. If you're trying to be hip, Dirk would be my old man, but since we clearly don't want to go there . . ."

Thomas told her all about his new job. She didn't interrupt once, and when he finished, he couldn't even hear her breathing. He wondered if the connection had been lost. But finally she spoke.

"That is really interesting," she said, and it was clear she meant it. "I'm impressed, Dad. You know I wanted you in the private sector, but I couldn't imagine you selling insurance or becoming a clerk of some kind. Forgive me, but are you tough enough for this? Adamsville is a supermax, right?"

Thomas told her he had the same hesitation, as did everyone else involved. "I realize I'll have to grow into this. But otherwise it seems to play to my strengths, and I do feel for these men."

Ravinia was silent again, but the sense that she needed to get going had faded. "I haven't told you, have I, Dad, where my educational emphasis has turned?"

"No."

"Criminal justice."

"Seriously?"

"Dirk laughs at me because I'm actually considering becoming a public defender. He says altruism is one thing, but even becoming a prosecutor would pay a little more. Those are the bottom two rungs on the legal ladder, you know."

"But it sounds like rewarding work."

"Thankless is more like it, but I've shifted my coursework, and the whole area really resonates with me. Dirk is big on victims' rights, which are hard to argue with, but many of these perpetrators are victims too, you know."

Thomas knew how Grace would feel about that and was grateful she didn't weigh in.

"I'm no longer so black-and-white even about capital punishment, Dad. I know where you are on that, but you'd be stunned by all the evidence and arguments against it."

Thomas didn't feel in the mood to pursue it just then. "At least I'm not as knee-jerk on that subject as the people I'll be working with," he said.

"I can imagine. 'No liberty, but justice for all,' right?"

"Something like that."

"Who knows, Dad? If I become a public defender someday, the cases I lose may end up in your chapel services."

"They don't even have chapel services at ASP," Grace said, but Thomas cut her off.

"All in good time, dear. We'll let you go, Rav, but we just wanted you to be up to speed."

23

Friday | Forest View High School

Brady was worthless all day Friday. Three midterms, none of them easy, and all he had done during the week was rehearse, work, and have his suit cleaned. After the audition, three dress rehearsals, and an hour of cast photos, he wanted it as crisp and dramatic as the first time he had appeared in it.

The night before, he had spent half an hour shining his shoes, and he had carried them to school, wearing sneakers. Now *there* was a look. He flipped off more than a half dozen friends and strangers—anyone who made a comment about him in tennies. They'd see who deserved jeers and who deserved cheers after tonight. If he was big now, imagine then.

All he could think of all day was his first real appearance onstage. Everybody was talking about it, and most seemed as familiar with the musical as he was. All he had to do was stand and deliver. The exams were afterthoughts, and he was already long past dreading their outcomes and feeling awful for being utterly unprepared. Like an idiot, he knew, he hoped his talent would somehow miraculously spare him. If one—just one—of the people in charge had an ounce of mercy, maybe . . .

Most exciting about tonight was that Alejandro and his girlfriend were coming. Brady had tried to shame his mother into coming too. "You've got a car. The ticket's free. You could bring Petey instead of me having to get my old boss to do it. And now even Alejandro is coming and is excited for me. You don't think people are gonna wonder where my ma is?"

"They don't care about me any more'n you do. Anyway, we always have a party Friday after work."

"And that's more important than your own son. Someday, when I'm a star and you see me on some talk show talking about my career, you're gonna wish you had a story about the first time you saw me onstage."

"Yeah, and that I knew you were going to be big."

"It could happen."

"And this trailer could grow white pillars."

Brady sat back and studied his mother. She looked way older than her years, though she had been a teenager when he was born. "Seriously, you're not gonna feel funny if everybody's talking about me and wants to know what you thought?"

"Who's going to ask me that?"

"Anybody could. Everybody else's parents are coming. Can't wait. And if you had any idea how popular I am at school, I swear you'd be amazed."

"You got that right. Well, if Petey's going with the Laundromat guy, he can tell me all about it."

At school Brady found a sassiness creeping over him. After each midterm, on his way out of class he shook hands with the teacher and smiled and told him or her that he hoped to see them at the musical that night.

Each looked surprised at this new, gregarious personality and asked how he felt about the exam.

"Oh, I have no doubt about that," he said. "I bombed royally, flying colors. Not a prayer. Hardly recognized any of it, and what I recognized I couldn't remember. And the one time I could've got a good look at my neighbor's paper, you were watching."

He laughed loudly, but somehow not one of them seemed to find that in the least amusing. Each said they were indeed looking forward to seeing him onstage but hoped he hadn't irreparably damaged himself academically.

"Well, I'm sure I have," he said. "But it's been fun."

Adamsville

"You sure you're feeling better?" Thomas said.

"I've never lied to you," Grace said. "I'm afraid these discolorations on my arms are a sign of age, though. I use creams and everything, but it just seems my blood vessels are closer to the surface, my skin thinning, or something."

Thomas studied the fresh marks that looked like bruises. "And you don't recall banging into something or putting pressure on them by pushing anything?"

She shook her head, apparently eager to change the subject. "It'll happen to you too, as you age."

"Grace, we're not that old, despite that everybody thinks we are. Those aren't age spots, and I don't think your skin is thinning. It worries me."

"Well, I feel fine, and I'm done talking about it, all right? Now go change out of your suit and come put your feet up. I want to hear all about your day."

In truth, that sounded great. Not that there was anything so special about that Friday. But for the first time in years, it signaled the end of Thomas's workweek, and it nearly made him want to dance. He and Grace could enjoy a casual dinner, take a walk, watch the news, read the paper, talk, whatever they wanted. And then Saturday was wide open. He could handle all the chores a normal husband handled, things Grace always had to take care of before.

She had always insisted that he use his first day off to crash after all the weekend church activities and the second to just read and study. Thomas had never been idle, but he welcomed this new season of life where he could really be a fully functioning partner to her. The first thing he was going to do was scour the classified ads for a used desk.

When he emerged from the bedroom, Grace was curled at one end of the couch, looking eager to hear whatever he had to say. She patted the cushion next to her and he settled in.

"Learned a little more today," he said. "Like every day. Gladys has really been helpful."

"She sounds wonderful. I like that type. Wish I could get to know her."

"She's got a passel of kids, and her husband loves to cook—owns a barbecue place, in fact. She lives for the weekend. It's church all the time for them. She's big into the music program."

"Should we look into her church one of these weekends?"

Thomas laughed. "I suggested that. Told her we wanted some recommendations. She implied that you and I probably would not be comfortable in her church."

"Really? Why?"

"Because of the part of town it's in. And because it's almost 100 percent black."

"You told her, didn't you, that we went to college in Chicago and we're not afraid of black people?"

"I did. She said, 'Well, I have lots of friends who would be afraid of *you!*' When we got serious, she said she had to admit that she was ashamed of some of her brothers and sisters there. She said there can be as much racism from within her community as without. Said she's seen members get up and move to another pew when visiting white people sit down."

"No! Really?"

"I was surprised too. She told me she'd sure welcome us, but did we like three-hour services, dancing in the aisles, people being slain in the spirit, nurses on call, all that?"

"Hmm."

"Hmm?"

"Well, I mean, I appreciate their passion and I love their music. . . ."

"Gracie, listen to yourself. *Their* this and *their* that? That sounds awful."

"You know what I mean. Still, I'd love to meet her, even if maybe she's right about us and her church."

Thomas told her how Gladys had been so helpful in the office that he almost considered her his surrogate boss. "I report to Warden LeRoy, but he's gone so much, and when he is there, I don't want to bother him. But Gladys knows everything anyway and seems happy to help."

"Like with what?"

"Well, today I finally got clearance on six of nine requests for a visit. Two of the inmates wanted private meetings, which were turned down and changed into just a stand-up outside their cells, and three were turned down because they didn't convince the reviewers they were sincere."

"But you saw six? That's a good start."

"Yeah, but every time I visit one of these guys, I come back with more questions. They all want something. No one just wants counsel or prayer or teaching. They all have an angle."

"And you're finding it hard to say no."

"I have learned to tell them that I'll have to check on things. It's nice to be able to hide behind that for a while. I tell them I'm still learning and that I don't want to promise anything I can't deliver. That's what

I meant about Gladys. She told me to stop worrying so much, that there are rules to protect me and that's all there is to it. I don't have to apologize or wonder. I'm protected by what's called 'administrative regulations,' which is what staff can and cannot do. No matter what anybody asks for, begs for, pleads for, whines for, finagles for, my hands are tied if the ad regs don't permit it. I can hide behind that without a second thought."

"What do all these guys want?"

"Some just want to talk about their cases or their lives. You'd be amazed, though, at how nothing is private there. Even if we're whispering, everybody else quiets down, turns down their radios and TVs, and listens to the conversation. They all chime in, boohooing, teasing, jeering. And it's obvious they've heard everyone's stories before.

"One guy was telling me about his childhood, and from another pod a guy hollers, 'Here comes the part about his mom treating him like dirt!' Well, the first guy cusses out the other, I try to calm him down, others start fake bawling, and now he's screaming at them all to shut up."

"Sounds like elementary Sunday school."

"That's where the similarities end. But I'm finding that the one thing I have to offer these guys that they want the most is a free fifteen-minute phone call. It has all kinds of restrictions, but it's entirely up to me whether to grant it. It has to be for a family emergency. Gladys tells me Russ granted just a few each year in all the time he was there. If a parent or a child is deathly ill or dies, we have to see bona fide verifiable documents. Then I can authorize a prearranged time when the inmate is strip-searched, bound, extracted from his cell, delivered to the phone bank, and allowed the call. He must talk to an immediate family member or someone principally involved in the matter, like a pastor, a funeral director, or a lawyer. And there's no leeway on the fifteen minutes. The phone goes dead right on the second."

"How often is there such a death in the immediate family?"

"Well, if you can believe these guys, four of the six today swore they had just lost someone."

"What are the odds?"

"Exactly. I told each what I needed from him, and they all earnestly pleaded with me to understand that by the time they got all the documentation in the mail, Mama or Grandpa or Baby or whoever would have been in the ground for weeks. I have to tell you, I'm glad I was warned about this."

"Or you'd have believed every one of them."

"Hook, line, and sinker. These are the most convincing, sincere liars I have ever met. I do have an interesting request pending from one con though."

"For a phone call?"

"No. Just a visit. It's for a private session in the separation room." Thomas told Grace all about the room with its Plexiglas barrier and its tiny slot for the transfer of documents. "Most requests are turned down or parceled out very sparsely, but I'm inclined to think this one will be honored."

"Because?"

"It's from a guy on death row who had regular weekly meetings with Chaplain Russ. And he's due for execution before the end of the year."

"Oh no."

"Calls himself the Deacon, and the warden thinks he might be sincere."

Forest View High School

The stretch between the end of the school day and the curtain that evening became the longest of Brady Darby's life. He found himself having to go to the bathroom every half hour, despite having hardly eaten all day. And it warmed him to see on the faces of all the other leads, and even the orbital characters, the same dread he felt deep in his gut.

He had looked forward to this all day, and now he had to talk himself into not escaping. All the confidence, the bravado, the eagerness to strut his stuff seemed to pool in his heart. Why had he thought he could do this? Yes, he knew his lines, his lyrics, his cues, his moves. But would they vanish in a wave of stage fright that would make an utter fool of him?

Of course they would. He would get out there and freeze, be unable to see the director or anyone who might believe in him or encourage him. He would be unable to spot Alejandro or any other friend. All of a sudden he was grateful his mother wasn't coming, at least for opening night. Each performance had to be better than the previous.

Could Brady survive this? Would he be able to somehow muddle through, get the opening-night jitters out of his system, and avoid all the calamities that came with them so both Saturday performances would be stellar?

No, this whole thing was ridiculous, a stupid idea. Why had he thought it made any sense? He felt his pulse increase and his breathing go crazy. He'd heard of panic attacks. Could this be his? If he didn't calm down, he wouldn't have a chance at pulling this off.

Just when Brady reached the point of seeking out Clancy Nabertowitz and telling him he wouldn't be able to go on, the director came rushing in, dressed to the nines, and called everyone together.

"All right, listen up," he said. It took longer than usual for the chatter to die down. "Those of you who have done this before understand what's happening to you right now. You newcomers are ready to bolt, I know. I've been there. But let me tell you something. No one is going anywhere. Any physical ailments you think you have are all in your mind. We have rehearsed this and rehearsed this, and you're all going to nail it tonight. The house is sold out. People can't wait. I know you're gonna knock 'em dead. In ten minutes I want everyone in full dress and right back here."

Brady didn't feel much better, but as Mr. N. had

said, nobody was going anywhere, particularly him. If this was the price for the future he fully expected, he would have to be willing to pay it before every performance. He hated it. It would be hard. It left a bitter taste in his mouth.

But he could do this, had to do it. Brady believed with all that was in him that this was his one shot, his only hope. He was going to make something of himself. He was going to be somebody.

He struggled into costume, his hands shaking, fingers trembling at every button and the zipper. *The zipper.* Yes, he was going to consciously raise the zipper and remember that he had so there would be no wondering onstage, in the spotlight, in front of everybody.

Would it look weird to study himself in the mirrors that covered the back wall of the dressing room? All the other guys were. Brady struck a pose, firing out one hip.

He was still scared to death, but hang it all, he *was* Conrad Birdie.

On with the show.

24

Little Theater

The beauty of Brady's role was that although Conrad Birdie was the musical's central figure—talked about, longed for, anticipated—he didn't actually appear until the demand for him was at fever pitch. The pressure was on because both Birdie and Brady had to deliver. Their entrance must not disappoint. In fact, it must be more than worth the wait.

With music, timing, and lighting, Clancy Nabertowitz pulled every string at his disposal. Now if Brady could just appear bigger than life when the spotlight hit him and show a sneer and a swagger that covered his fear . . .

Brady had a lot going for him as he tiptoed out to his mark. He had taken not one shortcut since the first day. He had memorized the script, every word of every part. He knew everyone's cues and stage directions, even the lyrics to songs he wasn't singing. He was as ready as he could be, but his eagerness had lost the battle with stage fright.

He stood there, heart hammering, gasping, sweating.

But he had one more advantage, and it was not lost on him. Nabertowitz had engineered the scenes in such a way that all the newcomers—except Brady—had already been on stage, singing and dancing in crowd scenes. Uplifting fun and funny stuff had brought the audience to life. The spectators were into the story, laughing at the right places and cheering every solo, dance, and punch line.

So when the spotlight finally hit Brady Darby in his Conrad Birdie gold lamé suit, the kids onstage jumped and squealed on cue, and the house erupted with cheers and applause. That gave Brady a beat to gather himself, to drink in the adulation, and to affect the knowing persona of the mega rock-and-roll star. He cocked his head, raised a brow, and winked, and the stage was his.

When he hit his first note on key, every distraction left him. He lived in the moment, playing to the kids, playing to the crowd, belting out his tune and dancing all over the stage as the teen actors swooned. When he finished with a flourish and both girls and boys lay at his feet, the audience rose as one, and he knew what people meant about a number stopping the show and bringing down the house.

As he exited, he saw Mr. N., clipboard tucked under his arm, jumping and clapping, tears in his eyes. Brady would never be able to get enough of this. He suddenly knew what he wanted to do with his life. Nothing could stop him. He imagined himself moving from the high school boards to community theater, a college scholarship, being discovered by a talent scout, getting to Broadway, then a TV series, maybe a recording contract, and the movies. He would have the same impact on the public that Conrad Birdie had.

He'd show everybody: Coach Roberts, Dean Hose, his mother, even Alex North and his snooty parents and snotty little sister.

The rest of the musical only got better. Yes, technically, Birdie was not the lead character. That was the agent/manager, and Alex was great in the role. But Birdie was the one who lit up the stage and brought squeals and laughter each time. And because Brady had been unknown before this, he could sense the wonder and mystery on the part of the crowd. He imagined them murmuring, "Who *is* this guy?"

Between scenes, as Brady waited in the wings or backstage, he realized he had a whole new image before his castmates. He had gone from curiosity to star. Nabertowitz kept grinning and giving him thumbs-up. Guys—except for Alex—clapped him on the back, shook their fists at him, mouthed "Way to go, man!" Best, girls hugged him, not once but often, and not one but several. This was the life.

With about twenty minutes left in the show, noise from the back of the theater distracted the crowd, and Brady noticed that even those onstage sneaked a peek. Brady moved to where he should have had a line of sight, but the spotlights blinded him.

Was it a fight? Mr. N. sent two stagehands running to the back of the house to deal with it. When they returned and whispered to him, he glanced at Brady, then shook his head. "No!" he said. "It'll wait!"

"What?" Brady said.

"Nothing to worry about," the director said. "Let's finish strong. Ignoring distractions is what being professional is all about."

Brady was in the middle of one of the final segments, a poignant train depot scene, when he heard loud talking from the back and people shushing the offenders. Soon there was shouting before security removed someone. Brady's heart sank. Had that been his mother's voice? Her drunk voice? There was no way, was there?

Whoever it was, he would not let anyone spoil this for him. He was going out with a bang. And as his character left the stage, rumbling away on the train, the laughing crowd bid him a warm adieu. As he disappeared into the wings and stood next to Nabertowitz to watch the final scene, he was so drained he felt he could melt all over the floor.

Mr. N. looked at him with such gratitude and admiration that Brady was intoxicated by it. But the director soon turned back to the stage to study every detail of the finale. Brady stood there fearing he might burst into sobs. He had been so uptight, so scared, yet so ready for this. And it could not have gone better.

He forced himself not to weep. The houselights would be up when he joined the rest of the cast for the bows, and there would be no hiding it if he was out there bawling. Talk about breaking character. His whole aura would be lost.

Yet he would not completely maintain the Birdie image. He would look the same, but he would not act the same. Now was the time for class, for a genuine, humble smile, a receiving of the adulation that was sure to come. He bucked himself up for it.

As the last song segued into the musical themes, the chorus burst back onto the stage, and the houselights came up. Mr. N. had said it was hard to read an audience for high school productions, because they felt obligated to respond with standing ovations just because the kids were young and had tried hard, regardless how good they were.

But there was no doubting the sincerity of this crowd. They cheered, they clapped, they stomped, they shouted, they whistled. And the crescendo grew as the chorus gave way to the gaggle of girls, then the female lead and her boyfriend, then her parents, the agent's secretary, the agent's mother, and Alex as the agent. He was thunderously rewarded, and though he had played the lead, he knew enough to allow Brady to be last to take a bow.

Alex turned grandly and generously gestured for Conrad Birdie, and as Brady jogged onstage, the audience let loose a new crescendo, and even the cast applauded. Cast members departed in the order they had appeared and were demanded back three times. Finally Brady forced Mr. N. to also make an appearance, and when that had gone on long enough, the director cued the curtain, and the cheering crowd finally, seemingly reluctantly, settled.

Brady had never been so high. The cast and crew congratulated each other as they slowly changed into street clothes, and as they made their way out of the dressing rooms and up the corridors to the front of the theater, parents and friends and fans slapped their hands and called out compliments. Everybody, it seemed, wanted to meet Brady, and his castmates appeared to love introducing him as if they were his dear friends.

He caught sight of Alex, crowded by his parents and little sister and surrounded by his friends; he also noticed they seemed to be sneaking glances his way and measuring the attention he was getting. The little girl, Katie North, suddenly appeared at his side and slipped her arm around his waist, beaming.

"This your sister?" someone said.

"Nah, Alex's," he said.

"I'm his lady friend!" Katie chirped, and everyone laughed. Even little kids loved the bad boy.

"Mother of the star, comin' through!" came the undeniable voice.

Erlene Darby was trailed by her boyfriend-slash-boss, and it was plain they both were drunk. Brady immediately shook free of Katie, moved past his mother to her boss, and squeezed his shoulder as he bent close. "You get her out of here right now, or I swear on my life I'll burn down your restaurant."

"They kicked us out of the theater, Brady!" the man said.

"And I'm kicking you out of *here*. Now go!"

"Made me stand to see my own son!" his mother said, and Brady saw people spin, mouths agape. He wanted to shout that he had never in his life seen this ghastly creature, still in her waitress dress. Seeing they weren't going to leave, he took each by the arm and marched them outside.

"Did you cause that ruckus in the back?" he said.

"I shouldn't have to stand to see my son in a play!"

"You were late! And you didn't have tickets! What were you thinking?"

"When they found out who I was, they put us in the corner behind the back row. Then somebody thought I

239

was cheering too loud. But why not? You were great, Brady."

"You're pathetic. You embarrassed me."

"How can you say that, you ungrateful little—"

"Where's Petey?"

"He's home, and he's fine. Don't you worry about him."

Alejandro approached. *Oh no!*

"This your *madre*?" he said, girlfriend in tow. "Bet she's proud of you tonight, eh, *muchacho*?"

"I'm proud o' him, but he's not proud o' me!" Erlene Darby slurred, and Brady saw instant recognition on Alejandro's face.

"Well, you did a good job, man," his boss said. "I'll see you Monday, okay?"

Adamsville

Thomas had talked Grace into retiring early, but the house was small enough that as he sat reading on an old couch in the tiny living room, he could hear her tossing and turning. He wondered whether it was better to let her fall asleep before joining her. He decided to memorize one more verse first.

But as he was working on it, he heard Grace begin to sing. As prodigious as he was in retaining the words of Scripture, she had hundreds of hymns—every verse—burned into her memory. He looked up from his Bible and lay his head back, closing his eyes as she softly sang.

O to be like You! blessed Redeemer,
This is my constant longing and prayer;
Gladly I'll forfeit all of earth's treasures,
Jesus, Your perfect likeness to wear.

O to be like You! O to be like You,
Blessed Redeemer, pure as You are!
Come in Your sweetness, come in Your fullness;
Stamp Your own image deep on my heart.

25

Sunday, 2 p.m. | Touhy Trailer Park | Addison

Barely a sliver of sunlight invaded Brady and Peter's tiny bedroom through the cheap, bent blinds, but it was enough to make Brady roll over and bury his throbbing head under his pillow. He let out a long groan. Why did he do this to himself?

Brady had never really liked beer, and when his friends had told him it was an acquired taste, he wondered why they bothered to acquire it. He drank only to look cool and get a buzz, certainly not for the taste. And hangovers like this—his worst ever—were the price. Every beat of his heart sent shock waves through his skull that reached his cheekbones. Why? *Why?*

To celebrate. Both shows Saturday had been as good as—some said better than—opening night. The local paper had shown up and interviewed everybody—cast, crew, relatives, fans—and taken pictures galore. Brady opened his eyes in the darkness afforded by the pillow and squinted against the raging pain. Before heading to Stevie Ray's to drink himself into oblivion, he'd had the presence of mind to leave Petey a note and a dollar so he could buy a Sunday paper. If he ever felt able to get out of bed, he'd see if it was there.

Oh no. He had wet himself in the night. And his breath tasted and smelled of vomit. How come they never showed that on the commercials?

How had he even gotten home? He didn't remember. Stevie Ray's wife had stomped out from their bedroom periodically to quietly but fiercely insist that they call it a night. And she kept saying that Stevie should get Brady home, as if he couldn't get there himself. But he could, couldn't he? *Hadn't* he?

Brady sat up and let the sheet and blanket slide off. He planted his feet on the floor and held his head in his hands. *Never again. Never, never, never.* He licked his lips, which made him gag.

"I got your paper," Peter said, and Brady looked up. Or tried to. He forced one eye open just a slit to see Peter in the corner, watching him.

"You read it?"

"Yeah. Cool. Lots of pictures and stuff about you."

"No kiddin'? Get it."

"You stink, you know."

"I know. You like the play?"

"Sure, 'course. But I didn't know where you were last night."

"I wrote you a note."

"But you didn't say where you were gonna be, so I didn't know till Stevie Ray brought you home."

"When was that?"

"I don't know. Really late. You were laughing and singing."

"Seriously?"

"Some song from the play, but not as good."

"I can imagine."

"Stevie Ray must really like you."

"Friends help each other."

"Help them throw up? He was in the bathroom with you while you were puking your guts out."

"Ugh."

"I think you wet your bed too."

"That's what booze will do to you, Petey. Don't ever—"

"Don't worry! But why do you?"

Brady shrugged. " 'Cause I'm an idiot. Don't be an idiot."

"I don't get it, Brady. You were so good in that show and everybody loved you. Why'd you go and get drunk after that?"

Brady shook his head. "Thought I was celebrating. Stupid. Just stupid."

"I don't want a brother who's stupid. I was telling everybody who I was at the play. They said I must be really proud. I've never been so proud."

"But not right now, huh?"

"Nope."

"All right. I'm sorry, man. I really am. Funny thing is, I don't even like beer. Stevie Ray does. Loves it. He's learned to drink only on weekends after his gigs so it doesn't affect his playing."

"Whatever."

"I said I was sorry. Now bring me the paper."

"Take a shower first."

"Just bring it!"

But when Peter went to get it, Brady staggered into the shower. At least they had water pressure. Not much heat, but the tepid liquid on his head offered some relief.

Adamsville

"I feel almost guilty, Grace," Thomas said, resting on the couch with his Sunday paper, an NFL game on TV. He had changed out of his church clothes after lunch.

"This is like heaven," she said. "You used to be so tired by now you'd doze off during dinner and nap the whole afternoon away."

"I may yet," he said. "What is it about doing nothing that is so exhausting?"

"It isn't as if you've taken the whole weekend off," she said. "You helped those boys move your desk in."

"Supervised is more like it. I don't remember ever being that strong."

She muted the television. "You haven't said a word about the church. How'd you like it?"

"It's close by. I like the service time. Nice building. Friendly people. About the right size."

"But?"

"The music was okay. I could have used another hymn or two and one or two fewer choruses."

Grace shook her head and smiled. "I think we're in the minority there, sweetheart. The hymns are going to die with our generation."

"Perish the thought."

"And the pastor?"

"Seems like a wonderful young man. Humble. I like that."

"Me too. But that sermon could have been more biblical and less anecdotal."

"It was a good bit of both."

"And that's the problem, right? Are you going to be content to sit under someone who tells stories more than he exposits Scripture?"

"He wasn't bad."

"I know. What I'm asking is, are we still looking?"

"Still looking, Grace. Don't you think?"

"I suppose."

He studied her. Wan. Eyes milky. She was the one who needed a nap. But she was right. This was heavenly. To be able to just sit on a lazy Sunday afternoon evaluating a pastor rather than knowing that's what everyone else was doing to you?

Thomas Carey could get used to this.

Brady drank in the looks from the other kids waiting for the bus, then reveled in the attention as the preppies all seemed to make room and want him to sit next to them.

At school it seemed everyone recognized him, called him by name, waved, smiled, high-fived him. Teachers he barely knew, custodial staff, office people—everybody seemed thrilled for him.

But Brady had no illusions. He knew the other shoe would drop, and soon. Because for all those who acted happy for him, some studiously avoided his gaze. They had to know what was coming. Brady finally had to admit to himself that he had not been celebrating Saturday night. He had been steeling himself against reality.

He had been telling himself that if he became the star of the play and the hero of the school, he would somehow be allowed to do the same the next weekend. But he knew better, even though he had excelled beyond even his wildest dreams.

He entered his first class to the cheers and whistles of his classmates, and just for fun he strutted like Conrad with a twinkle and tongue in cheek. But as soon as he sat down, his teacher entered and handed him a note. Dr. Hose and Mr. Nabertowitz were waiting for him in the dean's office.

Brady considered leaving his stuff at his desk, as if he would be back soon. But that wasn't going to happen. "Got to take a call from my agent," he said, rising as he studied the note. And everyone laughed but the teacher.

Even knowing what was coming, Brady had no idea how he would react. With anger? remorse? Would he beg? Nah. This was his own fault. They'd warned him. He couldn't be angry with anyone but himself.

The receptionist even looked sad when she ushered him in, and both Hose and Nabertowitz rose. Mr. N. would not meet his eye, but Hose stared directly at him. "Have a seat, Mr. Darby. You know why you're here."

When they were all seated, Dean Hose spread the Sunday paper before him and turned it around so Brady could see it. "I suppose you've read this."

"'Course. Nobody I know ever got a write-up like that before."

"And the pictures," Nabertowitz said, his voice weepy. "You had the world at your feet, Brady."

"Had?"

"If you think you still do, Darby," Hose said, "you're dumber than I thought."

"Now you think I'm dumb? I thought you said I was smart."

"Smart but stupid, son. It's long past time to be sugarcoating things for you. With the grade point average from your first two years, you had no leeway this fall. Everybody who cared about you made it clear what you had to do, and you didn't even try. Yes, you're smart. You proved that onstage. You can do whatever you decide you want to do. You decided not to try on the academic side, but that's a prerequisite for all the rest. Now you're done. You're out. No more musical."

"Oh, Brady!" Nabertowitz said. "You've let everyone down, but primarily yourself. We'll make do, but you know as well as I do that the show this weekend will be nothing like last. With just a little effort, you could have made this work. You could have switched to a work-release program, stayed in drama, made something of yourself. Now you've thrown it all away."

"No probation? No second chance? Can't I sign some sort of a contract, use a tutor, get help?"

"Too late," Dr. Hose said. "How can I ask any of these teachers to bend the rules for you when you ignored every piece of advice up to now?"

Brady searched his mind for a smart comeback, but what could he say? He shrugged.

"I informed your mother."

"She doesn't care."

"I got that impression. She did say she had hoped you'd be the first in the family to graduate high school."

"Her big dream, eh? Well, if you think I'm staying here without being in the play . . . My little brother will be first to graduate."

26

Thomas never wanted to get used to the ugly coldness of the ASP supermax, but already the prison clichés had become part of his daily routine. His practice became to pray in the car as soon as the great, sterile, impersonal compound loomed on the horizon. He was able to put his mind in neutral as he approached the guardhouse at the edge of the property.

This morning the hulking edifice nearly blended in with a dark, roiling sky. The news said thunderheads would roll through most of the state by noon. Thomas prayed for his day, for his colleagues, for the inmates, and mostly that he would somehow be used.

It seemed to Thomas that some good must come of the years he had spent in devotion to God and His Word. The praying, the studying, the memorizing, the preaching, the teaching, the witnessing, the counseling—up till now it had all seemed to come to naught. He could count on the fingers of one hand the people who had actually been converted under his ministry and whose lives showed marked change.

Was he simply no good at this? Was sincerity not enough? Thomas had made a decision, a commitment. He had turned his back on all the world had to offer. He didn't necessarily believe he would have been any good in secular pursuits either, but he had staked his claim with Christ. He believed Jesus had paid the ultimate sacrifice for him and for his sin, and just before he met Grace, he had pledged the rest of his life in service to God.

He was happy enough, he guessed. Grace was the greatest blessing he could have ever hoped for: a loving mate—if sometimes too perfect—who shared his values and encouraged his every step. They had never had much, had never wanted much. Beautiful Ravinia was currently a heartbreak, but Thomas believed she would come around. It was the years and years of seemingly futile ministry that really weighed on him.

He was finally in a position to perhaps do something about that. He was starting to get comfortable in his new role, learning the ropes as the warden and the former chaplain had predicted he would. Thomas was a man of order and discipline and schedules. He had designed a strategy. And while his ministry had the unusual wrinkle of requiring that his target audience seek him out, rather than the other way around, he could live with that.

His days were mapped out, his office organized. He was ready to try to serve in this difficult mission field if God would just open a few doors.

Thomas had to chuckle as he made his way to the administrative offices. One of the jokes at ASP was that not even God could open its doors. Well, he'd see about that.

Something began growing in Brady Darby's chest as he stood on rubbery legs to leave the dean's office. It suddenly became important for him to lock in his don't-care attitude. In truth he felt small, like a kid caught red-handed. Was it fear? shock? What would he do now?

He nodded at Hose and thrust out his hand to Mr. N. The theater teacher had a look Brady would never forget. He appeared about to burst into tears, which was how Brady felt but refused to show. "Thanks for everything," Brady managed.

Nabertowitz just shook his head.

Brady already felt like an outsider as he floated down the hall toward the front entrance. A few kids called out to him, hollering something about the play or Birdie. He just waved.

Brady stopped by his locker and cleaned it out, dumping everything—gym clothes, books, you name it—into the trash. He headed for the exit carrying only his jacket over his shoulder.

As he passed the security guard and pushed through the door, the guard said, "And where do you think you're going without a pass, Mr. Darby?"

Brady pressed his lips together and flipped off the man.

"You'll regret that, Darby! I'm reporting you."

What're they gonna do, kick me out?

Brady didn't even know where he was going. There

were no buses this time of the day, and he had no wheels. He lit up as soon as he was out the door, breaking the rule by doing so before crossing the road. He felt free. Like an adult. But with no prospects.

All Brady could think as he marched down the road, chin high, was, *Alex North as Birdie. Ugh!*

Adamsville State Penitentiary

Gladys spun in her chair as Thomas passed, head down. "Don't you be walkin' past me without so much as a good mornin', Padre!"

Thomas stopped and turned. "I'm sorry, dear. I thought you were busy."

"Never too busy for a man of God. Half expected you to show up at my church yesterday."

Thomas laughed. "You scared me off. I was afraid Grace and I would be turned away at the door."

Gladys roared. "Prob'ly woulda been! Here, I got something for you."

A slip showed that a request for a meeting with him in the separation room had been granted for that very morning.

"Henry Trenton?"

"The Deacon," she said.

"That was fast. Russ said these can take as long as—"

"Helps to have friends in high places," Gladys said.

"Thank Yanno for me, will you?"

"You want to thank somebody, you thank the woman you're talking to."

"You made this happen?"

"Who else?"

"You're the best."

"And don't you forget it."

Addison

A cool breeze kicked up and forced Brady to don his jacket. Soon he had zipped it to his neck and raised the collar. He could have hitchhiked, but he wasn't even sure where he was going, and few people picked up guys who looked like him anyway. He usually had luck getting rides only when Peter was with him because the kid looked normal.

The sun disappeared behind dark clouds, and now Brady bent into the wind. Perfect. Everything was going to go wrong today. He tried to tell himself he didn't care, that he had known this was coming, had had his fun, didn't want to be in school anyway, didn't see the value. He blamed his tears on the stiff wind, but when the rain started, he didn't pick up his pace, look for shelter, or even try to cover his head. Brady just lumbered on, shivering.

The rain ran off his hair and down his face, inside his jacket, chilling him. No one could see or hear his sobs, and he ignored even the occasional car that slowed and honked, offering him respite from the storm.

At least he could finally name his emotion.

Rage.

Brady felt like killing someone. Trouble was, he was the only logical target.

Adamsville State Penitentiary

The only place within the walls of the penitentiary where one had an idea of the weather outside was under the skylights in the corridor that led from the administrative offices to the first security envelope. For those on the inside, this was the last envelope, so for an inmate to reach this relatively less secure area was virtually impossible. In the more than ten years of the prison's existence, not even one envelope had been breached, let alone eleven.

On a normal day, the light-sensitive fixtures in that hallway often flickered off as the sun streamed through the skylights. But now the lights burned bright, causing Thomas to glance up at the black sky. Funny thing for a man with such an optimistic out-look: he loved rain, enjoyed being safely inside and peering out at a good storm. But there was no time for that today.

As he had been instructed, Thomas carried nothing but his Bible and his wallet as he passed through the various security checkpoints on his way to the separation room. He went through two metal detectors, and though he was greeted by name by all the officers, his ID was still compared to his face, and he was reminded that anything other than single sheets of paper was contraband. Four different officers fanned the pages of his Bible. He couldn't imagine what he might have hidden in there that would prove useful as a weapon to the Deacon.

Thomas told each new corrections officer, "This is my first time, so . . ."

And each rehearsed the procedure with him. He would be ushered into his side first and would sit in a chair facing the Plexiglas. Inmate Henry Trenton would be cuffed and shackled and brought to the other side in due time.

"Will he be uncuffed so he can use the phone?"

"There is no phone, Reverend. There's a built-in voice-activated intercom that allows you to hear each other fine. Just be careful to not talk over each other."

High-tech as the room was, as soon as Thomas sat he was struck by how old the place felt compared with the rest of the facility. The dull, gray-green walls were awash in a dingy light emanating from long, bare fluorescent fixtures. They cast a reflection on the Plexiglas that would force him to dip his head to see Trenton when the time came.

Thomas wasn't sure why he expected the prisoner to be brought within minutes of his own arrival. He had assumed that with all the computers and tracking devices in the place, there must be a record of his progress from his office all the way deep inside to this room and that someone would decide it was time to fetch the inmate.

No such luck. Fifteen minutes after sitting, Thomas began to idly page through his Bible. He didn't know what he would have done if he had not brought it. The only other reading material was painted on the wall.

Do not touch the glass.

Do not attempt to pass more than one sheet through the slot at a time.

Do not attempt to pass anything through the slot a corrections officer has not authorized.

Thomas heard nothing for fifteen more minutes, then finally poked his head out the door.

"Finished?" an officer said.

"Not even started," Thomas said. "Are they going to bring him, or what?"

"No idea. They don't tell us. They'll inform personnel on the other side when the inmate is ready."

"Can you call someone and ask?"

"I wouldn't know who to call, Reverend. Sorry."

After ten more minutes Thomas emerged again. A new officer stood in the hall. "I've been here forty minutes, and no prisoner. Could you please telephone the warden's secretary for me and ask her what I should do?"

The officer smiled. "You're gettin' a taste of what the cons go through every day. If he's still not here in twenty minutes, I'll let you use the phone down here."

The delay seemed so wasteful and inefficient, but

then Thomas realized that the Deacon didn't have any pressing appointments. And neither did he. It was up to Thomas to redeem the time. He turned back to his Bible.

Finally, just minutes before the hour was up, he heard muffled conversation, then a door open and close. Eventually, shuffling into view came the shackled and manacled Deacon. He looked small and thin and weak, no surprise for a man of nearly seventy who had spent half a lifetime in prison.

"Good morning," Thomas said, resisting the urge to stand.

The Deacon sat wearily. "Is it?"

"Well, I guess not. Big storm outside."

"Like I would know. I can't even verify it's morning."

"Trust me, it is. What can I do for you, Henry?"

"Call me Deke."

"Okay."

"First off, you won't be needing that." He nodded toward Thomas's Bible.

"If *you* don't need it, that's fine, Deke. But I always need it."

"Spare me. We won't be praying today either."

"As you wish."

"I need an emergency phone call, Reverend."

"You do? You know the rules. Is there an imminent death in your family?"

"Yes, mine. In ten weeks and a day, but who's counting?"

"And whom did you want to call? A family member?"

"My family abandoned me years ago. I want to call Chaplain Russ. Want him there when they string me up."

"I can't allow that, Deke. Sorry."

"Why?"

"He's retired; you know that. I asked him specifically if there were any loose ends, anything he needed to come back for, anything to finish up. He told me no, that he had promised his wife he was done and gone. He did say he would send you a note, remind you of a few things, tell you he'd be thinking about you."

"On my special day?" the Deacon said with a smirk.

"I suppose that's what he meant, yes."

"So I got to be alone up there with just a screw and an executioner?"

"You're permitted a spiritual counselor, but you're aware of that, too."

Henry Trenton looked away and shook his head. "You volunteering?"

It was the last thing Thomas cared to do. He did not know this man, didn't like him, and didn't need to be just a few feet from a hanging. "I'm willing," he said.

"I'll think about it," Trenton said. "I don't guess I want to be alone."

"Can I ask you where you are spiritually, Deke?"

"That's personal."

"As you wish. You know I only care that you're right with God. You wouldn't want to face eternity apart from Him."

"I'm sort of used to that by now."

Thomas prayed silently for wisdom and the right words. "He hasn't abandoned you, Deke. Not even in here."

"Well, I've abandoned Him."

"Have you? Someone told me they thought you were right with your Maker. I hope you are, and if you aren't, I'd like to show you how you can be."

"Do you know what I'm in here for, Chaplain?"

"I've seen your file."

"I told you I murdered those kids so they wouldn't rat me out. But most people think what I did to 'em before that was worse than killing them. Do you?"

Thomas hesitated but held the Deacon's gaze. "I suppose I do."

"At least you're honest."

"Tell me something. Why do people call you the Deacon?"

The old man shrugged. "I read the Bible. Pray. Talked to Russ a lot."

"Ever share your faith with other guys? try to get them to become believers?"

"Nah. That's rude. Anyway, I'm not sure what I believe."

"You want to be sure?"

"I don't know. I'm just tired. All I know is, I want to die, but I don't want to die alone."

Thomas sighed. "I can guarantee you won't have to die alone, Deke. But I can also guarantee you'll spend eternity with God if you want to."

"I'll think about it."

27

Dennis Asphalt & Paving | Addison

The work crews were huddled in the outbuilding out of the rain as Brady sloshed past and mounted the steps of the double-wide into Alejandro's cluttered office. The secretary was out, and Alejandro was on the phone, his back to the door. He spun and stared at Brady, holding up a finger as he finished his conversation. But the more Alejandro stared, the wider his eyes grew. Finally he covered the phone and said, "Grab a towel from the bathroom and get yourself dried off, man. You look like a drowned rat!"

Brady caught a glimpse of himself in the bathroom mirror as he toweled down. He ran both hands through his hair. What a mess. When he returned to sit across from Alejandro's desk, the foreman hung up and smiled at him. "I don't know where to start, dude. Did your brother love the play? Did you see the paper? No school today? What're you doing here?"

"Yeah, he loved it. Did you?"

" 'Course! And now you're a star, a celebrity!"

"Thanks."

"So, what are you doing here?"

"I quit school. I need to work full-time."

"Quit? Why, *muchacho*? You don't wanna do that! Best you can do around here is what you're doing, and maybe drive truck now and then. But I don't know how many more hours I can give you. Times are tough."

"I'll take whatever you've got."

"What do you need money for?"

"A car. And to live. I don't want to live at home any longer than I have to."

"The guys who work here live together in that shack at the edge of the property. You don't want to do that, do you?"

"I might."

"You'd be the only *gringo*, but they'd love to have someone help with the rent."

"I could get along with those guys."

"Sure you could. But do you really want to do this, Brady? I mean, I'll talk to the big boss and see what I can find, but I honestly don't know."

"I've decided, Alejandro. It's done. Let me know as soon as you can."

"You're working tonight, right? Maybe I'll know by then."

Brady had forgotten it was his mother's day off. No wonder she had been less than thrilled to be awakened by the dean's phone call. The last thing he wanted was to talk to her, but he was freezing and needed to

261

shower and change. He found her lounging in front of the television in her robe. She muted the TV as if relishing the chance to confront him.

"If it isn't my favorite failure. So you're out of the musical. That was one dream that needed to die, and you know it as well as I do."

"What're you talking about? You saw the paper. You know I was good. I could've become a star."

"In your dreams."

"I quit school too, you might as well know."

"Brilliant. Well, you can't live here without working because—"

"I'm working."

"I mean full-time."

"So do I."

"Good, because no school means you pay rent."

"What?"

"House rule."

"Since when?"

"Since now. Take it or leave it."

"Pay to live in a hole like this with you? You have got to be kidding me."

"What do you think *I* do, Brady? I pay to live in a hole like this with you."

"Well, I already got a place to live, so you don't have to worry about me."

"You gonna be working at the ash-phalt place?"

"Asphalt, Ma. Asphalt. Learn to talk."

"Yeah, tell me about it, dropout."

"Anyway, what do you care where I'm working?

Just know I'll be close enough to keep an eye on Petey."

"You can't protect him all the time."

"What are you saying?"

"Just that if he needs discipline, he's going to get it, especially with you not here threatening me all the time."

"The threat still stands, Ma. You keep your hands off him. You'll regret it if you don't."

"I'd have you in jail so fast your head would spin."

"It'd be worth it if I was paying you back for hurting Petey."

That afternoon, when the skies cleared, Brady walked all the way into Arlington to the storefront office of the Community Theater Players. A paunchy, middle-aged man was futzing about. He introduced himself as Walter. Brady told him he was an actor, working full-time, looking to audition for any roles they might have coming up for evenings and weekends.

Walter sat and studied him. "Are you even twenty-one yet?"

"Soon," Brady said. Five years was soon enough.

"You know, we do light comedies, that kind of stuff. Most of us are my age or older, and if we need young people, they are usually relatives. Do you like to do crew stuff?"

"Nah. I'm an actor."

"Um-hm. I can take your information and keep it on file."

"Any productions coming up?"

"*Kiss Me, Kate*, but I don't see a role there for your type."

"I'm not a type. I have range. I played the leads in all the shows at Forest View when I was there."

"You worked with Clancy? So did I! Well, let me call him and maybe something will open next spring you could audition for."

Walter was going to call Clancy Nabertowitz? That would be the end of that.

Brady had been free only a few hours, and already he was tired of walking. As soon as he could get out from under his Laundromat debt to Tatlock, he'd have to start a car fund again. He wouldn't need anything fancy. Just something to get around in.

Two things weighed on him as he trudged back to Addison. How was he going to tell Petey? And what would he do if Alejandro couldn't find more work for him or a bunk in the laborers' shack? Staying even one more night in the trailer suddenly sounded unbearable.

By the time Brady got back to the trailer park, Stevie Ray was pulling in from work. Brady jogged to his place. The baby was at day care, and Stevie's wife was still at work. Stevie had kicked off his boots and was sitting on the couch with a brew. "Grab yourself one from the fridge, Brady."

"You know what?" Brady said. "I appreciate it, but I hate beer."

"Yeah?"

"I do, man."

"If I drank like you, I'd hate it too," Stevie said. "You don't have to drink all you have, you know."

"I don't even like just one."

"That a fact? You know why I like it? I need something to take the edge off, mellow me out."

"Me too," Brady said, "but I can't stand the taste."

"What about weed?"

"Too expensive."

"But you like it?"

"Who doesn't?"

"In the can on top of the fridge. Go for it."

"No money," Brady said.

"I'm not selling, bud. I'm offering you one. Smoke yourself some dope."

Brady and Stevie passed the joint back and forth. It did mellow Brady out, but the combination of alcohol and marijuana made Stevie giggly. As Brady poured out his story, telling the truth to the only person he trusted, Stevie kept covering his mouth to keep from bursting out laughing. That made Brady mad, but he would never let it show.

"Man," Stevie said, eyelids heavy, "you're hosed. Listen, if nothing works out, you can crash here."

"You'd better talk to your wife about that, dude."

Stevie didn't seem to hear him at first, but then it seemed to dawn on him. "Oh yeah! Her! I am married, ain't I?" And he slid to where he was lying on the couch, laughing hysterically.

• • •

Brady showed up at Dennis Paving just before seven and found Alejandro at the door, pulling on his jacket.

"Bad news and good news," Alejandro said. "For a while I got no more hours for you than what you have now. But I like your work. The other guys like you, so next time we have an opening or a big job where we can add more hours, it's yours."

"Okay. Well, thanks. What's the good news?"

"The laborers have an extra bunk in the shack, and until you get more hours, they'll let you have it for a half share of the rent. You'll be helping each other out."

"How much is that?"

It was half of what Brady was making, and of course he still had payments due to Tatlock. He knew it was a foolish investment and probably twice what his own mother would charge. But something about the freedom it promised made him take it on the spot.

"When you're done tonight," Alejandro said, "check it out. Manny will show you. Those guys have fun over there, man. They live for the weekend, but they're good guys."

Brady worked with more enthusiasm and precision than he had in a long time, even with the weed still in his system. That was another thing. All the laborers talked about, besides their money and their booze and their women, was weed. He ought to be able to score some anytime he wanted it now.

Life was looking up. He still had to talk to Peter, and he was going to have to reassure him that he would still be close by and they would see a lot of each other. But things were going to work out.

28

Adamsville

Thomas and Grace Carey had never raised their voices to each other. Like their parents before them, they didn't believe in it. They had their arguments, their disagreements, their pet peeves. But these they discussed behind closed doors, and their goal—Thomas was proud to tell anyone he was counseling on marital issues—was to compete to see who could first clear the air. It was not about winning, he always said. It was about putting others above yourself, starting right there at home.

At times, he admitted—if only to himself—that the most irritating thing about Grace was her perfection. Worse, she wasn't even smug about it. She lived the life he strived for, and frankly it occasionally drove him nuts. Just once he'd like to see her lose it, raise her voice, stomp, slam a door. Lord knew, Thomas sometimes deserved it.

Living with a saint was sure better than the alternative. He didn't like tension, and there rarely was any. He found it easy to prefer her interests over his own, unless he was tired or cranky and, thus, selfish.

Of course, over the years, Thomas had learned that his idea of marital discord was markedly different from that of his parishioners. He joked about toilet paper rolls being set to issue from the front or back or whether husbands had it in them to ask for directions. Or who should do which chores and when. As he got older, the stares in the audience grew blanker when he discussed such knotty problems. When couples or individuals sought him out for counseling, their issues were pornography, affairs, second and third marriages.

For years, Thomas had felt hopelessly out of date and had learned the hard way that he had to give up his idea that most Christian couples wanted to please the Lord and each other and could learn to quit being so selfish. His last counselee had wanted to know whether he should tell his pregnant wife about his pregnant girlfriend. *Lord, have mercy.*

Thomas was grateful that little of what he discussed with inmates—at least so far—had to do with their wives or girlfriends. Those still married enjoyed rare visits, but there was no touching, not even pressing hands against the Plexiglas, let alone conjugal visits. Few marriages survived, and those that did were not seeking outside help, especially from a chaplain.

But now as Thomas sat across from the love of his life, he was as close to sharply disagreeing with her as he had ever been. She continued to insist that she was feeling better and had just been run-down, when it was vividly clear to him that she was deteriorating.

"Gracie, I love you and know you can't be well. You move in slow motion. The bruising on your arms is not going away. You're pale and drawn. Now you must see a doctor."

She asked to put it off for another few weeks. But the holidays were approaching—her favorite time of the year. She would want to entertain, to go caroling, to bake, to wrap and send presents. She was clearly not up to any of that.

"Promise me," he said. "Two weeks from today you'll get a checkup."

"We'll talk about it then," she said, and it was all Thomas could do to keep from slamming his fist on the table and demanding that she promise.

His last resort would be to enlist Ravinia's help. For all the heartache she had caused them both, Rav still deeply cared for and worried about her mother.

Addison

The laborers' shack was worse than Brady could have imagined. When he arrived, most of the men were crowded around the television, watching a boxing match, drinking, smoking, and cheering. The smoke-clouded place was a mess, clothes and garbage every-where, and it stank.

Manny, tall, bronzed, and in his early twenties, met Brady at the door wearing only sweat shorts. The others looked away from the TV just long enough to greet him. They appeared to be brothers, but he knew better. They teased each other and threw things. Trash and full ashtrays lay everywhere.

The shack was tiny, just two stories linked by a stairway so narrow that only those heading the same direction could move at one time. A small, hopeless kitchen and a foul full bath were on the first floor, along with the TV room and a small side room that seemed to be everyone's dumping place.

Upstairs was another full bath and two bedrooms, each of which had four bunk beds jammed in it. Hooks and nails on the wall served as closet space, and one bunk had a wood chest at one end.

Manny pointed out the lower bunk in the corner. "That would be yours, *amigo*, for half price until you get more work. You gonna get more work?"

"Hope so. Alejandro's looking."

"You got all day, man. Sling burgers or something."

"Good idea."

"So, you in? Everybody kicks in for beer and chips. Everything else, we're on our own."

"I don't drink."

"No? Oh, man! Well, if you don't pay, you can't even have one, *comprende*?"

"Sure."

"You do weed?"

"Some."

"That's on you. It's around, but everybody pays for his own. Pepe supplies us, if you don't have some-body. But don't take anybody else's. That's bad news, man."

"Got it."

"So, how about it? What can I tell the guys?"

"Well, the rent is gonna hurt me until I can find more work, but shoot, yeah. When can I move in?"

"Take a walk with me, Petey," Brady said a few minutes later. It wasn't easy, but he carefully explained everything.

The boy was silent.

"I know it's gonna be hard, but I'll be around."

Peter shook his head and appeared to be fighting tears. "I can't believe you're doing this. Leaving me here with Ma?"

"I warned her again. She knows I'll be close by."

"She's gonna take it out on me."

"Take what out on you? She doesn't care if I stay or go."

"Wanna bet?"

They headed back to find Peter was right.

"Why would you wanna stay with a bunch of Mexicans when you've got your own place right here?" she said.

"You said you were going to charge me."

"Well, yeah! There's no free lunch in this life, you know. Now what kind of a dive is that?"

"It's nice. None of the guys smoke, at least inside, and one of 'em cooks dinner every night." Brady amazed himself with his own imagination. "It's a big place, two guys to a room, and there's four bathrooms."

"Don't think you can be coming around here and mooching off me, raiding the fridge and all that."

"What, you don't have any mold I can have? I'll be around to see Petey; that's all. And I'll be checking up on him."

"Checking up on me, you mean."

" 'Course."

Brady couldn't wait to go. He started packing that very night, but he soon realized he had way too much stuff. There would be nowhere to stash it at the shack. He began giving things to Petey, including clothes that wouldn't fit the kid for years. Even some sports equipment.

Finally he rummaged around atop a closet and dug out the sawed-off shotgun his father had left him. It likely hadn't been shot in ten years, but a box of ammo lay near it.

"Where do you think you're going with that?" his mother said.

"It's mine."

"You're not even old enough to use it."

"It's still mine. Dad left it to me."

"I think he thought you'd be here with it to protect us."

"From what? There's nothing in here worth stealing."

"You never know. I feel better knowing we got us a weapon anyway."

"Then get your own, Ma. You might have to defend yourself against me someday."

"Don't flatter yourself. You don't have the guts."

"Just give me a reason."

Brady threw the big cardboard box containing all his worldly goods onto his shoulder and kicked the door shut on his way out. He couldn't bring himself to look one last time at Petey. He kept telling himself he'd come by often. It wasn't like they were going to become strangers.

He set the box down next to the stoop and wriggled beneath the trailer to retrieve the carton of his mother's cigarettes he had stashed near the back axle. On his way out, he brushed the underside of the trailer, which brought his mother stomping to the door.

"What're you doing under there?"

"Never mind, I just dropped something."

"Stay out from under my house. You don't live here anymore."

"Thank goodness!"

Brady waited until she had closed the door again before he slipped the carton into the big box. By the time he got to the shack, his whole body ached. None of the Mexicans gave him so much as a second glance as he hauled his stuff upstairs and hung some clothes on the wall and stuffed most everything else, including the shotgun, under the bed.

He wandered back down and sat behind everyone else to watch the fights, only to realize that they had the Spanish translation on. Well, that made sense. But was this all they ever watched? No, he found out they also watched an all-Spanish station and lots of soccer. He was more than a guest, but he was also the single minority. Freedom was all this place had to offer, but he would take what he could get.

When no one seemed to be going to bed by midnight, Brady, bored and exhausted, went upstairs. He couldn't sleep. The place was drafty, and he wasn't used to the cheap bunk yet. And when the others did finally begin drifting up between one and two in the morning, they were noisy. Drunk and high, they seemed to fall asleep quickly, but several also snored.

Wonderful.

In the morning, Brady walked the main drag a couple of miles until he got to the fast-food joints. Unfortunately, they were all busy with the breakfast rush and told him to come back midmorning with his résumé.

"Don't have one," he said.

"That's all right. Fill out this form and bring it back."

Talk about a creative imagination. By the time he got through with those forms, he'd have hired himself.

By noon he had learned that none of the places had any manager or assistant manager positions open. In fact, they didn't even have supervisory roles. But each place offered him a job, including a cheesy vest and jaunty cap, if he was willing to dunk fries and wrap burgers and learn the cash register.

Burger Boy offered ten cents an hour more than the rest, and he could work 10 a.m. to 6 p.m. Monday through Friday. At that rate, he could pay off Tatlock, pay his room rent, and start saving for a car. The trick was going to be keeping this from his housemates. If they knew he had work, they'd want more rent.

He could tell them no one was hiring, but what would he do with his yellow and white Burger Boy outfit? Maybe he could stash it at Stevie Ray's. He'd leave it in a box under the steps and pick it up on his way to work and drop it off on his way back. Then he could go straight to the forklift truck and get in his shift at Dennis Paving.

Alejandro finding him more work couldn't come soon enough. It was going to take every last ounce of Brady's dignity to stand behind a counter looking like an Up with People singer.

Brady arrived at Stevie Ray's and told his wife he'd just wait outside till Stevie got home. She brought the baby out and sat on the steps next to him.

"What're you up to these days, Brady? Still getting hammered?"

"Nah. That was just a one-time thing. Sorry if I kept you up."

"You weren't the first and you won't be the last."

"Just got a job managing Burger Boy," he said.

"No kidding! Good for you."

He told her where he was living and that he didn't want to make his coworkers jealous. Brady laid out his plan of how to hide the uniform each day.

"No problem with me," she said. "But what do you care what they think? You should tell them to buzz off.

Just 'cause you're more industrious than they are is no reason for them to be jealous. If you can get a job like that, so can they."

"You're probably right. After a while I'll tell them, but meanwhile . . . ?"

"You can leave it here every day, sure." She looked at her watch. "Gotta get Stevie Ray's spaghetti on. You want to join us? We've got plenty."

29

Adamsville

Thomas was alarmed to arrive home from work and find Grace napping. He actually bent close to be sure she was breathing. She was normally a light sleeper and roused at any noise, especially if he was moving about. But now she did not stir.

Thomas changed and headed to the kitchen to prepare them a light supper. Surely she would hear him eventually. But this was good, right? She needed her rest. He chastised himself for agreeing to let her wait two weeks before seeing a doctor.

Thomas brought a tray in to her with tea, soup, and a grilled cheese sandwich. He set the tray on her bedside table and put a hand on her shoulder. Nothing. He carefully sat between her and the edge of the bed. Her breathing remained even and deep.

Noise, movement, the smell of food, his touch—nothing woke her?

Thomas sighed and moved into the living room, where he phoned Ravinia. As usual, she sounded rushed. But she fell silent when he informed her of his concerns.

"As long as she's resting, let her, but, Dad, you can call a doctor yourself. Who cares if she gets upset? It's what's best for her."

"What does it sound like to you, Rav?"

"I don't know. Something in the blood? Some kind of a deficiency? She's too young for it to be age-related. Likely something easily treated. Keep me posted, will you?"

"Of course."

"And I suppose you're eager to know how Dirk is . . . ?"

Thomas had to smile. Caught. No, he had not been wondering about Dirk's welfare. He had been guilty of avoiding the elephant in the room. Thomas was hoping and praying for a miracle, that Rav would come back to her faith, that Dirk would become a believer, that they would marry. "Yes, how is Dirk?" he said, painfully aware that his awkwardness was obvious.

She laughed. "Fine, thanks. I'll tell him you asked."

"When will we be seeing you again, Rav?"

"You never know. I might be coming your way in the spring. Some of us in criminal law will be visiting the county seat up there in Adamsville."

"Not till then? Not Christmas?"

"Don't think we can swing it, and it doesn't sound like you can either."

"Likely not." He told her of the prospect of his witnessing a hanging before New Year's.

"Henry Trenton? I wondered about that. Big, noisy case here, as you can imagine."

"I had no idea."

"Oh, sure. The capital cases get a lot of attention in law school. That guy is a poster boy for your type."

"My type?"

"C'mon, Dad. You haven't softened on capital punishment already, have you?"

"Well, I still believe Satan is the author of death."

"I think capital punishment is satanic too, Dad, though I doubt that's what you were implying. Still, it's hard to argue against in this case. That monster still call himself the Deacon?"

"Yes, but I have my doubts about his salvation."

"Wow, I wonder why."

"No one is beyond re—"

"Redemption, yeah. But can you see why most of the people I know think there's something wrong with the prospect of sharing heaven with a child molester and murderer?"

"Degrees of sin," Thomas said, wincing. Why was it so hard to talk to his own daughter?

"Well, get him saved, Dad, so he doesn't have to have his neck broken *and* burn for eternity."

Thomas closed his eyes and rubbed his forehead. "Rav, I know we don't see eye to eye on much anymore, but I'd appreciate it if you wouldn't be so flippant about things I hold sacred."

"Point taken, Dad. Sorry. I do find it interesting that we're going to wind up in virtually the same field, maybe on different sides of the same fence. Now get Mom some help and let me know how it goes. Don't put this off."

Touhy Trailer Park

Something was distracting the usually mellow Stevie Ray, but Brady wasn't sure what it was until his wife had to leave the dinner table to tend to the squalling baby.

"One of those guys you're living with is my weed guy, man."

"Pepe?"

"He's the one."

"He told me he's looking for help selling. What do you think? I could make a lot more with him than I will wearing that monkey suit at Burger Boy."

"Dealing dope? It's your call, Brady. You do want a car and all that."

Brady nodded. "Selling grass to rich kids? Like shooting fish in a barrel. They're gonna get it somewhere anyway. Why shouldn't it be from me so I can get my cut?"

Brady left Stevie Ray's an hour before he was due on the forklift. Sober and subdued, he didn't look forward to the work like he had even the day before, and he dreaded a long evening at the laborers' shack, then trying to sleep there. But no way would he humble himself and move back home.

He wandered over to the trailer and found Peter alone. How his mother could just leave the boy there every evening until she and her boss/boyfriend were finished partying—or whatever it was they were up to—was beyond him.

Petey glanced up from his video game and blinked at Brady. "Wanna play?" the boy said.

Brady shrugged and sat next to him. They played in silence until Brady was hopelessly behind, as usual, and tossed away his controller. Peter shut down the game. "I don't like it when you're not here," he said. "Lonely."

"I can come by every day."

"That'd be good. Hey, you think Ma knows my birthday's coming up?"

Brady snorted. "You'd think she'd remember that. She was there too, you know."

"When I was born? Yeah. I get it. All I got last year was a shirt. And I've never had a party."

"You want a party?"

"Sure."

"But not here," Brady said.

"No way. I don't even want kids to know I live here, let alone have them see it."

"Then where would you have a party?" Brady said.

"What about Burger Boy?"

"I practically run that place! I'll check it out."

"Ma would never pay for it."

"I can handle that, too."

"Meals and treats for everybody?"

"Sure, how many?"

"Twenty?"

"Twenty! Wow. Can you cut it to twelve?"

Brady hadn't seen Peter this animated in ages. "Yeah, I can do that. I'll invite my favorites. Just the guys. You'd really do this for me?"

" 'Course. What are big brothers for?"

Brady was doing the math in his head. This was going to be over a hundred dollars. Brilliant. Him and his big mouth.

But somehow he felt warm all over as he left. There was nothing like doing something for somebody else, especially when that somebody was your little brother.

Funny thing about Brady's mood, though. Something deep in his gut still niggled at him. His life, which had never been much to speak of, was spinning, spiraling. Brady felt as if he were sinking, and somewhere inside simmered a fury he feared he would not be able to control.

Right now it was focused on himself. He knew he was the reason for all his own problems. But it made him want to lash out. Even his grandiose offer to Petey had more to do with showing everyone else that he could be thoughtful, generous, than it did with pleasing his brother. And even if it wasn't true, he could appear to have the means to pull it off. That ought to show somebody something.

Thomas had barely touched his own meal. He peeked in on Grace, and she had not moved. The soup and sandwich and tea were cold, so he took the tray back to the kitchen. He didn't want to wake her. Would she sleep through the night? That would be okay too. But he wouldn't forgive himself if he didn't do all he should for her.

He leafed through the yellow pages, finding listing after listing for general practitioners. That was no way to find a doctor.

Thomas phoned Gladys. After she determined exactly what part of town he and Grace had settled in, he could hear her rummaging through some papers.

"I think you've got a family clinic not far away," she said. "Friend of a friend knows one of the doctors there. Worth a try. Here it is. Plum Creek Medical Center." She gave him the number.

"I owe you, Gladys."

"I'm keeping a tab," she said, chortling.

Thomas reached the after-hours answering service, and the woman on the other end seemed to be reading from a manual. "I can contact the physician on call and ask him to call you. Otherwise, you're advised to check the patient into a local emergency room if necessary. We recommend Sky Ridge. Would you like me to have the doctor call you?"

"Uh, no, not yet. Would I be able to get his number, in case—"

"I'm not authorized to provide that, sir. But you can call back anytime, and I will have him call."

Grace appeared in the doorway. "Who are you talking to, Thomas?"

30

Adamsville

Grace was none too pleased with Thomas's initiative, despite his loving motive. She convinced him that she had just needed a long nap and that it had done the trick.

"I feel 100 percent better," she said. "I have pep I haven't had in ages. And don't you think my arms look better?" She moved close and raised her sleeves.

Thomas wouldn't have sworn to it, but there could have been some lightening in the bluish marks.

"I'm serious, Thomas. I feel like a new woman. In fact, I think I'm up to a walk. Are you?"

In truth Thomas was not up to it, but what could he do? He was eager to test her claims. He changed clothes and joined her, and she seemed to maintain a brisk pace with no ill effects. He did not let on that he had discussed her health with Ravinia. When they got home, he reminded her that she still had a commitment to see a doctor very soon.

"If I need to," she said.

Things had not gone well at Burger Boy. Brady wondered what he had been thinking when he agreed to dress like an idiot and smile at demanding customers all day. The work looked easy enough, but people with just a little more experience seemed to be able to do it in their sleep. Everything felt clumsy to Brady, and he took every complaint as a personal attack.

He snapped at customers and was sarcastic, which bought him meetings with his shift supervisor, a woman in her early twenties who looked like a young teen. He promised to do better, but he had already been officially warned, and she told him he would be carefully watched.

Worse, not one of the kids on the Burger Boy team looked like a druggie or even a prospect. This would be no place to start a career as a pusher.

Brady made sure he removed his vest and hat before visiting Petey each day. His brother would never see him in that getup if Brady could help it.

Every visit saddened Brady more. Petey seemed so down, so unhappy. And why not? He said he had fun and had friends at school, but there was nothing for him at the trailer park. Brady wanted to get rich somehow and get them both out of there.

He was distracted that evening trying to do his work at Dennis Paving. For the first time in days, he broke two stops and was tempted to try to hide them, though he knew better. No, it was best to be honest and stay on good terms with Alejandro, prove himself worthy of more work if any ever arose.

With nothing to do between work and bed, he hung out at the Laundromat, hoping to see Tatlock. He thought about seeing Petey again, but his mother would be home by then, and he didn't need the aggravation. Anyway, desperate to find the money for the party he had promised, Brady didn't have any for even taking his brother to a movie, so there was no sense getting Petey's hopes up.

As he sat waiting, Brady thumbed through the entertainment magazines, reminding himself how much he missed the stage. Mr. Nabertowitz had referred to him once as a *dilettante,* making Brady ask for a definition.

"It's someone who likes an area of interest and dabbles in it but is not an expert."

"Then I don't want to be that," Brady had told him.

"That's on you. You're brand-new and you seem to have unlimited potential, but there's only one way to move from dilettante to pro, and that's a lot of work."

Brady had already royally screwed that up, and now as he followed the exploits of the young hunks of Hollywood, he realized he had made his odds of getting there about as remote as they could be. He was deep into an article about a young director and his lofty ideals when Tatlock interrupted him.

"Conrad Birdie," the man said as he swept in.

Brady rose quickly. "Need to talk to you."

Tatlock looked at his watch. "No payment due for a few days. What's up?"

"That's what I wanted to talk to you about. I need to skip just one payment if I could." He told Tatlock what he planned to do for his brother.

"Come with me," Tatlock said, and they went to the back room and sat. "And you're no longer at home why?"

Brady explained, embellishing everything as usual.

"Makes no sense you would give up the last three performances at school."

"Yeah, that. I wanted to give the other guy a chance. He's going for a scholarship and all."

Tatlock seemed to study him, squinting. "Well, I like your thinking—about your brother, anyway. Nothing more important than family. But you know what, Brady? I'm going to challenge you to follow through on that promise, but I'm afraid I'm not going to let you postpone even one payment."

"What? Why not?"

"Because you have responsibilities, obligations. Plus I see something in you. I think you can do the hard things. Find a way to earn extra money while still paying your bills. Someday you'll be a husband and a father, and you'll have car payments and a mortgage, and something will come up. An injury, an illness, a repair. You'll have to adjust. That's life, son."

Brady could not remember ever having been so conflicted. Tatlock was talking to him like a father, respecting him almost as an adult. He knew this was wise counsel, surprising because it came from someone Brady had wronged, someone who had no reason to give him the time of day.

And yet Brady was so frustrated, so angry that Tatlock would not budge, that he imagined himself attacking the man. Except he knew Tatlock could tear him in two. Unless Brady stabbed him. Or shot him. Or something.

Brady felt himself flush and his muscles tense. What was he thinking?

"So I have to pay you and still try to pay for my brother's birthday party?"

"You can do it. I know you can."

"I'm glad *you* think so. How about a loan?"

Tatlock laughed. "That makes a lot of sense. I lend you money so you can make your payment, and you still owe me? What's the difference between that and letting you postpone?"

Brady had had a chip on his shoulder for as long as he could remember. And the absolute worst thing he could imagine was being laughed at.

He glared at Tatlock and his grin. "You're lucky I didn't steal more from you," he said.

Tatlock's smile faded. "You're the lucky one, Brady. You could be in jail right now."

"I should have broken the windows here, trashed the machines, slashed your tires."

"Careful, son."

"I still should."

"You threatening me, Brady? I think it's time for you to leave. And remember, I expect your payment this week."

Brady rushed out, kicking the push bar of the front door and bending it.

"And you can add a payment for that, Darby!" Tatlock called after him.

Brady cursed him and kept moving. That guy would be lucky if he saw one more payment.

Brady was quivering in the darkness by the time he reached the laborers' shack. What was wrong with him? Tatlock was the one guy who had treated him better than he should have, the one who could have called the cops on him, and now Brady had turned on him. He was his own worst enemy. If it wasn't for Petey, Brady would be better off dead.

When he entered the shack, the din before the TV suddenly died and someone muted the set. The Mexicans looked at him and at each other.

"Hey," he said.

"Hey, Burger Boy," one said.

Brady smiled as if he found that funny and headed up the stairs. He nearly froze when he realized they were following. Every last one of them. He sat on his bunk and began taking off his shoes as they all crowded into the room.

"What?"

Some leaned against the bunks. Some sat on the floor. Manny took charge.

"You were supposed to tell us when you got a job, man. Start paying your full share."

"I will. No problem."

"How long you been at Burger Boy?"

"Just a few days; why?"

"Meter's been running."

"Yeah, that, well, I'm on probation, so the job isn't guaranteed until they watch me for another week or so."

"That's bull and you know it. Why didn't you tell me you had a job?"

"Didn't I tell you? I thought I told you. I meant to tell you. That's my bad."

"No good, *gringo*. We got to be able to trust you. You want to live here, you tell us what's going on, and you take your responsibility for your share."

"I don't get paid for another week. I couldn't pay you till then anyway."

"Yeah, but we got to know how much to expect. Full price started when you started work."

"Fine. No problem. Now, we okay?"

"We'll let you know. Anything else we should know about?"

"Like what?"

"Like anything. You don't want to be a stranger here. We got to be like family."

"Okay. Good."

"You need anything from us?"

Brady laughed. "I need money, man."

"You got two jobs and you need money?"

Brady said he had debts and wanted to throw his brother a birthday party. "I also wouldn't mind a little weed, but I know you don't do that on credit."

Everybody turned to look at Pepe, who stepped forward and smiled. He was a young-looking, round-faced man who was probably carded at every bar. "I might be able to work something out, *amigo*," he said. "We can talk in private."

The rest of the Mexicans took that as their cue to head back downstairs.

"Somebody said you got a shotgun," Pepe said, sitting uncomfortably close to Brady on the bunk.

"Yeah. A sawed-off. My dad left it to me."

"I love guns. Can I see it?"

Brady shrugged. He wanted to talk business, but Pepe spooked him—so young and innocent-looking, yet clearly afraid of nothing and no one.

Brady dug out the shotgun, and Pepe weighed it in his hands, turning it this way and that, expertly breaking it open.

"Got any shells?"

Brady nodded. "Not sure how old they are."

"Lemme see."

Pepe deftly popped two shells into the chamber at once. "One way to find out if this works," he said.

"Hasn't been shot in ages. And that's really old ammo."

Pepe smiled and shrugged. "Plug your ears."

"What're you, serious? You're going to shoot that inside?"

And before Brady could cover his ears, Pepe pointed the weapon at the ceiling.

The explosion deafened Brady and left his ears ringing. He could feel the rumble from the stairs as the rest of the guys in the house charged up.

Pepe laughed loud and long and pointed at the hole in the ceiling, from which drifted bits of drywall and insulation.

"You're crazy, man!"

"Pepe, you're a fool!"

"You want the cops all over this place?"

Pepe just kept laughing. "Nobody heard that but you," he said.

He lifted the shotgun and swept it toward his friends. They all dove for cover. Then he broke open the mechanism again, slid the empty and the live shell out, and handed everything back to Brady.

They hadn't even talked business yet, but Brady had been sent a message.

Pepe was capable of anything.

31

Christmas Eve | Adamsville

December had broken cold and snowy in Adamsville, and the holidays saw freshly shoveled sidewalks tunneling through drifts and piles from snowplows.

Thomas loved winter almost as much as he loved Christmas. Brightening his spirits this year was that it appeared his fears for Grace's health had been unfounded. Though Ravinia checked in frequently and kept badgering him to force her mother to see a doctor, Grace had convinced Thomas she was better.

Her energy level seemed back to normal, and they were walking nearly every night, bundled up, laughing and talking through white vapor. The marks on her arms had disappeared, and except that she slept a little longer each night than she had in years, he was satisfied she was herself again. Maybe she had needed more sleep in previous years and either didn't know it or didn't feel she could afford the time.

Thomas was also satisfied that after a lengthy search, he and his wife had found their new church home. Their first visit had been at Thanksgiving, and he wondered how they'd missed the tiny chapel set at the back of a small lot just three blocks from their home. Its nondescript name had made it invisible, he guessed. But they almost immediately believed they had been led to Village Church.

The congregation numbered fewer than ninety adults, but they were salt-of-the-earth types, lower to middle income at best, and with bunches of kids running all over the place. Despite its modest size, the nondenominational church had a lot going. Kids' programs. Men's activities. A women's group. The congregation gave generously to missions. And they had a young pastor who was seminary trained but didn't talk over their heads. Will Kessler was a Bible man, a real expositor, and he and his wife—carrying their first child—seemed to live what he preached.

Thomas had been almost immediately pressed into service, substitute teaching the adult Sunday school class. And he and Grace had even been asked to sing a duet one evening. Thomas agreed only out of a sense of obligation and was grateful that Grace's sweet tone carried the melody while he reached for a nasally high harmony. Their new friends clapped politely.

Tonight, as they strode—early as always—toward Village and its Christmas program, Grace's tiny hands enveloped Thomas's arm, and she drew him close as they crossed a lamp-lighted street. "You know what I want for Christmas this year?" she said.

"Of course."

"You do?"

"It hasn't changed in decades, has it? You never want anything for yourself."

"I don't need anything but this."

"Me too."

Every year it was the same. She'd ask the question, he'd bite, and she'd say, "That my daughter love and serve the Lord."

That it went unspoken this year made it only more poignant. Neither spoke the rest of the way, and as they entered the cozy sanctuary, where squealing kids in bathrobes and bandannas ran up and down the aisle to find their places, Thomas noticed Grace brush a tear away. He had to do the same, though he hid it in one motion as he removed his hat and scarf.

Thomas remembered when Rav was the age of many of these kids and had played Mary in one Christmas program and John the Baptist's mother, Elizabeth, in the next. He would never forget the Christmas—when she was eight—that she came home with the box of treats each child received each year from the deacons. She laid out the hard and soft candies and the orange and a Brazil nut, planning to parcel them out so she could enjoy one a day for a week. Always organized and pragmatic. Thomas had known Ravinia would one day make something of herself.

But that was also the year Rav had suddenly paused in her candy chore and stared out the window. Then she turned and gazed at the Christmas tree, and her eyes seemed to focus on the star at the top. Finally she seemed to study the cheap Nativity scene Grace helped her set out each year.

The stable was made of cardboard and the figures of plastic. But Rav had always enjoyed arranging them just so. As Thomas watched, determined not to interrupt her reverie, she carefully moved aside the wise men and the shepherds and a cow to reach into the manger and pull out the tiny Jesus.

Ravinia held it before her eyes for the longest time, then began humming "Away in a Manger." Finally she replaced the baby and set the figures back in place, and when she turned to face her father, she appeared surprised to see him.

He smiled.

"You know what, Daddy?"

"Hm?"

"I really, really love Jesus."

Thomas recognized a teaching moment. "The baby Jesus, because He was so cute and His birth so special?"

"No. Well, yeah, that too. But I really love the grown-up Jesus who died for my sins."

Thomas, normally stoic, had dissolved into tears as he embraced his daughter.

Oh, God. Oh, God, he prayed silently now. *Bring her back!*

Leave it to God, he decided, to arrange that the very first thing on the program that night was the preschoolers singing "Away in a Manger." Thomas hoped Grace wouldn't look at him. He refused to hide his face, but tears ran as he forced his lips together and fought not to sob aloud.

Addison

Brady's Mexican housemates were going to Mass and then to get drunk. Brady had a quarter kilo of grass stuffed into his belt at the back and was heading to Stevie Ray's to share a joint with Stevie and his wife—who indulged only on holidays—then go with Stevie to a midnight gig. He and his band were playing a local rich guy's party until 2 a.m. But first, Brady wanted to stop by his mother's trailer to give her and Peter each a cheap gift.

Where's the wench now? Brady wondered as he

crossed the empty carport and mounted the steps to the trailer he had hated for so long. He found Peter watching television and eating something he had clearly prepared himself. Peter reported that their mother was at a party.

"Shocking," Brady said flatly. "She forgot we were going to do Christmas tonight?"

"She said you could wait."

"Till when?"

Peter shrugged.

"So she just leaves you alone on Christmas Eve," Brady said.

"She knew you were coming."

"But that's just it. I can't stay. I have plans."

"I'll be okay."

Brady put a wrapped carton of cigarettes on the kitchen table for his mother and tossed a festive envelope to Petey. The boy tore it open and smiled. "Ten Burger Boy bucks! Cool!"

"Just promise not to come when I'm working so you don't see me dressed like a dork."

That made Peter laugh as he ran to the back and brought out his gift for Brady, a huge color photo book about Academy Award–winning movies.

"I didn't know what else to get you."

"It's perfect, but how'd you afford it?"

"Mom still gives me a dollar a week. I saved up."

"Thanks, man. This had to cost—"

"Only $6.95 on the bargain table. Regular price is over thirty bucks."

"That's a really cool present, little man."

Brady heard a car pull up and hoped it wasn't his mother. She had already missed the gift exchange, and she'd probably come in drunk anyway. He didn't need that. He pulled back the blind.

Oh no! "Petey, kill the TV and go play a video game, will ya? I'll handle this."

"Who is it?"

"Just go!"

As soon as Peter was out of sight, Brady yanked the grass out of his belt and tossed it high into a kitchen cabinet. A rap came on the door.

Two uniformed officers.

"Hey, how you doin'?" Brady said. "I was just leaving."

"We could use a few minutes if you could spare them," the larger of the two said.

"You got a warrant?"

"Do we need one?"

"No, I'm just saying . . ."

"We just want to talk to you. You got something to hide?"

"No! No! Come on in."

"You alone?"

"My little brother's in the back."

"But you're leaving?"

"My ma's gonna be home any minute."

The three of them sat awkwardly in the cramped living room.

"You know a man named Tatlock?" Big Cop said.

"Sure. Used to work for him. Is this about my debt? He didn't get my last payment? I dropped it off at the Laundromat."

"You can stop the bull anytime you want," the officer said. "Now, he doesn't want to embarrass you or mess up your holiday, so if you'll be honest and convince us you're prepared to work something out and really get this taken care of, he won't press charges."

32

Adamsville

Pastor Will Kessler stood shivering in the doorway, shaking hands as the congregation filed out. "My closing was a little long, wasn't it?" he said.

"Oh, it was fine," Thomas said, but Grace squeezed his elbow.

"I think he wants you to be honest, Thomas."

"I do, sir! Please!"

"All right; I do feel you made your point long before you finished. And the point had been made throughout the program anyway. All you needed was to make certain it was clear. . . ."

"And get out of the way."

"You said it; I didn't."

"I really want your counsel, Reverend Carey. I want to get better."

Thomas and Grace chatted the whole way home about what a wonderful man Pastor Kessler was.

"Strange though," Grace said. "It's different to have a pastor so much younger. I mean, *he's* supposed to be *our* shepherd, not you his. And would you feel comfortable going to him with our heartache?"

"No, I wouldn't, but that's just pride. I'm ashamed to say we've lost our own daughter."

"We haven't lost her, Thomas. Don't say that. I'll never concede her to the enemy."

A few minutes later Grace was puttering in the kitchen as Thomas was changing in the bedroom. Noticing something sticking out of one of Grace's bureau drawers, he opened it to tidy the contents and found a packet of pamphlets—all about natural treatments for leukemia symptoms.

Thomas stopped breathing, stepped back, and slumped onto the bed. He felt violated, betrayed, almost as if he'd discovered she was seeing another man. What kind of a husband did she take him for if she did not feel free to confide her deepest fears?

She seemed better lately, so maybe these natural treatments, whatever they were, were working. But Thomas couldn't shake the feeling that his beloved had left him out of the most dire season of her life.

Addison

"We're happy to hear your side, Darby," the cop said. "But it's only fair to tell you that we know Tatlock. He teaches self-defense at the police academy. He was an

Eagle Scout, then a marine, then an Olympian. Not so much as a parking ticket on his rap sheet. He's told us the whole story, and your pretending the check somehow didn't get to him isn't going to fly. Now, you owe him; you threatened him; you vandalized his door. Yet he'd rather ask us to talk you into making it right than hurt you. And he could hurt you. He could rough you up or press charges, and he wants to do neither. So, is he lying?"

Brady suddenly felt a lot younger than sixteen. "He's not lying. I'll make it right."

"How? And when?"

"How much is it for the door?"

"Fifty on top of your balance." The cop checked his notebook. "Which he says was down to eighty bucks before he quit hearing from you altogether."

"So a hundred and thirty?"

"You're better at math than I am, kid."

Brady pulled out a wad of twenties. "I can take care of that right now and be done with it."

The cops both eyed him without smiling. "You got a good job?"

"Two of 'em. I'm a supervisor at one and a foreman at the other."

"Uh-huh. And you take your pay in cash?"

"Nah, not usually. I just cashed my checks this week because of Christmas. I gave my ma several hundred and my brother a hundred for gifts."

"Nice. And now you're gonna take care of this with Tatlock?"

"Sure. Can you give it to him for me?"

"You ought to do it yourself."

"I'd rather not. I'm kind of embarrassed, you know."

"I understand."

"I mean, once he's paid off I won't feel so bad running into him around, see?"

The cop nodded and took the cash. He looked at his partner, and neither moved.

"Anything else?" Brady said, standing.

"Matter of fact, there is."

Brady sat back down. "What?"

"Are you really this stupid, or do you think we are?"

"What are you talking about?"

"You'd trust us with $130 in cash?"

"Why not? You're cops."

"So we take this and give it to Tatlock and when we get back to headquarters, what, we find you're charging us with shaking you down?"

"I wouldn't do that."

"We can't take your money without giving you a receipt. You really don't know that?"

Brady shook his head.

"Tatlock says he sees something in you if you can control your temper. I hope he's not just seeing naiveté."

"Well, I wasn't trying to pull anything on you. I'll take a receipt, sure."

"And it will stipulate what we're to do with the money."

"Okay, good."

The cops left shaking their heads, and Brady waited a few beats before retrieving his grass from the kitchen. He tucked it back into his belt, then hollered to Petey, "Headin' out, man. Be good!"

Peter padded out. "What was that all about?"

"Oh, they're checking out one of the Mexicans I'm living with. They think he's pushing drugs or something."

"Is he?"

"Not that I know of. I just told them I didn't know anything. They were cool."

"Don't forget your book, Brady."

"Yeah, that's right! I'll start it tonight."

Brady arrived back at the trailer park with Stevie Ray about three in the morning, noticing that his mother's car was parked askew near the trailer. He considered checking to be sure Petey was all right but decided against it.

"Want me to drop you at the shack?" Stevie Ray said.

"Nah. I'll walk." He retrieved his book from Stevie Ray's living room and lit out.

As Brady approached the shack, he was not surprised to see lights on. These guys knew how to party, especially when they had no work the next day.

But when he entered, he met the same scenario as when they confronted him about his job at Burger Boy. Someone turned off the TV, everyone went quiet, and Pepe pulled Brady into a corner. "You a snitch?" he said. "A cop?"

"You kiddin'? I'm sixteen!"

"What were the cops doing at your place tonight? They on to you? asking about me?"

"No, it was about my mother. She's late on some payments or something. They got it all straightened out."

"You sure? We can't have 'em coming around here."

"They won't."

"They'd better not. It'll be on you, *muchacho*."

"Don't worry."

"Now, Manny's looking for the rent, and I'm looking for *my* money."

"Yeah, about that. I'm a little short. I had to help my ma with her late payment, so this is all I have." Brady produced about half what he owed each guy.

"Manny, come're, man," Pepe said. "Look at this garbage."

"Oh, no, no, no," Manny said. "This isn't going to go, Brady. What do you think you're doing? You got three jobs, dude, and what you do for Pepe pays more than the other two put together. And now you're short? No."

"It's just temporary," Brady said. "In fact, a guy owes me. I can have it by tomorrow."

"Tomorrow?"

"Promise."

"No credit this time," Manny said.

"From me either," Pepe said. "You give me the money tomorrow or you owe me a kilo."

Giving back the kilo would have been easy and gotten Brady off the hook. But he needed some weed himself, and he could make a lot more selling the rest than returning it.

When Manny and Pepe and the others lost interest in him and turned back to their partying, he slipped away to find his favorite customer. The college kid lived above a garage, and Brady woke him.

"What're you doing here?" the kid said. "I don't need anything."

"You can help me out."

"Why should I?"

"'Cause I always get you what you need."

"I don't have any money to lend you."

"I'm not looking for a loan. I have a bargain for you because I need some quick cash."

"What kind of a bargain?"

"Twenty-five percent off of almost a kilo. Let me smoke two joints with you, and you get the rest."

The kid seemed to study him. "No deal."

"Why not? Come on."

"I don't have that much money here, and I don't want you smoking dope here. Make it 50 percent, roll yourself a couple, and get out."

As Brady made his way back to the shack, he stepped in not one but two puddles of slush, freezing his feet to his shins. He couldn't wait to get back and smoke one of the joints. Maybe the high would curb his fury. He hated everybody in his life except Petey and his aunt and uncle. Even Tatlock drove him crazy. What was with that guy?

He sees something in me? What a sap!

It made no sense, Brady knew, to be so bothered by a man who kept giving him breaks. But Tatlock's kindness made him face himself and realize that he had become a criminal. He was a bad kid, a horrible brother. He hated his jobs, hated his bosses—and that was ludicrous too. Alejandro was one of the good guys. But why hadn't he found more work for Brady so he could leave Burger Boy and quit selling dope?

It wasn't Brady's fault he'd had to resort to that. Hadn't Alejandro promised him? Pretty soon he was going to have get tough with the foreman and tell him he needed more work or he was going to have to move on.

But where would Brady go? He'd have to find a new place to live. That would be all right too, if he found work that allowed him to afford someplace half decent. It was no fun living with a bunch of scary guys who didn't like him anyway.

By the time Brady got to the trailer park, he was so antsy for a joint that he was about to burst. And when he passed the Laundromat, he was reminded of everything Tatlock was and he wasn't.

He stopped and stared at the place, all quiet and dimly lit under a single fixture over the sign. Tatlock was tidying the place himself these days, and it looked like it would pass military inspection.

Livid, Brady looked around till he found a frozen

chunk of dark snow. He hefted it in his bare hands and guessed it weighed at least twenty pounds. When he heaved it through the plate glass window, it set off a ringing alarm that sent him slipping and sliding into the night.

33

Adamsville

Thomas Carey couldn't sleep but didn't want to disturb Grace. He eased out of bed and into the living room, where he sat in the dark, watching the snow fall and thinking about how to confront his wife about what he had discovered. Maddeningly, he couldn't keep his mind from drifting to Henry Trenton.

Thomas wondered if he should have called Chaplain Russ and told him what the Deacon wanted. If he did that, he would also have to tell the man that he didn't believe Deke was ready for eternity. But he guessed Russ was fully aware. Aside from everything else, Deke didn't seem to be one who would hide his opinions.

Deep in his gut, Thomas knew Trenton would ask for him late, and he would be pressed into gallows duty. But the child sex offender and murderer—Thomas still had difficulty ranking one crime over the other—had already clarified that he didn't want prayer or Scripture or even any counsel about his fate. Short

306

of those, all Thomas had to offer was company on the night the Deacon was to die.

Thomas didn't want to be selfish—it wasn't about him, after all—but, unable to provide any of the services he was trained to offer, what was the point? He had never seen a man die, and he certainly didn't relish hearing a neck snap. Imagining it was bad enough. How long might the bite of the trauma stay with him?

Thomas prayed that God would at least allow him to somehow minister to Henry Trenton, to be more than just a companion on that terminal night. If he knew the man had repented, had prayed, had been reconciled to God, Thomas believed he could stomach the ordeal.

He shook his head. *Forgive me for thinking of myself again, Lord. Is it possible to give me a love for such an awful man? I know You love him.*

Thomas stood and moved to the window, finally noticing that the only light reflected in the glass was the tiny bulb at the top of the ancient Nativity scene Grace had laid out on the piano. He turned and moved to study it, reminded anew of Ravinia and her childhood fascination with the figurines. He prayed for her as he did every time she came to mind, more and more often lately.

And then Thomas Carey went a step further than he had before. He also prayed for Dirk. Thomas had no idea how serious Rav's relationship with him was or how long it would last, being forged in ways foreign to his sensibilities. But given that Dirk Blanc might one day be his son-in-law or even the father of his grandchildren, Thomas was desperate to pray him into the fold as well.

As for the Deacon? Well, he owed it to the condemned man to at least call Russ in the morning. The hanging was set for just a few hours short of seven days away.

Addison

The laborers' shack had a cockeyed Christmas tree with lights askew. That and the muted TV, showing some old black-and-white yuletide movie, illuminated a bottle-strewn living room full of snoring men. It was as if they had partied until they couldn't move.

That was all right with Brady, still panting from his dash from the Laundromat. For once he could just slip upstairs unnoticed, smoke his dope in the bathroom, and crash. He kicked off his soggy shoes and socks and headed up.

A sweat-stained bandanna hung on the doorknob of the bunkroom, indicating that someone had a woman in there. Brady pressed his ear to the door. If she was still there, nothing was going on. When he finished his grass, he would just tiptoe in and go to bed.

As he emerged from the bathroom, Brady heard loud banging on the door downstairs. Whoever this was or whatever it was about couldn't be good for him. He hurried into the bedroom and stripped down, sliding under the covers.

From downstairs he heard arguing, then shouting, then his name. That was Stevie Ray's voice. "Just let me get him out of here," Stevie said, then called up the stairs, "Brady! You gotta go! Now!"

Brady dressed on his way down. "Get your shoes on, man," Stevie said. "You think the cops wouldn't be able to tell you just got here?"

"Don't bring no cops here!" Pepe said, coming to life on the couch. "I told you, man!"

"Cops?" Brady said.

"Just come on!"

Brady followed Stevie out to his car.

"Somebody saw you break the window, dude."

"What?"

"Don't start with me, Brady. I don't need this. I came to help. Who knows you live here? Does Tatlock?"

"I don't think so. Take me to your place."

"You know better'n that! I got a family, not to mention I'm on parole."

"What's going on?"

"Somebody called the cops, said it was you. They've already been to your mom's trailer."

"Great!" Brady swore.

"What were you thinking?"

"I don't know! I'm such an idiot! You know my ma's gonna rat me out, tell them where I live. And Petey! Oh, man!"

"Where you wanna go? I can't be driving you around."

"Where do you think they'll look?" Brady said.

"The shack, the paving company, my place."

"You won't say anything, will you?"

"I'll tell 'em the truth. I'll tell them I heard they were looking for you, so I tried to find you, knowing you wouldn't do something like that."

"That's a lie."

"So is telling them I couldn't find you. Now where do you want to hide?"

"Agatha's?"

"Will anybody think you'd go there?"

"Nah."

"You'll owe her."

"She's got a thing for me. It'll be cool."

Agatha lived on the far edge of the trailer park. Brady could see revolving police car lights bouncing off the low cloud cover through a light snow. As Stevie pulled away, Brady crept to the back of the trailer and tapped on Agatha's tiny window. He didn't want to scare her, so every time he tapped, he whispered her name. "It's me, Brady!"

Finally she pulled back the curtain and raised the blind. "What do you want?"

"Just wanted to be with you on Christmas Eve, that's all."

"It's nearly Christmas morning, Brady. What are you, drunk?"

"No, I just miss you."

She squinted at him, and in the dim light he saw hope in her eyes. He wondered if there was no end to his evil.

"You wake my dad, he'll kill you."

"Then be quiet and let me in."

He met her at the front door and followed her back to her room. A huge, ugly girl, she repulsed him.

"You got to be out of here by dawn," she said.

He nodded, removing only his shoes and socks.

"Does this mean we're on again?" she said.

"You and me?"

"Who else?"

"Yeah, sure."

"Really?"

" 'Course. But could you drive me somewhere?"

"Right now?"

"In the morning."

"Maybe. Where?"

"My aunt and uncle's. My ma and Petey are already there, but I had to work, and now I got no way of getting there."

"My dad's girlfriend and her kids are coming for Christmas dinner tomorrow, Brady. Why don't you join us?"

"Nah. I promised. Now can you take me or not?"

Adamsville

"Merry Christmas to you, too, Thomas," Russ said. "But something tells me you didn't just call for that."

Thomas chuckled and apologized, saying he hoped he had caught Russ before his celebration had begun. He told him all about the Deacon.

"I told Henry and I told the warden and I told you,

Thomas, that I'm out of there. Now I'm partial to the man, and I care for him, and I'll want to know when the deal goes down. But no, I can't be there, and yes, I have the same misgivings about his soul. I don't know what more to do about that, but let me tell you this: he knows the score. He can feint and dodge and play word games all he wants, but he knows the truth and the gospel and what he has to do. Don't let him play you."

Thomas told Russ of his frustration at having to play nursemaid to a condemned man when the man wanted nothing Thomas had to offer.

"Welcome to prison, friend. I'm sorry. Even now, just by getting you to call me, the Deacon is trying to work a guilt trip on me for abandoning him at his hour of need, but—"

"I'm doing this on my own."

"Well, you'd like to imagine you are, but don't think he's not working on you. Just tell him we talked and that I'll be thinking of him and praying for him, hoping he makes the right decision."

Why did all this have to come when Thomas was consumed with fear over Grace? He wrestled with how to approach her. Part of him wanted to scold her, yet that didn't jibe with his dread over her fate. He didn't know how long he could put off the confrontation.

Two Days Later

Aunt Lois, who had expressed delight when Brady showed up for Christmas, took a call from her former sister-in-law that sent Brady toward the door.

"Wait right there, young man," his aunt said. "Yes, Erlene, he's here, but he clearly doesn't want to talk to you. What's up?"

Brady was determined to escape, but something in Aunt Lois's eyes held him fast. "Trust me," she said, "we'll get him to do the right thing."

The woman hung up, cocked her head, and beckoned Brady with one finger, then pointed at the couch.

"I'm not going back," he said.

"Just tell me what you did and who Tatlock is."

Brady sat and told her he and his friend had been throwing snowballs and he'd accidentally thrown one through the Laundromat window.

"That's why you're here?"

He nodded. "Somebody saw me and called the cops, and I got scared."

Aunt Lois took his hands in hers. "Listen, this Mr. Tatlock sounds like a wonderful man. He told your mother he's not interested in pressing charges. He just wants to talk to you. He swears he'll keep the cops out of it if you'll come back and see him. Just tell him the truth, Brady. Your uncle will drive you back tomorrow morning, okay?"

Adamsville State Penitentiary

The day before New Year's Eve, Gladys stopped Thomas on his way to his office. "Like clockwork, who do you think wants a visit to his house today?"

"The Deacon."

She nodded.

"Can't you just tell him he didn't ask in time?"

Gladys narrowed her eyes. "Sit down a second, Thomas."

"I know," he said.

"Sit."

He did.

"You're not seriously considering dissin' this man two days before he meets his Maker, are you?"

"Problem is, I don't think he's going to meet his Maker."

"All the more reason to see the man."

Thomas nodded. "You know I'll see him. But—"

"Russ told me all about him, Reverend. But we don't give up on 'em till they're gone, do we?"

He shook his head.

"Now, I'll be thinking of you and praying for him," she said. "A ticking clock has a way of focusing a man's thoughts."

"I hope so."

Thomas called Grace, who said she would call Pastor Kessler and several others in the church. "We'll all be praying."

Thomas dumped the rest of his stuff on his desk, gathered up his Bible, and headed for the security envelopes that would deliver him to the Deacon's house.

34

Glass company workers were removing sheets of plywood from the gaping hole at the front of the Laundromat when Brady's uncle Carl dropped him off. He offered to stay, even to attend the meeting with Tatlock, but Brady said no. "He'll understand it was an accident and that I was scared. He's a good guy."

But as his uncle pulled away, the all-too-common tingle up his spine overtook Brady and made him want to bolt again. Unfortunately, Tatlock had already seen him. "The back room," he said. Brady followed him, silently rehearsing the account he'd been inventing for hours.

Tatlock sat across from him, looking more sad and confused than mad. "First I'm going to listen; then you're going to listen. Go."

"Well, okay, see, my friend and me came home late from a party and we were horsing around—"

"Who's your friend?"

"I'd rather not say. He didn't do anything."

"Fair enough. Then?"

"We started throwing snowballs at each other, and he hit me with one, so I threw the next one a little harder as he ran past your window."

"Uh-huh. You guys been drinking? doing drugs?"

"No, sir. I don't do that. I know better."

"So, what, he ducks and you chuck the snowball through my window?"

"Exactly. Then I got scared, even though I knew you'd understand. I'm sorry I ran, and I know I owe you, but you know I'm good for it."

"You have any idea what a plate glass window costs?"

"No, but whatever it is, I'll pay it. I appreciate you not getting me in trouble."

Tatlock sat shaking his head and scowling. "I ought to kick your tail."

"I know. I'd deserve it. But like I say, I appreciate—"

"Just cut the bull, will you? Why do you think you were caught?"

"Sir?"

"There was an eyewitness, Brady. Somebody saw you. Somebody I know and trust. And she says you were alone. No friend. No snowball fight. Just you staring at my place, finding a big chunk of something, and heaving it through my window."

"Well, I don't know how she could say that, because—"

"Because it's true, and you know it. Rumors are you're not even living at home anymore. You aren't even seventeen yet, are you?"

"No. But I'm living at home. You can ask—"

"I can ask who? Your mother? Who do you think told me you're living with the dope pushers?"

"Dope pushers?"

"You smoking, pushing, too?"

"No! I just stay there sometimes because I work there."

"You don't work there anymore, son."

"What? 'Course I do!"

"You missed work and didn't call in. I went to Alejandro looking for you, and he said if I saw you first, I could tell you to clean out your stuff."

Brady felt blood rushing up his neck, and his ears and face burned. "Well, I, uh, I still got my shift supervisor job at the burger place. . . ."

Tatlock snorted. "You're a shift supervisor."

"You don't believe me?"

"Should I? Have you ever, *ever* told me the truth?"

"Well, it's up to you whether you believe me, but—"

"You got any money on you?"

Brady still had the cash from his bargain sale of the marijuana, but that would cover only Manny and Pepe and leave him nothing.

"No, but I can get some."

"Where from?"

"Well, even if Alejandro fired me, he owes me. And my check is due at Burger Boy."

"Empty your pockets."

"What?"

"You heard me. Do it or I turn you in right now."

"Okay! I've got a little, but I need it."

"I don't expect to ever see you again, Brady. This is my last chance to get anything against the cost of this window."

Brady rose as if to reach in his pocket and lunged

toward the door. In a flash, Tatlock was in front of him. "Don't do this, Brady. I don't want to have to hurt you, but you're not getting out of here without paying me."

Ten minutes later, his pockets empty, Brady stormed into Alejandro's office and demanded his last check.

"Sit down and be quiet," Alejandro said. "The way I see it, you owe *me* money."

"What're you talking about?"

"The company owns the shack, man. Manny says you haven't paid your rent, and Pepe says you owe him money too."

"That's my business, but I just got mugged and my rent money was stolen."

"Not my problem."

"C'mon, Alejandro! I need money to live on. Can't you loan me some?"

"No way, man. You've really disappointed me."

"Well, you're disappointing me!"

"Brady, don't make this worse. You screwed up. Now just get your stuff out of the house and don't come back."

On his way out, Brady slammed the door so hard it flew back open. He wanted to kill someone, and he didn't care who. Maybe he was the one who ought to die. He marched to the laborers' shack and clomped up the stairs. Manny was alone in the house, but when he started to follow Brady, the boy turned on him.

"Don't even start with me!" Brady said. "Just stay

out of my way right now if you ever want to see your money."

"Pepe's looking for you too, Brady."

"Tell him to watch out too."

Brady grabbed his clothes and his sawed-off and stuffed the ammunition into his pocket. Manny ducked out of his way as he trotted down the stairs and bounded outside.

Brady ran back to his mother's trailer and found Peter watching TV.

"Hey, Brady! Is it true that you—?"

"All a big misunderstanding, buddy. I'm moving home though."

"Cool!"

Brady stowed the sawed-off and ammo in the closet and hung his clothes.

"Gotta go to work."

"Bring me home a shake?"

"Sure."

Adamsville State Penitentiary

One of Thomas's prayers had been answered. Beyond all reason, while going through the arduous process of getting from his office into the bowels of the prison, God had granted him what Thomas and his ilk called a "burden" for Henry Trenton.

It made no sense, and Thomas knew it could only be from the Lord. The Scriptures he had been memorizing all his life made clear that no one was righteous, but if ever there was a man who tested the unconditional love of God, it was the Deacon. Monster, predator, abuser of the helpless, murderer. Even the most ardent anti–capital punishment activist would sooner not talk about Trenton.

But something had come over Thomas. As he thought and prayed about what to say, he never once doubted that justice would be meted out the following night. The tragedy would be that a man would also be sentenced to hell. Oh, the so-called Deacon deserved that too. But so did Thomas. So did everyone.

But how great was the love of God available even to a man such as Henry Trenton. Like the thief on the cross, Trenton would have no time to do good, to live for God, to tangibly thank Him for His unspeakable gift. But grace was available even to him. What a God Thomas served, who would pour out His love on the basest of sinners if they would sincerely repent and believe.

Thomas picked up his pace, so eager was he to plead with Deke to listen, to understand, and to comply. It would be a mistake, he knew, to allow his emotions to show. Or would it?

Thomas had been warned by everyone to never show weakness, but was that what it would be if his urgency and compassion became obvious? Knowing that Russ and Gladys and Grace and Pastor Kessler and others would be praying caused Thomas to expect a miracle. He wanted Henry Trenton for the Kingdom, an example of the deep, deep love of Jesus.

The Deacon stood near the front of his cell, leaning against the wall, arms crossed. Thomas knew he should stand far enough away to avoid tempting the man to try to grab him. But that seemed counterproductive to everything he was expecting from God. So Thomas approached the front wall and leaned close. His face was inches from Trenton's. If the man wanted to spit at him, throw something at him, grab him by the tie and try to choke him, he could go ahead. Many officers were watching and would immediately come to Thomas's aid.

"You just can't go anywhere without that, can you?" the Deacon said, nodding at Thomas's Bible.

"I could, but I wouldn't. Especially when there is such important news in it."

"I know as well as you do what's in there, Reverend."

"Well, I doubt that, but who knows? You just might. If you do, then you know what is available to you."

"I don't want to talk about it."

"You don't? I'm here at your request. What *do* you want to talk about?"

"I hear Russ isn't coming, even though he promised."

"Don't start with that now, Deke. He never promised that. In fact, he made quite clear—"

"Whatever. So I got to die alone."

"That is your choice."

"You got plans for New Year's Eve?"

"Of course, but I am here to serve you, sir."

"Don't call me *sir*."

"To tell you the truth, Henry, I'd rather call you that than 'the Deacon.'"

"I understand."

"You do?"

"Sure. You know me too well."

"I don't know you the way your Maker knows you. And in spite of everything—"

"I told you, I don't want to talk about that."

"Your time is running out, Henry."

Trenton moved away and shook his head. "You think I don't know how much time I have?"

"Of course you do. I'm sorry."

"You're sorry. You said something out of line, and you're sorry. You're standing here in front of a man who is unforgivable, and you're—"

"Don't ever say that, Henry. When you say you're unforgivable, you besmirch the name of God Himself. Forgiveness is His job, not ours."

Trenton was silent for more than a minute, and while it was awkward, Thomas felt he should wait the man out.

Finally Trenton lifted his eyes. "So you'll be with me tomorrow night?"

"As you wish."

"You will do as I wish?"

"Certainly."

"I don't want you to bring your Bible."

"Are you sure?"

"You think I haven't thought this through? Yes, I'm sure. That's what I want."

"May I bring my heart?"

"What?"

"I have hidden His Word in my heart, so I will bring those Scriptures."

"Whatever. I just don't want to hear any of them, all right?"

"If that is still your wish at the end, I will reluctantly honor it."

"Count on it."

35

Addison

Brady picked up his cornball Burger Boy smock and cap at Stevie Ray's and began the long walk to the fast food place. His festering trip-wire rage abated somewhat as he tried his well-honed lying on himself. He would turn on the charm, lay out a sad story for the shift supervisor about why he'd had to miss work, assure him he would call if it ever happened again, and beyond that, tell him he was ready for more responsibility, like supervising.

By the time he arrived, shivering and embarrassed by the road-salt residue on his shoes, Brady had convinced himself he could pull this thing off. He would be more conscientious, make more money, pay down his debts, and start over in his quest to get out of the cursed Touhy Trailer Park.

His supervisor for that shift was Red, a usually

perky, pudgy, late-twenties guy with a sandy crew cut. He didn't appear so chipper just now. "Well, look who decided to finally show up."

"Yeah, sorry about that, sir. I gotta talk to you."

"Just turn in your uniform," Red said. "I've already cut this for you." The man held out a check for just under fifty dollars.

"You kiddin' me? I miss one shift and you can me?"

"I don't want any trouble, Brady. Now let's just trade and be done with this."

"You got to hear me out first," Brady said, taking and folding the check.

"We're about to get busy. Make it quick."

"Can we talk in private?"

"Just for a minute."

They went into the cramped office behind the kitchen, and Brady sat. Red didn't, which made Brady feel strange. He stared up at the supervisor. "I woulda called you; I really would have. But when I got word my uncle was near death, I just forgot everything else. I hitchhiked all the way to my aunt's house, and we were taking care of him around the clock until his medicine kicked in. I'm really sorry."

"I'm sorry too. I hope he's okay—that is, if you're telling me the truth."

" 'Course I am. I owe you; I know that. I also want you to know that I like my work here so much that I want to commit myself to Burger Boy and make it full-time. I quit school, and I quit my job as foreman at a paving company because I want to prove I'm serious about getting onto a management track here, like you. I think I'm ready to be your assistant, and I promise I'll give you and the company everything I've got."

Red crossed his arms and glared down at Brady. "What do you take me for?"

"A great boss. I've enjoyed working for you and I want to learn more, learn to get ahead, like you."

"You're so full of it, you can't even see straight."

"I'm serious, Red. Give me a chance to prove it."

"Listen, Brady. You've been nothing but a bad apple since the day you started. You don't listen; you don't cooperate; you don't follow instructions. You do as little as possible to get by. All you care about is punching out and collecting your pay. Well, the last of your pay is in your pocket."

"C'mon, Red! You're right, I know, but I see how wrong I've been. I want to start over, to make things right. I'll even work New Year's for you!"

"Don't you read? Don't you listen? We've told the staff, and it's all over our windows for the customers. We close at midnight New Year's Eve, and we reopen for breakfast January second."

"Well, I'll work New Year's Eve, then. That's time and a half, isn't it? I need all the income I can get, now that I've decided to make this my only job."

Red shook his head. "You think I'm as dumb as you are, and that's insulting. You think I don't know all the trouble you're in? Everybody knows, man. Dropped out of school, in hot water at the trailer park, sus-

325

pected of pushing drugs, and you were never foreman of anything. I've even got parents of workers here calling me, telling me to watch out for you, that you're trying to get their kids to smoke dope."

"No way! I would never do that! I got a little brother myself, you know, and—"

Red held up both hands. "It's over, Brady. Just cash your check before headquarters calls in a stop payment on it. And do yourself a favor. Take that line you were trying to shovel me and try it somewhere else. Only mean it this time."

Brady hung his head. "All right, Red. But let me just ask you one more thing. I promised I'd bring my brother a shake, and I got no money, not even any change till I cash this check."

"Tell you what I'll do, Brady, if you'll promise to think about what I said. Since that's a company check, I'll cash it for you. And on top of that, I'll give you the shake."

"For real?"

"My word is my bond, Brady, a policy you ought to adopt."

Brady handed over his outfit and followed Red out to the counter.

"Excuse me, Mike," Red said to a behemoth teen manning one of the registers. The kid, six foot six and on his way to three hundred pounds, stepped aside as Red used his key to open the register. "Give Brady a shake," Red said as he counted out Brady's money.

"Flavor?" Mike mumbled.

"Strawberry."

"Ninety-nine cents," Mike said.

"I got it," Red said.

And Brady headed back out into the cold, unemployed and broke, save for forty-eight dollars and change.

Adamsville

Thomas Carey found himself in a good mood that evening after dinner, so convinced was he that God would answer his prayer—and those of so many others—and make a trophy of one who had to rival the apostle Paul when he was Saul, the murderer of Christians, as "the chief of sinners."

Grace seemed more cautious, but late that night as they were getting ready for bed, she softly sang:

> Alas! and did my Savior bleed
> And did my Sovereign die?
> Would He devote that sacred head
> For such a worm as I?
>
> Was it for crimes that I have done
> He suffered on the tree?
> Amazing pity! grace unknown!
> And love beyond degree. . . .

As he lay in bed, hearing his beloved's breathing fade to the deep cadence of sleep, Thomas read through the entire book of Romans, which he had committed to memory years before. After each chapter he turned the Bible over and silently recited it word for word. He prayed Henry Trenton would change his mind, even as late as when he reached the top of the gallows stairs, and would allow Thomas to quote the sacred words of redemption.

Finally he laid his Bible on the nightstand and shut off the light, turning onto his back with his hands behind his head. Romans chapter 4 was the answer for Henry Trenton. Paul had written to the church in Rome as if writing directly to Deke, speaking to his crisis.

And as Thomas drifted off, he was running over in his mind the verses he planned to quote to the condemned:

The Scriptures tell us, "Abraham believed God, and God counted him as righteous because of his faith."

When people work, their wages are not a gift, but something they have earned. But people are counted as righteous, not because of their work, but because of their faith in God who forgives sinners. David also spoke of this when he described the happiness of those who are declared righteous without working for it:

"Oh, what joy for those whose disobedience is forgiven, whose sins are put out of sight.

"Yes, what joy for those whose record the Lord has cleared of sin."

Knowing he was ready as he could be for the Trenton crisis, Thomas found himself still troubled in his gut about having to confront Grace. But he simply couldn't complicate either of their lives more with that until the execution was over.

Addison

Brady Darby, his mind full of ideas and possibilities, arrived back at the trailer with Peter's strawberry shake. The fury was still with Brady, but now plans were attached. He would ask for Stevie Ray's help. Was there something he could do at the garage or for the band? Did Stevie know of anyone else looking for help?

But all those dreams vanished when he realized his mother's car was there, and he heard the shower running as he entered. Petey wouldn't look at him. The boy's face was red, his eyes moist. He took the shake and put it in the refrigerator, then returned to his perch before the TV.

"She do something to you?"

Peter shook his head. "She's got the day off 'cause she's working all night tomorrow."

"Working, then partying, more likely," Brady said. "Now what's wrong?"

"Nuthin'."

"Tell me, Petey," Brady said, shutting off the TV.

Peter buried his face in his hands and sobbed. "A guy named Pepe was here."

"Here? What'd he say?"

"He said you owed him money and he wanted you to know he knew where you lived and that he also knew your mom and your little brother lived here."

Brady swore. "I'll kill that—"

"*Do* you owe him money, Brady?"

"Yeah, but not much, and he's really making way too big a deal out of it."

"What do you owe him for?"

"Oh, uh, just some shotgun shells."

"He was threatening us, Brady."

"Ma was here?"

Peter nodded.

"He's gonna regret this."

"Just pay him, will you? He said he has to have his money this year. That means by midnight tomorrow."

"I know what it means. I always pay my bills, but I can't have a guy coming over here—"

The shower stopped, and his mother called out, "Who's that? Brady?"

"Yeah!"

"Don't you dare leave! I got to talk to you."

Minutes later she emerged in a ratty terry cloth robe. Their loud exchange sent Peter to his room. Brady told her he had just been promoted to assistant manager at Burger Boy and would have plenty of money to pay his small debt to Pepe for the ammo. "So just stay out of my business!"

Erlene screamed that his business became her business when people came to her house and threatened her and Petey. "And if you plan on moving back in here, you're gonna pay!"

He demanded to know why she had ratted him out to the police.

"I wasn't ratting you out, you idiot. I was worried about you. I didn't know where you were or if you were guilty or what. They asked if you lived here and I told them you lived at the paving company's shack, that's all."

Her tone had softened, and Brady was sure it was because she liked what she had heard about his having a full-time job, an income, the ability to pay rent. That could only be good for her if they could stand living under the same roof. They were hardly ever there and awake at the same time, which suited him.

Of course, if he didn't come up with some real cash soon, she would realize he'd told another whopper.

And there were only two ways to get out from under Pepe's threat. Brady could pay him. Or kill him.

36

New Year's Eve | Adamsville State Penitentiary

Knowing he would be there until well after midnight, Thomas didn't arrive at work until early afternoon. Protesters were out in full force, marching in circles outside the fences and huddling around fires in fifty-five-gallon drums. They displayed banners and waved posters for the ubiquitous press.

One long, painted sheet proclaimed, "If murder is wrong, murdering the murderer is wrong."

Thomas saw an interview he was hearing live on the radio as he pulled up to the guard tower. One of the protesters was telling a reporter, "No one believes Trenton is innocent or that he should be freed. But killing him is hypocritical."

Warden Frank LeRoy was in his office for one of the few times since Thomas had joined the staff. Thomas asked if he had a moment, and the warden waved him in.

"Been on the phone most of the morning," LeRoy said. "Press wants to know if I expect a call from the governor. 'Course I don't. Trenton's one of the reasons we're here. I want to see him hang, and so does George and anybody else with a brain in this state. The Deacon is what the death penalty is all about."

"Surely you're not saying that publicly."

"Not in so many words, but people know where I stand. What are you telling the press, Thomas?"

"Nothing so far."

"No calls?"

"I just got here."

"Aah. Gladys! Any phone messages for the Reverend Thomas Carey?"

"Just one," she called out. "One stack." She bustled in with an inch-high pad. "I tell 'em you're busy, you know, with preparations."

"Well, that's true," Thomas said. "I'm certainly not looking forward to this."

"It's a valuable service, Reverend," the warden said. "Just do your duty."

"Has the Deacon asked for me?"

Gladys shook her head.

Thomas turned to the warden. "We both know he needs counsel and some sort of company today. Can I just take the initiative and visit him?"

"Yeah, no. We can't start bending the rules now."

"Can't make an exception even on a man's last day on earth?"

The warden shook his head.

This was going to be a long day. Besides praying and reciting and planning what he would say when—and if—he was finally given the opportunity, Thomas couldn't free his mind of his own dread of what was to come. He was going to watch a man endure an ugly death. He shuddered every time he thought of it and used it as a trigger to pray for a miracle—not that Trenton would be spared or justice thwarted. Just that God's unconditional love not be spurned.

Thomas began to watch the clock as he knew Henry had to be. For the latter, the second hand must have seemed to speed. For Thomas, the day dragged. He took two media calls and felt overmatched in both, finally telling Gladys he would accept no more. Death, even in this circumstance, was a decidedly personal affair, and Thomas had nothing to say.

Reporters did not want to hear of a God who would forgive such a subhuman creature, and short of that, anything Thomas said sounded absurd.

Strangely, Thomas felt most concerned for Henry when he heard that the man had asked for a huge last meal of all kinds of treats. It didn't sound like him at all.

When the workday was over, the only lights burning in the administrative offices were the warden's and Thomas's. Yanno eventually moseyed in and sat on Thomas's desk. "So this'll be a first for you."

Thomas nodded miserably.

"They're never pleasant. It won't make my day either, but there's something fundamentally right about it."

"I know. But it's sad. As you can imagine, I believe I have comfort, even salvation, to offer Trenton. I can only pray a man in his position will listen."

"Salvation? For him?"

"Certainly."

"I'm a Christian, Reverend, but I don't buy that."

"Really? You're saying God's grace and love are limited?"

"Yeah, no. I hear what you're saying, but I don't know that I'd want to share heaven with a guy like that. Doesn't seem fair to me. Does it to you?"

"Of course not. That's the point. There's not one thing fair about grace."

"Well," Yanno said, "if God forgave Henry

Trenton and let him into heaven, that would sure not be fair."

"You think he'll call me, Warden? Before the walk to the gallows, I mean?"

"They usually do. The Deacon's a hard one to read, though."

Touhy Trailer Park

Brady's chat with Stevie Ray did not go well. Stevie said he needed to stay away from troublemakers. "I told you, man. Pepe's my supplier. I know what's going on. I'd be a hypocrite to tell you not to use when I'm a user. But dealin'? You gotta get out of that. Keep your nose clean."

"I will. I just got to pay him off is all."

"Well, I got no money for you and I can't hire you, and I don't know anybody who's hiring."

Back home Brady wished he could get drunk or high, but he still hated the taste of booze and didn't have any weed. Besides, he didn't want to do anything in front of Peter, who kept begging to go out with him somewhere.

"Nah, there's nowhere someone your age can go tonight. And I gotta go to work."

"This late?"

"Yeah. I'm closing up. I'll be home after midnight."

"I'm staying up. Gonna watch the year change on TV."

At a little after 11 p.m., the warden left Thomas's office at the sound of his phone.

He returned a minute later. "The process has begun. We'd better go."

It surprised Thomas that even being with the warden didn't get him through the security envelopes any faster. With all the media surrounding the place, nothing was left to chance. By the time he and Yanno reached death row, Henry Trenton had been dressed to kill.

The Deacon smiled self-consciously at Thomas. "Haven't worn a diaper since I was a baby. How do you like my new jumper?"

The man's khakis and tee had been replaced by a pea green jumpsuit that made him look like a hospital orderly.

"You look fine, Henry."

"Doc's been here. I'm healthy and 170 pounds. Know what that means?"

Thomas shook his head.

"Means the drop will be exactly seven feet five inches so I go instantly from a broke neck. Any shorter, I suffer. Takes a while to strangle, you know. Nice of them not to want me to suffer, eh? If the drop is any longer, I could be decapitated. Wouldn't that be a mess?"

Thomas didn't know what to say. Was this normal, this macabre conversation just before the end? "Can I do anything for you, Henry?"

Trenton looked irritated. "Do anything for me? Short of getting me out of here, no."

"You know what I mean. I could read to you, er, recite for you, anyway. Pray for you. Whatever you want."

"I told you, Reverend. You know what I want. No Bible. And no prayer."

"If you change your mind—"

"I won't be changing my mind."

"People are praying for you, Henry."

"I don't need to hear that either. Most people are praying something goes wrong and this is the most inhumane sentence ever carried out. They hope the rope snaps and I survive the drop, only to strangle to death on the floor with my legs broken."

"No, no—"

"Oh, stop. It'd be too good for me and you know it."

"Do you want to discuss what I know, Henry?"

"No! Let's talk about something else."

"What would you like to talk about?"

"My family."

"Tell me about them."

Henry called them vile names. "They abandoned me. Can't blame them, I guess."

"When was the last time you heard from them?"

"Got a letter about seven years ago from a nephew I'd never met. Said he wanted to come visit me. I actually looked forward to that. Got it all approved and set up, and then I got word that he had not cleared it with the rest and they were refusing to allow it. The kid was of age, could make his own decisions. Guess he finally did. Decided to obey. Never heard from him again."

"I'm sorry."

"So am I," Henry said.

Thomas looked in his eyes. "Are you?"

"That they turned their backs on me, sure."

Corrections officers arrived and asked Henry to slide his hands through the meal slot so he could be cuffed. Then they entered his cell and manacled his ankles. He emerged, led by one officer, flanked by two, and trailed by another. The warden hung back, allowing Thomas to follow the last officer.

Dreading the final moment, Thomas decided the mere sight and sound of the approach was awful enough. Henry Trenton didn't look so monstrous now. A thin, pale, aging man, he shuffled along in that tell-tale shackled way, chains around his waist and between his legs tinkling in cadence with his gait.

The shouting and catcalling of all the other prisoners died away, and all that could be heard over the footfalls of the entourage was a light, rhythmic tapping on cell walls with pencils or slippers. That was how the only acquaintances Henry Trenton had had for years said their good-byes.

Thomas, his throat constricted, prayed desperately for a chance to somehow minister to the Deacon beyond simply being there at his end.

When they arrived, all but one officer peeled away, and the warden joined the witnesses on the other side of the window. The executioner, a stern-looking old man, stood on the platform. He nodded to Thomas and motioned with his head that he should ascend the gallows stairs and join him.

Finally the remaining officer put a hand gently on Henry's back and guided him slowly up to the tiny platform. There was room for only the four of them, and Thomas found himself wishing the corrections officer were not so large.

Thomas could not keep himself from shaking as he prayed desperately for Henry to somehow falter, to break down and ask for something, anything—a prayer, a verse. The condemned was shaking now too, which gave Thomas hope.

Finally Henry spoke, whispering to the executioner, "Can I thank the chaplain?"

The old man nodded, and Henry awkwardly turned to face Thomas. Raising one hand to shake Thomas's made him raise both because of the cuffs.

Thomas shook the Deacon's hand and found it frigid. He held the grasp for as long as Henry Trenton would allow.

"Thanks for coming," the Deacon said, finally letting go and turning away. Thomas found himself staring at Henry's back.

Suddenly the curtain opened and Thomas saw over Henry's shoulder a dozen or so witnesses, including a man in a physician's smock, stethoscope around his neck, bag on the floor at his feet.

Henry snorted. "So they came after all. I recognize at least three of 'em, Reverend."

Thomas put a hand on Henry's shoulder and found it bony and cold.

With a tiny shrug, Henry shook him off. "Family reunion. Maybe they'll have meat loaf and potato salad after."

The executioner pulled from his pocket a black hood. "Any last words, Mr. Trenton?" he said.

"Let's just do it," Henry said.

The old man lifted the hood above Henry's head.

"Do I have to wear that?"

"I believe you do," the executioner said. "It's for the sake of the witnesses."

"Ask the warden. These sons-a-guns come to watch me swing, they can see it all."

The old man peered out at the warden, who waved his permission to skip the hood. He stuffed it back into his pocket and lowered the fat hangman's knot over Henry's head and down onto his neck. Thomas was amazed how thick the rope was. It seemed much less would have done the job.

"About sixty seconds, sir," the executioner said.

"Don't rush on my account," Henry said, but no one so much as cracked a smile.

Please, Thomas prayed silently. *Please!*

Addison

Brady stood in the shadows beyond the Burger Boy parking lot, watching the night shift stream out to their cars. Soon the only two left in the place were Red and

Big Mike. Red seemed to be giving the young man last-minute instructions, including how to set the burglar alarm.

Soon the supervisor donned his jacket and hurried out to his car. When he had pulled out of sight, Brady jogged toward the entrance.

37

Adamsville State Penitentiary

Thomas Carey's mind whirred as if everything he saw and felt were in slow motion. All the while chastising himself for finding this nearly unbearable when it was hardly he who would suffer most in the next few seconds, he prayed fiercely that the Deacon would break down and plead for forgiveness or at least for prayer. Simultaneously he thought of all the others who were praying and noticed the witnesses' grim visages, the doctor's impassive gaze, Henry's rigid but quivering body.

Oh, God, oh, God, please . . .

Thomas's breath was short, his heart stampeding. He saw Henry inhale deeply and slowly let it out. He hoped the executioner would tarry a moment, for another breath might mean Henry had one more thing to say. But the man glanced briefly at the warden, who turned slightly and nodded. Thomas had not known what to expect, but the thunderous bang of the trapdoor made him jump, and he had to grab the corrections officer's arm to keep from toppling himself.

Henry Trenton disappeared in a flashing stream of color. The rope stretched tight with a loud snap that told Thomas Henry was gone, then briefly slackened as the body bounced and then hung, swaying.

To a person, the witnesses stared; then some closed or covered their eyes. The executioner signaled the officer to draw the curtains as the doctor entered, pressed the stethoscope on Henry's chest, and soon announced the time of death.

As Thomas descended the stairs, rubber-gloved aides rolled in a gurney and lowered Henry onto it, removing the noose. Because bones in his neck had snapped and severed his spinal cord, as designed, except for ligature marks, he showed no signs of crisis. He appeared to be sleeping.

The warden was signing documents as Thomas made his way out of the death chamber and back toward the first security checkpoint. Yanno said something as Thomas passed, but whatever it was did not register with the chaplain. He was unable to speak or even acknowledge the warden.

The officers at each security envelope tried to engage Thomas, but he could not look at them, let alone respond. Finally alone, he dully made his way back to his office, opened the door, and turned on the light. There on his desk lay his Bible and his car keys. He stood staring at them for a moment, then turned off the light and shut and locked the door.

Thomas walked the corridor to the parking lot,

passed his car, and walked all the way to the main guardhouse.

"Car trouble, Reverend?" the officer said.

Thomas shook his head, showed his ID, and kept walking. It would take him more than forty minutes to walk home, but he neither buttoned his coat nor wrapped his scarf around his neck against the frigid winds. It just hung there, flapping. He was way more cold inside than out, and he couldn't even pray.

What a waste. What was that all about? Justice was done, sure. But what a point could have been made to a skeptical world! Oh, few would have believed a fox-hole or deathbed conversion anyway, but Thomas could not make it make sense that a soul had been lost for eternity.

Without question Henry Trenton had gotten what he deserved. And as Thomas silently passed the pro-testers, now cupping tiny candles and singing softly, he was grateful none tried to talk to him or criticize him or ask him anything. Someone stepped in front of him and stuck a microphone in his face, but he brushed it away and kept moving.

The questions were all his.

What about the effectual fervent prayer of a righteous man? It had availed nothing, so maybe Thomas wasn't righteous. What about all those believers agreeing in prayer in the name of Christ? It was all for naught.

What kind of a ministry could Thomas have at this godforsaken place? Few prisoners wanted to talk to him. None wanted to listen.

Thomas had seen few results during his decades in the ministry, yet Grace had encouraged him to stay at the task, to remain faithful, diligent, disciplined, devoted. Hadn't he done that? He'd prayed, he'd studied, he'd read, he'd memorized. He was always ready—in season and out of season, as the Bible said—to say a word for the Lord.

He'd been mistreated, used, and abused, but Thomas had never allowed himself to be defeated by one defeat. One battle was not a war. But this—he didn't know what to make of it. Here was a valley; here was the shadow of death.

Thomas had been disappointed before. He'd been bereaved, hurt. But he had never been this low. He felt isolated, alone, abandoned. Depression swept over him like a bitter, ugly shroud.

Normally Grace was his tonic. Within minutes of an insult or a bad board meeting or an unfair assessment of his gifts, she could find just the right verse or lyric or tune that would keep him in the game. Now he dreaded facing his wife—who, he knew, was keeping her own secret these days.

She would be eager to hear what had happened, ready to rejoice. What would he tell her? What could he say?

Addison

"Hey, Brady," Big Mike said. "We close in about a minute, you know."

"I know. Shake machine still running?"

"Nah. Shut down and cleaned up already."

"Shoot."

"You want something for your brother?"

"Yeah. Promised."

"Pie?"

"It'll be cold by the time I get it home. Got any cookies? He loves those."

Mike tossed him a package. "No charge. I just closed the register too."

"Thanks, man. So, Red's got you on night deposit duty tonight, eh?"

"Yeah."

"Congrats, Mike. He must really be happy with you."

"I guess."

"They paying you pretty good now?"

"Nah."

"Hey, you want to make forty bucks?"

"Sure. How?"

Brady pulled four tens from his pocket and spread them on the counter, as if the deal were already done. "Takes you a few days to make that much, huh, Mike?"

"What do I got to do?"

"Hardly anything. Mostly say only what I tell you to say and nothing more. Can you do that?"

"Depends."

"Here's the deal: you give me the deposit bag. How much is in there?"

Mike shrugged. "A few thousand."

"Perfect. You just drive over to the bank and park near the night deposit drawer. Then call Red and tell him some guys—in fact, make it a man and a woman, and say one of 'em's black. Anyway, they pulled up and held a gun on you and took the bag. You gotta sound all scared. Can you do that?"

"What? That'll never work."

"'Course it will! Red'll call the cops, and you can tell them you were too scared to think about what kind of car it was and say they wore ski masks or something, but you could tell the guy was black. C'mon, man, forty bucks!"

"I do all the work, you get all the money, and I get forty? No way."

"How much then?"

"Half."

"But it was *my* idea!"

"You're gonna skate, Brady."

"I'll give you a fourth, then."

"Deal."

"Really, Mike?"

"I can use the money."

"Me too. Good man."

They went to the back and counted the money, and Brady was thrilled to see that his part of the deal would give him more than forty-five hundred dollars.

"That's more'n fifteen hundred for you, Mike."

"Plus the forty."

"What?"

"You're gonna be rich, Brady. I'm taking all the risk. . . ."

"All right, fine."

After a few more words of coaching for Mike, including a little acting advice, Brady headed back to the trailer park. Along the way he tossed the bank bag in a ditch and stuffed the wads of cash in his pockets. Then he went directly to the laborers' shack and paid off both Manny and Pepe.

"And let me have a quarter kilo too," Brady said.

"I still got work for you," Pepe said, handing him a taped cellophane package. "As long as you keep up with your bills."

"Or what? You'll threaten my family again? I don't need that, and I don't need you."

When he got home, Brady left the cookies on the kitchen table for Peter and a stack of cash for his mother with a note telling her he was paying his rent a month in advance. He stored the remaining booty deep in the closet with his sawed-off and ammo, smoked a joint, and dropped into bed.

But despite the grass, Brady was so wired he wondered if he would ever sleep again.

38

"I saw you on the news," Grace said, padding out in her robe. It was one in the morning. "They showed you walking past the demonstrators. Something wrong with the car?"

Thomas shook his head. She helped him shed his hat and coat and scarf and led him to the couch. He buried his face in his hands.

"You don't need to talk about it, Thomas. It's written all over you."

He leaned over on her and she enveloped him.

Thomas was so glad he didn't have to go to work in the morning. He would request Thursday and Friday off too, meaning he wouldn't have to return to the prison until Monday. If there was any getting over this despair, he ought to be able to manage it in five days. But just now he couldn't imagine returning to the grind, the routine, the bureaucracy. If it were up to him, he would issue a challenge, hold prison-wide meetings, tell these desperate men to show up if they were serious about getting to know God and to otherwise stop wasting his time with their games, their requests, their endless challenges and minutiae.

"Let's get you to bed," Grace said.

He allowed her to lead him to the bedroom like a

sleepwalker. The phone startled him. An officer from the penitentiary was asking about the car. He told Thomas it was okay to leave it there, but that he should have cleared it first.

Brilliant, Thomas thought. *All these days off and I'll have to walk back.*

Defeated. He could think of no other way to put it. He was beat, his tank was empty, and he couldn't even conceive of how to muster the energy to try to refill it. Oh, he'd show up at church Sunday, and Pastor Kessler would preach the Word, as they both were wont to say. And if God's promise was true that His Word would not return void—whatever that meant—maybe something would knife its way through.

Thomas had so counted on that promise. How was it that God had not allowed him to utter even a word of Scripture to a dying man? What was he supposed to do if not minister to someone on the brink of eternity?

Finally sitting on the edge of the bed in his pajamas, Thomas would normally have read some Scripture, quoted some, prayed, kicked off his slippers, and stretched out on his back. But he had left his Bible at the office. That would be embarrassing come Sunday morning. And he didn't feel like quoting. Or praying.

He just sat there, lower than he had ever been, trying to muster the wherewithal to bare his feet and pull back the covers. Was Grace going to have to do even that? Before the thought was fully formed, here she came, kneeling to take his slippers, helping him stand so she could make room for him under the covers.

"Thank you," he said quietly, too spent even to weep.

Thomas stretched out on his stomach and pressed his face into the cold pillow. He felt as if he'd been strained through a cyclone fence. He should pray for the release sleep would bring, but he didn't much feel like talking to God.

Touhy Trailer Park

Brady Darby had nearly drifted off when he heard a car slowly roll up to the trailer. It wasn't his mother, unless she was half in the bag, as it stopped on the wrong side. Now whispering, then a flashlight, then another car in the front.

Brady sat up and peeked out. He swore under his breath.

Already?

He reached over and grabbed Peter's toe and twisted. As soon as the boy roused, Brady shushed him. "Whatever you do, don't answer the door. We're not here, got it?"

"What? Why? What's going on?"

"The cops are after a friend of mine, and I don't want to lie to them, but I don't want to rat him out either. Better if they just think there's no one home."

"What if they break in?"

"They can't do that without a warrant."

"Where's Ma?"

"Probably won't come staggering in till morning. Now be quiet."

Brady heard footsteps on both sides of the trailer. He hid under the covers, showing Peter how to do the same. Soon came three sharp knocks on the door.

"Police department! Open up!"

"Brady!" Peter whined.

"Shh!"

"Brady Darby! If you're in there, open the door!"

"You gotta answer it, Brady!"

"Shut up, will you?"

"We know you're in there, Darby! Don't make us damage your place!"

"Brady! Answer the door!"

"Shut up, Petey! They're bluffing."

"No, they're not!" Peter cried out. "Now go!"

They had to have heard that, and Brady lost it, cursing his brother in desperate whispers. "You answer it and tell 'em I'm not here! You let 'em in, you're dead meat!"

Peter ran to the door as Brady locked the bedroom. He leaned against the door so he could hear.

"Coming!" Peter hollered.

"No problem, ma'am!" a cop said. "We just need to talk to your son."

"I'm not a ma'am, sir," Peter said, opening the door. "I'm a kid."

"So you are," a female officer said. "Your mom here?"

"She's working all night. Waitressing."

"Uh-huh. This is the Darby residence, right? And your brother is Brady Darby? We need to talk to him."

"Yeah, but he's not here either. He worked late too."

"Where?"

"Burger Boy."

"He's *working* at Burger Boy?"

"Yup."

"Who else is here?"

"No one. I was just sleeping."

"Who were you talking to?"

"Oh, that must have been the TV. I like to have it on when I'm here alone."

"Even when you're sleeping."

"Uh-huh."

"Yeah. Do me a favor, son. Grab a blanket or a coat and step outside here a minute, will you?"

"It's awful cold."

"You can sit in the squad car. It's toasty in there."

"I'm not supposed to let anyone in."

"Son, we have a warrant to search this place and to arrest your brother. Now do what I say."

"Arrest him? I thought you were just going to ask him about his friend."

"We might. Who's his friend?"

"I don't know," Peter said, pulling on his jacket and slipping into his shoes.

"Where is Brady?" the woman whispered as Peter stepped outside.

"In the back bedroom, but don't tell him I told you."

"You're a good boy and a good brother," she said, leading him to the car. "Don't worry, we won't hurt him. Does he happen to have a weapon?"

"A sawed-off shotgun, but it's way up in the closet."

"You stay right here."

She unholstered her gun and joined two other cops as they entered. "Potentially armed," she whispered.

Brady heard them approach. He crept back under the covers and pulled them over his head. A cop knocked.

"We got a man outside the window and there's three of us here, Brady. Open up and show us your hands."

The lead man's radio crackled and word came from the post at the window. "No movement inside."

The cop knocked louder. "You got five seconds, scumbag. Open this door or we kick it in."

Brady fought not to stir when the door burst open, the flimsy wood frame breaking into pieces and flying about the room. He could feel the room fill with bodies. A huge boot pushed his rear end. "Get up, you faker!"

Brady groaned and rolled over, shielding his eyes from an overpowering flashlight. "What? What do you want?"

"You're the worst actor in history," the woman said. "Get your tail out of that bed and get dressed."

"What's up, officers?" Brady said. "Something wrong? This about my ma?"

The biggest of the cops grabbed Brady as soon as he stood and threatened to cuff him in his underwear if he didn't get dressed immediately. Brady pulled on his shirt and pants and slipped into his shoes, trying to smooth his hair.

"If you've got any of the money left, you'll do yourself a favor and produce it right now. Don't make us find it."

"I have no idea what you're talking—"

"Okay, find it, people."

"All right, all right, I'll get it."

"You gotta be the dumbest perp in history, Darby. You recruited the wrong guy. Mike What's-His-Name had his share of the take in his car, man! The first thing we do in a robbery like that is suspect the caller of being in on it. Kid sang like there was no tomorrow."

Brady spent the night in the county jail. His mother refused to come, let alone to try to bail him out. He was assigned a public defender who didn't look much older than he did.

Despite the pleading of his lawyer, Brady refused to help himself by telling where the rest of the money had gone. Even though it was a first offense and he was a minor, the judge gave him six months in juvenile hall, reminding him that he could have gotten off with a few weeks plus probation if he had decided to exhibit even a little cooperation.

Consecutive sun-drenched winter mornings, even without having to go to work, had not budged Thomas from his funk. This was a new one on him—a wilderness experience, he called it. He tried to hide at church Sunday morning, glad the Sunday school teacher was there and he didn't have to substitute.

After the service Pastor Kessler asked if he would wait around until the others had left. Thomas knew what was going on. He could see it in Grace's eyes. She was worried about him and had clearly confided in the pastor. But hadn't she herself said that the pastor was too young to be their shepherd?

Grace waited in the car while Kessler walked Thomas back to his office. "What's going on, friend?" the pastor said.

"I don't want to keep you from your family, Will, really. I'll get through this."

"Nonsense. Now you've suffered a blow, and it'll be good for you to talk about it."

"I'm afraid I can't yet. Sorry."

"You upset with God?"

Thomas let his head fall back and stared at the ceiling. "I don't think that's the way I'd put it. Disappointed maybe. Frustrated. Puzzled for sure. Not upset. Not angry at Him. How could I ever be?"

"It's okay to be, you know. He can take it."

"I know. And I've told people what you're telling me. But how could I ever be angry at the One who has lavished so much on me? We both know I deserve Henry Trenton's fate, not the life I enjoy. No, I could never really be mad at God."

Kessler seemed to study him. "Thomas, I'm in a rather awkward spot, trying to counsel a man with your experience. But I'm going to ask you to consider something—just consider it. Allow for the possibility that you're so low because you're in denial about your thinking about God right now. Now, don't look at me that way. I know all the denial stuff sounds like psychobabble. But I just have to wonder if your crisis, your inability to start seeing this in context and perspective, is because you're not allowing yourself to be honest with the Lord."

Thomas lowered his head and gazed at the pastor. The young man was trying so hard. And he seemed to genuinely care. "I appreciate your concern," Thomas said. "And I will think about what you've said."

PART TWO

39

Addison

Brady Darby spent much of the next two years in and out of juvie hall, then was tried as an adult at eighteen for a botched escape attempt when he was just days from having served his time. He spent most of the next year in the local jail, which he would not have survived without having earned his chops in juvie.

One place he didn't want to wind up was back in the county jail. That, many said, was worse than the state's supermax, because rather than being isolated from each other, prisoners were crammed together all day every day.

Every time Brady had been released from juvie—once for good behavior, twice due to overcrowding—he had used the new criminal knowledge gained inside to find more and more creative ways to ruin his life. Petty theft, a clownish armed robbery (which he claimed he didn't realize he could be charged with since he was faking a weapon with his finger tenting his jacket pocket), and finding himself in the middle of a very real drug bust had turned him into a jail rat, on his way to becoming a career criminal.

At yet one more sentencing, a judge clearly at the end of his patience cocked his head and squinted at

Brady. "Listening to you will spoil my lunch, Mr. Darby. To hear you tell it—" he grabbed a sheaf of papers and waved them about—"none of this is ever your fault. Misdemeanor, misdemeanor, petty crime, felony, felony, felony. But no, in your sedated mind, it's always a misunderstanding. You were in the wrong place at the wrong time, blamed for someone else's crime, victim of bad counsel or an overreaction from a hanging judge, you name it. Well, I'll gladly serve as your excuse this time, son. I'm tired of your sorry face."

Even Brady's aunt and uncle had given up on visiting him, having heard, Aunt Lois said, "one too many tall tales. Just know that we will continue to pray for you, Brady. But you won't be seeing us again until you're out and make the effort to come to us."

That last hurt Brady, because they were the only ones who ever brought Peter to see him.

His mother made a huge show of disowning Brady and bad-mouthing him to everyone she knew:

"He knows better."

"He wasn't raised like that."

"I don't know where he learned that kind of behavior. Must have got it from his no-account dad."

When such comments got back to Brady, he just shook his head. *As if she's ever been a real mom.*

Truth was, Brady had given up on himself. Since his brief, so brief, season in the sun as Conrad Birdie, he seemed to be at the mercy of his impulses. He found it hard to admit, even to himself—and certainly never

358

to anyone else—that he seemed incapable of making good decisions.

Not even his old friend Stevie Ray would have anything to do with him anymore.

Brady hated himself for the example he was setting for Peter. When his brother visited, he looked more and more like Brady each time, and he talked tougher, sounding more cynical. Brady tried to tell him to be good, but who was he to talk? While Peter was no longer listening to Brady, it was clear he liked being known as the brother of a bad guy.

Terrific.

When he finally got out for what he hoped was the last time, Brady talked his mother into taking him back and letting him live in the trailer. He accomplished this by promising to pay rent. Embarrassed and humiliated though she might have been because of him, he knew she could never turn down the lure of cash.

Brady promised himself he would never smoke dope again, and when he landed a job driving a truck (or, as the drivers called it, *driving truck*), he was ready to get back on the straight and narrow once and for all.

Funny, what he'd missed most while in the joint (he loved calling it that, and it seemed to come up frequently in conversation) was seeing movies. He still fancied himself an actor, a natural, as Clancy Nabertowitz had once said.

Who knew? Maybe once he got on his feet financially he would be able to get his own car and be mobile enough to try some community theater after work. He would be just as much a curiosity there as he had been on the boards in the Little Theater at Forest View High School.

As soon as he got his first paycheck, Brady paid his mother, put a down payment on a junk car, then found he was forced by law to insure it. And so he did. Which put an idea in the back of his head. A bad place for any idea.

The new leaf he had turned over crisped up and blew away when "just one or two joints to relax" made a little crack cocaine sound interesting. Soon he began showing up late for work, then lost his job, then began missing car payments. When the loan company threatened repossession, Brady hid the car at Agatha's, reported it stolen, and tried to collect the insurance.

When Agatha made the mistake of borrowing the car and was pulled over for a bad taillight—and possession of a stolen vehicle—she quickly broke down and admitted that Brady had put her up to it. Had he not recently tried to dump her by having someone else tell her he had enlisted in the army and been killed in a training accident, she might have been more loyal.

Brady turned on the charm—along with producing cash (from yet another drug sale—this time to three junior high girls, no less) for the missed payment and the next one—and talked the company into dropping the charges and letting him keep the car. It had all been a misunderstanding, you see.

Money talks, he learned.

As soon as he had the car back, Brady bought a can of charcoal lighter fluid, stuffed a rag in the top, set it afire, and tossed it into the backseat.

Fortunately, the automobile was insured for more than it was worth.

Unfortunately, it was all the fire department could do to keep the blaze from burning down Brady's mother's trailer, not to mention the rest of the park.

Most unfortunate? It took arson investigators less than an hour to identify the accelerant and trace it to the convenience store in the trailer park.

"Anybody buy charcoal lighter recently?"

"Yeah, matter of fact. We don't get much demand for it this time of the year, but I just sold a can this morning to Brady Darby. Why?"

Brady tried to tell the cops he still had that new can, unless somebody stole it, and, yeah, hey, come to think of it, there *had* been a suspicious guy hanging around the trailer.

But Brady had been apprehended at the insurance office, where he had hitchhiked to file his claim. And he had both marijuana and crack on his person.

Two weeks later Brady stood before the same judge. "Last chance, Darby. Sending you downstate for eighteen months. You don't succeed there, you're on your way toward County, and it wouldn't surprise me to see you graduate with honors from Pen State University."

At the medium-security prison Brady found enough mischief and dope to keep him high and in trouble— and behind bars—for the next six years. Every time Brady involved himself in a fight or a scheme, time was added to his sentence.

By his release, Brady was a full-grown man, twenty-five years old and—he believed (along with most others)—beyond hope.

Peter, now seventeen and a junior in high school, looked like a full-fledged hoodlum himself, and he refused to be called Petey any longer. But despite dressing the part and talking a big game, he had never been in trouble, worked at a local grocery, and had his own car.

Brady's mother, now working at her fourth different restaurant since he had been sent up, was heavy into alcohol and spent her off hours sleeping when and if she was home, according to Peter. There was no steady man in her life, as far as he could tell, but he told Brady, "There must be at least one somewhere, because she can't be working all the hours she's away."

Brady again moved back home. He strung his mother along for a couple of weeks, promising to find a job and pay rent. But he slept most of the time, and while Peter seemed to enjoy the novelty of sharing a room with his big brother again, he soon told Brady he didn't want to lend him his car all the time. "I gotta keep it running good if I ever want to make something of myself and get out of here."

Brady told him he would pay for gas and mileage when he needed to borrow it, but he had to use it to try to find a job.

But everywhere he went, the application asked if he had ever been convicted of a felony. When he answered honestly, he didn't even get an interview.

At a landscaping firm he checked the NO box and during the interview spun a story of how he and his father had had their own little nursery in Indiana before his dad died a few months before. Brady said he could do anything they asked, humbly admitting that he was "not the creative one; that was Dad. But I know what it means to do hard labor in the sun."

He was hired on the spot, asked to cut his hair, and issued two sets of colorful work clothes.

This time, Brady thought. *This time, for sure.*

Adamsville

While Brady Darby was trying to turn his life around, Thomas Carey was growing old. People always said he had aged before his time anyway, and the mirror did not lie.

In the nine years since Thomas's crisis of faith, much had changed in his life, but not nearly enough in his heart. If he was honest with himself, he had never recovered from the disappointment the night Henry Trenton was hung. But as he ruminated about it over the years, Thomas realized—or at least felt he got closer to understanding—that it was what God's silence had revealed to him about himself that had sent him into such a tailspin.

Thomas remained as devout and disciplined as he had always been, but still nothing seemed to really work for him. He wondered what he was doing wrong. It was as if God had turned His back on Thomas.

If his despair over the Henry Trenton debacle had birthed anything, it was a steeliness in Thomas that made him finally able to confront Grace about her health. As lovingly as he knew how, he had put his foot down and told her they both knew what her continuing bouts with fatigue and the return of her inexplicable bruises meant.

Against her wishes, he drove her to the doctor. "Don't rob me of a healthy wife. You're the only thing I care about anymore, Gracie."

She lectured him about that, reminding him that there was his calling, his ministry, his daughter, his future son-in-law. "I know you care about all of that. You must. I'm as heartbroken as you over how a lot of our life has turned out, but we have many miles to go."

The doctor, half Thomas's age, confirmed their fears, and Grace was put under vigorous treatment for a slow but steadily debilitating form of leukemia.

Thomas met with the young man alone and demanded to know how badly he had erred by not forcing her to come earlier. The doctor was kind enough to phrase it gently. "Of course we always like to have as big a head start on treatment as we can. But if it makes you feel any better, early symptoms are often mild and indeterminate. The important thing now is medication and treatment."

"What is her prognosis?"

"You have a difficult time ahead, sir. Her demise is not imminent, but it's unlikely she will improve. There will be the occasional remission where she'll feel herself again, but over the long haul, say the next decade, she will need more rest, more treatment, more medication. Eventually you will want help and perhaps a hospital bed in your home, unless you choose to institutionalize her."

Thomas bit the inside of his mouth to steady his lips. "Oh, never. No. I will take care of her until I am unable."

"Well, thankfully, that is a long way off, sir."

Thomas could only hope.

It was clear Grace worried about Thomas too. He wanted to be chipper, to keep her happy and motivated. Her enthusiasm and spirituality never flagged, but her body was simply unable to keep up most of the time, and Thomas regretted having taken so long to do what he knew was right.

Another thing he was unable to forgive himself for was Ravinia. Grace continued to pray for her, and Thomas did too, of course, but he despaired over having lost her. When she and Dirk, after several years of living together while slaving in low-paying jobs after law school, finally decided to marry, Ravinia actually asked Thomas if he would conduct the wedding ceremony.

Thomas had decided he would not even attend, let alone be a part of it, but Grace's cooler head prevailed. She told Ravinia it was not fair to ask her father to appear to condone this unequal yoke, but that of course they would attend so as not to cause an irreparable tear in the relationship.

"Well, without Dad, it's going to be a civil ceremony. I thought he might want to pray or something."

"Believe me, we'll be praying."

"And you need to know too, Mother, that this is not an unequal yoke. I don't mean to hurt you, but you cannot claim me for the faith."

Thomas and Grace had attended the tiny ceremony, held in the home of friends of the bride and groom. There Ravinia proudly announced that her new last name would be Carey-Blanc, obviously assuming this would please her parents.

Thomas forced a smile. His name would carry on, despite his never having had a son, but he feared what kind of spiritual heritage might be passed down.

Thomas and Grace agreed privately that the wedding was one of the most difficult ordeals of their lives, and it only exacerbated his spiritual doldrums. Would God ever again work in his life, answer a prayer, give him a victory?

Every day he rose early to read and study and pray, and then it was off to the prison, where he slogged through the monotony of days and weeks and months and years of the same old same old. The few convicts who asked to see him had their own agendas and didn't care about his. They were all angling for something.

If nothing else, Thomas had changed in one regard. He was no longer a softy, a pushover. He could see the cons' games coming a mile away. And while he was known as a gentle, devout soul, no one could work a scam on the chaplain.

He gradually allowed himself to be drawn back into work at Village Church, especially when the little flock had to replace pastors. That happened four times in nine years, not unusual for a small church. They saved money on interim pulpit supply because Thomas was there and willing. But just as in every other area of his spiritual life, he found little to encourage his own soul.

What was he missing? What more could he do? He had made an irrevocable commitment to spend his life—and he meant that—in the service of God. Was there to be zero payoff for that this side of heaven? If the answer was yes, so be it. It wouldn't change his decision. But his enthusiasm for the task waned with the years and showed in his graying hair and the deep lines in his face.

At work, too, despite the monotony of his chores, things had changed. Governor George Andreason, after serving two full terms, retired to sit on a number of corporate boards and ended up filling a vacant seat on the state's Department of Corrections board as well. Eventually he came out of retirement to replace Frank LeRoy as head of the DOC, moving that office out of the Adamsville prison and into the nearby state capitol building.

This had actually been Warden LeRoy's idea, allowing him to concentrate solely on running the penitentiary. *Well,* Thomas thought, *at least someone around here looks and acts like a new man.* He decided that if he himself were in a better frame of mind, he would have been inspired by Yanno's seeming new lease on life.

Now Yanno was at the prison all the time, freshly committed to the task. Adamsville State Penitentiary was going to remain the jewel in the state's DOC crown, financially strapped as it was, and Yanno kept asking Thomas if it didn't make him proud to be part of it.

"You bet it does," Thomas said, coming as close to lying as he had as an adult.

Thomas was shocked one afternoon when his daughter knocked and entered his office. He leaped to his feet.

"Rav! What brings you here?"

"You won't believe it. Dirk and I are moving to Adamsville."

"Seriously?"

"Dirk is working for the county, and I have just been hired as a public defender. You can guess where a lot of my caseload will come from."

"Here?"

"I trust we won't get into each other's way too much."

"You could never be in my way, sweetheart. You look fantastic, by the way."

"Well, this suit is Penney's, not Saks, as it would be if I were in a big firm. But I like to look the part."

"And you certainly do. I need to coach you on dealing with men like these, Rav."

"Wide open to input, but I suspect I'll have to learn as I go."

"Your mother will be thrilled to have you so close. You will come visit, won't you?"

"Of course. I think we can all be civil."

Addison

For a time it appeared Brady Darby might actually have turned a corner. It didn't take long for his new employers to catch on that he might have exaggerated his history of landscaping experience, but he proved, at first, to be diligent and hardworking. As long as someone told him what to do and walked him through it a time or two, he found he could learn anything.

He planted trees, laid sod, moved trees and shrubs. He mowed, weeded, edged, fertilized, even created rock formations.

Brady found the work—the first he had really done in ages—exhausting and painful for the first few weeks. And when Peter could not drop him off or pick him up, he had to hitchhike several miles to the office, where he rode with a crew to the various job sites.

He loved his uniform and found reasons to delay removing it at the end of the day. Brady liked to be seen in it here and there, especially around the trailer park. The old Laundromat had been replaced by a filling station, where he bought his smokes and snacks and dreamed of someday again having a car he could pull into there for gas.

With his history, Brady had zero credit and could get neither a credit nor even a debit card and thus had to run his entire personal financial life on cash. His expenses consisted of only a stipend to his mother for rent—they barely spoke and when they did were rarely cordial—and the occasional five or ten to Peter for the use of his car, which was infrequent.

Poor Peter was charged with making sure Brady got up in time to get to work every morning, and that became more difficult all the time. Brady was proud of his job and his steady, if not generous, income, but he had come to reward himself every evening by going to the movies, smoking some dope, trying to find a one-night—or more likely a few-hour—stand, then lounging in front of the TV until the wee hours.

He knew if his parole officer knew he was even associating with people who sold grass, he'd be right back in the joint. But at least he didn't drink or do the harder stuff anymore. Life was boring, no question, and Hollywood was a forgotten dream. But this was better than doing time.

The only person in the world Brady cared about was Peter, but the kid was not blind to Brady's weaknesses. That left him with little basis to teach or counsel his brother, but for sure he had enough experience to warn him. He told Peter to stay away from cigarettes, let alone grass and coke and booze. He praised him for holding down a steady job and keeping up with his car payments. He urged him to stay in school and graduate.

"You know the old line about doing what I say and not what I do?" Brady said.

Peter nodded.

"That's what I'm saying. I know I've screwed up. You don't have to. Promise me."

Peter shrugged. "Aunt Lois has been asking about you, Brady. Wants you to come see them if you want."

"What have you told her?"

"The truth, mostly. I told her you're doing good, working, making a little money, behaving yourself."

"So not the whole truth."

"Well, I didn't think it would make her day to know you like the occasional joint and that you sleep around, no."

"Good man."

"She wants to know where we're going to church."

"There's a surprise. Did you tell her Church of the Inner Spring with Pastor Blanket and Deacon Sheets?"

Peter roared. "I'll tell her that next time. I told her we've both been real busy."

Brady nodded. "And she told you that if we're too busy for God, we're too busy."

"Exactly."

40

Late September | Adamsville

Having Ravinia Carey-Blanc and Dirk over for the first time was about as nerve-racking a proposition as Thomas could imagine. He and Grace agreed that despite their discomfort over their daughter's marriage, it was unconscionable that they had never hosted the couple.

"Should I say that?" Thomas said. "Just confess it and ask their forgiveness?"

"I don't know," Grace said. "I'd leave it alone. Let's just be as gracious and warm as we know how. Make it clear we're finally recognizing them as a couple. She'll always be our daughter, regardless, and it's time we started treating her like an adult free to make her own decisions."

Thomas was as nervous as he had been in ages. Worry about Grace's stamina niggled at him, but mostly he was trying to frame his meal prayer. He always prayed; they would expect that. But he didn't want to offend them either.

What was the point of this? He would be talking to

God, not to them. He questioned his own motive for wanting to mention them, and he knew it would be wrong to hint what he really wanted God to do for them.

This was all too disconcerting, and as their arrival approached, he and Grace seemed nearly frozen from anxiety.

"Let's just be good hosts and let it play out as it plays out," Grace said.

With everything ready and dinner cooking, Grace sat on the couch, looking as if she could use some sleep. Thomas sat in his easy chair, trying to read the paper but unable to concentrate. He couldn't sit still and began to pace.

"You're making me more nervous," Grace said. "Just relax."

"Sorry. I can't. Has it been getting dark this early already?"

She looked at her watch, then out the window. "Storm brewing?"

Thomas moved to the picture window and scanned the sky. "How perfectly appropriate," he said.

"Oh, Thomas."

Addison

Despite being sleep deprived as usual and logy from smoking too much grass, Brady actually didn't mind his work so much that day. He was mostly mowing and bagging, and the weather forecast showed potential for their getting off work early.

373

Peter didn't have school that day, so Brady was using his car. No hitchhiking. He would ride back to the office in the company truck and be able to drive back to the trailer park. Peter said he was going somewhere with friends, but Brady begged him to be back at the trailer by five. "I need you to be there to take a delivery for me. Very important. Guy will give you a sealed-up cookie tin. You give him the envelope from the freezer."

"The freezer?"

"Just do it. Don't let me down."

"What are you buying?"

"The less you know the better."

"I don't want to get involved in anything like that."

"It's cookies, okay? A gift for Mom."

"You're buying cookies from some guy for an envelope full of cash."

Even Brady had to laugh. "Just tell me you'll do it, Peter."

"I will, but if this blows up in my face—"

"We can both say honestly that you were just doing what I told you and that you had no idea what was going down. You don't, do you?"

"I have a pretty good idea."

"But you don't know."

"No, I don't."

As Brady worked that day, he couldn't stop thinking about having run into Agatha at the convenience store that morning. She had really let herself go. She had walked her five-year-old to the free day care bus stop and had her two younger ones in tow. Without makeup and under a pink baseball cap, she looked twenty years older.

"Jim's on the road overnight," she whispered. "In case you wanted to drop by, I mean."

Brady couldn't imagine anything he'd less rather do.

As he watched her leave the store in her too-short shorts, especially for a big girl, and her flip-flops—even on a chilly autumn morning—he saw his future. The Touhy Trailer Park was like a jail term, and he feared he was a lifer.

But today Brady's ship would come in. There would be enough dope in that afternoon's delivery to set him up as a real player. He could quit this crushing job, get his own car, even his own place. He hated dragging Petey into the middle of it, but it would be only this one time.

Adamsville

"Let's see what the TV is saying about this," Thomas said, flipping on the set.

Just as he did, a flash of lightning killed the power and a horrific clap of thunder shook the house.

"Oh no," Grace said.

"Temporary," Thomas said. "Always is."

"Find some candles. They're going to think we changed our minds and aren't even here."

Thomas laughed. "You don't think they'll see that the whole area is affected?"

He found the flashlight and put candles in the kitchen, the living room, and on the front windowsill.

Addison

The first flash of lightning sent the landscaping crew racing for the truck. The last two there had to ride in the bed—no fun once the rain began—but Brady didn't mind. The only thing he didn't like was that he was an hourly worker, and cutting out early meant less pay. Another reason to get on with his other career.

On the other hand, today was payday, so his check would be waiting at the office. He always splurged on payday, only this time he hadn't even decided how yet. With the profit he could make on the delivery Peter was accepting for him, right about then as a matter of fact, he could party all the time.

About a mile from the office the rain turned to hail, and Brady and his cohort rapped on the window of the cab of the pickup. The driver and the other two workers at first laughed and trash-talked, but finally the truck pulled over and the two in the back squeezed inside.

Five dirty yard workers crammed into a truck made it almost impossible to drive, and of course there ensued endless laughing and jabbing and swearing.

When they finally rolled into the parking lot of the office, however, no one was getting out. The tiny hail pellets had been growing steadily larger, and now they rained like golf balls, drilling deep dents in the hood and imprisoning the laborers.

Suddenly a chunk of ice as big as a lemon shattered the windshield. The five men ducked and tried to elude the freezing gusts blasting through the truck. When the wind rocked the rig and threatened to roll it over, somebody said, "We gotta get out!" and they opened both doors and dashed for the office.

Brady covered his head, taking fierce, stinging blows to his hands until he got inside. As they listened on the radio and watched from the window, the truck was lifted off the ground and rolled up onto its side, then slammed back down. In the distance, high-tension poles swayed and wires snapped, shooting showers of sparks across the highway.

The lights went out, but Brady could still see the havoc as the pea green sky roiled. A generator kicked in and the radio came back on, filled with news of twisters in the area.

Brady ran to the back and looked out into the employee parking lot for his brother's car. Strangely, in that one spot, except for the weird light, no one would have suspected a storm. Hardly any wind. No damage. As soon as the hail stopped, Brady was going to try to get out of there.

Dirk parked at the curb in front of the house, and he and Ravinia came bounding up to the door through the rain, a quickly sogged newspaper serving as a makeshift umbrella. Thomas waited with the door open and helped them in.

"You need a lighthouse!" Dirk said, vigorously shaking Thomas's hand. He embraced Grace, and Thomas noticed her stiffen before hugging him back.

As Thomas expected, Dirk and Rav were in business attire, but Dirk immediately accepted Thomas's offer to shed his suit jacket and tie. He was a hard man not to like, effusive, loud, articulate, funny. He was smart enough to have to be aware of the elephant in the room, but it was apparent he had adopted the son-in-law role and planned to relish it. It was as if he thought the in-laws could hate him if they wanted, but he was theirs to hate.

When the power came back on, Thomas had a fleeting wish it had stayed off. Awkward as this was, it was worse in full light.

Grace served tiny meatballs pierced with toothpicks.

"A nice cold one would go great with these!" Dirk said. "Oh! Sorry! My bad. A nice cold anything, I mean."

Grace brought him a glass of water, which he ignored.

"This is so nice, Mom," Ravinia said, and it warmed

Thomas to see that she too was working hard to make the best of a tense situation.

"We're serving your favorite tonight, Ravinia," Grace said.

Rav grabbed Dirk's arm. "Didn't I tell you?"

"You did. She did, Mom and Dad. Any wonder she's the brightest lawyer in her firm?"

"My firm! In my so-called firm, the partners share cubicles."

Dirk howled. Thomas and Grace smiled. Dinner could not come soon enough.

Addison

The storm blew past the landscaping office as quickly as it had come, and except for the driver's-side mirror and some creasing of the door, the pickup looked little the worse for wear.

Brady picked up his check and hurried out the back. The wind was quickly dying, but on the horizon in the direction he was heading, the sky was pitch-black. He supposed he ought to stop by the restaurant and check on his mother, though she probably hadn't given his safety a second thought.

The highway was crowded, and with six miles to go on Touhy Avenue, it was stop-and-go. Cars from both directions took turns avoiding downed power lines and branches. Emergency personnel were obviously overtaxed; in some intersections civilians were directing traffic.

Brady pulled into the packed parking lot of Judy's Feed Bag, a hash house owned by a guy who had named it after his granddaughter. The place was hopping, every table occupied, but most patrons stared out at the storm as they ate.

"I'm lookin' for my ma," Brady told a girl at the counter. "Erlene."

"Went home. She was worried about you. Said you were off school today and might have been home when the tornado hit."

"One touched down?"

"Tore up your trailer park, so they say. But at least you're all right."

Brady burst from the place and jumped in Peter's car. He tried driving on the shoulder to pass lines of cars, but when he came to obstacles, no one would let him back in. One guy shot him the finger and screamed, "We're all in a hurry, pal, okay?"

Adamsville

Thomas decided on a simple prayer, thanking God for all the blessings of life, including Dirk and Ravinia, and for the provision of food and a wonderful wife and mother to prepare it.

"Amen to that!" Dirk said. "I'm starved."

Thomas found Dirk charming. And while the man seemed to know how to make Grace feel good about herself and her cooking, he seemed a little less affectionate toward Ravinia than Thomas remembered. Of course, he hadn't seen them together all that much, and the first time was before they had even moved in together. The last time he had seen them was at the wedding, and naturally they had been affectionate there.

Maybe they were just settling in, as happened to most couples. And while they were still relative newlyweds, they had been together a long time.

"We have news," Ravinia said.

"Well, hon," Dirk said, "it's not really news yet. I mean, we may have news in a while, but do we really have news yet?"

"What?" Grace said. "You have to say now."

"We're going to try to have a baby next year."

Thomas just sat staring and could tell Grace was doing the same. Why did this surprise him? Wasn't it the natural course of events? Had he hoped that since they were both career people they might put this off, maybe forever, or at least until Ravinia came back to her faith and Dirk became a believer? "Well, that's something, isn't it?" he said.

"You know what trying means!" Dirk said, too loudly. "But that's why it's not really news yet. It'll be news when it works and we have a date to announce. But, as long as we're talking about it, we're hoping something will happen early in the year so we might have a child by this time next year. Cool, huh?"

"Will you stop working then, Rav?" Grace said.

"Oh no. Nobody does that anymore, Mom. No need.

I'll take the appropriate maternity leave; then I'll jump right back in."

"And who will care for the baby?"

"The county provides day care right at the office," Ravinia said. "I can work and see the baby anytime I want. I can take it with me in the morning and back home at night."

Thomas knew Grace's gears were turning and she was deciding how she might care for her own grandchild at least several hours a day.

He knew she was not up to it now and would be even less so in a year, but this was all moot unless and until, as Dirk said, there was anything to report come the new year.

What Thomas was afraid to ask was what, if anything, Dirk and Ravinia had in mind for their child's spiritual life. Would they allow him and Grace to take their grandchild to church? If they were like most modern nonreligious parents, he decided, they would talk a lot about exposing the child to all sorts of ideas and letting him or her decide what to believe.

When that happened, the child generally grew up like the parents and believed either a mishmash of conveniences or in nothing much at all. This was going to be one delicate balancing act. Thomas knew well that this would not be his child. But it would be his grandchild, and he wasn't about to retreat from trying to see that he or she was raised, as the Bible said, in the nurture and admonition of the Lord.

Thomas had left the TV droning in the living

room, and in a brief lull in the conversation, Dirk said, "Did you hear that? Where's the Touhy Trailer Park, and why is it that tornadoes seem to aim at those things?"

"The same funnel that blows through a neighborhood and takes out a tree or two can rip those foundationless little boxes to pieces," Thomas said.

Addison

Brady thought he had been hardened by his years inside. How long had it been since he had felt anything but anger or lust?

But now, as a rent-a-cop in an orange vest vigorously waved him over about two hundred yards from what was left of the gaggle of motor homes that had been his neighborhood, Brady was sick from his gut to his throat.

A thin, halting line of traffic snaked past the place, drivers gawking. Brady had to stay out of that line, because once in it, he would be corralled past, unable to stop, unable to run home, find his mother and brother, and see what had become of the single-wide that had housed them for as long as he could remember.

He pulled off the road, only to find he was blocking an ambulance. The driver blasted his siren, pointing, shouting. Brady moved as far to the right as he could, only to have his right front tire drop off the shoulder and the car slowly slide deep into the ditch.

At least he was no longer in the way.

The ambulance crept past, and there Brady sat. He could imagine it being days before he would be able to find anyone to tow him out. The hail had given way to a cold, steady rain that cocooned the car. On the one hand he was desperate to get home, and on the other he dreaded what he might find.

He couldn't just sit there. If he could help, he had to try. But his door opened only a few inches before striking the side of the ditch. In that instant he was drenched. Brady pulled the door shut and wrenched himself across the seat, tumbling out the passenger-side door into frigid water over the tops of his work boots to his shins. Every step in the sucking mud was an effort.

His first couple of attempts to scale the incline found Brady sliding back down. Finally he climbed atop the hood of the car, then the roof, and leaped up onto the shoulder, nearly into the path of a car. He zigzagged through the traffic to the other side, clods of mud flying up behind him.

He gave a wide berth to the trailer park sign, hanging by a single chain and swaying madly in the wind. The asphalt seemed to boil as millions of huge raindrops caused tiny splashes to rise from the sur-face. Emergency vehicles rimmed the place, and from one high vantage point as Brady began his path toward home, he could plainly see where the twister had barreled through. He had seen carnage like this only on television.

Again, part of him wanted to flee, to race back to the car and fling himself across the backseat. There he would hide his head and try to stay warm and keep any horrible news from invading. He had been close, so close, to a new life. Sure, he was taking risks, getting back into the unhealthy lane, consorting with dope pushers, living on the edge. But so far so good. Brady had a little money with the promise of a lot more on the way. And his parole officer seemed pleased, if wary.

But what if he'd lost a place to live or at least to crash? What would he and his family do?

Brady knew all this worrying was just delaying the inevitable. Deep in the recesses of his soul he was terrified at what he might find at home. It wasn't really his life and his income he was worried about. It was his brother.

"God, please," he whispered as he hurried that way. "I know I don't deserve a thing from You, but please. Not Petey. Please."

If Peter had been home when this happened, it was because Brady had begged him to be. Couldn't the kid have been irresponsible, selfish, rebellious, disobedient once in his life?

Please.

Many trailers lay on their sides, some on their tops, some pushed several feet from their moorings. People Brady knew milled about, eyes vacant, crying, holding each other. The convenience store had had its roof blown off, its front door and window obliterated.

People streamed in and out, apparently still able to buy things.

Emergency workers hurried through the crowds, barking orders, searching for the injured and the dead.

The gas station, where the Laundromat had once been, seemed the lone unscathed place, a strange oasis that had somehow escaped the worst of the damage. Men and women in uniform on squawk boxes made it obvious some emergency crew or another had set up a command post there.

The ravages from the funnel seemed to worsen the deeper Brady got into the park. Two entire streets, once made up of tight rows of modular trailers with tiny picket fences and indoor/outdoor carpeting that had served as pretend lawns, were now just empty ribbons of blacktop. In the distance towered a macabre pile of twisted aluminum carcasses. It was as if the homes had been tossed atop each other one by one.

Such was the devastation that Brady found himself suddenly disoriented, unsure exactly where he was. But there lay a street sign, marking an intersection he knew well. His trailer should be just ahead and left two blocks.

Adamsville

Except for the disconcerting news about a potential addition to their family, Thomas found the meal and the evening going better than he had expected. That

386

was due, he had to admit, to the people skills of Dirk Blanc. Oh, maybe the tall man with the shaved head was a little out of touch with how he came across to others, but he proved gregarious and solicitous. He so praised the dinner that Grace had to finally scold him into stopping.

And he asked Thomas all about his work at the prison, maintaining eye contact and at least acting fascinated, even though Thomas had done all he could to make it sound mundane. Dirk actually convinced Thomas that he had learned much from what little the chaplain had shared about life inside the supermax.

"Thank you, Dad. That gives me a real picture of what Ravinia will be encountering over there. Hey, big ball game on tonight. You follow baseball, do you?"

"Sorry, I can't say that I do," Thomas said. "Just never really got into it."

"Really? Because it looks like there could be a New York subway series this year."

"Subway series?"

"You know, both teams from the same city? New Yorkers can watch all the games just by taking the subway between Shea and Yankee Stadium."

"No kidding."

Dirk threw his head back and laughed. "You have no idea what I'm talking about, do you?"

"I used to watch the Cubs and the Sox now and then when I was a student, if somebody got free tickets."

"Well, you see? If they had both been in the World

Series the same year, that would have been a subway series in Chicago."

Thomas looked puzzled.

"You see what I mean, right?"

"I think so, but what would be the odds they would both make it the same year?"

"I wouldn't even want to try to compute that. But, anyway, Dad, I guess you're not interested in watching the game tonight?"

"Oh, I see! You want to watch a game. By all means."

"Oh no, not if it's only me."

"We can watch, sure."

Thomas tossed Dirk the remote, and as he began changing channels, Grace and Ravinia emerged from the kitchen. "Oh, Dirk," Ravinia said. "Now, no, you promised."

"It's okay with Dad," Dirk said. "Let me just see if there's any score yet."

Thomas had called his late father-in-law Dad. But Grace's father had actually seemed like a second father to him. Thomas didn't feel like Dirk's father at all. Maybe that would come.

41

Brady's little street proved nearly as bad as the obliterated neighborhood he had just come through. Where his trailer had once stood lay only the concrete two-step riser that had led to the front door. Even that was gone from most of the little homesteads.

Brady had always loathed this park and the ugly metal box he called home. But now he felt as devastated as the acreage he stood in. It hadn't been much; in fact it had been a depressing, desolate place he had always longed to escape. But it was also where he'd grown up and the only real home he had ever known.

Would Touhy Trailer Park rebuild? He couldn't imagine it. If he owned a park like this, he'd just leave it in his rearview mirror and make a new start in Florida or Texas or California. What did owners do in situations like this?

Worrying about everything and everybody other than the matter at hand worked at keeping Brady from awful realities only so long. He forced himself to keep moving, and as he scanned the debris for anything resembling his trailer, he came across the figure of a thin, trenchcoat-clad woman, shivering in the rain with her back to him.

Her arms were folded across her chest, and she wore a transparent plastic rain hat. She was staring at the wreckage of a trailer about forty feet away and was apparently unable to talk herself into moving closer.

Brady moved next to her and startled her by putting his arm around her shoulder. It struck him that he had not touched his mother in years.

"Brady," she said, her voice thin and raspy. "You heard from Petey?"

"No. You?"

She shook her head. "No school today. He's with friends somewhere."

"I wish. I think he was here, Ma."

She turned to look at him, and Brady pulled away, hunching his shoulders against the cold.

The trailer was broken in half, lying on its side, familiar contents appearing to have gushed out. Kitchen appliances lay about, closets broken open, clothes and junk spilled here and there. Furniture was soaking up the rain.

"I got to check, Ma. Got to look for him."

"He's not in there, Brady. No possible way."

"I need to make sure. You coming?"

She shook her head.

The closest emergency crew was two blocks away. Brady didn't like the silence that pervaded the pile of former homes that had made up his neighborhood. Some of the residents were elderly. Others were young mothers who stayed home with little kids all day. Had no one survived?

When Brady got to the ripped and shredded aluminum that had been the skin of his trailer, he saw his sawed-off shotgun and some shells strewn about. The toilet lay on its side. The kitchen table was on its top, three remaining legs pointing skyward.

And there, protruding from under the refrigerator, were the torso and legs of Peter.

Brady climbed through the junk and pushed with all his weight, rolling the giant box off his brother. Peter's head had been crushed, and a metal rod of some sort had run him through, just above the abdomen. Unable to keep from shaking, Brady forced himself to press his fingers to the boy's neck, feeling his carotid artery for a pulse.

Brady slid to sit next to the body and hung his head. Racking sobs attacked him, and he rolled over to embrace his bloody brother. Suddenly realizing his mother could see him, he looked up quickly to see her slowly approach.

"Stay there, Ma!" he wailed. "You don't want to see this!"

"Is it Petey?"

"Yeah!"

"Is he dead?"

"Yeah!"

She stopped about halfway and stood staring, hands deep in her pockets. She had never been much of a mother, Brady knew, but nobody deserved this.

He realized the kitchen table was askew and grabbed a leg to see what was underneath. And there it was, that thing that was so important that Brady had made Peter promise to be there to take delivery of it. The top of the cookie tin was gone, but the rest was otherwise intact, packed tightly with small bricks of marijuana, and the bottom—if the pusher could be trusted—lined with packets of metham-phetamine.

Tears streaming, Brady put the tin in his lap and sep-arated the cellophane packs of grass. Sure enough, crystal meth.

If anything should have made Brady Darby fling this garbage into the debris, it should have been the body of his own brother not three feet away. But, Brady realized, the dope and the check in his pocket constituted the entirety of his worldly goods. That and his brother's automobile.

What in the world kind of a brother was he? *Forgive me, Petey. I'm hopeless.*

Brady couldn't just leave his mother standing there in the freezing rain. He emptied the tin and stuffed everything into his pockets, then covered his brother's head with a shirt. He pulled Peter's wallet from his pocket, emptied it of cash—about twenty dollars—and took the driver's license.

"Just a minute, Ma!" he called out, then jogged to an ambulance down the way. He told an EMT about his brother, left the man his own name and Peter's license, and asked him to call his work number to tell him where they would take the body.

Then Brady went back and retrieved his shotgun, tucking it down his pants and grabbing as many shells as he could fit into his jacket pockets.

When he got to his mother, she said, "We had insurance, you know."

Insurance? That was what she was thinking about with her son lying dead? Well, he was no better, covering his own tail and worrying about his dope deals.

"Yeah?"

"Um-hm. I think the trailer was worth like four thousand dollars. That'll give me a down payment on a new one."

Brady wanted to smack her, scream at her. Truth be told, he wanted to shoot her. But maybe this was how parents reacted when they were in shock.

"Where'd you park?" he said. "I'm stuck in a ditch and will need a tow, so . . ."

She started walking. "You think Petey's school insurance covers this?" she said.

"Covers what?"

"An act of God. Sometimes it doesn't, you know. And I don't even know if it's life insurance. Maybe it's just personal injury, something like that. High schools don't insure kids against death, do they? I mean at home?"

Brady glared at her. "What if they do, Ma? Would that be good news? Would that make your day?"

"Well, sure, 'course, in a way. I mean, I don't know how much it'd be, but maybe with that and the four grand, I wouldn't need a loan on a new place."

She was as bad as he was, maybe worse. "So, you remember where your car is?" he said.

"Over there."

"Okay. I'll see ya."

"Thought you needed a ride. I don't even know where I'm going. Do you?"

"I'm sure one of your boyfriends will take you in," he said. "And I'll figure something out. I'll call you when I find out where they're taking Petey."

"And then what am I supposed to do?"

"Have a funeral, Ma! What do you think? Were you just gonna leave him there, hoping somebody would dispose of the body?"

"Well, I can't afford that."

Brady turned on her and found himself screaming, cursing, calling her the vilest things he could think of—and he could think of plenty. She looked surprised, as if she couldn't imagine what might have triggered this.

"Well," she said, "if that's how you feel, don't come crawling to me, looking for a place to live. And by the way, you owe me last month's rent."

"Sue me," he said.

When he got back to where he'd left Peter's car, he prevailed on a tow truck driver to pull him out. He told the man he could pay cash and that he didn't want some other car sliding in there and crushing his. The guy seemed perturbed but apparently agreed it was better to just get it done right then or it might not happen for days.

"I'm going to be living in this car," Brady told him. "Just lost my trailer."

But as the car came sliding up the embankment, a

police officer approached. "I'm going to need to see some ID and proof that this vehicle is yours."

Brady pulled out his wallet and gushed the story of all that had just happened.

"I'm sorry to hear that, son, but until we can confirm your story, I'm going to have to search you, and—"

"Search me why? What did I do? I just lost my home and my brother and—"

"That may all be true, Mr. Darby, but you were seen looting a disaster site, including the body of a victim."

"That was my brother! And that was my place! Whatever I took from there is mine! You can ask my ma! She was just here. And I was giving the EMT my brother's ID, that's all."

"That should be easy to confirm," the officer said. "But meanwhile, hands on the car, feet back and spread 'em."

"You don't need to search me, man."

"You gonna make this hard?"

"No, but see, you're gonna find stuff I'm not supposed to have on me. I just got out of the joint and am on probation."

"What have you got on you?"

"A weapon and drugs, but they're not mine. They were my brother's. He was in deep trouble, doing crimes, and I was trying to help him, you know?"

The cop got on his radio. "I'm going to need backup," he said.

"We're a little thin on personnel," came the reply.

"Roger that, but this is a felony arrest."

In the back of the squad car, hands cuffed behind him, bloody from embracing his brother, Brady lowered his head, praying he could die. If his hands were free, he would have found a way to kill himself. His life as he knew it was over anyway, and he had blamed the drugs and the shotgun on his own dead brother.

42

Adamsville

When Summer Grace Carey-Blanc was born, she was just the tonic for Thomas. It thrilled him to hold the tiny princess, and he chortled at her every look and sound. With an exotic mix of fair skin, dark eyes, and wisps of dark, reddish hair, she was intoxicating. He could barely look away from her curious expressions.

And to see Grace become immediately maternal toward both Ravinia and the baby, well, Thomas found his whole attitude and demeanor changed. Even at work, Gladys said she noticed Thomas's new enthusiasm for life.

"We all wanna see that new baby," Gladys said. "See the little woman what put a smile on your face. But don't you dare bring her to this cesspool. You got to invite us someday, that's all."

Little had changed with Dirk and Ravinia. Thomas sensed more distance between them, yet they both doted on Summer. Grace had the temerity to ask if she and Thomas could have the baby dedicated at Village Church sometime soon, but Ravinia put her foot down. "I don't want to go all lawyerly on you, Mom, but I can use your own logic against you."

"Well," Grace said, "I do want to talk about it."

"Fine. I grew up in church. I know what baby dedication is all about, and it's hardly about the baby."

"Pardon me?"

"Dad said it every time he conducted one of those things. What you're really doing is dedicating the parents to raising the kid for Jesus, right?"

"Well, sure, but—"

"And we're supposed to stand up there pretending to be good soldiers, committing ourselves to the task?"

"I'd certainly like to think the people at Village Church will get to know Summer and love her and want to commit themselves to teaching her and—"

"And so do you."

"Of course," Grace said.

"Then dedicate yourselves, but leave us out of it."

"You mean we *can* dedicate her?"

"Without us? Not on your life! How would that look? You and Dad up there with our baby, making it plain to the world that the heathen parents are nowhere to be seen and oh, the poor child . . . ? No way. You just privately dedicate yourselves to having whatever influence you want on your granddaughter, and yes, we'll let you take her to church now and then."

Thomas and Grace did just that, hoping the day

would come when Summer was old enough to be involved in a church program that Rav and Dirk would be unable to miss.

Brady had really done it this time. Violating his parole in just about every way possible, being found with a deadly weapon *and* ammunition *and* too many drugs for personal consumption, he found himself in the county jail before he could catch his breath.

His aunt and uncle buried Peter at their own expense, and Brady was allowed to attend the funeral, sitting in the pew between two sheriff's deputies. He saw his mother there only briefly, just long enough for her to report that there had been no clause in Peter's school insurance to cover death by act of God. She told him she was taking possession of Peter's car, selling hers, taking the tiny insurance settlement on her trailer, and moving to just outside Nashville, Tennessee, to work in an auto manufacturing plant.

Brady nodded as she talked and shook his head as she left, then was escorted to an unmarked squad car for transport back to his cell. The county jail rivaled Los Angeles County and Cook County in Chicago as the most crowded such facilities in the United States—jam-packed, understaffed, and full of violence, gangs, and drugs.

Brady used his acting skills and gift of gab to get next to, of all people, the head of one of the most notorious black gangs. He told the glowering, heavily tat-tooed fat man—who called himself Tiny—that he wanted to become a member.

"You? Pasty white boy? Prove it."

"How?"

"Lemme give you a tat."

"A tattoo? Oh, I, uh, can't do that, 'cause of my career."

Tiny laughed, his big belly jiggling. "You got a career?"

"Yeah, I'm an actor."

Tiny squinted. "I watch a lot of TV. Never seen you."

"Uh, just regional commercials so far—mostly West Coast—but my agent says I have big potential, so, you know, no tats. And you want me to keep my options open on that front, Mr. Tiny, because it can mean a lot of money for you guys when I get out."

"That so?"

"Yes, sir, and I also have a lot of money stashed away from an armored car robbery I engineered, which was what got me sent here."

Tiny's eyes lit up. "*You* pulled that job?"

With that enticement and more every time he thought of something, Brady bought himself protec-tion from one of the most feared cons in the place. He had no idea what would become of him when he got out and never came through on all his promises. But why worry about tomorrow today? The story of his life.

Of course it was not beyond Brady to play both ends against the middle, putting him in position to risk his life every day. As the only white aide to Tiny, he became both a target of other gangs and vigorously protected. And when the antigang unit at County called Brady in, he saw the opportunity to help himself in new ways.

Lieutenant Dale, head of the task force, sat Brady down and told him that since he was a known gang member, he was missing out on an important opportunity.

"Such as?"

"Early release."

"How would I qualify for that?"

"Few do, but we're processing in over a thousand new inmates a week, and fewer than that are being processed out. We can't expand, and we can't add cells, so all we can do is add newcomers to the cells we have. How many cellmates you got now?"

"Six."

"See? Your cell was built for two, and by next week, you'll have a seventh in there. Guys with worse records than yours are getting out, just due to over-crowding. Don't you want that? 'Cause as a known gang member, you don't qualify."

"But if I don't have protection, I'm dead anyway. See, I'm not really part of the gang. You gotta believe me. I'm just playing Tiny to stay safe."

Lieutenant Dale sat back and slowly looked Brady up and down. "Fact is," he said, "I'm inclined to believe you. You don't look the type. Amazing you've kept from getting hurt this long."

"It's true!"

"You want to prove it? Help us out."

"I'm listening."

"We need information. We have a pretty good idea who's who and where they all fit. But we have to know for sure. If you're as wired in as you say you are—and if you're really just using them—then you can tell us things we would otherwise have no way of knowing. Is that right or not?"

"Sure, and I'd be happy to help. But aren't they going to notice if I keep getting called in here?"

"We can fix that. We'll spread the word that we shook you down for information, even offered you early release, and you turned us down flat out of loyalty. How's that sound?"

"Beautiful!"

"But you have to give us straight stuff on as many of these guys as you can."

Over the next two years, Brady became the most reliable informant the antigang unit had at County. He had been scheduled to be sent to state prison for eight years, but Dale worked to get him released after five, provided he could serve it all at Adamsville County.

"This is where we need you most, and if you stay helpful, it'll shave three years off the other end. But you have to be honest with me, man. You're getting dope, aren't you?"

Brady pressed his lips together, considering his options. He had been honest with this guy all along. So far it was paying off, and if he could really be free in a few years, that's what he wanted. But no one was supposed to stay at County that long. He only hoped the other cons never figured that out.

"Drugs? Me? What makes you ask?"

"I can see it in your eyes, Darby. I just need to know the truth, man."

"Yeah, I'm getting what I need."

"At some point, we're going to need to know how that stuff gets in here."

"You don't want to know."

"You think I'm naive enough to be surprised it's coming from our own people?"

"No, I'm just saying—"

"Here's the thing: you know it's a crime for a convicted felon to possess, let alone use. That alone could get you five or ten more years tacked on. But we both know that if you all of a sudden go clean, you give yourself away.

"Now, we're trying to help each other, Brady, and I like you. So here's what I want from you: a pledge. You promise that when we finally get you out of here, you won't go straight back on the streets as a meth head."

"I don't want to."

"That's not what I said."

"Yeah, but I know myself. I want to be straight with you, and I'm telling you, if I don't have some kind of help, I could be in trouble as soon as I get out. I got no job waiting for me, no family, no girl, no place to live."

"How do you feel about a halfway house?"

Brady shrugged. "Better than nothing. I mean, I got zero else out there."

"There'd be accountability. They'd know where you are, and you'd have to stay clean. They'd help you find work and eventually a place of your own. It won't be much, but you can build from there. Start making yourself a real life."

"I'd try. I sure would."

"Is that a deal? We do what we say we'll do, and you'll do what you say?"

Brady was suddenly overwhelmed with the need to remain transparent with Dale. He was the first since Clancy Nabertowitz who really seemed to believe in him.

"I got to tell you the truth, sir. They're going to really have to keep an eye on me. And I'm going to be going through withdrawal and all, you know. I mean, it's a few years away, but like you say, I can't all of a sudden turn clean in here."

Lieutenant Dale leaned forward. "You ever heard of Hug-a-Thug?"

"No."

"Name came out of LA County. It's a program they have for ex-cons who really want to get their lives turned around. You got to qualify; then you join the program, live in a halfway house, work some, go to

403

classes, study a little, and actually graduate. By that time they have found you some kind of work, and they stay in touch, keeping track of you after that.

"They're pretty proud of their record. Listen, you know how many times you've been in and out of jail. Well, these guys have a good record for avoiding recidivism. Know what that is?"

"Keeping on coming back?"

"Exactly."

"Why they call it Hug-a-Thug?"

"'Cause that's one of the things they do. The teachers and counselors there are handpicked. They're empathetic. They really care, really want to help people."

"And they do a lot of hugging?"

"Can you handle that?"

"As long as I don't have to hug back."

Adamsville

Grace was beginning to really slow down. Her doctor's visits became more frequent, her prescriptions stronger, her treatment more vigorous. The doctor told Thomas to start insisting that she cut her daily activity by at least half and begin a nap regimen.

It was obvious Grace found that restraining, but Thomas enlisted Ravinia in helping enforce the new rules.

"Mom," she said one day, "I will quit bringing

404

Summer if I don't have your solemn promise that you'll let Dad do most of the work, including keeping an eye on her."

As Thomas knew she would, Grace promised anything to keep seeing Summer. She was even allowed to have a third birthday party for her, including inviting Summer's day care friends. Everyone seemed to think it strange that the party was held at Grandma's, but Thomas knew that Ravinia feared there might not be many more such opportunities for Grace.

It wasn't that she was dying, but her strength was ebbing.

That Saturday party marked a new highlight in Thomas's life. Ravinia agreed to let him invite coworkers, and six showed up, including Gladys, who became the life of the party. Summer seemed fascinated by the chocolate-skinned woman in the loud clothes, though the birthday girl kept her distance.

"Come on, little one!" Gladys said, cackling. "I know you've seen my color before!"

"Of course she has," Ravinia said. "The day care center is totally cross-cultural."

"Then where are they? You invite only your kind?" Gladys's eyes were dancing.

Ravinia seemed troubled. "You know, I gave Mother all the names, and we really did invite everybody."

"Maybe they're as scared of this neighborhood as I am," Gladys said, laughing. "What street corner are we on, anyway? Mason and Dixon?"

Thomas was amused by all the activity but had to admit it didn't break his heart to see his friends and the toddlers and their mothers finally leave. The mothers mostly reminded him of Ravinia, and why not? They were all career women in the legal field.

But Summer, despite her friends being there and all the attention lavished on her, had stayed close to Thomas all day. It was as if she had all of a sudden gone from being Grandma's girl to Grandpa's. And it seemed nothing could have pleased Grace more. "I've been praying for this, Thomas," she said.

"So have I. You see how she talks with me, looks at me, smiles at me? And she's so articulate. Did you hear her say she wants to come back to Sunday school soon?"

Grace nodded. "She's going to be a lifelong friend."

Thomas could imagine nothing better, though it pierced him to recall that he and Ravinia had been best friends when she was Summer's age too.

When it was about time for Ravinia and Summer to leave, the toddler fell asleep in Thomas's arms. "Don't go yet," he said. "Let her sleep."

"I don't know, Dad. I promised Dirk he could see her on her birthday."

Thomas shot her a double take. "You what?"

Ravinia clearly looked frustrated with herself. "This wasn't exactly how I wanted to tell you," she said. "Stupid, stupid, stupid."

"Tell us what?" Grace said.

"In here," Thomas said, moving to the living room,

where he sat carefully in his chair, cradling Summer to his chest.

Ravinia and Grace sat on the couch.

"Dirk and I are taking some time apart," Ravinia said.

"You're separated?"

"Not formally."

"What does that mean?" Grace said.

"What?" Ravinia said. "You're not happy? I thought you'd be ecstatic. I know how you feel about Dirk."

"Don't say that, Rav," Grace said. "The last thing we want is for Summer to become the product of a broken home."

"Well, it's not broken yet, but we've got work to do."

"What's the problem?" Thomas said quietly. "Is he seeing another woman?"

Ravinia looked down, and Thomas knew. "Rav, not you."

She nodded.

"Ravinia!" Grace said. "What are you saying?"

"It was nothing serious. It just happened."

"Don't give me that," Grace said. "Nothing just happens. You violated your wedding vows?"

"Yes, and I'm going to hell and will pay for it for all eternity, okay? Does that make you happy?"

"Rav, please. What happened?"

"Dirk and I were both working long hours and not seeing each other much. I thought he wasn't spending enough time with the baby and certainly not with me.

I was lonely. We argued. He stormed out. He'd spend a couple of nights at a friend's and then come back. We'd work it out, forgive each other, and then it would happen again. Just getting on each other's nerves, you know? Well, no, I don't guess you do know. You never did that. I used to think that was so phony, that you were just faking it, not sticking up for yourselves just so you could say you were getting along. I thought normal couples fought. Well, they do. Everybody I know does. Hardly anybody I work with is still even on their first marriage."

"Sad," Grace said.

"But true. That's life, Mom. Real life."

"You're supposed to put others above yourself, and that starts at home."

Ravinia stood and moved to the picture window. "You know what, Mom?" she said, her back to them. "I'm not even going to argue. You guys have always done that. I have to hand it to you."

"I can never tell whether you're being serious or sarcastic, Ravinia," Grace said.

Ravinia turned to face her. "Dead serious, Mom. I admire your commitment to each other. I really do."

"Well, thanks for that, but let's get back to you and Dirk. Have you ended this other relationship?"

"It wasn't a relationship, Mom. It was a one-time thing. But I did tell Dirk about it."

"And what did he say?"

"He didn't say anything. I have never seen such pain in his eyes, and I never want to again. I've written him, talked with him. I feel terrible. I mean, I don't think it was entirely my fault. Don't say it; I know how you feel about that. But he had emotionally left me some time ago. But he's a good man and a pretty good dad. I do love him and want him back. We're working on it."

"How?"

"Counseling. We meet at the counselor's office and we take turns with Summer."

"No wonder she's become so attached to your father."

Adamsville State Penitentiary

On Tuesdays and Thursdays, it was Dirk's turn to pick up four-year-old Summer from day care so she could spend the night with him at his apartment.

On those days, Ravinia arranged her schedule to spend the afternoon meeting with her various charges at the supermax prison. At the end of the day, she found her way to the administrative wing, spent a few minutes bantering with Gladys, the warden's secretary, and then wandered into her father's tiny office at the end of the hall.

Like clockwork, Thomas would hear Gladys's high-pitched cackle and Rav's chuckle, knowing he would soon enjoy—was that the right word?—another melancholy chat with his only daughter, a county public defender.

At some point or another—he couldn't remember

when this started—they had taken to embracing each other when she arrived. Ravinia had said something once about how amusing she found her dad's courtliness, evidenced in his rising when she entered. And one day she had simply wrapped her arms around him, resting her head on his shoulder.

At first it had been awkward. Thomas loved Ravinia deeply and always had—even through her rebellious years. But he had never been physically affectionate with her. He was making up for that with Summer, but he had long feared he could not change the way things had begun with his own daughter.

Ravinia was still not "walking with the Lord," but he had long since quit attributing that to rebellion against her parents. She was, after all, in her late thirties now. He had long believed—and preached—that adults were free, independent moral agents. She had chosen her path, and while she was still at the top of his prayer list, Ravinia Carey-Blanc was certainly free to conduct her life any way she saw fit.

The problem was that it was clear she was not happy. That saddened Thomas to his soul. Ravinia's daughter, his granddaughter, had become the light of his life. She deserved parents who loved each other, lived together, and loved her. One out of three just didn't cut it.

Thomas and Ravinia's twice-weekly chats always seemed to begin and end the same. They would embrace, which after a while he came to cherish. Just looking at her made him smile. She was attractive in her own understated way, well-dressed, and perfectly groomed. And smart? He and Grace had been good students, but Rav was off-the-charts bright.

They would discuss her clients and how hopeless most of their cases were. They laughed at the naiveté of men who could not face the truth about themselves and seemed incapable of telling the truth about anything. Rav had become a fierce opponent of capital punishment and a proponent of convicts' rights—to a degree—and Thomas was pleasantly surprised to find that they could engage in vigorous debate without offending each other. She was full of statistics and arguments and usually quoted them verbatim without notes.

On the home front, Ravinia continued to insist that she and Dirk cared for each other, and while the counseling had become inconsistent, they still talked about someday trying again to make it work. Meanwhile, he lived in a tiny apartment and swore he had never cheated on her, despite, by now, more than a year of separation.

Ravinia claimed the same fidelity, though it had been her unfaithfulness that had led to their problems. Ravinia still insisted that Dirk take some of the blame for that—reasonable at some level, Thomas conceded, but probably also the reason they had not been able to repair the breach.

Thomas never hesitated to tell Ravinia that he saw hope for her marriage only if she returned to a spiritual base and became an example to Dirk to do the same. And she seemed to accept that her father's view would never change and appreciated that he seemed less judgmental all the time.

"In fact," she said one day, "I suppose I would be disappointed if you weren't so consistent."

"Predictable, you mean."

"Well, you're nothing if not that. But your weakness is also your strength."

"Thanks, I think."

Then the discussion always moved to Summer and what a precocious child she had become. Like her mother, she was full of curiosity, peppering every adult in her life with endless questions followed by more questions based on every answer. The mere thought of her brightened Thomas, and Ravinia never seemed to tire of hearing him repeat, "That one, she's going to be something."

Their frequent conversations had so freed Thomas emotionally that he had even taken to letting his guard down and admitting to Ravinia that now, at fifty-nine, he had many regrets. He allowed that his current work—fourteen years being the longest he had ever invested in a single ministry—was the hardest he had ever done. And that the lack of much to show for it wore heavily on him.

Today he was on that theme again, and his daughter seemed to study him. "What were you dreams, Dad, your hopes when you got into the ministry? Did you expect to have some global impact, 'win the world'?"

"Not really. I think I've always been fully aware of

who I am and who I'm not. And if I ever wondered, there was always someone there to tell me."

"Not Mom. She's always been in your corner."

"That she has. We've always known that the journey is more important than the destination, as they say. I just wanted to win people, you know."

She nodded. "Working here has to be awful, then."

"It's pretty rough. Some men pretend to listen. Some have even prayed with me and then started a study program with me. But not one has persuaded me in the end that anything took or stuck or that he was serious. Each had his own agenda."

"And yet you're still at it. Still singing with Mom?"

"You bet. Those are the most precious times we have these days. Mostly we just continue our love affair with our eyes."

Ravinia cocked her head and covered her mouth. When she pulled her hand away, her lips were trembling. "That's about the sweetest thing I've ever heard you say."

Thomas realized, to his great delight, that after more than a year of these regular meetings, he and his own daughter had become friends and confidants. In many ways this unexpected relationship so late in his life had become an oasis. He looked forward to their every meeting and was disappointed anytime it was postponed.

Ravinia, despite the pressures of being separated and shuttling her daughter back and forth between her husband and her parents, not to mention helping out with the care of her mother a couple of times a week too, also found time to do pro bono work.

Thomas was more than impressed; he knew that work as a public defender—especially regularly defending some of the dregs of society—was not much more than pro bono in itself. She and Dirk had to be struggling to make ends meet, especially with both of them having to pay rent.

Ravinia's helping with Grace fell into the same category. She could have easily begged off of that or cut way back, citing time pressures, Summer, marriage counseling, whatever. But she never shirked her duty. Whenever she was at her parents' home, she was cooking, cleaning, waiting on Grace.

Rav would sit with her mother, talk with her, read to her, bathe her, even do bedpan duty. Nothing was beneath Ravinia. Amazingly, when Grace asked, Ravinia would even sing old hymns with her, harmonizing as she had learned as a child.

From the leased hospital bed Thomas had moved into their bedroom, Grace was often too weak to converse. But she would sing softly or hum all hours of the day.

The highlight of her week, however, was Saturday, when Ravinia would bring Summer by to see Grandma before carting her off to Dirk's. Somehow the rambunctious youngster had come to understand that she had to tone down her enthusiasm when visiting Grace. She would sit still and talk softly and— when allowed—actually crawl into bed next to

414

Grandma and assure her that she was there and that everything would be all right.

Thomas wondered if Summer would always possess that gift of mercy and maybe someday become a doctor or a nurse.

"Grandma," Summer said, "who watches you when Grandpa is at work?"

"Wonderful friends from church," Grace said. "They love Jesus and they love me."

"If they ever can't come, I will."

43

Adamsville County Jail

Brady Darby was being processed out after his longest single stretch ever behind bars.

A black girl with a look that said she had seen and heard it all sat behind a computer and passively gazed at him, perched on a chair with one of his knees bouncing. He needed some meth, and he wasn't likely to get any before arriving at the halfway house in his new civvies with a modest amount of cash in his pocket.

Thirty years old, and that constituted the extent of his worldly goods.

"Anybody need to be informed of your release?" the girl said, long, ornate nails poised on the keyboard.

"Haven't heard from my ma since I been in here," he said. "Maybe my aunt Lois."

"You got a phone number for her?"

"No, but I remember her address."

"Let me have it and we'll try," she said. "You know where you're going, right?"

"Some Hug-a-Thug place is all I know."

"Serenity in Addison."

"Addison, really? That's where I grew up."

"Mm-hm."

Well, that clearly made her day.

She gave him a thick manila envelope and instructed him to follow a colored line on the floor to a waiting area for a van. A corrections officer used a wand to scan the bar code on his envelope, and Brady was directed out a door that led to an underground garage.

As he joined half a dozen others waiting for the van, Brady shivered in the cool air. A couple of the others chatted, but Brady avoided eye contact. He just wanted to get aboard and see sunlight for the first time in years.

When the van finally emerged at street level, Brady shaded his eyes, and when he grew accustomed to the light, he didn't recognize the area around the county jail. Everything had changed. Five years before, he had arrived at a facility that seemed isolated in an industrial park. Now the street was crowded with chain restaurants, shops, and condos.

The first parolee was dropped at a Greyhound station and greeted by a couple of thugs who would no doubt have him back in the joint within twenty-four hours. The same would be true for Brady if not for this program.

He was cautiously hopeful. He had a craving for dope and a woman and any kind of excitement he hadn't had for five years. But he was going to give this thing a chance. Still, he'd learned not to turn over any new leaves or even make any unrealistic promises to himself. His only goal was to never get himself busted again.

Brady knew he wasn't ready for total freedom and might not be for a long time. Accountability, Lieutenant Dale had emphasized. Well, if that's what it took to transition a guy like him from the joint to sobriety and then to real outside freedom, Brady could handle that. He wanted that.

Two more men were dropped at the airport, met by men in suits. Brady had no idea what that meant. Relatives? Friends? Someone who had promised them help or jobs? Flying somewhere—that sounded cool.

"Next stop, Serenity!" the driver called out.

Brady glanced at the other three parolees. Maybe they'd be program mates.

"That where you're goin'?" one said.

The others nodded.

"Me too," Brady said, and they all traded fist taps.

"Should be interesting," the first said.

"I'm not expecting much," another said.

I am, Brady thought as he peered out the window. The van cruised past his old haunts on Touhy Avenue. He felt like an alien.

And the old trailer park? It was now the Addison RV and Camper Resort, jammed with row after row of all manner of the same, hooked up to power and water for the weekend or for a few weeks. Looked like a nice place to live, only no one lived there longer than a few days at a time anymore.

Adamsville

One Saturday Ravinia insisted on coming back after dropping Summer off.

"You don't have to do that, Rav," Thomas said. "You know I can manage."

"No, I want to talk to you. I'll be back."

Thomas did not understand how Grace slept through the night anymore, after having been in bed most of every day. Even now, as he sat in the living room watching for Ravinia's return, he could hear Grace's deep breathing.

When Rav arrived, she strode from her car with a look that evidenced a serious purpose. What was it that could not wait until their next meeting at ASP? Bad news about her and Dirk? Thomas hoped not. He believed the best chance for Rav and Dirk spiritually was for them to come back together.

Ravinia breezed past her father with a "Be-right-with-you-do-you-want-anything?"

He shook his head and heard her making herself some tea. Something felt right about his daughter treating their home as her own.

Finally she sat across from him in the living room, cup and saucer in her lap. "This may surprise you, Dad, but I need to tell you there are things I miss about my faith. Now don't go getting excited. I'm just saying I miss . . . I don't know, I guess I miss Jesus. He was the best part of the whole deal."

"I can't argue with that. He *is* the whole deal."

"How I wish that were true, but I'm not here to reignite old arguments. It's just that I want you to take Summer to church and Sunday school every week, starting tomorrow. I'll watch Mom Sunday mornings."

"Oh, Rav, come with us. I can easily get someone from the church to—"

She held up a hand. "Don't, Dad. I just don't want to be responsible for Summer missing out on something that was once so important to me. I'm not coming back, maybe ever. I'm not ready, and that's what I want to talk to you about."

"I'm listening."

She had been speaking directly and quickly, as if she had something specific on her mind, and yet now Ravinia suddenly stalled.

Finally she set her cup down. "Dad, you and Mom are the reason I'm no longer on good terms with God."

Thomas had heard that before, years ago. As it would with anyone, it triggered his defenses. He fought to keep from challenging her, defending if not himself then Grace for sure. He knew what he and his wife were: old fogies, conservatives. Some called him and his kind fundamentalists. And sure, of course they had made mistakes with Ravinia. But she couldn't, shouldn't, blame them.

Yet this was as close as they had gotten to any real discussion of God in years. "I'm still listening," Thomas said.

She raised her brows. "I know you are. You've been saying that a lot lately, and I sense it's true. I didn't feel listened to a lot as a child, especially as a teenager. I mean, I know I didn't have much to say, much of value anyway. But you and Mom had an answer for everything. Some verse or some hymn or some platitude. It didn't have to make sense, as long as it was common knowledge. But you're listening more and talking less these days, Dad."

"Glad you've noticed. You know, the older you get, the less you're sure about."

"Tell me about it. But here's what I'm saying: your faith is so simple and pure and straightforward that I can't criticize you for it. My problem is that God seems not to care about you."

"How can you say that, Rav? Having Summer here is a gift from God. And I have work, a decent income. We love our church. We're fine."

"You're *not* fine! You've said yourself that you haven't seen any results for your labor in years! And it hasn't been just since you started working at ASP. I don't see much accomplished there from my efforts either, and I don't expect to. But what about all your years in all those pastorates? All you've got to show for that are horrible, petty people who took and took and took and used you and Mom up, never once giving."

"Oh, there were those—"

"Of course there were, but they were outnumbered by the ones who wanted you as puppets, to keep things the way they had always been. For as long as I can remember, and even after I had left home, every one of your pastorates ended the same way. In disappointment. In unfairness."

"People are human, Rav. You can't expect—"

"You *can* expect better than that, at least once, somewhere along the line. Dad, I saw you give and give. You never quit, and if you ever even got discouraged, you never let on. But how long does the wilderness experience have to continue? Is it literally going to be forty years for you, and then, what, will God still not allow you to enter into any promised land?"

"The only land promised me is on the other side."

Ravinia sighed. "A nice sentiment, but not good enough."

"Heaven is not good enough?"

"Well, if you buy into that and it turns out to be true, I'm sure it will be wonderful for you, but I'm talking about the here and now. You should have more than two good decades left. Can't God cut you some slack, give you a break, let a few crumbs drop off His table? Maybe you can handle this; that's your nature. But watching from my vantage point just makes me bitter."

Ravinia was plainly fighting emotion. Was it possible there was more?

"What is it, Rav?"

"It's Mom. I can hardly bear to see her this way. Why her? What has she done? I mean, all right, if I'm going to be honest, she has driven me crazy over the years. It was as if she never let me grow up, be my own person. She had an answer for everything, and frankly, I never thought she used the brain God gave her. Did she ever acknowledge the other side of any issue? To her there was always one and only one answer to every question. It must be nice to be that sure of everything, and I know she meant well.

"But I wanted her to think. I didn't expect her to be so open-minded that she changed her bedrock views. I wouldn't have respected that. But to at least acknowledge that people who disagree have brains and hearts and souls too—was that too much to ask?"

"There's something to be said for simple faith."

"I'm not just talking about that. And after all that vitriol, this next isn't going to make sense, but just bear with me and let me get it out. Where I was going with all that frustration over Mom and the way she thinks—or doesn't think—is that I have never once questioned her motives.

"All right, as a bratty teenager, I probably did. But not once since I left home have I doubted that Mom

422

loves me and you and God, and that with her, what you see is what you get. Believe me, I've learned the hard way that there aren't too many people you can say that about these days. But she's pure gold."

"When you talk of her like that, Rav, that's the woman I recognize. That is the love of my life."

And finally Ravinia broke down. "Don't you see, Dad? I love her too! I have come to accept her just as she is—pure, selfless, loving, a servant. Maddeningly perfect. But look what's happened to her. How does any of it make sense? If anyone deserves to be in that bed, becoming dependent on others for their very existence, it's me! Don't you *ever* question God? Look what He's done to—okay, look what He's *allowed* to happen to Mom, the love of your life.

"You have pledged your life to God, and this is what happens to your wife? I don't get it, and frankly, I'm not going to get over it, Dad. How can I respect a God like that?"

"Please don't say that, Rav. You know your mother and I believe we deserve nothing but death and hell, so anything short of that is a bonus. We have so much to be thankful for."

Ravinia rose and stretched and took her cup and saucer back to the kitchen. "Thanks for hearing me out. I know it wasn't what you wanted to hear, but at least I feel like I can be honest with you."

"You can. And you must know I'd like the opportunity to debate the point. . . ."

"Maybe someday. I've got to go."

Brady had hoped Serenity, especially with a name like that, would look like the idyllic facilities he'd seen on TV and in movies. Maybe it would have a long, tree-lined road leading to a huge circular drive before a massive pillared colonial brick building. People in white coats would be strolling with bathrobed patients as they worked together to fix all that ailed them.

In fact, Serenity proved to be a three-story brownstone, though not the kind you'd see in the ritzier areas of New York City or Chicago. No, this was a rather stark structure with heavy-gauge steel screens on the doors and windows and a very shallow front lawn—if it even could be called that—of shrubs and sod, enclosed by a tall, heavy, black iron fence and locking gate.

As soon as the van rolled up outside, the driver chirped, "Welcome to your new home, gentlemen, and I wish each of you all the luck in the world."

He leaped out to open the side door, and as Brady and the others got off, a couple emerged from the brownstone, went through a rather complicated procedure to unlock the gate, and held it open.

The man was tall and broad with a black goatee and curly hair to match. He wore a sleeveless denim jacket that exposed tattoos from his hands to his shoulders.

The woman was only a couple of inches shorter, also dressed in denim, and was robust with sandy blonde hair going gray.

424

They appeared to be in their early to midforties, and both were beaming. She did the talking. "Welcome, welcome, welcome," she said, shaking each man's hand. "I'm Jan and this is my husband, Bill. Introduce yourselves to him. I know even a broken-down old lady like me looks good to guys who have been locked up as long as you have, so I like to show off my guy and make it clear from the get-go that I'm not available. Everybody clear on that?"

"I am," Bill said, and Brady got the impression that was their stock joke.

When Brady shook Bill's hand, the man's eyes bored into his and made him look away. "You're welcome here," Bill said. "You do your part, and we promise to do ours."

The men were led inside and introduced to other staff, who appeared to be mostly just custodial or clerical. A few other men milled about, some sweeping, one mopping, and they seemed happy enough.

Brady noticed that Bill never left Jan's side as she asked the four newcomers to follow her upstairs. "We like to give each of our new guests their own small room after you've been living in a steel dorm for so long," she said. "The bathroom is down the hall. Be considerate and work out with the others when you want to use it."

Brady liked being called a guest. But he was getting antsier for some dope. His last taste of meth had been just before he processed out, and that was too long ago. He had come prepared to fight through his cravings and start right in on staying straight, but just then he would have done any drug in sight.

As if he could read Brady's mind, Bill waggled a finger and beckoned him to follow. He showed Brady to his room, no bigger than a cell at County, but with a wire-meshed window, drapes, a nice pastel yellow on the walls, a single bed, and a chair and desk. There was also a small closet. "I know you haven't got anything to store in there yet, but you will."

Brady couldn't stand still.

"Listen, Darby, you suffering?"

"Yeah."

"What've you been on?"

"Meth."

"At County?"

Brady nodded.

"That's the good news. You weren't likely getting good stuff, so you might have it a little easier. We got something that can help. You need it right now?"

"Unless you want me to go out that window, yes, sir."

"All right, settle in here and I'll be back to get you."

"Settle in?"

"Just get used to your surroundings. Bet it's been a while since you've been in a room by yourself."

"Try five years."

"There you go. Just take a breather. I'll be right back, I promise. I know what you're going through."

"Seriously?"

"Oh yeah. Drugs? I did 'em all, pal."

426

"You serve time?"

"Time was my middle name."

"How long you been straight, sir?"

"Coming up on ten years. And call me Bill."

"Thanks. And your wife? Same history?"

"Not even close. I met her in a house like this one. She's a social worker, been straight and sober her whole life. Got me cleaned up, then got me into this work. Nothing better. This succeeds, man, if you do your part, as I say."

"Think I can find a wife here?"

Bill laughed. "You never know. 'Course our guests are all men, but when we have group sessions, we get a mix of all kinds from the outside. Keep your eyes open. Just remember, the worst love combination of all is two addicts."

Brady opened the drapes all the way and squinted into the sun. He raised the window. Wow. Except for the wire mesh, it was nice.

He opened his envelope and spread the contents on the desk. It was good to just sit and read something, even if it wasn't much, just stuff about the halfway house. It said that Bill and Jan were in charge and pretty much handled everything—the counseling, the classes, all that. And they had all kinds of orbital professional personnel to help with physical and mental issues.

Brady was so used to doing what he was told, going only where he was allowed, and keeping his nose clean that he wasn't sure he should even venture out of his room. He just wanted to wander down the hall and check out the bathroom. He hoped it had a nice shower. Did he dare?

He poked his head out and looked both ways. No one was around. He crept toward the bathroom, feeling free but also nervous. Could he get in trouble for this? Bill had told him to wait, that he would be right back. But Brady would be able to hear him coming up the stairs.

The bathroom proved plain but big, and the shower looked great. He would enjoy that.

When Brady heard footsteps on the stairs, he rushed back to his room, getting there just as Bill appeared. "Sorry, man," Brady said. "You said to wait, but I was just—"

Bill put a hand on Brady's shoulder. "Chill, bro. It's all right. At orientation we'll tell you the only places around here that are off-limits. Otherwise, treat this as your home. Okay?"

"Okay, I just—"

"It's your home, Brady. Really. Stay out of the kitchen and the medical office unless invited, and of course you can't leave without an escort. Otherwise, inside you need to get used to coming and going as you please. Now the nurse is on duty and she has something that will help your cravings. Follow me."

On the way down the stairs and through the large dining room, Bill told Brady, "You know, you earned your spot here. If you were doing dope inside, you couldn't have been doing it without your sponsor's knowledge, so it was part of whatever you were doing to cooperate. You're here because they believe they can trust you and that you're a good candidate for success. It's time you started looking at yourself in that way."

"I appreciate that. Man, something smells good."

"Dinner is family style, and believe me, it's always good."

Bill introduced Brady to a plump young nurse he guessed to be Italian or Greek. If he hadn't been so strung out, he might have concentrated on her. On the other hand, despite all the talk about trust and coming and going as he pleased, it was not lost on Brady that there was at least one sweeping camera in a corner of the ceiling of every room. No one was getting away with a thing in here.

The nurse proved efficient. She shook his hand and pointed to a chair. Once he was seated, she pulled out a card. "Methamphetamine?"

He nodded. "Not good stuff, though," he said.

"Of course not. Not inside. Pill or powder?"

"Just pills."

"So, no snorting or injecting."

"No, ma'am."

"How long?"

"About three years."

"How dependent?"

Brady shrugged. "I need it and want it; that's all I know."

"What's it like when you don't get it?"

"Like now. Anxious, irritable, want it more than I want anything else."

"Your release physical shows you in fair health despite the dependence. That's good. We have medication for you. It'll help, but you're going to go through withdrawal for about forty-eight hours."

"Really? That's all? I can handle that; I know I can."

44

Adamsville

Thomas assiduously avoided burdening Grace with his troubles. But she didn't appear to need him to keep up her spirits. While her body deteriorated, her mind seemed sharp and her interests keen. She always wanted the latest news from the church, from the family, and from his work.

The women's missionary society had taken on what they called the privilege of attending to Grace during the day when Thomas was at work. He took over later in the afternoon, and of course Ravinia spelled him Tuesday and Thursday evenings. Needless to say, it fell to him to be with her the rest of the night until a volunteer arrived at dawn. Though by nature a private person, Thomas couldn't imagine being able to cope without the help.

He had traded his and Grace's old double bed for a single he pushed to the wall to allow plenty of room to come and go from her bedside. The doctor urged him to use the bedpan only as a last resort and to help her to the bathroom at least twice every twenty-four hours, averring that even that little exercise would do wonders for her circulation, her soft tissue, and—as important—her state of mind.

Thomas was amazed at the latter, as she never seemed to complain except to rue that she had become so dependent on so many people. "Oh, to be able to simply do things for myself again," she would say.

Thomas fought to hide his despair over her condition. It did her no good to see it in him, and he could tell that his discomfort troubled her more than her own. Her voice was weak and she spoke softly, often seeming to have to recover and build strength before speaking again. But she loved to ask questions and seemed fascinated—and hopeful—about his frequent conversations with Ravinia. "I keep praying," she said.

"I know you do."

"I pray for you all day. Do you feel it?"

Thomas hesitated in spite of himself. He wanted to tell her that yes, of course he felt her prayers, was buoyed by them, energized, encouraged, uplifted. "I, uh, know you pray for me, Gracie, and I appreciate it more than I can say."

That was hardly convincing, and he knew it. And if he wasn't sure, he could see it in her face. "Don't spare me, Thomas. You're still struggling in your work, aren't you?"

He shrugged and nodded. "I know I'm doing what I have been called to do, so I have not lost any of my resolve."

"But you have lost the joy."

How he wanted to deny that. She didn't need this burden. "I just want to reach someone," he said. "Anyone."

He lowered his head, then had to cover his eyes when she began to sing, slowly and softly:

> Sometimes I feel discouraged,
> And think my work's in vain,
> But then the Holy Spirit
> Revives my soul again.
>
> If you cannot preach like Peter,
> If you cannot pray like Paul,
> Just tell the love of Jesus,
> And say, "He died for all."
>
> There is a balm in Gilead
> To make the wounded whole;
> There is a balm in Gilead
> To heal the sin-sick soul.

Serenity Halfway House

A week into Brady Darby's time at Serenity, he noticed a new spring in his step, and for the first time in years he believed he understood what hope was.

At orientation, he and the other newbies were treated like men, like adults, like the responsible citizens they were expected to become. Brady learned he would be required to be up at a certain time every day, to be showered and shaved and dressed and ready for chores immediately after breakfast. He would sweep and mop and do yard work, as well as take his turn doing kitchen duty and even laundry.

Brady wondered if anyone would rebel against this. At times it felt juvenile and confining, but he knew he had brought this on himself. With every motivational class taught by Bill and every group therapy session led by Jan, the men were encouraged, treated with respect, and expected to succeed.

That had helped during his first forty-eight hours, through all the side effects that went with the medication prescribed to treat his meth addiction. At least they didn't expect him to kick cigarettes. The men had to smoke outside and clean up their own mess, and they were reminded often that if they failed here and were ever sentenced to a supermax facility, they would have the fun of quitting smoking without any help. No nicotine patches or gum, no counseling, no tapering off. Just cold turkey and all that that entailed.

Brady was fascinated to see men who looked like younger versions of Bill—muscled, tattooed, defined features, a deep, painful look in their eyes—turn from scowling to smiling. It was as if they were eager to please. He felt it himself.

Was it possible he could get through all these classes

and courses and therapy sessions and actually graduate, get a certificate of completion? Before, that
would have seemed silly, a sorry substitute for a high
school diploma. But now Bill was urging the men to
start thinking about getting their GEDs and then even
considering junior college or a trade school.

Brady had for so long been just a druggie, he had to
think about what he might do with his life in the
straight world.

He envied Bill and Jan; they seemed to genuinely
care for each other. Life had passed Brady by in many
ways, and now he wondered if he would be attractive
to any woman. Being a con had been no kind of life,
but at least it was an identity. People who knew him
knew him as a bad guy, a tough guy, somebody you
didn't want to mess with.

What was he now? Happy, hopeful, earnest, perhaps
finally getting some traction in the real world. But
who was he? There were days, he had to admit, when
he felt like a sap, like the yokels he had always criti-
cized. Dorks, stooges, nerds. He felt like a goody two-
shoes, whatever that meant. Was that the price for
staying out of prison and actually making something
of his life? Could he be cool and respected without
being a criminal?

One afternoon following a class Bill taught on maintaining one's composure during a job interview, Brady
was in his room studying—actually studying—his
notes. He had scribbled the list from what Bill had
written on the board, trying to memorize or at least

settle in his mind all the things one had to know to impress a potential employer. Could he do it?

He had to be well groomed, dress appropriately, maintain eye contact, smile, listen, not talk too much, be open and honest . . . the list went on and on. It had been almost comical to see tattooed Bill with his goatee and long, curly hair talking about how to present oneself in a corporate setting. "Rule number one," Bill had said, "you definitely don't want to look like me."

Most intriguing to Brady was Bill's counsel on being straightforward. "I would tell the interviewer, 'Look, I no longer have anything to hide. I'm an ex-con, and I served this many years for this crime. I have no excuses and no one to blame but myself, but I'm a new man, and I'm eager for a chance to prove it. If you give me this opportunity, I will accept any safeguards or restrictions that make you feel comfortable until I earn your trust. I successfully completed the intense rehabilitation program at Serenity Halfway House, and here are my certificate and my references, whom I encourage you to call personally.'

"See?" Bill said. "Everything on the table. No surprises. The first time they suspect you've left something out or are trying to pull something, they move to the next candidate."

Brady felt as if he was really digesting this stuff. He couldn't imagine himself sitting across from a hiring agent without making up some shiny history and ignoring the fact that he was a career criminal, but it was a concept.

"Brady Darby?" It sounded like Jan calling from the bottom of the stairs.

Brady rushed to the landing. "Yes, ma'am."

"There's a Carl and Lois here to see you."

Brady bounded down the stairs. He embraced his aunt and vigorously pumped his uncle's hand. He couldn't quit smiling or telling them how great it was to see them and what a surprise it was. "I thought you'd make me come your way again," he said, laughing and leading them to a front room where they sat on couches to talk privately.

"Well, I would have, Brady," Lois said, "but we kept checking on you and heard good things. We had to see for ourselves, and I gotta tell you, you look great."

"You do," Carl said.

"Do I really? I feel good. I'm learning a lot. I don't know where I was when I was younger, but I sure hated sitting in classes. Now I'm soaking up everything these people have to offer."

"We're trying to see if we can come get you some Saturday night and have you at our home overnight so you can come to church with us."

Brady's smile froze. It was always about church. "Yeah," he said. "That'd be cool. What'd they say?"

"There's all kinds of hoops we've got to jump through. We have to prove we're blood relatives, sign our lives away promising to not let you out of our sight, report any suspicious activity, have you back here by a certain time, all that."

"That's way too much hassle, Aunt Lois. It's all

436

right. I'll be out of here in a few months, and I can come then."

"Nonsense, Brady. You need to start gradually seeing what the real world is like again. Anyway, you want to meet some nice girls, don't you?"

"You have no idea. 'Course, whether they want to meet me is another thing."

"Oh, you'd be surprised. If they know you've served your time and are on the straight and narrow again, loving Jesus, going to church, all that . . ."

"Yeah, well . . ."

"Where do you go around here?"

"They've got a list we can choose from, but you have to arrange for somebody to go with you. I just join the—what do they call it?—interfaith deal they have right here."

"What's that?"

"Some guy from a local seminary comes in and gives a thing he calls a homily, kinda like a sermon. Just as boring but a little shorter, know what I mean? Doesn't say much. Then he tells us to have a quiet time and pray to whoever we want to however we want to. It's all right, I guess."

"It most certainly is not, Brady. He doesn't even sound like a Christian, does he, Carl? I'm going to keep pushing to take you to our church, okay?"

It wasn't okay, but what was he supposed to say? "If you want."

"There's a girl we know," Aunt Lois said, "about your age, maybe a year or two older, whose late father became a rescue-mission preacher and jail minister when he came back to the Lord after serving time. She would be sympathetic to what you're going through and wouldn't judge you on your past."

"Never been married?"

Carl shook his head, then turned and looked out the window. Brady wondered what to make of that until Aunt Lois said, "She's got a bit of a weight problem, but she's a wonderful person and has a nice smile."

"Yeah, well, maybe I'll meet her sometime."

"I'll send you a picture. By the way, what do you hear from your mama?"

Brady snorted. "Ma? You couldn't prove by me she's even alive. I know she's in Tennessee. Haven't seen her since Petey's funeral."

Aunt Lois and Uncle Carl glanced at each other. "You seriously haven't heard from her since then?"

"Can't blame her. Who wants a son behind bars?"

"You really don't know she's married again?"

"You kidding me? I know nothing."

Carl leaned forward. "She's on husband number three, Brady. And Nashville's a distant memory. She's waitressing again. In Little Rock. Her husband drives truck."

"Hold on. Number three?"

"My," Lois said, "you *have* been out of touch. She married some guy in Nashville a few months after she got there. Said he owned a grocery store. Turned out he just worked there, and not often. He beat her, and she eventually had to get a restraining order on him."

438

"That doesn't break my heart."

"Brady! She has her faults, but nobody deserves that."

"She does."

"All right, we're not going to discuss this. Thing is, this new guy at least has a steady job, but he's gone most of the time. She's not well, you know."

"No?"

"Some kind of a lung thing, and of course she still won't quit smoking."

Brady hoped it would kill her, but he knew Aunt Lois wouldn't want to hear that.

"Well, Brady, it's great to see you doing so well. We have high hopes for you. Pray our request will go through and we can come get you for church one of these weekends."

He'd pray about it all right, but certainly not in the way Lois hoped.

On the other hand, they were the only family Brady had and maybe his only friends too. It had been wonderful to see them, even if it meant his mother would be on his mind for a few days until he could find something else to think about.

A brief letter arrived a few days later, including what Aunt Lois referred to as good news and bad news. Brady agreed but would have ascribed opposite adjectives to each.

Aunt Lois's good news was a picture of one of the plainest women Brady had ever seen. If she was less than ten years older than he was, no one could tell. He shook his head. She probably was wonderful, devout, and who knew, might make a great wife. But even though he knew he was shallow to be so concerned about mere looks, a guy should be attracted to a woman to consider a future with her, shouldn't he?

Aunt Lois's bad news was that they had received a cordial but definite rejection of their request to take Brady away from Serenity overnight "at this time." The Department of Corrections had reminded them that Brady Darby was still officially a ward of the state but that it would be happy to reevaluate the request in due time.

"They didn't say when 'due time' was," Aunt Lois wrote. "But if we all keep praying, it'll happen. Meanwhile, you hang in there. I have enclosed your mother's address, in case you want to get in touch with her. I'm sure she'd be glad to hear from you and know you're out and doing well."

Fat chance. If his mother wanted to hear from Brady, she'd have to let him know herself. He didn't expect to hear a thing from her until she thought he had a job and something to offer.

Aunt Lois closed: "I have also included the address of the young woman in the picture. Why not get acquainted by mail? You never know what might come of this."

Brady tossed everything in the trash.

45

Adamsville

Thomas stood cautiously and without expectation outside the cell of a short, forty-year-old illegal from Guatemala. Jorge Lopez had been incarcerated at the Adamsville State Penitentiary for six years, though Thomas had a hard time imagining this innocuous-looking con pulling six armed robberies and making four escape attempts from other facilities before being sentenced to life here.

Jorge had never asked to see Chaplain Carey.

Until now.

Jorge had studied English as a second language by correspondence, resulting in a strange but most understandable accent. Thomas thought it made the man sound sophisticated, almost courtly. He didn't slur or use contractions, and he pronounced every syllable with care.

"I appreciate very much your honoring my request, Reverend Carey. I am curious as to what privileges might be afforded a lifer such as myself who converts to your brand of American evangelical Christianity."

"Let me be sure I understand what you're asking, sir. Are you curious about the Christian faith, Jorge, and specifically evangelicalism?"

"Oh no. I was raised Catholic, was baptized and confirmed. But I understand that evangelicalism is more accepted and may win me privileges that Catholicism may not."

"In the system, you mean."

"Yes. I am not scheduled for even a parole hearing for thirteen more years. Is it true that if I were to convert, I might see that expedited earlier?"

"No. In fact, the opposite is true. I'm afraid it would appear manipulative on your part and could work against you. You wouldn't want me vouching for you."

"Very well, then. Thank you very much and I apologize for taking your time."

"Not at all. Tell me, Jorge, do you understand the differences between Catholicism and Protestantism?"

"Oh yes. I have studied both very carefully."

"How would you characterize the differences?"

"Well, the one seems more liturgical, creedal. The other more personal. I believe there are more similarities than differences, but I also understand where Protestantism originated and what Martin Luther believed was needed to reform the church."

"You do?"

"Yes."

"And does one or the other appeal more to you, prison privileges aside?"

"Yes. Catholicism."

"Interesting. You know, many men here misunderstand Protestantism to be the faith of grace and see Catholicism as the faith of works."

"Misunderstand?"

"I mean," Thomas said, "that they carry the differences to the extreme, thinking that if you are saved by faith and not works, you are free to live however you wish, once you have your eternal destiny decided."

"I see. And yet I find Catholic literature also emphasizes grace, though perhaps not as exclusively."

"You are very perceptive, Jorge. I find that many who choose between Catholicism and Protestantism choose the latter because they find it more accessible, even in a way easier."

"I can see that. But I suppose I prefer the faith I grew up in as a child."

"Do you still practice it? You have never asked for any literature that I am aware of."

"No. I am no longer a religious person."

"Yet you were once?"

"Yes, as I said, as a child. I loved going to church with my parents and brothers and sisters."

"Do you fear for the fate of your soul?"

"No. I believe when we die, we are simply gone, body, mind, and soul."

"You realize your religion does not teach that."

"Of course. As I have said, I am no longer religious in any manner."

"So your question was wholly based on whether a new allegiance might benefit you somehow here."

"Correct."

"I appreciate your honesty, Jorge. I would be remiss if I did not tell you that I believe God loves you and that the Jesus you worshiped as a child died for your sins that you might have eternal life by believing in Him."

"I know that is what your faith teaches."

"Yours too, Jorge."

"No. As I told you, sir, I have no faith."

"Might you reconsider?"

"I cannot conceive of it."

"Well, you know how to reach me."

Thomas could barely put into words, even for himself, how he felt heading back to his office. The man had not been contentious or antagonistic. He was not despairing or angry as Henry Trenton had been so many years before. But Thomas thought Jorge's views were the epitome of the thinking of these men. It was all about what was in it for them, yet they thumbed their noses at the greatest benefit of all: the forgiveness of their sins and the promise of heaven.

That night at home, when the volunteer had left and Thomas enjoyed uninterrupted time with Grace, again he found it impossible to hide his angst.

"I know you, dear heart," she said. "Talk to me."

Thomas told her as much of the conversation as he could remember.

"I don't understand it any more than you do, Thomas. But I still believe you are there for a reason. What these men do with the gospel is up to them. Your responsibility is to tell it. Jorge's response saddens me too, but what you said to him reminds me of how I cherish my faith."

Thomas rubbed his forehead. "I wish it did the same for me."

"Doesn't it? When you talk of Jesus' sacrifice, doesn't it thrill you?"

"Don't worry about me, Gracie. I'm just as low as I can be right now."

"I have a song for you but not the strength to sing it tonight. You should sing it."

"I'm not up to it either."

"It's a favorite. 'In the Cross of Christ I Glory.'"

"Yes, wonderful," Thomas said. "Sing it for me tomorrow."

"But I want to hear it now. Please, for me."

It was the last thing he felt like doing, but there was nothing he would not do for Grace. So Thomas sat a little straighter and took a deep breath, and in his pedestrian but serviceable voice, he began to sing for her. And in the middle of it, tears streaming, and with her reminding him of the lyrics here and there, he began to sing it to God.

In the cross of Christ I glory,
Towering o'er the wrecks of time;
All the light of sacred story
Gathers round its head sublime.

When the woes of life o'ertake me,
Hopes deceive, and fears annoy,
Never shall the cross forsake me:
Lo! it glows with peace and joy.

Brady liked the days when Jan conducted group therapy sessions solely for the drug addicts. And while he had been clean for weeks, not only was he still required to go, but he also wanted to. He found it helpful to hear from so many others who faced the same struggles and temptations he did. And while he felt self-conscious at first when he too admitted his triggers and weaknesses, in time it became easier for him.

But who was he kidding? He liked the sessions because, unlike the classes under Bill, they were coed and drew not only from the immediate community but also from the entire county.

Brady liked checking out the ladies, though most of them looked so strung out and wasted that they didn't appeal anyway. The ones who seemed to be succeeding and were attractive appeared way too young for him. But he was closing no doors, as long as they were of legal age. Up till now he had just been looking.

Today one of the outsiders had upper crust written all over her. Oh, she had the streaky hair and pierced tongue and showed a tattoo on her midriff, but Brady had never seen those kinds of clothes on a typical junkie. Funny thing was, she looked vaguely familiar. Or maybe he was only hoping. One thing was for sure. This woman had her eye on him too.

He casually looked around the circle—they always

sat in a circle—and noticed who seemed engaged, who was slouching and looking elsewhere. Each time his gaze landed on her, she was looking back, brows raised. Once she even smiled.

Hello.

Finally Jan flipped open her notebook and said, "Let's greet each other."

"Hi, I'm Brady, and I'm an addict."

"Hi, Brady."

And so it went. Most of the names flew past without Brady catching them or caring to. He knew his housemates, of course, and he wouldn't likely be getting to know the outsiders anyway. Though he held out hope for "her."

"Hi, I'm Katie," she said, "and I used to be an addict."

Some returned her greeting, but most waited for the inevitable reproach from Jan.

"Katie," she said.

"Okay, I'm still an addict. Always will be."

"No, but you may always be in recovery."

"Whatever."

Brady liked her spunk. Was there a chance he could speak to her before she boarded the van back to wherever she came from?

Halfway through the session Jan raised the issue—as she often did—of the future. She had established early that one thing many addicts lost was a dream, a plan, a view of what might be in store for them. After living only for the next hit for so long, that was as far ahead as they could look. "And when we finally start to think further ahead than our next score, where else should we look? Anyone?"

"Our past," someone said.

"Exactly. Search the recesses of your mind for your innocent years, your curious years, your best years. What was it you loved to do? What was it that was lost to you when you lost your way? What would you go back to if you could? I know maybe some of it is unrealistic now. Maybe you wanted to be an Olympic gymnast and those days are gone. But you could enjoy the sport in another way. Could you teach, coach, judge, just help out somewhere?

"That's the same with any sport. Or maybe you were a ballerina. It isn't likely you're going to dance at the Met, but let's not put any boundaries on our thinking right now. What did you once love to do that you would do again if you could?"

"Race cars."

"And why not?"

"Work construction."

"A clean and sober guy can do that. Go for it!"

"Be a model," Katie said.

"You've kept your figure," Jan said.

Brady wanted to shout, *Amen!*

"What's in your way?"

"My parents. I already just about got disowned 'cause I didn't make the Ivy League. To them modeling would be only one step down from druggie."

Everybody laughed.

Several other dreams were revealed and encouraged. Finally Brady said, "Acting."

"You were an actor?"

"Believe it or not."

"As a child?"

"High school. Actually played Conrad Birdie once."

Suddenly Katie was on her feet. "Get out!" she squealed. "I knew I knew you! Brady! I'm Katie North, Alex's sister!"

"No way!" Brady jumped up to embrace her. "I don't believe this! You were nothing but a snot-nosed kid back then."

"And you were the bad boy everybody had a crush on. Just look at you now."

"Yeah, same guy."

"How long ago was that, Brady?"

"Only fourteen years."

"I was like nine," she said.

"All right," Jan said, "you two can catch up later. Now who else can look back to look ahead?"

Adamsville State Penitentiary

"I think Dirk has a girlfriend," Ravinia told her father that afternoon in his office. "He's begged off of taking Summer twice in a row, claiming he had to work both nights."

"Hmm. Have you ever known him to lie?"

"No."

"Then why not take him at his word?"

"Maybe I'm paranoid. But Summer asks for him every evening."

"Tell him that. He needs to see her. He can't keep doing this to her. Listen, Rav, do you *want* him to have a girlfriend?"

"What are you saying? You mean so I wouldn't be the only guilty one? No. Would I be jealous? Yes, I would."

"Then you do care for him."

"I've said that all along."

"But his having someone else *would* take a little of the load off of you for, you know, what happened."

"For what triggered all this, you mean? Sure. But if he's guilty, that doesn't make me any less so. Just makes us even. Except mine really was a one-time fling, and who knows what his is?"

"Or even if it's anything."

Ravinia shook her head. "I can't believe I'm talking with my own father about this."

Serenity Halfway House

Brady and Katie had only a few minutes to talk before she had to go. He had so little experience with women, he hardly knew what to say. "So, you're all grown up, eh?"

"Yeah, you like?"

"Who wouldn't? Can't believe you got into drugs. I wouldn't have expected that in a million years."

"You kidding, Brady? There's as much booze and dope in my part of town as there is in yours."

"Seriously?"

"Oh yeah."

"So, where've you been, Katie? What have you been doing all these years? What's Alex up to?"

"He's got two wives and three kids between 'em."

"What?"

"Well, not at the same time. Had one with his first wife, two with his second. He's a financial planner. Already a big shot for my dad's firm."

"Figures. He ever get anywhere with his acting?"

"Nah. Couldn't make any money at it, and that's what it's all about for us Norths."

"Community theater?"

"Maybe someday. He says he has no time now. When he talks to me, that is. I'm the black sheep, you understand."

"You still live at home?"

"In a manner of speaking," she said, lifting her designer jeans pant leg and showing an ankle monitor. "They know where I am all the time. But I could come visit."

"Visit?"

"Here. You know I've been in love with you since I was nine."

Brady roared. "Right! Now admit it, you haven't given me a second thought since."

"You'd be surprised. I told all my girlfriends you were my guy. I even cut your picture out of the newspaper and carried it around to make them jealous."

"C'mon, I bet you've had a ton of real boyfriends since then."

She was being summoned to the van.

"True, and every last one of them has added to my dad's ulcers. Do me a favor. Soon as you get out of here, beg, borrow, or steal a Harley and come rumbling up to my door. Guaranteed, it'll make my mom a widow."

Brady couldn't wait to see Katie North again.

46

Adamsville State Penitentiary

Gladys poked her head into Thomas's office. "Got a minute, Reverend?"

He followed her to her cubicle outside the warden's office. Yanno was out.

"The boss thought you might want to see this," she said, handing Thomas a beat-up videocassette that appeared to have been used several times. "Documents the Guatemalan's extraction and transfer to isolation."

"Jorge? What'd he do?"

"The usual."

Gladys led Thomas into the warden's office, where an ancient combination TV–VHS player sat atop a small stand in one corner. Thomas pulled a chair away from the conference table. "Have you seen it?" he said.

Gladys shook her head and emitted a low chuckle. "No, thank you. Got my initiation years ago. One is enough. I don't know these guys and don't want to know them. I don't feel any sympathy, I can tell you that. And I don't want these images in my brain."

Thomas smiled sadly. "And I do?"

"Mr. LeRoy said you recently talked to the man, that's all. Thought you'd be interested."

Thomas shook his head as he shoved the cartridge into the machine. He couldn't understand why they didn't record these things on DVDs.

Gladys left and shut the door as the video came to life.

The bored voice of the videographer announced the date of the action, gave the prisoner's full name and number and the location of his cell. Each of the five corrections officers was shown and identified as well. "Subject assaulted an officer through his meal slot with a feces bomb to the face constructed from toilet paper and remnants of a juice box. Officer had not been wearing a face mask due to no incidents in this pod for more than six months. Extraction commenced at 2:10 p.m."

Every member of the team wore a helmet with face mask, rubber gloves, and all the protective gear they seemed to have been able to amass. One carried a huge Plexiglas shield. The team leader instructed Jorge to back his way to the meal slot to be cuffed.

He remained passively on his bunk at the back of his cell.

"Don't make us come in there!"

Jorge responded with an obscene gesture.

"Show your hands."

Jorge hid his hands behind him.

"Could be armed," the leader told the others. "Watch yourselves." Then, to the prisoner, "Last chance."

Jorge let loose a stream of expletives, whereupon the team leader pressed a can of gas through one of the openings and filled the cell with a white cloud. Through the haze Thomas could see Jorge cover his face.

"He's unarmed!" the leader shouted. "Come on, Jorge. Just back up to the slot."

Jorge just sat there, gagging and coughing.

"One more," the leader said, reaching behind him and accepting another canister from a teammate. This one made Jorge stagger to the door and thrust his hands through.

"No! Turn around. We're cuffing you in the back!"

Jorge would not move.

The leader shrugged and cuffed him in front, then released the manual lock, thrust his key into the main lock, and nodded to the officer in the pod, who tripped the remote so the key would work. As soon as the door was open, the team surged in.

Jorge swung his cuffed hands and kicked and tried to bite the officers. One circled behind him and wrapped a spit mask around his face while the others each grabbed a limb and the one with the shield drove him to the back of the cell.

When Jorge hit the bed, he crumpled to the floor with the shield and the officer atop him, but still he thrashed and screamed and grunted. Someone rolled in a gurney, and he was soon strapped down, legs also shackled.

"Subject transported to isolation," the videographer said.

Thomas pressed his lips together. When would he learn to read these men? He could easily have been the victim of the initial assault, but who could have predicted it?

And why did Frank LeRoy think Thomas wanted to see this? Just because he had chatted with Jorge at the prisoner's request? Or was Yanno still trying to educate him? Thomas figured he'd been in the system long enough to understand that these things happened. He guessed the warden would always consider him the new guy, even after all these years.

Thomas emerged and gave Gladys the tape.

"He wants to see you," she said.

"Jorge? In isolation? He knows better."

"When he gets out."

"When will that be?"

"Who knows? This will be the end of any hope for parole for him. Ever."

"Well, let me know. I'll talk to him. As long as there's a window between us."

"I heard that."

Brady began to live for Thursdays, when the outsiders came in for group therapy. Katie North would rush from the van and straight into his arms, though they kept their embraces short and friendly so they would appear simply like old friends. Bill and Jan both seemed encouraged by Brady's rekindling an acquaintance. Brady was hoping for a whole lot more than that.

Katie seemed to make sure to sit next to Brady, and they whispered asides and winked at each other throughout every group session.

One Thursday she leaned close and said in his ear, "I have a gift for you, but it's contraband."

Brady didn't want to even wonder if it was something unhealthy. Surely she could see he was doing well. He had kicked every addiction except nicotine and was determined to stay straight. For the first time in ages he felt hope that he could really turn his life around. He didn't ever want to go back to the joint, of course, but the truth was, there were people he wanted to impress. Bill and Jan, to start with. His aunt and uncle too, though he wearied of their efforts to get him to their church and to introduce him to their friend. Even his mother. He didn't care if he ever saw her again, but something in him wanted her to hear—at least secondhand—that he was succeeding.

But at the top of his list?

Katie. He knew himself well. She would be worth

throwing over the whole reforming thing. In a flash.

She had become all he could think about. She looked better, smelled better, sounded better every time he saw her. There was a hint of danger about her, and she hadn't hidden her interest in him. And Brady was sure she was as committed to sobriety as he was. He'd seen enough people strung out to know that she seemed clean. And if she wasn't? Well, with her, he was open to anything.

As people milled about chatting, waiting to board the van, she said softly, "Don't let anybody see you take this."

They talked and joked and locked eyes, but she also kept glancing at the Serenity staff. Suddenly she reached into her pocket and then shook his hand. "Get it out of sight right away. I have it set on vibrate. Just don't get caught with it."

A cell phone.

"Do they search you, Brady?"

"Not anymore."

"Still, you'd better keep it hidden in your room. Call me when you're alone. We can even text each other."

"Listen, I've never used a cell phone. I don't know the first thing about—"

"Hmm, I never thought of that. I'll send you a manual. Do they go through your mail?"

"No."

"I'll overnight it. Then we can talk every day."

"How long do the batteries last?"

She swore.

"What?" he said.

"You're going to need a charger, too."

"A what?"

"I'll send you a box of cookies. Everything you need will be in the packaging. Gotta go."

She cares.

It was all Brady could think about. Aside from ugly Agatha, shallow high school girls who loved the novelty of squealing about the bad boy, and his series of one-night stands, real women had rarely given him a second glance. And Katie North was hot. Not to mention rich. How much must a cell phone cost?

Within a few days Bill and Jan were teasing Brady about having a girlfriend who sent him cookies in an overnight package. He was careful to share them with everyone. He was left with just one, and it wasn't that great. But it wasn't the cookies that mattered. He also found the charger and the phone manual, and he forced himself to read it until he figured the thing out.

He plugged it into a socket next to his bed and kept everything hidden. Several times a day he stole away to his room, locked the door, and checked for messages. Texting was a frustrating chore, but he learned the shorthand and enjoyed keeping up with all of Katie's exploits. Despite her ankle bracelet, her girlfriends brought her everything she needed and wanted.

"It won't be long," she told him one night, "before I'll be able to use my car again."

And it wasn't just any car. She had a Mercedes, the big four-door sedan.

When do they let u out 4 rides? she texted him late in the afternoon one day.

Free 2 come and go, but curfew, he keyed back. *Long as ur not a felon.*

Make sure. Tomorrow at 2.

Brady met with Jan and Bill. They seemed amused at the budding relationship, but their smiles faded at his request. "We can't really say no," Jan said. "But your parole officer needs to know. And we have to know where you're going and exactly when you'll be back."

"Is there any way I can transfer?"

"Transfer?"

"Parole officers. It'd be a whole lot easier if one of you could take over for my guy. He works down by County, and it's hard to get there. And I don't think he likes me or trusts me."

"Trusting you isn't his job," Bill said. "He's supposed to suspect you and keep an eye on you."

"But you guys always talk about trust and respect, and I feel that here."

Jan looked at Bill. "You have served as parole officer for a few of the guys."

"Once they've completed the course, yeah," Bill said. "Never before."

She shrugged. "Maybe the county would make an exception."

"I'm willing," Bill said. "But no promises."

"I'd sure appreciate you trying," Brady said. "When I get out of here, I want to find a place to live right here in town."

"You're doing well, man," Bill said. "I'll see what I can do. Meanwhile, why don't you and Miss North just plan on an hour or so tomorrow."

"Let's be specific," Jan said. "Make it ninety minutes. You're back here at 3:30 sharp. And where will you be going?"

"Just out for a snack, I guess. No big deal."

"Good idea. She has to sign some papers, you know. And we have to see documentation that she's no longer monitored and is free to do this."

The next morning, Brady raced through his chores, showered, shaved, and dressed in his best and cleanest clothes. Katie showed up early with a letter from her parole officer and signed everything Bill and Jan required, promising to have Brady back right on time.

It was all he could do to keep from running to her car, but she kept telling him to just stay cool. She pulled away slowly, Brady marveling at the interior of the coolest ride he had ever enjoyed.

"First time in a Benz," he said.

"Really?"

"You kiddin'? 'Course."

"You wanna drive?"

"I don't even have a license."

"Then don't do anything that would get you stopped."

She pulled over.

"You're not serious," he said. "Are you?"

"As serious as this." She climbed from behind the wheel directly into his lap, wrapping her arms around his neck.

After a few minutes of passionate kisses, during which Brady worried about dying of a heart attack, she said, "Your turn to drive, bad boy."

Brady found himself relieved that the car was not a stick shift. "Where to, ma'am?"

"Harley-Davidson," she said, eyes dancing. "Can't think of anyplace more fun than that."

"Got another gift for me?" he said, laughing.

"All in good time."

47

Adamsville State Penitentiary

When Thomas pulled up to the guardhouse at the end of the day, the officer was busy with another car and driver. He turned to Thomas and shook his head as if in apology. "Tried to see if I could get him to leave, Chaplain. Couldn't shake him."

The man approached. "You Reverend Thomas Carey?"

"I am."

"Little mail for you," the man said, handing Thomas a large envelope. "Consider yourself served."

"Served with what, for what?"

461

"Those answers, sir, are beyond the boundaries of my job description. Good day."

Thomas considered leaving the envelope in his car and dealing with the contents in the office the next day. Whatever they were, Grace didn't need to be burdened by them. But curiosity got the better of him, and Thomas removed the legal papers while the officer logged him out.

"Surely this is not the first time you've been served," the officer said.

"Believe it or not, it is."

"By an inmate, of course."

Thomas nodded.

"Join the club."

"You too?" Thomas said.

"Most all of us at one time or another. Get yourself a good attorney and try to keep the thing short."

"Don't worry." *An attorney?*

Thomas couldn't afford an attorney, and he hated to ask Ravinia. By the time he got home, he was distracted beyond reason, knowing he would have to at least tell her what was going on and seek her counsel. His thank-yous to the volunteer lady from the church were perfunctory. He would have to remember to be more effusive next time. He barely listened to her report, knowing that if anything had gone wrong or turned worse with Grace, the woman would have brought that to his attention first. Why did life have to be so complicated?

Thomas pasted on a smile and kissed Grace's cheek.

"I need to sit up," she said, gripping his arm as she slowly swung her legs off the side of the bed. She sighed heavily and slumped. "Feels better, at least for now. Something's on your mind, Thomas. You know I can tell."

"Just work."

"Tell me."

"Routine."

"Nonsense. Now, come on. It's bad enough I'm isolated from everything in your life. I can take it."

The sad fact was, she could. She rolled with these things better than he did.

"I'm sure I can deal with it quickly," he said, "but an inmate is filing charges against me for treating him 'with malicious disregard and contempt.'"

"That will be hard to prove."

"He says I disparaged his attempt to convert to Christianity and refused to represent him before the parole board. That led to extreme emotional distress that caused him to lash out at corrections officers and get him sent to isolation and cost him any further chance at parole."

"The man from Central America? Ravinia will take care of it."

"I hate to—"

"Come, come. She'd be hurt if you didn't ask."

After sharing a light meal with Grace, Thomas moved to the living room, where he phoned his daughter.

Ravinia paused after hearing his side of it. "You

know who loves this kind of case? Dirk. This will get his back up, and the guy won't know what hit him."

"Dirk? Are you sure?"

"Trust me."

"I can't afford—"

"Dad! Whatever Dirk is or whatever we are going through, he's not the kind of a person who would charge you. And believe me, he won't do this halfway. He'll flood this guy's lawyer's mailbox with so many motions and demands, the guy will wish he'd never gotten involved. Tell me you'll call him."

"I don't know. Won't it be awkward? How are you two doing? Is he seeing Summer more, going to counseling with you? I certainly don't want to get in the way of—"

"Well, one out of two ain't bad. We've let the counseling slide for a while, because it turns out he really was swamped when he had to beg off from taking her those times. I threatened to get him cut off forever if he treats her that way again, and he cleaned up his act."

"You no longer suspect him of—"

"Seeing someone else? I don't know. I guess I couldn't blame him if he was, after all this time. But we're cordial, and honestly, I do think he's behaving. I know I am."

"Are you?"

"I am, Dad. It's not easy. And don't think I don't have my opportunities."

"I'd really rather not discuss it, if you don't mind."

"I know. Sorry. I just thought you'd want to know that I'm doing the right thing, even by your standards."

"Well, I appreciate that. But you say Dirk is so busy. . . ."

"Dad, if you're not going to call him, I will."

"How would that look?"

"It'll look like what it is. That you don't want to bother him but that I knew he'd jump on this. Now I'm calling him, and that's all there is to it."

Addison

Brady Wayne Darby was helplessly, haplessly, hopelessly, head over heels in love. He couldn't wipe the grin off his mug, and everyone teased him about it.

He and Katie were careful to follow most of the rules, especially the ones that showed. She had him back at Serenity on time every time, and while she allowed him to drive the car, it was rarely on the open road, and he drove like an old lady.

On one of their afternoon outings, after they spent their first twenty minutes making out, she drove to the motorcycle dealership. Katie made all kinds of noises to the salesman about looking to buy one of the top models if she could just get used to riding it.

Since Brady didn't have a driver's license, she left hers and the Benz at the shop while he climbed on the back of a top-of-the-line Screamin' Eagle V-Rod. She

465

drove, but once they were out of sight of the dealership, they changed places.

Brady was skittish as a new colt, reminding her that if he tipped it or caused any damage, she was going to have to take the heat or see him sent back to prison. "Where'd you learn to ride anyway?" he said.

"My boyfriends have always had Harleys."

"Am I gonna have one too?"

"I actually prefer the Fat Boy," she said. "And, no, I'm not buying you a bike. I will rent one, though, as soon as you prove you can handle it. I want us to come flying up to my house, rattling every window on the street. Then I'll tell my dad I just met you, that you picked me up at the mall and gave me a ride."

Brady was howling. "What I wouldn't give for one of these," he said.

"Stay close, sweetie."

Oh, Brady loved this girl. She was crazy, but so was he. And best of all, just the thought of her was keeping him on the straight and narrow. Of course, had she said the word, he also would have committed any felony she asked. But for now he studied like he never had before, was diligent at his every chore, and was earnest and forthcoming with Jan and with Bill, his new parole officer. Well, as forthcoming as he dared. He wasn't about to tell anyone about the phone, driving, and riding the Harley.

Brady was up at the same time every day, starting to work out (he actually ran a few blocks, but he was so new to it and his system so wracked by cigarettes, he wasn't sure he had a future in jogging), and was cleaned up and ready to go early.

Bill had a list of local employers willing to take a chance on the top Serenity members. "It won't be much at first, but as you gain their trust and prove yourself, who knows?"

It sounded good to Brady. He didn't want to get ahead of himself when it came to Katie North, but he would have sworn she felt about him the way he felt about her. It didn't add up, and he found it hard to believe. But she never talked about other guys, and they text messaged each other all the time and talked by phone when they could. And every few days, she picked him up for a couple of hours of fun.

Life could hardly get better.

Adamsville

Thomas found himself thinking about the pastorate again. In the prison system, if it wasn't one thing, it was another. But at sixty, his energy level was already keeping him from diving into the daily grind, the same problem he would have if he switched careers again. And who but a tiny congregation without much money would want a man his age in the pulpit anyway, especially one whose ailing wife would come with the package? He felt stuck.

There was no getting around it: churches got free labor when a pastor brought along a healthy wife, whether she was into music or teaching or running a children's or women's program. Who was he kidding? Becoming a pastor again would virtually mean providing charity work for a struggling congregation, and they would be offering precious little to a needy, over-the-hill preacher.

"Man waitin' in your office," Gladys told him as he passed her one morning.

He stopped. "Another process server?"

She beckoned him close and whispered, "Your son-in-law. Calls you Dad."

Thomas found Dirk had draped his overcoat over a chair, opened his briefcase, and laid his legal pad on the edge of the desk. "Hey, good to see you," Dirk said, pumping Thomas's hand. "Rav's told me everything she knows, and I'm honored you would let me help."

"Well, I—"

"I've already been studying this, Dad, and I think it's a slam dunk. These guys love to drag these things out and make your life miserable, I know, but we're going to put a stop to that, believe you me. First of all, you're not to meet with him."

"No? Won't that play right into his hands?"

"At least not until he drops the charges. Meantime, he talks to his counsel, you talk to yours."

Thomas removed and hung up his coat, held up a hand, and sat behind his desk. "Dirk, we really must talk first. I mean, here I haven't seen you in ages, and we can't just pretend everything is hunky-dory at home, can we?"

Dirk was finally silent. Then he threw back his head and laughed heartily. "Did you just say *hunky-dory?* Haven't heard that in years. No, I guess we can't, Dad. But the truth is, every minute I spend on your case, I have to make up for at the office. So can we do that another time?"

Thomas shook his head. "You know, Dirk, I don't think we can. Maybe people of your generation can go about their business as if nothing is wrong, but I find it distracting. Now, I'm sorry this is causing you more work, and if you want to drop it and leave me to find my own lawyer, I'll just have to bite the bullet and—"

"No way. If that's a deal breaker, fine. Let's talk. And if it helps me get Ravinia and Summer back into my life, it'll be worth any sacrifice."

"You serious?"

"Serious as a supermax. Nothing I want more than to be back home with my family."

"Where do things stand? Does Rav know, and is she turning you down?"

"I haven't told her."

"You tell me and not her? What kind of a lawyer are you?"

48

The Harley salesman was apologetic but said his manager had put the kibosh on Katie's test-drives until she was prepared to commit to a purchase. "We'll then be happy to enroll you in classes so you can become proficient," he said.

"Sounds like you'd be happy to have me buy from another dealer," she said.

Brady saw panic in the man's eyes. "Oh no, not at all. But you understand there's a limit to how many times we can have you—"

"And my fiancé . . ."

"Look, if you need one more spin to help you make your decision, I can talk to my—"

"Do that. We've pretty much made up our minds about the metallic blue Fat Boy, and—"

"Really?"

Now Brady saw something else in the salesman's eyes. Dollar signs.

"And we're prepared to pay cash."

"Let me get the key."

As the man jogged into the showroom, Katie squeezed Brady's shoulder. "Too good to be true!" she said. "We're not even going to have to rent!"

"You're not really going to buy—?"

"Of course not. Once you start working, you can buy your own."

"Yeah, like that'll happen. I'm really gonna buy a bike worth twice as much as the best car I could afford. And in the winter . . ."

"I'm just saying, I like a man on a Harley. And you're getting awfully good on 'em. You ready to buzz my dad?"

"I'm up for anything you want," Brady said.

Once again Katie left the Benz and they took off on the big bike. Half a mile away, they switched places, and she hollered directions in Brady's ear as he headed north to the exclusive suburbs. He felt that familiar tingle up his back, the one that told him he was on the edge of danger, or disaster.

Adamsville

Dirk Blanc proved as engaging as ever, and in spite of himself, Thomas simply liked the man.

"Have you forgiven Rav?" he said.

Dirk squinted at him. "So you know everything."

"I know enough."

"Apparently. Tell you the truth, forgiveness was hard. We'd been drifting, like couples do. Well, most couples. To hear Ravinia tell it, you guys are next to perfect."

"Oh no, now—"

"Just telling you the standard that has been raised before me. Fact is, my parents are pretty tight too,

471

though in some ways I think my mother is an enabler. Life pretty much revolves around Dad. 'Course he loves it, and she seems okay with that. But back to us. I know I contributed, okay? We were both trying to gain traction in our careers, and yeah, I can see where she was lonely and I was the reason—or a big part of it. I mean, it falls to me to be sure she's not lonely, am I right?"

"I see it that way, yes," Thomas said. "Unless there's something pathologically wrong with the wife, it's the husband's lot to be sure she's happy."

Dirk shook his head. "I'd love that chance again."

"But you never answered my question."

"Formally, no, I guess I haven't actually forgiven her. I was deeply hurt, sir. You cannot imagine."

"Has she asked your forgiveness?"

Dirk shook his head. "Might open an old wound if I announce forgiveness that hasn't been asked for."

"Let me talk to her."

"Is she going to think I want her to ask?"

"Give me a little more credit than that, Dirk."

"I'll leave it with you. And I appreciate your interest more than I can say."

Dirk proved as energetic about Thomas's case as he would have been for a paying client. He came to the penitentiary with court documents allowing him to conduct his due diligence—seeing the pods, the cells, and even interviewing anyone within earshot of the conversation between Thomas and Jorge.

"I found the other prisoners understandably close-

472

mouthed, protecting their own. But they also seemed reluctant to cast you in a bad light, and that's a good thing. Not one would say that you were mean or cold or acrimonious to Jorge. And while there is no tape of your conversation, we have the next best thing. Two officers in the control unit for that pod overheard the entire exchange through the intercom."

"Then they know."

"And their recollections are just disparate enough to pretty much prove reliability without collusion. The only drawback is that they would naturally take your side against an inmate. But if it comes to needing witnesses, we've got them. Once I get their depositions, I may be able to get a summary judgment, a decision by the court before it even gets to trial. If I were Jorge's counsel, this would persuade me to stop wasting my time."

49

Addison

"Won't your dad be at work?" Brady hollered as he rolled the big Harley into a sprawling subdivision with colossal mansions on generous lots. Already drapes were being pulled back here and there as the machine roared through the otherwise quiet streets.

"He works at home! This is going to be perfect! Pull over so I can call him!"

Brady carefully parked the machine at the curb and

shut it down. As Katie entered her father's number, a couple of yard workers wandered over from across the street, eyeing the bike.

"Nice," one said.

"Thanks."

"New?"

"Yeah."

"Sweet."

"I know."

"Don't get caught with it around here though, dude. We even have mufflers and governors on our edgers and mowers. Lots of what they call 'noise covenants' around here."

"That right?"

"Yep. 'Course, by the time they call the cops, you'll be long gone. Nobody's gonna catch you, man."

"You got that right."

Katie nudged Brady and put a finger to her lips. "Daddy, you home right now? I have a surprise for you. . . . Yeah. See you in a minute. . . . Well, tell 'em you'll call them back. Watch for me out the window."

Katie slapped her phone shut and hugged Brady so tight around his chest that he felt the bike tipping and had to put all his weight and hers on one leg. At the last instant he shrugged her off and wrestled the cycle back into balance. "Sorry," he said. "No way we'd be able to right this thing ourselves if it goes down."

"I'm just so excited," she said. "This is going to be too cool for words! My dad's going to flip out!"

"Yeah, about that. I'll do whatever you want me to,

but remember, I haven't seen him since I was in high school, and I don't think I made a good impression."

"You think I want you to make a good impression now? C'mon, Brady. You couldn't impress him without an Ivy League degree and hiring potential. Short of that, he'll never accept you anyway."

"Wow."

"Wow what? Welcome to my world, big boy."

"Don't you think it's kind of important I get off on the right foot with him?"

"Why?"

"Because I expect to be seeing a lot more of you."

"He's not even impressed with me, Brady. Why would he be impressed with you? Even if you had a résumé, he'd be suspicious just because I chose you."

"Have you chosen me?"

"We gonna do this thing or not?"

"Sure. But after I've done it, can I at least try to get him to see me in a good light? I mean, things are looking up for me right now. You don't think he'd be interested to hear how I'm trying to turn my life around?"

"You can kiss up to him all you want after you turn this bike around a couple of times in the street in front of our house. Can you do that, revving it as loud as you can?"

"You're sure that's what you want?"

"Did I stutter?"

"No ma'am. One bust for disturbing the peace, coming up."

Brady fired up the Harley and gunned the engine before engaging the gears.

"Yeah!" she shouted. "That's what I'm talking about!"

The front tire rose an inch from the ground as he took off, making Katie squeal. "Go, Brady, go!" She pointed to each turn, and when they finally rounded a corner that led to a cul-de-sac, Brady was glad to see he could make a quick escape if necessary.

"It's the big one in the center," she said.

The big one? The houses were all monstrosities. He'd seen smaller hotels. The house in question was three stories and had a four-car garage and what looked like a half-acre yard.

"His office is on the lower level. That's him staring out the window."

"What does a place like that cost?"

"Later! Go! Go! Go!"

Brady had not liked where the conversation had gone, but there was nothing he wouldn't do for his love. He slipped into neutral, topped out the RPMs, then let the engine settle before dropping it into gear again. He raced up the street, slowed just enough to make the wide circle around the cul-de-sac, and kept the noise at peak decibels.

"Again!" she screamed, and he kept going, afraid to peek at the face peering out. "Faster!"

He thought he was leaning into the circle as far as he could, but what Katie wanted, Katie got. Brady took the next swing faster (and of course louder), but he had been right. No matter how far they leaned, the bike was just an oversize gyroscope with centrifugal force that would not be tamed, and this time it drifted up the curb and onto the Norths' lawn.

"Perfect! Again, but this time, leave a mark!"

"No!"

"For me! I'll make you glad you did!"

Brady stole a glance at the window, and it was empty. As he made the circle again, a touch faster, the front door burst open and here came Jordan North in his stocking feet. Ashen-faced with fury in his eyes, the man hesitated on the porch as the Harley reached the expansive lawn again.

Brady slowed enough to let the bike lean, then rammed the throttle, making the back tire sink into the sod and dig its way out, throwing grass and dirt all over the house.

"Katie!" her father screamed. "What do you two think you're doing?"

Brady motored to the end of the street as Mr. North marched up and down the porch, looking as if he wanted to explode, while at the same time apparently hoping against hope that none of his neighbors had seen this.

"Time to meet Daddy," Katie said.

"I'm not going back there."

"Oh yes you are. This is the payoff, darlin'. If I don't get to see the full reaction, this has been a waste."

Brady had been less scared dealing with the cops.

"Go, Brady. I'll take the brunt of it."

"I don't like it," he said.

"For me."

"Here goes nothin'."

Brady slowly cruised up the block and into the driveway, shutting down in front of one of the garage doors. Mr. North approached slowly, as if fearing Brady was armed. Brady couldn't look at him.

"Hi, Daddy! Meet my new boyfriend. We were thinking of getting married tonight. Want to come?"

Brady looked up.

Mr. North, shaking, glared at his daughter. "You want me to call your parole officer, don't you, Katie? You want to be back in that ankle bracelet. I could have you behind bars again inside ten minutes."

"So you won't give me away tonight?"

"Who's this lowlife anyway? Whoever you are, I hope you know she's just using you to push my buttons. You're going to pay for my lawn and cleaning up my house."

"Actually, you know him, Daddy. You met in another life. Remember Brady Darby?"

"Should I?"

"Think Conrad Birdie."

"You've got to be kidding me. That's you?"

"Yes, sir."

"Well, you've come a long way from that failure. Didn't Alex have to take the role because you bombed out or something? Nice to see you've grown up and made something of yourself."

"Actually, sir, I need to tell you—"

"You need to tell me nothing. If you know what's good for you, you'll leave Katie here so I can drive her back to her car. And you'd better never so much as show your face here again, let alone that motorcycle."

Brady turned to plead with Katie to help defend him, but she had a look he hadn't seen before. It was plain she was loving every second of this. "Brady can take me back to my car. Now you're sure you don't want to come to the wedding?"

"You're going to regret this, Katie."

"Sir, I—"

"Don't you talk to me. Don't even look at me. I ever see or even hear you again in this neighborhood, I'm calling the cops."

"Sorry," Brady said, letting the Harley roll down into the street before starting it again.

As he rode off as quietly as possible, Brady felt Katie's arms around him, her hands clasped over his stomach, her head pressed against his neck. "Hope you're happy!" he called over his shoulder.

"It was everything I dreamed," she said. But her enthusiasm was gone.

Brady stopped a couple of blocks from the dealership. "We're going to have to get this thing cleaned up before we take it back," he said.

"No way. I can't wait to see the look on the guy's face when he sees all that mud. He'll be all cool about it, thinking I'm about to drop a bundle on one of these. Then I'll just tell him I've changed my mind and might get back to him."

"You're not really going to do that."

"Watch me."

"I'd rather not."

"What? You don't want to be there? Don't tell me you're a wuss, Brady."

"C'mon, nobody deserves that."

"Fine, I'll do it without you. Pick you up in a few minutes. Anyway, I owe you one, right?"

"Sorry?"

"I said I'd make you glad you did what I asked."

"You did, didn't you?"

"Be right back."

She roared off, leaving Brady at the side of the road. He felt conspicuous.

What could he make of this woman? He thought he had a mean and bitter streak, but she beat all. What could have made her so spiteful toward her dad?

Whatever. Brady had only half an hour before he had to be back at Serenity, so whatever she was planning as his payoff was going to have to be quick.

Ten minutes later he spotted the Benz and stepped into the street. But as Katie passed, she flashed him a beautiful smile and gave him the finger.

Funny. She'd be back. He knew it. He hoped. He wondered as she disappeared from sight.

C'mon. No longer funny. If she wasn't back soon, he'd have to hitch a ride. And what if he was late? That would spoil everything he'd accomplished.

But this was part of what he liked so much about Katie. You could never tell what she was going to do next. On the other hand, he didn't want to be played. Wouldn't be.

Brady hurried to a pay phone and called Bill, telling him Katie had car trouble and that he would hitchhike. "I didn't want you or Jan to wonder or worry if I was a little late getting back."

"You need me to come get you?"

"No thanks. I'll call if I run into any snags."

And just as he was hanging up, here she came.

"Hilarious," he said, climbing in. "Better let me off a block away. I told Bill you had car trouble."

"Brilliant. With a Benz."

"It happens."

"Hey, Brady, I gotta borrow that phone and charger till I see you next, all right?"

"Sure. It's yours. What's up?"

"A girlfriend and I are going on a little trip, and she doesn't have a phone. It's just a few days."

"You still coming for group therapy Thursday?"

"Of course."

She pulled up to the center right on time, and Bill looked confused as he opened the gate.

"Mercedes responded right away," Brady said. "Took care of it just like that. I'll be right back down. I got to give her something."

Brady wrapped the phone and charger in a shirt and slipped past Bill. "She's gonna have this cleaned for me at some special shop." It was lame, but what was he supposed to say?

Brady had a bad feeling as he approached the car.

481

What had this all been about anyway? Did he and Katie not have what he thought they had?

Bill was standing there holding the gate open and watching. Brady opened the passenger-side door and put the stuff on the seat.

"Come around to my side, sweetie," she said.

He looked at Bill, then back at her. "What?"

"Come on. Just a taste of what's to come."

He moved to her window, and she reached for him. He bent, and she grabbed him around the neck with both arms, nearly pulling herself out of the car. She planted a deep, passionate kiss on him and smiled. "I don't care who's watching," she said. "You ought to know that by now."

50

Adamsville

As much as Thomas longed to see Grace at the end of every day, lately it seemed a weight settled on his shoulders and grew only heavier as he neared home. He had come to know well the six or so women who rotated tending to Grace, which one was her favorite, which she merely tolerated. Both he and she were deeply grateful for all of them, of course, and Thomas wondered how other people in their economic situation coped at all.

Today the caregiver informed Thomas that she had had to call the doctor late in the morning when

Grace's blood pressure dipped alarmingly. "He actually came to the house. And he said something about her blood sugar too."

"When was this?" Thomas said.

"A little before noon."

"Did you try to reach me?"

"I mentioned it, but Grace forbade me to interrupt you at work."

Thomas sighed. He wanted to overrule his wife and set a policy with the caregivers that he was always to be informed of any change in her condition, but how would that look? There was no sense putting these volunteers in the middle of his frustration with his wife. Gracie was only thinking of him, but still he very much wanted to be informed of everything.

Later he said, "Grace, do I have to check in here by phone every few hours?"

"You need to trust me, Thomas. I know my own body and whether I'm really in trouble. The doctor has said for ages that our goal is to get me to at least a temporary state of remission. He thought we were making progress. The blood pressure thing was a setback, and he tested my sugar level just as an afterthought since he was here anyway."

"Tell me you're not diabetic or even prediabetic."

"He doesn't think so, but he's asked me to test for a while so he can put me on oral meds if necessary."

Thomas didn't like the sound of that. Already it seemed he had to fight with his insurance company over anything new.

"Don't look so glum. I feel better now. And don't worry about the house call either. The doctor said it was gratis because he knew our insurance didn't cover it."

"Something free from a doctor? Will wonders never cease?"

"Oh, I think he does fine and would even if I were his only patient."

Not wanting Ravinia to feel as left out of the loop as he did, Thomas called her and brought her up to date.

"How do you explain this, Dad? Why does something like this happen to someone like her?"

"We are not promised tomorrow."

"I just don't like it, that's all. Well, let me talk to Mom when we're done. Are we done?"

"In a minute. I wanted to thank you for recommending Dirk. He's been amazing."

"That's no surprise. He's gifted and thorough."

"I'll say. He misses you, Rav."

"He said that? Unsolicited?"

"I didn't put any words in his mouth. Have you asked his forgiveness, hon?"

"For?"

"Don't be coy, Rav."

She fell silent. Thomas waited her out.

"He needs to ask my forgiveness too, Dad."

"That's not going to happen unless you two make it happen."

"I'm not ready."

"You don't miss him?"

"I don't want to talk about this right now. Let me talk to Mom."

Thomas busied himself preparing dinner and bringing it to Grace, catching snippets of her side of the conversation with Ravinia. As usual, Grace was assuring her daughter that she was not bitter, did not feel she deserved to be spared anything God allowed in her life, and she finally asked her daughter if she could sing to her.

"Just listen to this," Grace said. "May I?"

Thomas could imagine Ravinia rolling her eyes, but she would not be so rude as to deny her mother's request. And so Grace sang softly.

> Abide with me; fast falls the eventide;
> The darkness deepens; Lord, with me abide!
> When other helpers fail and comforts flee,
> Help of the helpless, O abide with me!
>
> I fear no foe, with You at hand to bless;
> Ills have no weight, and tears no bitterness.
> Where is death's sting? Where, grave, your victory?
> I triumph still, if You abide with me.

Serenity Halfway House

Brady found himself distracted, waiting for Thursday. He still went about all his activities and responsibilities with enthusiasm, but it seemed something was wrong with him.

He was on a group outing when he missed a call from his aunt Lois, and the message Jan had scribbled for him and left on the desk in his room read simply, "Says she and your uncle are praying."

He knew he should call her, but he didn't need all the church mumbo jumbo just then. Something was happening to him, something he couldn't describe. Brady had pulled a lot of stunts in his thirty years, most much worse than tearing up a lawn with a motorcycle. Yet he couldn't seem to get past this. Every time it crossed his mind, he felt worse.

Brady loved Katie and hoped he had impressed her and convinced her he would do anything for her. But whatever was between her and her father had nothing to do with him—at least until now. He'd been able to explain away every other crime he had ever committed, but this one made him feel like a juvenile—and he was hardly a kid anymore. It had been stupid, senseless. He felt he owed Mr. North for the damage, just as the man had said.

Brady also felt as if he wanted to come clean and tell the whole story to Bill. Oh, he wouldn't. Couldn't. He would lose every step he had gained and would get his beloved in trouble too. Maybe the best he could do would be to talk to her about it and see if she didn't agree that he should somehow make it right.

Thursday couldn't come soon enough. He had not heard from Katie for several days, not even on the house phone. She had said she was going on some sort of a trip, but couldn't she have called and at least left a message?

Unable to clear his mind, Brady noodled a letter to Mr. North. He would ask Katie to deliver it personally. But even as he got into it, he couldn't find it in himself to simply take responsibility for what he had done. He would not blame it on Katie, even though she had put him up to it. How would that look?

No, he would offer to pay, but he would have to creatively explain the incident.

Dear Mr. North,
I want to say I'm sorry for what happened to your lawn and to tell you to send me the bill for fixing it. I didn't realize how loud the bike was going to be, and I sure didn't plan to tear up your yard. That was an accident.
Please send me the bill and forgive me.

Your friend,
Brady Wayne Darby

Brady found sleep next to impossible Wednesday night. He hadn't realized until he was out of daily contact with her that Katie had become a lifeline for him, a purpose, the reason for everything he was doing. He wanted to succeed for her.

In the morning he rushed through every activity, then found the clock crawling as he watched out the window for her car. She didn't have to take the van anymore, unless her father had followed through on his threats. He certainly had enough on her to get her in real trouble.

Too much time on his hands made Brady shift from longing for Katie to dreading his own fate. What was he going to do if Mr. North reported him and everything came crashing down? Katie would have to agree that his letter and his offer to make amends to her father was the right thing to do, end of story.

Driving herself, Katie had been showing up early on Thursdays, but not today. And when the county van pulled up, a shy, dark-haired girl emerged and slipped Brady a note.

Hey, Lover:

My dad is absolutely refusing to let me come back to group there. He got me reassigned. I pitched a fit, telling him I was of age, but he got my PO involved. Let's just lie low for a while and be patient.

Love, Katie

With just minutes before the session was to begin, Brady raced upstairs and scribbled a reply.

Katie, I'm putting a note in here for you to give your dad. We've got to make a truce with him, right? I love you and need you and want you. You're all I'm living for. Call me.

Love, Brady

The girl agreed to deliver the notes back to Katie, but that didn't make Brady feel much better. He was sullen during the meeting and found himself slouching and scowling, unable to participate. It was so unlike him that it seemed to rattle Jan. She kept calling on him for comments, and he would merely shrug or mumble an "I don't know."

When the session was over and the others had left, Jan told Brady she and Bill needed to speak with him.

They sat in an anteroom off the kitchen. Brady was not content to wait for Jan to ask him what was wrong. He just dived in. "Sorry about my attitude. I just miss Katie, and her dad is not happy about me."

"That's not unusual for future fathers-in-law of ex-cons," Bill said.

That he even mentioned the possibility of Brady and Katie's getting married raised Brady's spirits. "Maybe you can put in a good word for me."

"Keep your nose clean and complete this program the way you've been going, and I'll be happy to tell anyone who asks that you've done everything required of you. I need to tell you something, though. We heard from your contact at County, the antigang guy."

Brady held his breath. Had Jordan North already

squealed on him? And if so, how did it get to Lieutenant Dale and not to Bill? Or did Bill know too? "You heard from him?"

"Yeah. He wants you to know that Tiny is out on some technicality, so you'll want to keep your distance. You made a lot of promises to that guy, apparently, and he may come calling."

"He doesn't know where I am."

"Brady, he's the most connected gang leader in the state. Unless you're in the witness protection program, he'll find you. He thinks you're on your way to Hollywood to find your fortune. You know what that means."

"He'll expect a piece of it."

"Of course. For all those years of protection."

Brady studied the ceiling. "This is all I need. Once I'm out of here, where do I go to stay away from Tiny?"

"Anywhere but the city. The west side in particular."

Brady's smile was gone. He felt tired and achy all the time. Couldn't concentrate. Wasn't eating. Hardly slept.

As days passed without word one from Katie, he felt himself changing. Something roiled deep within him, a restlessness. First it seemed like simple impatience, but soon he was testy, defensive, angry all the time. When he called Katie's cell phone and got only her voice mail, he pleaded with her to call and tell him how her father had responded to his letter.

And he reminded her how much he loved her and couldn't live without her.

The next Thursday the same girl emerged from the outsider van with a note for Brady. He ducked into a first-floor bathroom and locked himself in a stall to tear it open. Desperate for any word from Katie, he found only a terse letter, typed on Mr. North's business stationery.

Mr. Brady Wayne Darby:

Be advised that this is the last communiqué you shall receive directly from me. Anything further will come from my legal counsel.

The damage you caused has been repaired at my own expense, and while I appreciate your offer of reimbursement, allow me to counterpropose: you never see my daughter again, and we will consider the matter closed.

Do yourself a favor and don't imagine you and Katie as star-crossed lovers. She has made a habit of attaching herself to your type over the years, but wake up. No one like her could really be seriously interested in someone like you, and the sooner you accept that, the better off you will be.

If you find this difficult, grow up. If you violate my wish in this, you'll regret it.

Direct any further correspondence to my attorney, but I guarantee that effort will be futile too.

Most sincerely,
Jordan North

51

Serenity Halfway House

It had been years since Brady had wept. In fact, he hadn't shed a tear since his brother's funeral.

But now he found himself on the verge of sobs—not tears of remorse or sadness or disappointment. No, this was fury. This was making Brady take a good look at his real self again after playing the going-straight game for too long.

This man was not going to come between him and Katie. No way. What did Mr. North know of what his daughter felt for Brady? If it was anything remotely like what Brady felt for her, nothing and no one on earth could keep them apart. If she wasn't interested in a future with him, everything she had said and done was a lie. He would have to hear it from her lips.

The problem was, Brady could not wait. He simply could not stay at Serenity without knowing where he stood. And if it meant a fight—of any kind—between him and Katie's dad for his right to continue their love affair, he would stop at nothing.

That evening, just after dark, Brady used the house phone to call her one more time. "Katie, I know you're screening calls like you always do. Maybe you can't talk because your dad is there, I don't know. But you had better get yourself somewhere where you can call me here at the house. I have to know where I stand, and I have to know now. If I don't hear from you in an hour, I'm coming to talk to you. I'm waiting by the phone, and I love you with all my heart."

Brady paced up and down the stairs, in and out of rooms, avoiding eye contact with anyone. He mustered an "okay" when Jan asked how he was doing. "Heard from Katie?" she said.

"Yeah. We'll be getting together soon."

"Great! Keep me posted."

When the hour was almost up, Brady was so exercised he was afraid to look in the mirror. Something beastly and savage had been born in him that seemed almost physical, and he knew it would show in his eyes. He gathered up all the small amounts of cash he had earned doing menial tasks and stuffed into his pockets about forty dollars and change. As he hurried down the stairs, he ran into Bill. "Need to get out for a walk, man. Gonna pick up some cigarettes. Want anything?"

"No, thanks. Be back before midnight though, hear? Otherwise, somebody's got to get out of bed to let you in."

"No worries."

Despite a chill in the air, Brady was sweaty by the time he reached the highway and thumbed for a ride. A trucker stopped.

"Trying to get into the city," Brady told him.

"That's where I'm goin'."

"West side," Brady said.

"You kiddin'? I don't go in there. I can get you within about half a mile."

"Perfect."

As they rode, the trucker said, "Seriously, man, unless you know someone in there and they know you're coming, you don't want to be caught alone, know what I mean?"

"I know someone."

Forty minutes later Brady was on the street again, second-guessing himself. His fury had not faded. Neither had his resolve. He just hoped someone would believe he knew who he said he knew.

Almost as soon as he entered the run-down section, he felt eyes from everywhere.

"You lost, boy?"

"Wrong neighborhood, son!"

He kept moving, unsure where he was going. An old woman, bundled up and sitting on her front steps, called out to him. "Young man, you best know your business if you gonna be 'round here. What you up to?"

"Looking for Tiny."

She snorted. "You mean *the* Tiny? He at County."

"Heard he was out."

"For real? Well, I know somebody who would know. Stay right there."

Brady could hear her on the phone. "Yes, a white boy . . . I don't know, normal I guess. Not that big . . . No, I don't think he's carryin', but he might soon wish he was. . . . Okay, I'll tell him."

She returned to the steps. "Well, you knew something I didn't know. My nephew says Tiny's back where he belongs. Where you know him from?"

"County."

"If you're looking for some kinda revenge, you gonna be shipped outta here in a bag."

"He's a friend, only I don't know where he lives."

"Lives? He lives where he works, boy. Sixteen blocks north, four blocks east. But you better tell everybody along the way where you're going, or you'll never get there."

Brady did just that, only once warned that if it turned out he wasn't really a friend of Tiny's, he'd get himself messed up. Everybody he talked to was on a cell phone, and by the time he got within a quarter mile of Tiny, it seemed everyone knew he was coming.

"Here he is!"

"Almost there, bro."

"Tiny expectin' you by now."

He came to an abandoned four-story building with a dozen guys milling about out front. Each reminded him of guys he'd met at County. "Hey, Hollywood! You Tiny's buddy from the joint, right? Follow me."

As Brady mounted the inside staircase, he was glad he wasn't up to anything, because as he followed the man up, the rest followed him. Apparently his life was in Tiny's hands already.

Had this been a movie, Brady would have expected Tiny to be sitting on a throne, wearing bling and surrounded by beauties. It turned out Tiny was wearing a sleeveless T-shirt and lounging on a dilapidated couch, watching TV. He looked even bigger than Brady remembered. Being out seemed to agree with his appetite.

Tiny grunted as he leaned over to shut off the set. "My brother," he said, and they traded the handshake Brady had learned inside.

"How do you get cable in here?" Brady said.

"I get anything I want wherever I want. Don't ask, don't tell. You a brave boy, comin' into this neighborhood."

"Your turf," Brady said. "That makes it mine too."

Tiny grinned. "My man. You bring me anything? You owe me for a lot of years. You get your stash from the armored truck job?"

"Actually, I need your help on that."

"Oh, man!"

"The guy who's got my share has it in the suburbs and won't give it to me. If I can just borrow a car and a cell phone . . ."

Tiny laughed, his fleshy arms jiggling. "Oh, is that all? I'm supposed to trust you with that?"

"For fifty percent of a hundred large."

"Seventy."

"Deal."

Tiny nodded to one of his associates. "We got any legit rides available? I don't want my boy pulled over for grand theft auto. And let me borrow a cell phone." He turned to Brady. "For how long, brother? When's this go down?"

"Tonight. I bring back everything, including your share, before midnight."

"Cool. You need any help?"

"Uh, no. Your guys just might stand out in the suburbs."

"What're you sayin'?" Tiny said, laughing. "I been trying to get into the suburbs for years. What you gonna leave me for collateral?"

"I got nothin', man. Like forty bucks if you need it."

Tiny snorted. "If I need forty dollars, I need more help than you can give me. You know what happens if you do me wrong."

"You don't even have to think about that, man. I know I owe you big-time."

"Yeah, and a lot more than this."

"I know."

"You gonna be carryin', right? You don't stand for somebody trying to stiff you."

This was exactly what Brady had hoped for, a weapon without having to ask for it. He knew Tiny would think of everything.

"What do you suggest?"

"Got to take a piece, man. Don't have to use it. Just wave it in his face. He'll have to go change his pants."

"You got something I could use?"

"Yeah. The bigger the better. You ever see a sawed-off?"

"Used to own one."

"Double-barrel over/under with double trigger?"

"You're kidding."

Tiny turned to another lackey. "Get him that gun and make sure both chambers are full. Put the safety on. This boy likely to kill hisself."

Everybody laughed, including Brady.

Tiny walked him down to the car, handed him the phone, and tossed the shotgun into the backseat.

"Anything goes wrong, you stole this car and this weapon and this phone, you understand? You don't know who ever owned any of 'em."

"Sure, 'course."

"Don't let me down, Darby."

"You kidding? I brought you this job, chief."

"Yeah, and it could be a good start, depending on how it goes. Make this one work, we'll talk more business."

More business. As Brady pulled the late-model sedan out of the west side, he knew he'd never see Tiny again. He would kill Jordan North if he had to, ditch the car, the shotgun, and the phone. Then he and Katie would be off to wherever they had to go to be sure no one traced them to the murder. And where Tiny could never find him.

Brady had no idea where that might be, but Katie would know. She knew everything. Best of all, she could afford anything.

52

After a lifetime of lying and a fascination with acting, Brady Darby had an imagination that wouldn't quit. It had landed him behind bars more times than he cared to count, and it was at full throttle now as he care-fully—sans driver's license—drove toward the sub-urbs and the North mansion.

Despite the scenario playing out in his mind, Brady wasn't thinking about the consequences. He rarely did. All he imagined now was rescuing the love of his life from her spiteful, overbearing father. He meant only to scare the man, if it even came to that, but Brady was so saturated with passion that he ruled out nothing. All he could see in the future was him and his soul mate waking up next to each other somewhere—anywhere.

One of the coasts would be cool. But even if it was just a hotel in the middle of nowhere or even some abandoned hideaway, that was okay too. The system, Serenity, Tiny? They'd soon give up looking for him. The Norths? Katie could call them from here or there to assure them she was fine and to tell them that she had made her choice and was following her heart.

Brady didn't know why Katie hadn't called or taken his calls. Of course, she had caller ID. That was the advantage of his having the phone of one of Tiny's girlfriends. When Katie saw the strange number with the downtown area code, she would have to pick up out of curiosity alone.

Within a mile of Katie's subdivision, Brady was so excited he could barely sit still. What could be better than this? He had given his all at Serenity, had even considered the straight life if that's what it took to win Katie. But though she had been raised to be a good girl, the straight life sure didn't seem to appeal to her.

Brady had been making progress, had proved he might even be a candidate for normal life as a free man. But that would soon be a distant memory. He didn't really want to be a sap anyway, a working stiff, a nine-to-fiver. He was smart enough to hide in plain sight, get himself a new ID, start a new life. With Katie at his side, all things were possible.

As he pressed her number into the phone, he allowed himself for the first time to wonder if she was even at home. Was it possible her father had kicked her out? So much the better. Brady would pick her up wherever she was.

Her number was ringing. *Don't go to voice mail! Please!*

"Hello?" Katie said.

"It's me, babe."

"Brady? What phone are you calling from?"

"Borrowed it."

"Oh. Uh, hi."

"Hi, baby. I got that letter from your dad and I've just got to see you."

"Letter?"

She had to know. "All official and everything, threatening me, talking about his lawyer, telling me to never see you again and that you weren't really interested in me. Can you imagine?"

"Oh, man. Well, you know, he's just upset. He doesn't speak for me."

"I know! I know! I've just got to have you tell me to my face that we've still got something going. In fact, I'm ready to get married if you want."

"Married?"

"C'mon, we've been talking around it forever. I've got wheels, and I'm ready to go. Where are you?"

"I'm home, but—"

"I'm almost there. Pack a bag and sneak out. I'll pick you up a block away."

"Brady, no. My dad and I are half getting along right now, and there's no sense—"

"I thought you said he didn't speak for you."

"He doesn't, but I'm not ready to just up and—"

"We're still okay though, aren't we? I mean, I'm glad if you're getting along with your dad better. And I've got to find a way to do that too, don't I?"

"Um-hm."

"But I can't just show up there after getting his letter," Brady said. "We've got to figure this out, make a plan. You've got to work on him for me."

"Um-hm."

"I'm pulling into the area right now. I'll wait at the corner, all right?"

"I can't go anywhere tonight, Brady."

"I know. I just need to see you and talk to you, that's all. We can figure out the rest later."

"He's going to be suspicious."

"What do you care? Tell him anything, but just come and talk to me in the car."

"How'd you get a car?"

"Never mind, from a friend, who cares? Now I'm parking and I'll be waiting. You coming?"

"I'll try."

"Don't try! Just do it. Tell him you're going for a walk."

"I don't go for walks."

"Katie, I'm serious. I am not leaving till I see you. You want me to come there and start something with your dad?"

Silence.

"I didn't think so. He's not ready for that and neither am I. Don't make me come there. Because I will and I mean it."

"No, don't come. I'll see if I can slip out."

"That's my girl."

Brady sat there aware that this had to be one of those neighborhood watch areas and that concerned eyes could be peeking at him from any number of windows. He kept wrenching around, looking for Katie, all the while recalibrating his plans. If she wasn't ready to run off with him tonight, he'd have to get back to Serenity. But then Tiny would soon know where he was.

Maybe he should pull a heist in this neighborhood. Problem was, who knew if anybody had cash lying around? Maybe Katie had an idea. Brady had never burglarized a home, though he'd heard enough stories from guys inside who had. He would be a lot more comfortable with a partner or even a team.

Katie seemed tentative as she approached, and he realized she wouldn't recognize the car. He waved and leaned over to open the passenger door, and she slid in. Brady reached for her, but she wasn't her usual self. She seemed to halfheartedly return his hug, and when he went to kiss her, she turned and took it on the cheek. "Man, I've missed you, babe," he said.

She smiled thinly. "Thanks."

"Where've you been, Katie?"

"Busy. Whew. Dad's really clamping down, and I guess it's time to start acting like an adult."

Brady cocked his head and squinted at her. "Hello? I'm looking for Katie North. Where's the rebel I knew?"

"Oh, you know. Growing up."

"In just a few days? It wasn't that long ago you had me cutting Harley cookies on your lawn."

"I know. But enough's enough."

"What happened?"

"Nothing."

"Your dad got to you, didn't he?"

"I guess."

"What, he threatened to cut you off?"

"Only if I see you."

503

"So we're both taking it in the teeth from this guy."

"*This guy?* Brady, you're talking about my father."

"I know who I'm talking about. What do you think, I don't know? Oh, I know all right. This is the guy who threatened to report me if I tried to see you again. Told me someone *like you* wouldn't ever really be interested in someone *like me*. Well, what does that make me, Katie? What does that say about your taste in men? You gonna let him decide who you're going to be in love with?"

"In love? Brady, we've had a lot of fun, but we're not in love. At least I'm not."

"*What?*"

"It's been fun, a game."

"It wasn't a game to me! I want to get married."

"Married? Oh, Brady, no. Now, come on."

"What, so it's true? A girl like you could never—?"

"I didn't say that."

"No, your dad did, and you're proving he was right."

"Seriously now, Brady, did you really think there was a future for us?"

"There is!"

"Um, no. There isn't. And I'm sorry if you didn't get that, but there never was."

"You were playing me?"

"Brady, please. I thought we were both just playing. How would it have worked out? I marry you and then what? What do you do? Where do you work? What happens next?"

"So the whole thing was a big joke?"

"I didn't mean to mislead you, I really didn't."

"You were conning me!"

"No, that's not it. Now I'm sorry, but I've got to go."

"Wait! So now that you know how I really feel about you, that's it? It's over?"

"I'm flattered, really I am, but I don't feel the same, so I think it's better that we just—"

"Wait!"

But she had opened her door and the interior light came on.

"Wait! I've got something for you."

"Brady, listen, now, come on. Do you need me to be clear that we're officially over?"

"Don't say that! I love you!"

"Stop! Okay, I admit it. I used you to tick off my dad."

"We had way more than that going, Katie."

"No! We didn't."

She turned to leave. He grabbed her arm. "Please," he said.

"I helped him write the letter, Brady, okay? I know that's hard to hear, but you need to hear it."

Brady reached into the backseat and grabbed the sawed-off, flicking off the safety as he brought it forward and stuck it within inches of her face.

He saw the panic in her eyes. She opened her mouth but couldn't seem to make a sound.

He loved her so much. Wanted her so badly. Needed her so desperately.

When she turned to flee, he pulled the trigger.

The explosion deafened Brady, and the twelve-gauge pack of buckshot had barely escaped the muzzle and had no time to release and spread before it hit her. The concussion removed most of Katie's head, drove her body into the half-open door, and blew it off its hinges onto the grass.

She lay next to it in a motionless heap.

Brady sat quivering as the acrid smoke cleared, sickened by the blood and tissue left inside the car. Lights came on all over the neighborhood, and he heard shouting.

He turned the weapon and pressed it to his heart.

Click!

He had emptied both barrels into the love of his life.

Anyone else might have thrown the car into gear and raced away. But Brady didn't want to live. If only Tiny had given him one more shell . . .

Nothing had ever gone right for Brady Darby. And now he couldn't even kill himself.

With the car still idling, he opened his door and rolled out, landing on the pavement on his hands and knees. He vomited and howled like an animal, heaving great sobs in the night. Soon he was surrounded by men in bathrobes, one on his cell phone to the police, two others leveling hunting rifles at him.

He was vaguely aware that a couple was making their way around to the other side of the car. The woman screamed.

506

53

Katie North was not really an heiress, except in the usual way rich kids would benefit from the passing of their parents. But the press dubbed her the Murdered Heiress, and thus, Brady Wayne Darby became the Heiress Murderer.

The newspapers and magazines and news shows dug up everyone anywhere who knew the victim or the perpetrator, alternating interviews between the upper crust and the other side of the tracks. It made for interesting television, if little else.

Friends of the Norths called Katie a troubled rebel who had recently reconciled with her family.

Acquaintances of Brady—some from as far back as Touhy Trailer Park, even his own mother—called him a dreamer, a career criminal, selfish, heartless, and cruel.

"He was always up to no good," Erlene Darby said, her shy husband shifting nervously in the background. "Hasn't spoke to me in years."

Brady's aunt Lois told the TV people that despite his troubled past, he had been doing well and that "this was a surprise and we wouldn't be shocked to find out it was an accident."

One of the first questions Brady was asked when he was processed into isolation at the Adamsville County

Jail was whether he was suicidal. "You have no idea," he whispered.

"Is that a yes?"

He closed his eyes and nodded.

Brady was put on suicide watch and issued prison garb that contained nothing he could fashion into a death tool. He spent the night in a padded cell with recessed, grill-covered lights that never went off. A guard sat outside, and a small video camera in the ceiling slowly swept from corner to corner with a quiet whine.

The next morning Brady was escorted to a room where a tall, thin man in his early thirties introduced himself as Jackie Kent. Everything about Kent was straight and narrow—his dark, short hair, his nose, his ears, his chin, his tie, his suit, even his trench coat and shoes.

He proved to be one of those get-to-the-point guys.

Jackie pulled a sheaf of papers from his briefcase as he sat across from Brady. "Know that part in the Miranda warning where they tell you that if you can't afford a lawyer, one will be provided for you, blah, blah, blah? That's me. I'm what's called a contract attorney. Firm I work for contracts for a certain number of these cases a year and assigns them to people at my level. We each get about one case a day for every day of the year, including weekends and holidays, and I'm not exaggerating. I had exactly 365 cases last year. All that for about twenty-five hundred dollars a month, not a dime of which comes from your pocket."

"I'm guilty," Brady said. "What do I need you for?"

"Everybody deserves representation. You did yourself no favors by spilling your guts to the police and trying to plead guilty."

"I *am*."

"So you've said. But you don't plead your case to the police. You plead it to the court. If you decide to plead guilty—"

"Aren't you listening?"

"If you decide to plead guilty, you do the county a big favor, and that ought to be worth something. It might even be worth your life. You see? You withhold your plea until that offer is floated before you. They say they could try you and put you to death or you can plead guilty and get life without parole. You might rather be dead, but—"

"I would."

"—but you have to admit that of the two options, one is clearly better than the other."

"I admit it. Only I wouldn't choose the one you'd choose."

"I won't even pretend I know how you're feeling right now, Mr. Darby. But let me say that I have one job here, and that is to do the very best legal work I can for you. I happen to be anti–capital punishment, but even if I wasn't, my goal would be to do everything I can to keep you from the death chamber."

"You're wasting your time."

"So I've been told and more than once. But do not discount that over the next few days, while the public and the press variously call for your life or your protection, you may change your mind. I have seen men and women go from what you're professing now to where they'd agree to anything to not be sentenced to death."

"I can't imagine."

"Okay, here's what happens next. I will ask for a continuance so we can start working together. If that is granted, it won't be for long because of the high profile of this case. Already the capital punishment abolitionists, among whom I count myself, have cranked up their newsletters in your support. I walked through a band of demonstrators to get inside this morning."

"What are you talking about?"

"People who oppose the death penalty. They know it's coming. They're marching outside on your behalf."

"They're supporting me. I blew a girl's head off, and they're on my side."

"Don't misunderstand. No one is condoning what you claim you did."

"I'm not just claiming it. I did it."

"Fair enough. No one in his right mind condones murder. But do you realize that the United States is the only democratic society that still executes its citizens?"

"Sure glad I live here, then."

"Listen, Mr. Darby. Why should only the rich benefit from the courts? You know what they say about capital punishment? 'If you have the capital, you don't get the punishment.'"

Brady stood and shook his head. "I want the punishment, man, okay? I don't know how else to say it."

"You're going to be on death row for years as it is. You might as well redeem the time by fighting for yourself. There are nearly four thousand waiting to die in this country right now and twenty-five thousand more serving life without parole."

"How fast can I be put to death?"

"I wouldn't answer that if I knew. It's counter to my purpose."

"Your purpose is to keep me alive?"

"Of course. It's my job."

"You're not supposed to represent me, try to get me what I want? Because I want to die and soon. All I want to know is how soon you can get that done."

Jackie Kent sat back and sighed. "Even if you plead guilty and don't try for life, there are mandatory appeals of death penalty sentences at all levels."

"Mandatory? You mean they appeal for me even if I don't want them to?"

"Exactly."

"How long does all that take?"

"Years."

"No good. What's the shortest amount of time?"

"If you don't cooperate with the process and keep going public with your guilt and your wish to die, maybe as short as three years, the way it was back in the forties, fifties, and sixties."

"The good old days."

"Let me fight for you, sir. I've read your file."

"Then you know what happened."

"You made that fairly plain, yes. There'll be no getting you cleared. But it wasn't your car. It wasn't your weapon. You were not in your own neighborhood. You have been a habitual drug user. You could have been high. Your relationship went sour; an argument became heated. You meant only to scare her, maybe make her think you were going to shoot yourself. The shotgun went off. You didn't mean to do it."

"Except none of that's true. I was stone-cold sober. Do I regret what I did? 'Course I do. I want to die for it. But she played me for the fool, and I killed her because I wanted to."

"Temporary insanity. A crime of passion. That fine line between love and obsession. If you couldn't have her, no one could." Kent looked at his watch and began refilling his briefcase. Brady wondered if he had finally convinced the man. "In case you change your mind, let me enter a plea of *nolo contendere*. That's just Latin for not admitting anything but accepting punishment as if you were guilty. The judicial system of the county, in its gratitude for your willingness to spare it considerable time and expense, will come back insisting that you plead guilty in exchange for life without parole over a death sentence."

"No deal. Now, I been pulling schemes and scams

my whole life, and I'm done. What do I have to do to be guaranteed the death penalty as fast as I can get it?"

Jackie folded his arms. "I can't believe you're asking me this. I have an ethical and professional obligation to—"

"All right, I'm tired of hearing that. I know what your job is. I know you don't need or want this case, and I'm going to ask for someone else if you won't get me what I want."

"Truth is, Mr. Darby, the fastest way to get what you want is to plead not guilty, make the county prove its case, and don't cooperate in your own defense. Everybody will love the publicity, and all they have to prove is motive, which you just told me you had; method, which has your fingerprints all over it; and opportunity. Can you be placed at the scene? A no-brainer."

"But wouldn't any trial take longer than no trial?"

"If they'll let you plead guilty and still sentence you to death, no. But if I go to the judge with that plea, without asking for life, he'll find you or me unstable, and then you'll be interviewed by batteries of shrinks trying to get a handle on your death wish."

"Handle? There's no handle. There's a death sentence for murderers. And I'm a murderer."

Jackie Kent told Brady it surprised even him, but within a week, the Heiress Murderer got what he wanted. He was sentenced to die at the Adamsville State Penitentiary, method to be determined. As his lawyer had predicted, a schedule of mandatory appeals was drawn up, despite Brady telling the judge in plain language that he opposed these, would not cooperate, and hoped they would all fail.

With cameras rolling, the judge said, "Mr. Darby, as you have pleaded guilty, there is no cause for me to lecture you regarding your thoughtless, wanton act. Do you wish to make any statement before being remanded to the penitentiary?"

Brady spoke so softly that the TV stations had to run subtitles. "No. I did it and I'd do it again."

As Brady was loaded into a county van for transport to ASP, reporters and cameramen surrounded the Norths near the steps outside the courthouse. Jordan and Carole looked ten years older than their fifty years. She stared at the ground as her husband spoke solemnly.

"No death will be slow or painful enough for that animal. I pray he burns in hell, and my biggest regret is that I can't kill him myself."

54

Adamsville State Penitentiary

Dirk Blanc was in Thomas's office celebrating with him the summary judgment throwing out Jorge's case against him when Frank LeRoy knocked and entered.

"Hear the news, sir?" Dirk said, rising and shaking the warden's hand.

"Yeah. Thrilled. Good job. Gettin' tired of these frivolous wastes of time. You guys want a peek at our new celeb?"

Thomas rose. "He's here?"

"Should be by the time we get down there."

Like everyone else in the state, Thomas had followed the Murdered Heiress case from the beginning. People were naturally fascinated by a condemned man without an excuse, let alone one who insisted on paying the ultimate price for his crime. Pundits everywhere had proffered every reason imaginable why a young man from the wrong side of town would fall for a socialite and wind up slaughtering the very one he claimed to love.

Others wanted to blame everything and everybody but the perpetrator: poverty, drugs, culture, society, the school system, the courts.

As they left his office, Thomas grabbed his Bible off the desk. He would not be allowed to engage the new man for at least ninety days, and in fourteen years as chaplain he had learned never to take his Bible with him unless visiting a cell at a con's request. But it seemed the thing to do this time. Maybe it was just for himself, a security blanket. Some things never became routine here, and one was the sobering experience of seeing a death row inmate processed in, even though most of the condemned men in the supermax would outlive Thomas. But not this one. If the press could be believed, he would die in three years.

"Ya gotta hand it to the kid," Dirk said as they made

their way through all the security checkpoints. "Not trying to get out from under it."

"Yeah, no," the warden said. "I mean, okay, most of the guys in here, even on the Row, are innocent to hear them tell it. Friends betrayed them, lawyers blew their case, the judge made up his mind before the trial, and on and on and on. But hand it to this guy? You won't hear that from me. Vicious killer getting what he deserves, I say. And he's no kid. He's thirty, ya know."

"It's sad, that's all I can say," Thomas said as his ID was scanned yet again. "Two young people in the primes of their lives . . ."

"Yeah, no," the warden said. "Her maybe. He was in the prime of nothing."

The prison was, if anything, noisier than ever. There wasn't a man inside who didn't know who was coming. Everybody was talking, catcalling, hooting, hollering, or banging something. The place depressed Thomas more every time he stepped into it. God had once bestowed on him a deep burden for these men's souls. Oh, it was still there, but now it came to him in the form of a rolling wave of melancholy and frustration. The evangelist in him wanted to call for order and begin preaching right then and there, calling men to repentance and belief. But he could not. He could talk to one man at a time, and then only at the man's request. And to Thomas's knowledge, not one con had come to faith under his influence.

George Andreason, the former governor and now director of the state's Department of Corrections, waited near the intake cell. Yanno greeted him like the old friend he was. Thomas introduced to him Dirk Blanc.

"Nobody in Ad Seg I see," Andreason said.

"Had one with a coupla days to go and another on his way," the warden said, "but they'll wait. Give the new man his space."

"Good idea," the director said. "The press are here. They stay outside the overhead door."

Yanno nodded, and the four of them turned as one at the sound of the door opening a football field's distance away. The press was being held back as they shot live footage of the Heiress Murderer taking one last long drag on a cigarette, both cuffed hands to his mouth. Finally he flicked the butt away.

"Hope he enjoyed that," Andreason said. "His last forever. Think of it."

Maybe it was the distance, but Thomas had pictured a bigger man. This guy was of average height and lean build, and as a phalanx of heavily armored corrections officers brought him toward the intake cell, Thomas noticed he was dark-complexioned for a Caucasian. Dark hair and eyes too.

The officers seemed to be aware they were part of this center of attention and appeared to want to move faster. But the condemned man, garish head to toe in his Day-Glo orange county jail uniform, was slowed by his ankle shackles and chains. He was also bound around the middle, hands cuffed in front. Thomas had seen men jog along with mincing steps when so constrained, but this man was in no hurry. And why should he be?

Thomas could not help but think of the man's victim as the party drew near. She apparently had been no saint either, but as a father and grandfather, Thomas grieved with her family. He could not conceive of losing his beloveds, let alone in such a manner.

God, please grant me some compassion for this man in spite of everything.

Screaming, whistling, yelling seemed to come from every cell in every pod as the cavalcade passed. Some cons called out vile questions or insults. But neither the officers nor the new man so much as turned to look. Once the prisoner lifted his hands high enough to flash double obscene gestures, making the caged men shout even louder.

It appeared to Thomas that the officers were aware that the big bosses were waiting for them at the end of the line. Every uniform was crisp and clean, every boot spit-shined, every badge gleaming. Each man stood ramrod straight and bore a serious countenance. What may have started as each man putting his best foot forward for the press now took the form of showing the head of the DOC and the warden that they meant business.

The man leading the procession, the biggest and widest of the officers, stopped about ten feet in front of Thomas and the others and looked to the warden. "You handling it from here, sir?"

"Yes, thank you," Yanno said. "Assume your positions."

The officers formed a semicircle behind the inmate, and the warden approached him and introduced himself and Andreason. The con appeared sullen and only nodded.

"This is our intake cell, where you will spend your first twenty-four hours. Once you are inside and the door is secured, step to the meal slot so we can remove your cuffs. Then lie on your back and rest your ankles above the slot so we can remove your shackles. Then strip down to your underwear and pass your uniform out through the slot. When we come get you tomorrow for transfer to your cell, we'll reverse the process and you'll get your tee and khakis and slippers."

The young man peered into the cell, scowling. "I'm sleeping here? On the floor?"

"Hey!" Yanno shouted to the officers. "What happened to the king bed and the down comforter? And remind the maid about the mint on the pillow."

The officers laughed. The con didn't.

Thomas was not amused.

Yanno signaled an officer in the observation booth, and the loud click of the electronic lock echoed in the hallway. The warden removed the manual security device, and the lead officer used his key on the main lock. Throughout the process of getting the man inside, unbound, and undressed, Thomas looked away, noticing that everyone else, his son-in-law included, gawked at the murderer the whole time.

When the man was on his feet again, Yanno beckoned him close and spoke softly, informing him of when he would be fed (twice while in intake) and that someone would deliver an envelope. "Normally when someone is in this cell, it's for Administrative Segregation, and they get nothing to read. But when being processed in, you are expected to become familiar with our rules and regulations and procedures, understand?"

The man pursed his lips as if the question insulted him.

"One piece of advice," the warden said. "Do your own time. The less you listen or talk to anyone else, the better off you'll be. You'll be treated the way you act. Do what you're told, follow orders, and you'll get along. We're not here to judge you. That's already been done. Our job is to keep you, and we've never failed at that. You follow?"

"Whatever." The man's eyes seemed to fall on Thomas's Bible, then directly into Thomas's eyes.

The chaplain couldn't bring himself to smile, but he found himself instinctively greeting the con with a raise of his brows and a tightening of his lips.

This man certainly didn't look thirty. In fact, for an instant, he looked like a child. His eyes were distant, his cheeks hollow, and a great cavernous emptiness seemed to reside in him. He appeared to want to say something to Thomas, but Yanno interrupted.

"We're done here," he said. "Your packet will show you how you can talk to this man if you wish, provided you behave as required your first ninety days."

As the quartet made its way back through the

labyrinth to the administrative offices, Thomas wondered if this would be just another sad soul swept into the black hole of the ASP. He sure looked like he needed to talk with someone, but would he ever ask?

"If I had to guess," Thomas said, "I'd say that one is a real suicide risk."

"Only way he could off himself in intake," Andreason said, "would be to tie his underbritches around his neck and yank it as tight as he can before our guys get to him."

"I would hope our guys take their time," Yanno said. "Sorry sack of garbage. Save us the cost of feeding him before we get to kill him anyway."

"You don't mean that," Thomas said.

The warden looked genuinely surprised. "Oh yeah, I forgot. You want these monsters around long enough for Jesus to get to 'em."

Thomas had never spoken angrily to Frank LeRoy, but there was an edge to his voice now. "Well, that is my reason for being here, after all. Otherwise, what's the point?"

"Man, Dad," Dirk chimed in, "you know where I stand on capital punishment, but that guy . . ."

"I don't want to hear it," Thomas said, and as they emerged from the last security envelope, he hurried ahead of the rest and went directly to his office, slamming the door. Then he noticed Dirk's overcoat on the chair and knew he would have to face him again. He picked up the phone to call Grace, hoping to be busy when Dirk came in. But he had barely begun dialing when he heard the knock and the door opened.

"I apologize, Dad," Dirk said as Thomas hung up. "That was insensitive. I wouldn't want you making fun of my beliefs."

"Your beliefs? I didn't know you had any."

Dirk held up both hands. "All right, apparently not in the mood. I surrender." He began putting on his coat.

"Well," Thomas said, "I know you believe it's wrong to put a man to death, but I guess it's okay in this instance because, why, the victim was different from all the others of the men on the Row in here?"

"Dad, listen, really, I didn't mean to push your buttons. I'm sorry. Even if we don't see eye to eye on the God stuff, I admire what you're doing here or trying to do."

"I'm doing nothing here, Dirk. I have wasted my life."

"Surely you've brought comfort and inspiration to someone in here."

"That's not what I'm here for! I am here to introduce these lost men to God, and I feel like a blind man in a mine shaft, trying to show people the way."

"I don't know how else to say it, sir. I was out of line. I'm going to go now."

Did God still answer prayer? When was the last time He had for Thomas? Dirk and Ravinia were prime examples. Was Thomas praying in the wrong way for them? Was he really asking for something that was not in the will of God? And how could it not be?

As Thomas left at the end of the day, Gladys moved directly into his path.

"Excuse me, dear," he said, but when he went to slip past her, she blocked him again. He sighed.

"Hold on there a minute, Reverend," she said. "I need to tell you something. I like the new you."

"I really need to get going, Gladys. Can we talk tomorrow?"

"We can, but you're going to hear me right now. For a lot of years you've been known as the easy mark, the milquetoast man around this place."

"I've worked on that."

"And you've succeeded, at least with the inmates. But I'm talking about with your coworkers. I like to see a little fire in you."

"Well, thank you. Can I go now?"

"Don't ask, man. Just go. Be the new Thomas."

Thomas had no idea what that was all about. He certainly didn't feel new. He felt like a frustrated old man who'd been through the same thing so many times he could hardly imagine bearing it again.

And now he had this haunting encounter with the Heiress Murderer to plague him. Well, it was time to put God to the test once again. Apparently his first prayer about this man had been answered. There seemed to have been planted within Thomas some kernel of compassion or concern or care. But it meant nothing if the inmate never asked to see him again.

523

What kind of a policy was that anyway? Hire a chaplain, give him an office and a huge congregation, but don't allow him to talk to anyone without their permission?

Craziness.

But in spite of himself, Thomas felt led to pray for the young man. But how? And for what exactly? God knew. And so Thomas's petition took the form of simply repeating the inmate's name to God, over and over.

The newspapers always called him by all three names.

Brady Wayne Darby.

55

Brady didn't know what to make of how he was feeling.

First he was cold. He pressed his bare back up against the concrete block wall and endured the shock until a little warmth developed there. But he had to wrap his shins in his forearms and tuck his head between his knees to keep from shivering, and even that didn't help much.

He hated this about himself, but his need for a cigarette was actually allowing him to forget what he had done, at least for a few seconds at a time. Brady even considered pleading with a passing guard, offering him anything for a smoke. But as he understood it, not even the staff was allowed to bring tobacco into the facility. He was going cold turkey and that's all there was to it. And each time he got that into his brain, his body seemed to scream for nicotine all the more.

But then the horror of the murder came rushing back. How could it not? Desperate as Brady was to push it from himself and think of anything else, he could still smell the gunpowder, the blood.

He could still see Katie hurtling from the car in a torrent of flesh and gore.

He could still feel the cool pavement on his palms as he perched there, braying as his life too was ending.

All he wanted was to die, and if there was a way to accomplish that before three years passed, he would do it.

Brady was also lonely, but he couldn't think of a person he wanted to talk to except Katie. That was so strange. He couldn't expect a bit of sympathy from a soul, but did anyone understand that he had suffered a loss too? Yes, he had done it. He had murdered the Katie who so repelled him and had made clear that he had been duped, played, betrayed. But with her had gone the woman he had loved as he had never loved anyone else in his wretched life.

That was the Katie he missed, the one he could talk to, the one who teased him, flirted with him, held him, and kissed him.

Brady was smarter than people gave him credit for, evidenced by the high school teachers who always seemed surprised at his reading ability. But he had never considered himself an intellectual and so now wondered if there was a description for what had happened to him in all this.

Shock? Maybe. But not physical. He had not been injured. Yet as soon as he had moved from his hands and knees in the street to sit with his back to the borrowed car, it seemed his entire past and future passed before his mind's eye. Nothing was unclear anymore. It was as if he had taken his best hit of dope ever.

Brady had thought of every family member, loved one, friend, acquaintance he had ever had. And this had happened in an instant. He had been aware that the terrified people in the neighborhood, who kept their distance while making it clear he wasn't going anywhere until the cops showed up, were relentlessly talking, sometimes to him. But he wasn't listening.

Rather, Brady had been seeing his future as clearly as if he had already lived it. It never crossed his mind to try to get out of this mess to end all messes. Other than to kill himself, escape was not an option. He wouldn't lie, deny, excuse, anything. He wouldn't stay silent or demand a lawyer. No, for the first time in his life, he would accept the consequences.

He had committed an unthinking and unthinkable act, and as he heard the blaring sirens in the distance, he saw himself cuffed, searched, Mirandized, ushered into a squad car, interrogated, delivered to County, processed in, and assigned a defense attorney. That hadn't taken any special powers of foresight. He'd been through this many times, though not on this scale and never for anything with so many mortal repercussions.

Brady had to admit he had not expected it to be so hard to simply insist on a death sentence and have it finally come, and the mandatory appeal process still frustrated him. But otherwise, none of this had been a surprise. He had watched it unfold from some dark spot deep within his soul. Oh, the various personalities had been unique, and he had not imagined the supermax to look or be like this, but he knew this was where he would wind up.

No clock. No food. No cigarettes. Nothing to read. No clothes. He wasn't sure what the point was. Wasn't his accepting the ultimate punishment enough for these people? He didn't care, really. It just didn't make sense. Maybe they felt the need to personally make him pay. Fair enough. It simply irritated Brady that he began to long for those things that were deprived him.

"Excuse me, guard," he said, "what time is it?"

The man looked offended that Brady would even address him. "First of all, don't call me *guard*. I'm a corrections officer. As for what time it is, scumbag, it's time for you to shut that hole in your face before I come in there and shut it for you."

"Thank you."

"Get smart with me, you'll be in here for a week before you get a cell."

"Sorry."

"The only response I want from you is silence!"

Brady held up his hands. What did he care what time it was anyway? It wasn't like he had a schedule.

He guessed it was half an hour later when he heard guards—officers—making the rounds for roll call. What was he to say? "Here, sir," as he had done in phys ed class years before?

An officer stopped before his cage. "Brady Wayne Darby!"

"Yes, sir!"

"On your feet! This is the standing roll call so we can verify you're in one piece."

"I am."

"Shut up! You haven't received your induction packet yet, have you?"

Brady wanted to say, "Do you see one in here?" But he knew saying anything seemed to upset these guys. So he simply shook his head.

"I can't hear you!"

"No, sir, I haven't."

"Dinner's comin'."

Instinct told him to say thanks, but Brady resisted the urge. He was hungry, maybe for the first time since he'd been arrested, and even the mention of dinner made it worse. Funny, he hadn't slept or eaten much while at County during all the briefings and hearings and pleadings. He had lost weight, he was sure, and now wondered if he would ever be hungry again.

But the next visitor was an officer who slipped an envelope into the meal slot. It slapped onto the floor.

Brady decided he wouldn't be able to concentrate enough to read it before he ate anyway.

When his tray finally came, Brady found one slice of lunchmeat bologna between two slices of slightly stale white bread with neither butter nor any other condiment. This was accompanied by a room-temperature box of some kind of fruit juice that was more sugar than real. Had it not been for the tepid liquid, he would not have been able to force down the dry sandwich. And hadn't the warden said he would get only two meals here in twenty-four hours?

He set the tray aside and opened the large envelope. It was full of pamphlets and booklets. One contained page after page of hints on how to get along behind bars. He'd seen similar before, naturally, but Brady had never been in a supermax, where he would have zero personal contact with another inmate ever.

As he read, he learned of all the services offered and the procedures required to take advantage of them. He was stunned to see that he would have no electricity or reading material or exercise his first ninety days. It wasn't that he thought he was entitled to any privileges or even common necessities, but this was going to do nothing but damage to his state of mind.

Needless to say, no one cared about his comfort, including Brady. But when he allowed himself to consider merely existing until the state put him out of his misery, he knew it would require at least a few things to keep him sane. How ironic that they watched him constantly to be sure he didn't kill himself before they had the chance to do it.

One brochure, reserved for only the death row inmates, told him his method of execution was his choice: lethal injection (described as the most humane and the choice of 95 percent of the condemned), gas chamber, electric chair, and hanging.

Well, he didn't have to decide yet, but Brady was almost certain he would choose the first. He knew himself, knew that at his core he was a coward, that he was not really likely to kill himself and would want to go in the least painful way possible.

He wasn't ever again going to embody the courage he'd had when he thought that sawed-off still had a live shell in it.

Brady found one more pamphlet, this one outlining how to get counseling, medical care, a chaplain's visit, books or magazines, or a meeting with a lawyer.

Chaplain. The guy with the Bible had to be the chaplain. And one had to fill out a form and wait for a decision to get him to so much as visit your cell. Like that would happen.

Brady shook his head as he read the fine print. None of the above were available to the inmate during his first ninety days except in the case of medical or legal emergency.

It was going to be one long night and an even longer first three months.

56

Remission.

Such a technical, medical word, and yet how sweet it sounded to Thomas Carey.

For the first time in months, Grace was walking without help, getting in and out of bed on her own, able to get to the bathroom and even shower by herself.

It was temporary, Thomas knew. Everyone knew. Even the volunteer caregivers from Village Church who were now getting a few days off from the normal rotation. They still checked in on Grace when Thomas was at work, and she was careful not to overdo things. But it thrilled him to see her sitting in the living room when he got home from work each day.

She read. She sewed. She watched TV and DVDs. While they agreed she should not undertake baking or big meal-preparation chores, Grace enjoyed fixing herself snacks and often had something ready when Thomas arrived.

She had even taken to wearing a little makeup, and seeing her in anything but nightclothes during the day made life seem normal again. Once Thomas splurged and paid to have a hairdresser make a house call. The next day he drove Grace to church, where she sat weeping through the entire service.

"It was like heaven," she said.

The problem was, while Grace's leukemia was in remission, Thomas's spiritual life was in depression. He did everything he could to put a happy face on things, and there was no question he was warmed and encouraged by her rally—short-lived as the doctor warned it would be—but after nearly four decades of marriage, there was no hiding things from Grace.

She talked with him, counseled him, encouraged him, prayed for him, sang to him. "I'm no Pollyanna, Thomas," she said one day. "Frankly, I wish our lives and Ravinia had turned out differently. But I still believe we were called to serve and that we should do that and leave the rest to God. If our reward comes only in heaven and not here, so be it."

He knew she was right. Thomas also knew he would be admitting defeat if he allowed disappointment and frustration to interrupt his devotional life. His spiritual life needed to be fed.

And that was the rub. Many were the days at the state penitentiary where he felt incarcerated too. Maybe it was only eight hours a day, but it was in many ways as much a prison to him as it was to the men in the cages.

Only four inmates had asked to see Thomas in the past few weeks. All were lifers. One was a Native American complaining that the sweat lodge was inadequate and insisting that Thomas interact with tribal authorities and do whatever was required to bring it up to code, regardless what that meant.

Thomas did what was asked of him, willing to honor another man's faith, no matter what he believed. He just hoped that perhaps by doing his part, as required by his job description, he might earn the right to discuss spiritual matters with the man someday.

But when Thomas raised the sweat lodge matter with Frank LeRoy, the warden said, "Yeah, no. He knows religious rights extend only so far as they don't threaten security. You know what happened, don't you? That man lost his last chance at parole after assaulting an officer while being escorted to the sweat lodge."

The other three men Thomas talked with during that quarter told him of bad childhood experiences in church but pleaded for family phone calls—none of which met requirements. One settled for having Thomas lend him a couple of books from the chaplain's library, but these soon were delivered back, apparently unread. Thomas had not heard from any of the three again.

Was it too much to ask that someone would ask to see him who was sincerely interested in spiritual things? Apparently it was.

Death Row

After sitting twenty-four hours in his undershorts and ingesting as much as he could stand of two single-slice, dry bologna sandwiches and two lukewarm boxes of fruit juice, Brady had suddenly become the man of the hour again. Four officers showed up, one toting Brady's new clothes. But rather than allow him to change, he was instructed to back up to the meal slot to be cuffed, then was asked if he could be trusted to cooperate so they could open his door before manacling him at the ankles.

"Like I've got a choice," he said.

"You'll behave or you'll wish you'd never been born," one of the officers said.

I already wish that.

It made sense, he figured, that they would treat him as the murderer he was, but Brady wondered if there was another con in the whole place who was less interested in violence now that he had committed the ultimate violent act. Brady had been involved in a lot of brawls, in and out of jail, with cops and civilians, other cons, you name it. But these guys at ASP had nothing to worry about with him. He had lost the will to live, let alone to fight.

Brady found it hard to believe, but his need for a cigarette soon drowned out everything else in his mind. Maybe that was for the best. He knew he was just this side of insane anyway.

Why did they feel it necessary to parade him through the other pods and cells and security checkpoints in his underwear? He wanted to ask, but he had already learned that they resented questions. It was bad enough the whole place smelled and was variously too cold or too hot. Again, everyone seemed to know who he was. He was met with screams and whistles and comments all along the way. Brady just kept his head down and shuffled as quickly as he was able.

The reason for not letting him dress became clear when he was delivered to his unit and ushered directly to the shower, hands and feet unfastened, and handed a safety razor. "That comes back to us in one piece or you'll regret it."

His clothes were left just outside the stall. The water seemed to come on and go off on its own schedule, so Brady just hurriedly showered, shaved quickly in front of a reflective sheet of metal on the wall, handed the razor back, and reached for his clothes. He found strangely inviting the idea of finally being clothed.

"Not so fast. Body cavity search."

Brady complied with this humiliating exercise, wondering what bit of contraband he could possibly have found between the intake cell and here. Finally allowed to dress, he was hooked up again and led to his final home, which the people inside referred to as his house. His was on the lower left of a ten-man, two-level unit on death row. Every one of the other nine men would pass his cell when led to their thrice-weekly showers or to the exercise area for their one hour of each twenty-four.

Brady was released from the cuffs and shackles again, handed his induction packet, and finally locked away. Once the officers were gone, the noise became almost unbearable. Besides the radios and TVs and conversations, everyone within earshot began calling out to Brady, asking him obscene questions about the heiress, describing the murder, recounting everything they had heard and read about it, demanding that he answer.

Brady laid his envelope on the steel desk with attached stool, knowing it would probably be his only reading material for three months. He sat there, studying the cot and the combination toilet/sink in the corner, in full view of any passersby.

He decided not to answer, to say absolutely nothing. But as the yelling and the questions rose to a deafening din and he sat on his cot and covered his ears, Brady realized that some cons in certain cells of other units in the pod could see him. They told his unit mates every detail of what he was doing.

"Don't plug your ears, trailer trash!"

"Too early for bed, lover boy!"

"Tell us the story! Did you really think she loved you, Romeo?"

"Did you hear what Daddy North said? He wants you to burn in hell!"

Brady had seen similar hazing at County and knew of newcomers who wound up burying their faces in their blankets and crying themselves to sleep, opening them to even more ridicule. He decided to just busy himself in the farthest, most private corner of his cell, reading over the stuff from his packet.

But it was no good. He couldn't block the noise, and he had resolved not to respond.

"Miss your smokes, sweetheart?" someone hollered.

536

Boy, did he.

In some recess of Brady's mind, he realized that his nicotine addiction and all the racket were at least keeping him occupied. One thing he feared above everything else was having to face his own darkness.

Fighting the withdrawal and the unending harassment, Brady sat with his back to the wall, his head between his knees. He was unaware of having slept the night before and wondered if this place ever quieted enough for anyone to sleep. Brady was exhausted, and yet there would be no dozing, at least for now.

His absolute refusal to give the hecklers what they wanted eventually cooled them down. But even when the shouting was not directed at Brady, the noise level seemed to abate only during the counts of the inmates with every shift change and meal delivery. Like everyone else, Brady began to look forward to the food, meager and unappetizing as it was.

Each time the officers brought his meal, Brady was required to sit on his cot at the back of the cell. Holidays and weekends the men got just two meals a day. The rest of the time, three were delivered, almost always with the same fare: a simple TV dinner–style entree, salt and pepper packets, a fruit drink, a combination plastic fork and spoon, a packet of instant coffee, and a tea bag. The irony of the last two was that no hot plates or heating units of any kind were allowed in the cells, so the men had to mix these with barely warm tap water.

When the officers came to pick up his tray, again Brady had to be sitting on his cot, and his tray was searched every time to be sure everything was still there—all the packaging and the spork. That, he was told, was to ensure that he didn't keep anything he could use to fashion some hybrid weapon. If only he had the courage. He was barely eating anyway, and if he ate less, he knew he would be reported and likely hauled away for intravenous feeding.

At the end of his first month, the drone of Brady's life had been established. The sharpest bite of his withdrawal from a lifetime of smoking was over, yet he occasionally caught a whiff of something that reminded him of cigarettes, and the cravings came back.

The inmates all around him apparently found him no fun due to his silence and eventually gave up hassling him entirely. But his only respite from the other constant racket came in the evenings when those with televisions all watched the same show and then discussed it to death.

During that time, Brady could hear every word of dialogue from all the TVs, so he would stretch out on his cot and pull the end of his scratchy blanket up behind his head, forcing it into his ears. Sometimes that allowed him to doze, but only briefly, because then his hands would relax, the blanket would slip away, and the noise would invade.

TVs had to be off at midnight, and some of the men actually seemed to sleep, though Brady could hardly imagine how. The other clamor seemed to go on and on until it became white noise to him. Part of him wished he had not grown used to it, because when he had been unable to think, at least he was spared the wide-awake nightmares that showed him for who he really was.

What Katie North's father had told the press was right. He deserved to burn in hell.

Brady slowly came to understand that there were two types of prisoners—those who lived to make trouble for little other reason than that they were bored and craved attention, and those who were content to just get along.

He fit the latter category, but he could understand the others. They couldn't really be punished any more. Even being sent back to an intake cell for Administrative Segregation was at least variety. And the chance to fight and bite and spit and throw blood or feces or try to make some creative weapon out of whatever could be found—well, Brady wasn't interested, but something about the efforts of the desperate reached him. It reminded him of how he had felt at Forest View High School years before, when negative attention was at least better than none.

In his more fanciful moments, Brady had imagined himself simply passing his time doing nothing. But the deprivation of everything he knew—human touch, conversation, something to read, not to mention the ability to come and go as he pleased—changed his entire system of values.

While he could not sleep, never ate his entire meager portion of food, and felt nauseated all the time, still Brady found himself looking forward to every scheduled event that marked the passing of each day. He anticipated being roused by the banging on his door for first count, the delivery of every meal, even his short walk to the shower every week. The head counts helped him mark the time, and he was expected to stand and show himself at the predinner count. Hardly a week passed without someone refusing and having to be forcibly extricated from his cell.

Brady tried to be cordial to the officers, hoping one might engage him in other than just stilted conversation. Whenever he said anything more than please or thank you, however, he was quickly barked back into submission. Someone—he couldn't even remember who now—had told him, "Treat the officers with respect, but don't expect to talk to them much."

Hardest to get used to were the creatures that invaded his house. Sleep was so evasive that he didn't think he had to worry that something would bite him if he happened to doze. But he was wrong. In the weeks he had been inside, he had already seen roaches, flies, mice, crickets, moths, spiders, mosquitoes, and gnats. Brady suffered so many bites on his feet and ankles that he had taken to wearing his soft slippers to bed.

He looked forward to the end of his ninety-day probationary period so he could have a TV and something to read besides the juice boxes—which he had memorized. He had also read and reread his induction materials so often that he could have recited every word, subtitle, and page number.

Brady didn't know what he would do with his hour a day in the exercise kennel. There was only one man in there at a time, and each either strolled or just leaned against the wall or sat, apparently enjoying the slight change of scenery and more space. A few exercised, but Brady couldn't imagine doing that. He had already lost weight and muscle tone, and in his cell he moved as little as necessary. He knew that was unhealthy, but what was the point?

Brady was alarmed every time he was taken to the shower and got a glimpse of himself in the makeshift mirror. He had begun to look older than his years, gaunt, wasted. Three years and the lethal injection couldn't come soon enough.

Those first ninety days, he knew, were meant to break him. Again, that puzzled him. Break him from what? He supposed it was good for him to have quit smoking, though it had not been voluntary. But he didn't have to be persuaded to follow orders, do what he was told, not cause trouble, not trust anyone.

Apparently this initial period of deprivation didn't have its desired effect on every inmate, as many newcomers went crazy within a week or two, finding themselves dragged from their cells to Ad Seg and—depending on how much of a fight they put up—having years added to their sentences. Brady had no interest in making trouble. He found himself simply sad, depressed, and mostly sleepless.

One day his lunch delivery was accompanied by a letter from his aunt Lois. Brady's fingers trembled as he opened it, though it was clear it had already been read by the authorities.

> Your uncle and I are praying for you, Brady. We know it was an accident and that you would never hurt a flea on purpose. We asked if we could come visit you but were told only one person was allowed at a time and not till after your first ninety days, and then only if you put us on some list. Do that, and one of us will come as soon as it's cleared. Tell us about your appeals when you can.

The last thing Brady wanted was his aunt or uncle seeing this place. He wanted to answer, "It was on purpose, stop praying, and don't come." But he would not be issued pencil or paper until the ninety days were up, and he wasn't allowed to send any mail until after that anyway.

And his appeals? He didn't even want to know, let alone tell anyone else. What was to appeal? Any higher court judge or panel looking over his transcripts would see what everyone else saw. If anyone dared reverse his sentence, he would sue them. Whoever all these activists were, demonstrating and acting in his and other death row inmates' interests, they were going to be sorely disappointed at his lack of cooperation. In fact, he would be working at cross-purposes to theirs.

At the eighty-day mark, Brady began to really get antsy about reaching normal status. Wasn't that something? Whatever their motive for treating him like the animal he was, it had worked. He would still be a man condemned to death, living in a steel-and-concrete box, humiliated, deprived of almost everything, and relegated to public calls of nature, public showers, body cavity searches, and cuffing and uncuffing every time he left his house. And yet the TV and radio and writing materials and something to read began to actually sound like something, looming on the horizon like an oasis.

And he needed something to distract him. Because now that the craziness and the noise and the creatures and the smells had become a macabre amalgam of his daily existence, Brady's sleeplessness and nausea finally reached him in that far corner he had struggled so frantically to avoid.

He had searched desperately every minute for anything to occupy his mind so he could shut out the ugly truth about himself. He was a criminal, a murderer, a monster. He had snuffed out a life and destroyed a family.

Brady had allowed himself to somehow cover the worst of this in his mind by freely admitting his guilt and demanding death. By some far-fetched rationalization, he felt that should have squared it. But when he was forced to face himself, he knew better. Nothing could make it right. In one ugly instant he had gone from a liar, a lowlife, and a no-account loser to the worst thing a man could be.

And now that he had settled in to where he belonged and found that a few crumbs of privileges due him for ninety days' good behavior sounded like Christmas, he could shut out the despicable truth no longer.

Guilty, guilty, guilty was all he could think. Was he going crazy? Would he try again to kill himself? And why was it Katie's father and not Brady's aunt Lois who had mentioned his burning in hell? Lois really believed that stuff, that there was a heaven and a hell and that good people went up and bad people went down.

I murdered someone, and I'm going to hell.

Brady realized that he could not kill himself. Even the supermax had to be better than hell. Killing himself would get him sent there only earlier. And now all of a sudden the three-year mark didn't seem so far away either. Oh, he deserved it. He had never denied that. But what he feared would not come soon enough now seemed to be racing toward him.

Why hadn't he listened to Jackie Kent and considered that the day might come when he would change his mind? Life in this place would be awful, but if there was a hell, he'd rather be here than there—regardless what he deserved.

He knew Carl and Lois were sincerely into this stuff, but he had always just endured their church and Sunday school and the stories and songs. It was all okay for them, sort of quaint. Lois was known as a bit of a religious wacko, even among her family and friends.

But could it be true? If it was, Brady was in deep, deep trouble, not just with the county and the state, but with the God of the universe Himself.

He dug through his induction packet again, though he had committed it to memory. That black-and-white picture of the plain, old-fashioned-looking, broad-faced older man, the Reverend Thomas Carey. He was the chaplain. And to arrange a visit with him, you had to fill out a form and submit it to the administrative offices. If the decision was positive and the inmate in good standing, the meeting would be scheduled. The first would be at your cell, and if the chaplain deemed it appropriate or necessary, subsequent meetings, each subject to the same permission request procedure, could be arranged in an isolation unit. There the inmate and the chaplain could sit on either side of a Plexiglas window and converse through an intercom.

Brady understood exactly why he had this sudden interest in a meeting with the chaplain, though he wasn't sure he would want to say it aloud where other cons could hear. The bottom line was, he had to know. Was there any hope for a murderer?

57

Adamsville

It had been years—*years*—since Gladys had called Thomas Carey at home.

"Wanted to catch you before you left," she said now. "I still don't know what you have against cell phones, Reverend. I could have waited a few minutes and talked to you while you were driving."

"It's called a budget," Thomas said, hoping she could hear the smile in his voice. Plus, cell phones didn't work in the supermax with all the steel and concrete. And he wasn't going to invest in a phone and monthly charges so he could be reached anywhere else.

"How's your sweetheart this morning?"

"Still in remission," he said. "Believe me, we're enjoying it while it lasts."

"I'm praying it lasts forever."

"Thank you, but you didn't call to tell me that. I'm on my way out the door."

"You must have a long cord on that phone, then."

"Funny."

"I just thought you'd like to know whose request to see you has been approved and who you can visit whenever you want."

"I'll bite. Who?"

"Guess."

"A Muslim. A Wiccan. A Buddhist. Worse than that? A satanist? Surely not someone interested in what I'm selling."

"You never know, but you're wrong on all counts."

"Another one of those who's invented his own religion and wants me to get it cleared with the state so he can, what, worship girlie magazines or something?"

Gladys cackled. "I'll never forget that guy. Nope, believe it or not, it's the Heiress Murderer."

Thomas held his breath. The very one he had been praying for. The one with the vacant look. "He's been with us ninety days already?"

"Last week. Yanno just signed off on the request."

"You know, Gladys, one of these days I'm going to tell the warden that you call him that."

"You'd blackmail me?"

"If I could figure out a reason. But if I did, what would I get out of it?"

"My loud scarf collection. Any one of 'em would go well with your somber suits."

"That's just my uniform, Miz Fashion Plate."

"And you wear 'em well. Now get your tail in here and do your job."

"Can you do me a favor? See if you can get the man's file for me?"

"You didn't get enough of that story in the papers and on TV?"

"More than I wanted, actually, but there's always stuff the press ignores that can be enlightening."

Death Row

Brady got word late that morning that the chaplain would visit his cell at four in the afternoon. *Interesting timing,* he thought. *If he gets bored, he can leave at the end of his workday.*

They would have an hour and a half before the dinner count and then the meal delivery. Brady couldn't imagine it taking that long. He was curious was all. Just wanted to know where the local man of the cloth stood on this stuff. Brady had heard friends say over the years that when you're dead you're dead, but being a Christian or trying to live like one was good because it made you a better person in this world.

Well, he had certainly failed on that account, and long before he murdered Katie North.

Administrative Wing

Thomas spent the day busy but distracted. Brady Wayne Darby was the highest-profile inmate the penitentiary had had in ages. While there had been no trial to make the thing the media circus it might have become, the murder had been center stage for weeks.

Andreason and LeRoy were adamant about no information being leaked out of the prison about Darby, though a couple of corrections officers reported that they had been offered money by the tabloids to sneak a cell phone photo or any tidbit of news to them. The truth was, one of them might have taken the offer had the inmate been the least bit interesting. Word was he was quiet and cooperative, though still considered a suicide risk. But he was talking with no one, so anything sold to the cheap newspapers about Brady Darby would have to be invented, like most everything else in those rags.

At 2:00 Gladys swept into Thomas's office and plopped a three-inch file on his desk. "You owe me," she said.

"I'm hopelessly in debt to you already."

"And don't you forget it. Someday you'll pay, Padre."

"How would I ever?"

"Oh, trust me, I'll think of something. And if I can't, my hubby will. If nothing else, we ought to have a barbecue at your place while your darlin' is up and about."

"C'mon, Xavier wouldn't want to cook on his day off. That'd be like me preaching on my day off."

"I didn't say he was gonna cook. You are!"

"Then I'll *really* owe you."

Thomas found investigative files fascinating and had taken to watching real-life mystery shows on television when he had the chance. He might have enjoyed a career as a detective. He certainly couldn't have done worse than as a clergyman. Thomas had to smile at the memory of Grace's scolding when he had mentioned that.

He read through the entire corpus of the Darby case, which included the young man's whole criminal history. Everything was fairly straightforward. Like many other men at Adamsville State, he had been raised by a single parent, had suffered a loss in his immediate family, had a history of drugs and petty crimes before graduating to bigger ones, and had been in and out of all sorts of penal institutions from juvie to local lockups and even the notorious county jail.

Again, like many, he'd had the occasional bright spot—sort of like remission, Thomas thought. He had enjoyed stellar marks at his last halfway house and was on the verge of finishing, getting a certificate, and being recommended for job placement. Then came the murder, which had taken everyone by surprise.

Darby's lengthy rap sheet showed the telltale signs of almost every other inmate Thomas had ever studied. He had progressed in his career from little stuff to big, eventually pulling armed robberies, grand theft auto, assault with deadly weapons, and finally murder. He'd also had his share of escape attempts and violence against other inmates and staff at previous institutions.

Lord, Thomas said silently, *I still don't know what to ask You in regard to this man, but You put him on my heart, so I hope his request is an answer to my prayers.*

An officer met Thomas as he emerged from the last security envelope before death row. It still struck him that if one didn't know, he would not have been able to tell this pod from any of the others. It was different, there was no question. These men were all living by the calendar and the clock. But no sign or look or noise or smell distinguished it from any of the other units.

Thomas caught sight of Darby from about twenty feet away. Usually the sound of anyone walking nearby captured everyone's attention. They would at least look up, just for the change of scenery. But Darby was sitting on his cot, fiddling with his TV. He appeared thinner than Thomas remembered. Could he have lost that much weight in three months?

The officer rapped on Darby's door and called out, "Your chaplain visit!"

The young man immediately turned off the TV and stood, but he seemed to carefully approach the front of his cell, as if he had learned not to appear threatening. Thomas kept his distance but tried to welcome the approach with a smile. Brady Darby looked wretched, wasted.

From all over the pod, other cons began to stand and yell and whistle.

"Chaplain visit!"

"Lover boy has a meeting!"

"Gonna get right with your Maker?"

Thomas leaned close and spoke directly. "Thomas Carey."

"I'm Brady. You didn't bring your Bible."

As soon as they began, someone shushed everyone

else. Thomas and Darby whispered, but Thomas was certain some could hear.

"Happy to bring it, anytime you'd like me to. Lucky for you, I have much of it memorized."

"Seriously?"

Thomas nodded.

"I memorize too," Brady said. "You want to hear what it says on the juice boxes and in the induction packet?"

"You know one of the things I can offer you is reading material. You can borrow anything in my library and keep it for as long as you're here."

"What've you got?"

Thomas pulled a folded list from his suit coat pocket, showed it to the officer—who checked it for staples or paper clips and nodded—then rolled it and passed it through one of the openings.

Brady tossed it on his cot. "So you believe in Jesus and all that?"

"I do," Thomas said. "Helps in this job."

Brady nodded, either not catching or not appreciating the humor. "Heaven and hell? The devil? Satan?"

"Everything in the Bible," Thomas said. "Yes, I believe it."

"Sinners go to hell, good people go to heaven?"

"No, I don't believe that."

The con looked genuinely surprised, just as Thomas had hoped he would. "What then? Heaven and hell aren't real? They just stand for something else?"

"Oh no. Heaven and hell are real. Jesus talked more about hell than He talked about a lot of other things. You believe in Jesus, the afterlife is part of the package."

"Then who goes where?"

"Sinners go both places."

"Sinners go to heaven? How does that work?"

Suddenly the cacophony from men in the nearby cells erupted again.

"Get him saved, Reverend!"

"Bring him to Jesus!"

"Hallelujah!"

"Amen!"

Thomas beckoned him forward and the man turned his ear toward one of the openings. "You want to talk about this somewhere else?"

"Yeah, I guess we'd better."

"Because, listen to me, son, I'm going to give you the benefit of the doubt and assume you have serious questions. We both know you're not talking about *sinners,* plural. You're talking about you."

Brady hung his head.

"We're all sinners," Thomas said. "The Bible says no one is good enough. 'No one is truly wise; no one is seeking God. All have turned away; all have become useless. No one does good, not a single one.' So, we're all sinners, but it's the believing, forgiven ones who get to go to heaven."

Brady looked desperate. "What if you believe but aren't forgiven?"

"You're saying, what if you do your part and God doesn't do His? The Bible says, 'If we confess our sins to Him, He is faithful and just to forgive us our sins and to cleanse us from all wickedness.'"

"C'mon, not *all* wickedness. You know what I did."

"So does He."

Darby shook his head as if that was not what he wanted to hear. Had Thomas come on too strong too quickly? Had his years of seeing no response in this hellhole made him want to close the deal before the prospect was really sold?

God, don't let me mess this up.

The hollering from all around made it nearly impossible to hear the young man.

"He's starting to cloud up!"

"Here comes the waterworks!"

"Oh, man, get the boy some cryin' towels!"

"Pass the offering plate, Preacher! You got him right where you want him!"

Thomas put a finger through the opening and said, "Request a meeting in an isolation room."

The young man ignored his hand and looked down, nodding. But Thomas got the distinct impression he had not gotten through at all. He was sure Darby would not ask to see him again.

For the next two weeks, as Thomas enjoyed a season of normalcy with Grace and continued to talk with Dirk and Ravinia separately, plus get time with his granddaughter—whom he had taken to calling the light of his life—he was plagued with despairing thoughts about the man on death row.

He had heard nothing, not even a request for reading material. And Thomas had already set aside several books he thought would help, including a Bible in modern, easily readable language.

Finally he spoke with the warden. "Is there no way I can even send this man some books without his requesting them? I know he's curious and wants to talk with me, and I expected him to ask for a private meeting."

"Yeah, no. We can't start making exceptions. You know this guy's history. You really think he's redeemable?"

"What kind of a question is that, Frank? Is any one of us redeemable? The day I start deciding who's worthy of love and forgiveness is the day I've got to get out of here."

"Well, I don't want you to do that, but this has to be nothing new for you. You've been telling me for years that you can't get these guys to take spiritual matters seriously. Why should this guy?"

Thomas didn't know what to say. He couldn't tell the warden that he had felt more compelled to pray for Brady Darby than for any other con in a long time— in fact since Henry Trenton went to the gallows.

Oh, please, he thought, *don't let this turn into another of those.* He could just picture it. The kid wouldn't want to read or hear any more Scripture, couldn't see himself ever worthy of forgiveness, but would appreciate Thomas's interest just enough to ask him to accompany him to his death.

If it came to that, Thomas would quit first. He'd do what Russ did, and when he left, he would be done. No way in the world would he pray for this man for two and a half more years, only to see him go to his death as unrepentant and lost as the Deacon.

And yet, despite himself and his disappointment, Thomas could not shake the compulsion to pray for Brady Wayne Darby. He didn't even have to be specific. God knew what the man needed.

And God had to know what Thomas needed too.

I know You and You alone do the work, but use me. Please.

58

Death Row

The one simple visit from the chaplain alone opened Brady to days of harassment from his pod mates. Did he dare order books or request another meeting? If these guys saw him cuffed up and ushered out for anything but his shower or his exercise hour, he'd never hear the end of it.

Brady knew he was in trouble, however, when he quit looking forward to anything. *Anything.*

He used to enjoy TV, and when he was without it for the first three months, he had craved it. Now he watched because there was nothing else to do. And he was drawn to old movies, but nothing else really interested him.

Sleep still eluded him, and meals were so bland and same-ish that he blamed his nausea and lack of appetite on that. How was he going to endure this sentence if nothing would help him burn the hours and days?

Brady wondered if he was going crazy. Not that that would necessarily be bad. Who cared? He sure didn't. Losing his mind might be interesting; if nothing else, a distraction. The problem was that as fewer and fewer things even attracted his attention, he began to sleepwalk through his days.

Night was no different. Except that the noises changed because of no TV after midnight, little differentiated night from day. Everyone lived in noisy darkness and stench. Brady wished he could force himself to get interested in the news, comedies, sitcoms, documentaries, sports, anything.

He would sit staring blankly at the screen, determined to keep the black hole of memory from invading his brain. But it was futile. The scene always began with Katie North speaking to him as if he were an imbecile, amazed that he actually thought there had ever really been something between them.

Was it possible he had been wrong all along? He couldn't make it compute, couldn't convince himself that it was simply because his love for her was so deep that he had only imagined it went both ways. Had he wanted to believe it so badly that he read all of her politeness and friendliness and mischief as true love when she was, as she claimed, just having fun?

It couldn't be. And the more her questions from that final conversation echoed in his brain—the ones about what he thought was going to happen in the future—the more he dreaded what was coming next. Where would he work, what would he do, what would she do? He had no answers and she was on her way out of the car.

But wait!

Wait!

And he was reaching into the backseat, and now it all went to slow motion. Something had burned onto his mind every detail, every drop of sweat, the exact hue of her ashen face, the sweep of her hair as she turned to slide out, the sound, the horrid sound of the blast, and then . . . and then . . . everything else.

No matter how many times the ugly scene played out in Brady's mind, he couldn't get it to change, to fade, to adjust. It was as if the explosions from those barrels had torn his lover in two and killed him in the process. And yet he had not died. At least physically. But there was nothing left of him but a body and a mind. Everything else seemed utterly gone.

Guilty, guilty, guilty.

There was no excuse. Oh, of course, he'd had his reasons, but he had hit a fly with a sledgehammer. He could have simply told her off, screamed at her, slapped her. He could have cussed her out, pushed her from the car, even pulled her hair.

Brady would have been charged and prosecuted and punished for most or all of that too, but it might have at least fit the situation in some extreme way. But no. He had acted without thinking. He had let his rage, his shame, his humiliation, his abysmal disappointment over losing her lead him to take matters into his own foolish hands.

As soon as the detonation assaulted his eardrums, Brady had known. There wasn't a split second of wondering if this was real or whether there was some way to take it back, to start over. He knew his beautiful Katie was dead before she hit the ground and that his life was over too.

Guilty, guilty, guilty.

And he was going to hell.

This unending replay continued for days, and finally the morning arrived when Brady didn't even bother to turn on his TV. He didn't retrieve his meal tray when it was delivered, and thus he didn't have to return it to the slot.

But that was duly noted and reported, and he was warned that if he continued to starve himself, he would be moved to a psychiatric facility for diagnosis and therapy. He didn't care. Some cons looked forward to such diversions and even faked neuroses and psychoses, but this was anything but an act.

Brady didn't want any attention. He just wanted to die. And yet he didn't want to go to hell.

At the predinner count he took a little too long to rise from his cot and the officer shouted, "You want me to bring the extraction team in here, Darby? Don't tempt me. Because I'll do it and you'll wish I hadn't. Now get up and show yourself. And you'd better be eating tonight or we're shipping you out of here."

Brady just nodded. And when dinner came, such as it was, he forced himself to eat. Even after having fasted almost twenty-four hours, nothing tasted right, and it was all he could do to eat enough to make them leave him alone.

He put his tray in the slot and returned to his cot, lay in a fetal position, and closed his eyes. There would be no sleeping, and sure enough, someone from the end cell of another unit saw him and announced, "Check it out! The Heiress Murderer has assumed the position!"

"Curled up?"

"Yeah!"

"Crying?"

"Probably! Let it out, boy! Let us hear you!"

Brady did want to cry. He wanted to sob, to wail, to curse himself. He buried his face in his blanket, and from the depths of his soul came raspy, guttural moans. "I'm sorry! I'm sorry! I'm sorry!" he screamed, muffling his cries, shoulders heaving.

He could still hear the others taunting and teasing and berating him. Brady no longer cared. He wanted to bellow and curse them, but that would be playing right into their hands. They already probably thought they had pushed him to this point. But they hadn't at all. He had done it himself.

Loser, loser, loser.

He couldn't remember having made a right decision for as long as he lived. Even when things temporarily went right—when he landed the musical role, or got a job, or helped the antigang unit, or turned over a new leaf at Serenity, or loved his woman the best he knew how—eventually he messed it all up.

And now this.

Who was he that he suddenly belonged in prison, condemned to die? It seemed he had moved overnight from mouthing off in grade school to lying despicable and broken on death row. How had it happened? How had he let it happen?

Beyond hope.

Suddenly Brady sat straight up and let his feet hit the floor. He leaned forward, resting his elbows on his knees. He was through crying about it. He had brought this on himself. He was responsible, had done it, caused it all.

There was no one to blame but himself, and what future was there in wallowing in it? He had no future. Brady would cause no more trouble for himself or anyone else. He would park his mind in neutral and consider this a marathon, not a sprint. He would go through the motions one had to go through to do his time, and that was all.

Maybe he couldn't sleep or eat like he wanted to, but he would go to bed at midnight every night and lie there until awakened for the first count of the day. He would eat his breakfast, all of it, regardless how long it took to force it down. He would eat all his meals, watch TV all day—just to know what time it was— would shower and shave when it was his turn, stand around in the exercise kennel during his hour, and speak to no one unless it was absolutely necessary.

If he found himself going stir-crazy again, maybe he would ask for the occasional magazine or newspaper or book.

And when the terrible images invaded again, as he knew they would, he would simply watch as they flashed past. Brady was as sorry as he knew how to be, but there would be no apologizing to anyone.

Strangely, Brady found he did believe. He believed in God and even Jesus. And he believed in hell. Something must have stuck in that stupid brain years ago from church and Sunday school and hymn sings at Aunt Lois's little church, because there was no longer a doubt in his mind that he was going to wind up there, burning for eternity, just as Jordan North said he deserved.

When he settled into that routine, having essentially surrendered to his fate, Brady found himself flat, sad beyond measure. His only consolation was that he knew justice would be served. How did the cliché go? He had made his bed . . .

Mail call brought another note from Aunt Lois. She and Carl were still praying and still pleading with him to put them on the visitors list so they could come see him. At least she didn't mention any more about knowing he hadn't meant to do what he did.

Poor lady, he thought. *She really cares.*

Too bad he didn't.

Brady tore the letter and the envelope into little pieces and tried to flush them down his toilet. Didn't work. He couldn't do anything right. The commode backed up and flooded his floor, and when he called for help, the place went nuts.

He was forced to mop up the mess himself, then was accused of having done it on purpose and hauled off to Ad Seg while a plumber came in to repair the fixture. While in the intake cell, shivering in his underwear and living on the cold bologna sandwiches, Brady was informed that a review board had determined he would spend a total of three days and nights right where he was.

Brady was furious. No wonder men went crazy here. Why would he flood his own cell? And was seventy-two hours in an intake cell justified? On the other hand, who cared? According to most who knew anything about his case, death was too good for him. What was a few days of more discomfort?

Brady began praying he would fall sick and die. But then he remembered what eternity held for him and decided to go back to simply trying to endure his time.

Administrative Wing

"You hear your boy is in Ad Seg?" Gladys said.

Thomas shot her a double take. "Darby?"

She told him what had happened.

"Makes no sense," he said. "Was he belligerent?"

She shook her head. "Claimed it was an accident, but he's been docile as a lamb. Just like always."

Thomas had not felt released from his compulsion to pray for the man. Now he had an idea. Was it time to parlay his years in this place for a little privilege? He knew if he asked Frank LeRoy for permission to just mosey past the intake cell and see if he could strike up a conversation with Brady Darby, the warden would respond with the trademark answer that had given him his nickname.

So instead of asking, Thomas grabbed his Bible and a few books, just for props. He wanted to look like he was on an errand and would be careful not to lie; people could think what they wanted. In truth, he was just on his way past intake to the last pod on that floor.

For what?

For nothing. He hoped no one would ask. Thomas had simply decided to take a stroll to that location and come back. If he got a chance to whisper a word or two to Brady Wayne Darby, well, wouldn't that be an interesting development?

As he moved through the security envelopes, the occasional officer said, "Visiting, Reverend?"

"Just on an errand."

A hundred yards from intake, his steps echoing throughout the unit, Thomas was praying desperately. *Let him notice me and say something.*

And for the first time in years, maybe ever, it seemed God impressed something so deeply on

Thomas's heart that it was almost audible. It was as if God said, "Tell him how I feel about him."

Thomas's knees buckled and he almost stumbled. He wished God would repeat Himself, but there was no doubt in his mind what he had heard or at least felt. And he also knew how God felt about Brady Wayne Darby. That was one thing Thomas Carey did know after a lifetime in the ministry.

As he passed the only occupied cell, there sat Brady in the typical Ad Seg pose, backed into one corner, head between his knees, forearms hugging his bare shins.

Thomas cleared his throat. Nothing.

He peered in at Brady, tempted to say something but knowing he would be heard over the intercom in the observation unit. Someone banged on the Plexiglas behind him. Thomas turned and saw the officer waving him on.

Thomas played dumb. He raised his brows as if to ask what the problem was. The officer came on the intercom. "No visitors in Ad Seg, Reverend. You know that."

"Right. My mistake."

When Thomas moved past the cell, Brady looked up, clearly surprised. Thomas whispered, "Got to tell you something."

But the officer came on again immediately. "You're on the edge, Reverend. You got business down here?"

"Sorry, officer. It's just that God told me to tell this prisoner that He loves him, and now I realize I'm not at liberty to tell him that until he's back in his own house."

The officer laughed. "Yeah, okay then, God loves him. Think he heard that. Now keep moving before I have to report you."

Thomas saluted and hurried back the way he had come. How he wished he could have seen the look on Darby's face. That either piqued the man's interest or Thomas had lost him forever. He wouldn't know for two more days, minimum.

59

Ad Seg

Terrific, Brady thought. Just when he had cleared his mind and was determined to keep the horrific thoughts at bay, at least until he got back to his cell, now this.

God loved him. Uh-huh. That's why he was born in a trailer park, had an alcoholic mother, lost his only brother, and screwed up beyond repair every last thing in his life. Sure, made sense. That was how God showed His love.

Better yet, it wasn't just the chaplain, whom Brady had found kindly and seemingly genuine, who was telling him this. God *told* the man to tell Brady. *Great. Now we've got a God who ignores a guy for thirty years and now wants him to know He loves him.* Well, so much for the murder scenes playing and replaying every waking and sleeping moment. Brady had something new to stew about now.

By the time he was ushered back to his cell—again with the humiliation of making the entire trek shackled and in his underpants, then being unhooked and showering and shaving and being searched before dressing, then being hooked up again for the short walk back to his house—Brady realized he felt a normal emotion for the first time since the murder. Yes, there was some sense of satisfaction that he was dressed and back in his own place, privileges returned.

"Hey, Heiress Boy!" someone shouted. "You're on channel 5! Check it out!"

Brady was curious but wouldn't bite. He didn't need to. As soon as the others heard that, every set within earshot was tuned to the station where an anchor-woman on one of the celebrity roundup shows was telling the story.

"Authorities report that Darby put up no resistance when sent to and brought back from solitary, and while he was confined there for three days, there is no move afoot to have this incident affect his sentence. Of course, he has been condemned to death, though the mandatory appeal process is under way.

"An unnamed source says that while it was clear Darby was trying to flood the entire death row unit, he succeeded in making a mess only of his own cell."

Over the next few days the story was played out on all the newscasts and tabloid shows. Brady couldn't avoid it, though he tried to switch channels every time it came on. One station allowed viewers to call in and give their opinions, which ranged from "Why on earth should anyone care about such a waste of space?" to "He's getting what he deserves and shouldn't be appealing his sentence."

Appealing my sentence?

Brady answered every communiqué from Jackie Kent the same way, in pencil—a short, stubby one because a prisoner had killed himself with a long one. "I will never challenge my sentence and will not help anybody else try to."

As Brady began changing channels more than he used to, just to stay away from inaccurate stories about himself, he landed on a religious station just long enough to hear a preacher close his program with, "And remember, God loves you."

Couldn't prove it by me.

Anyway, God couldn't love everybody, could He? Brady had to be one of many exceptions. Why did God send some people to hell if He loved them? Brady dredged up a vague memory from his childhood when he had asked Aunt Lois the same thing.

"God doesn't send people to hell," she had told him. "The Bible says He's not willing that any should perish but that all should come to repentance. If people don't want to repent and turn from their sin and trust Jesus, they send themselves to hell. God made hell for the devil and his angels, not for us. He wants us in heaven with Him."

Brady turned on a classic movie channel and tried to interest himself in an old black-and-white. He always imagined himself as one of the actors and how he would have studied the script and done his research and performed the lines. But he couldn't concentrate. How could he?

Was it possible for a person to repent of murder? Brady figured he could repent of all the lying he had done to everybody he knew, repent of vandalism, theft, pushing dope, assault, sleeping around, all that. But no way God was going to hear him or believe him if he said he was sorry about killing someone. That seemed so cheap. Like, *Yeah, my bad, sorry about that.* Brady wasn't even sure he wanted to be forgiven.

But he sure didn't want to go to hell.

He asked for a chaplain's visit request form.

Administrative Wing

Ten days later, Gladys buzzed Thomas on the intercom. "Warden would like to see you, sir."

As he walked past her to knock at Frank LeRoy's door, Thomas mouthed, "What's up?"

"Darby."

"No need to even sit, Rev," Yanno said as he entered. The warden was peering at a single sheet of paper. "Review board's been sitting on this and wanted your input. This Darby guy's requested a private meeting with you. After you saw him last, he pulled that toilet stunt and got himself Ad Seg-ed."

"How long ago was this request?"

"Just after he got back to his cell."

"What, they're punishing him more than the seventy-two hours he spent in intake? Why wasn't this green-lighted?"

"Letting him cool his heels. These aren't automatic, you know."

"If it's up to me, I'd meet with him immediately. This is a man in crisis, sir. It's what I'm here for."

"All right, no need to overreact."

"Well, how long do I have to wait now?"

"I said all right, didn't I? How many times I gotta tell ya, I'm captain of this ship. When do you want to see him?"

"As soon as possible."

Yanno pressed his intercom. "Gladys, get word to somebody to have Darby delivered to an isolation room immediately." He looked up at Thomas. "All right, Mr. All-Business? See if you can beat him there."

Thomas rushed back to his office and grabbed his Bible, a book on basic Christianity, a booklet on personal salvation, an easy-reading New Testament, and a legal pad. As he hurried through all the prison checkpoints, he scribbled Bible references on the pad.

He should have remembered that no prisoner had ever beaten him to the isolation rooms. When Thomas arrived, the coordinating officer already knew whom he was there to see and in which room. "You know you can't give him anything but a single sheet that passes through the—"

"How long have you worked here, officer?"

"Coming up on six years."

"More than fourteen for me. I know the drill."

"Well, I have to see what you're planning on sliding through the slot."

Thomas showed him the list.

"What's this, some kind of a code?"

"Yeah. Tells him how to break out of this place in less than a minute."

"No, seriously, I can't let you give him this unless I know what it is."

"These are references to Bible verses. I have my Bible here. You want to look them all up, be sure I'm not trying to give him secret information?"

"Just doing my job, Reverend."

"So am I."

When Darby finally showed up and noisily sat on the other side of the window, chains rattling, Thomas was stunned at how a man could age in so little time. Every time he saw this guy, he looked worse. It was plain he was not exercising, not eating much, and likely not getting more than a few hours' sleep each night.

"You don't look so good, son."

"Yeah, fine, okay, listen, can we cut right to it? You know all about me and I think I know what you're about. I don't mind dying, I really don't. I know I deserve it and everybody else knows it too, you included. I heard what you said about God loving me, which is a laugh because He's had a strange way of showing it all my life, but here's the thing: I don't want to go to hell. Call me selfish, say I'm only thinking of myself, and you don't have to remind me that I'm never going to be forgiven by Katie's family or anyone else who cares. But I don't think I could feel worse about what I did, and if I could, I'd do anything to make it so it never happened. But it did and here I am. Does God still love me, and if He does, can He keep me out of hell?"

Thomas sat back and studied the man. "My, you do get right after it, don't you?"

"Just don't waste my time, Chaplain."

"You in a hurry?"

"I'm done fooling around. I can't change what I did, and I'm not trying to get out of what's coming to me, except burning forever."

"I have good news for you, Mr. Darby, but I don't want to sound glib about it. You bring up some interesting things, particularly about how God has never shown that He loves you."

"Would you do me a favor and call me Brady?"

"Honored. And you may call me—"

"Oh, I wouldn't feel comfortable calling you anything but Reverend Carey, if that's all right."

"Whatever you wish, Brady. You sound like you don't want to argue or get into a long discussion. You just want it to make sense that God is supposed to love you and yet you never saw evidence of that, right up until the time you were sent here."

"Exactly."

"Let me just ask you, Brady, what did you ever do to deserve God's love?"

"Nothing, I guess."

"Then why should He love you?"

"He shouldn't."

"Whom should He love?"

"People like you. People like my aunt and uncle. People who love Him."

"But the Bible says we love Him because He first loved us. What do you make of that?"

"I don't know! I don't know what to make of any of this."

"You want to know what I believe?"

"That's why I'm here, Reverend."

"I believe only what is in the Bible. Everything else is just someone's opinion."

"But isn't the Bible just someone's opinion too?"

"I hope not, Brady. I believe it is God's Word, His love letter to mankind."

"There you go with the love again."

"God loves us because He made us, and He proved it too, whether or not you felt it or were aware of it. Here's what the Bible says about that. Ready? I want you to imagine yourself as the object, the target of this. You with me?"

"I'm listening."

"And I'm quoting: 'When we were utterly helpless, Christ came at just the right time and died for us sinners. Now, most people would not be willing to die for an upright person, though someone might perhaps be willing to die for a person who is especially good. But God showed His great love for us

573

by sending Christ to die for us while we were still sinners.' "

Brady shook his head as if it was too much to grasp. "I'd like to read that for myself a few times, you know, to try to follow it."

"I've got a Bible for you and a list of verses you can look up."

"I'm not promising I'm going to buy into any of this stuff, but I heard all about Jesus dying on the cross for us when I was a kid. But now haven't I screwed all that up? He can't accept murderers into heaven. Who's going to hell if I'm not?"

"I would have, and I never murdered anyone."

"You?"

"Everyone, Brady. Like I told you. We're all sinners, only some of us are believers who have been forgiven."

"God can't forgive me."

"Like I told you, I believe the Bible. You want to know what He says in there about that? 'I will never again remember their sins and lawless deeds.' "

"Yeah, but—"

" 'I will never again remember their sins and lawless deeds.' "

"But I—"

" 'I will *never again* remember their sins and lawless deeds.' "

"But—"

"There are no *but*s, Brady. Here's more: 'Since we have been made right in God's sight by the blood of Christ, He will certainly save us from God's condemnation. For since our friendship with God was restored by the death of His Son while we were still His enemies, we will certainly be saved through the life of His Son. So now we can rejoice in our wonderful new relationship with God because our Lord Jesus Christ has made us friends of God.'

"Catch that? Isn't that what you've been saying is scaring you? Eternal punishment? Listen: 'So now we can rejoice in our wonderful new relationship with God—all because of what our Lord Jesus Christ has done for us in making us friends of God.' "

Brady looked away. "You telling me this even goes for people like me?"

"If not for you, who? Ever hear about the thief dying on the cross next to Jesus—the one Jesus said would join Him that very day in paradise?"

"Yeah."

"If him, why not you?"

"It just seems like—"

" 'I will never again remember their sins and lawless deeds.' "

Thomas sat watching as it appeared Brady was thinking deeply. Finally the young man said, "I don't get it. It's like this was what I wanted to hear, hoped to hear, but didn't really expect. And now you say it, and I can hardly believe it."

"And that's the key. You have to believe it and put your faith in Jesus and what He did for you. That's how people become friends of God."

"I've got to think about this."

"Of course you do. And as I said, I've got some things for you to read, including several verses." Thomas tore the sheet off his yellow pad and jockeyed it through the slot.

Brady sat studying it. "Bible verses, huh? So I look these up, and—"

"Yes, this is on you. I'm not going to do your homework for you. You have a lot of good and legitimate questions about what it all means, but if I was the best evangelist or salesman in the world, it wouldn't matter. No one can talk you into this. Just ask God to reveal Himself to you. If He's for real, and I know He is, how could He not answer a prayer like that?"

Brady narrowed his eyes at Thomas. "Did He really tell you to tell me He loved me?"

Thomas held up a hand. "He did. And let me be clear. He's never spoken to me like that before, and frankly, I don't expect Him to again. But I believe He compelled me to pray for you from the first day I saw you here. I was frustrated because I didn't know what He wanted me to do about you and I didn't know if I'd ever get the chance to talk to you. What was I supposed to do? Actually, I think He took pity on me and let me have that morsel of what is in His heart. It may have been as much for me as for you."

"But He really told you that and to tell me about it?" Brady held the scribbled sheet in his cuffed hands. "I'm gonna check all this out. And I hope to talk with you again."

"I hope so too, Brady."

60

Brady had a strange feeling as he was returned to his cell and uncuffed. He had hoped the chaplain could send the Bible and the other stuff with his escorting officers, but it looked like those would come later. Meanwhile, all he had to look at was the yellow sheet with the list of Bible references.

He should have been happy, he knew. He wanted with all his heart to believe Reverend Carey was right, and who was he to argue with a minister about the Bible? But happiness was no longer part of his vocabulary. Oh, if he could avoid hell and be forgiven and become a friend of God, yes, that would have to make him feel better. But none of this, at least so far, had dented the blackness that had invaded his mind and heart and soul the instant he snuffed out the life of Katie North. And he was sure it shouldn't. He didn't deserve to ever smile again after what he had done.

Every minute of every day the wickedness of it all seemed to crouch at the door of Brady's mind, waiting to pounce and overwhelm him. Regardless what else he thought about, he could hold it at bay for only so long.

This list, already wrinkling and creasing and softening from the oils in his hands, gave him something to look forward to besides counts and meals and TV shows and third-day showers and his hour a day out of his house. None of that really appealed anyway, but even the thought of being able to look up verses and read them and study them and think about them . . . well, if nothing else, maybe that would allow Brady to hold off the evil for a little while.

Adamsville

Though it was clear to Thomas that Grace was at least in the beginning stages of regressing, she was still up and about and seemed to rally with his report of the conversation with Brady Darby. She had always been proud of Thomas's gift of recall, and she insisted on every detail.

When he finished, her eyes were bright. "Let's call the church," she said. "Get people to pray."

Within an hour, Thomas had gained commitments from the prayer chain, the women's group, the men's ministry, and even the youth group to pray for a prisoner. He didn't dare say which prisoner, because if anyone told the wrong person, the press would have a field day. As it was, if this man became a believer, it was bound to get out, and everyone in the press and the public would weigh in with his or her opinion of Brady Darby's true motivations.

Death Row

Brady found himself depressed the next morning. The anticipation of real reading material with some substance had faded to frustration. There was no explaining the pace of prison procedures. For all he knew, the chaplain had left on vacation or had forgotten to get the stuff into the mail delivery system, or someone had absconded with everything, knowing it would frustrate him.

The bad thoughts came roaring back, and he was in a foul mood when officers came to lead him to his regular shave and shower. That never got easier—the humiliation of the cuffing and uncuffing, the pat down, showering in front of officers, the cavity search. He just gritted his teeth and tried to zone out, but even that opened him to the memories that had seemed to poison his mind.

It wasn't until he was back and his cell had been thrice locked, per procedure, that Brady realized the stuff from the chaplain had been delivered and lay on his table. This was better than all that had come to him following his probationary period.

He grabbed his sheet and gave it a look, noticing at the bottom a line that wasn't a verse reference. The chaplain had written, "The Romans Road." Was that in the Bible?

He tore open the envelope, only to hear men start to yell at him.

"Package from home, sweet cakes?"

"Get any cookies? Share the wealth!"

"Got a new honey? You gonna blow her away too?"

Brady turned his TV as loud as it would go—not very, as the volume gains on all the sets had been equipped with governors. But at least it kept him from hearing all the shouting.

Brady removed from the envelope a New Testament, which was brand-new and smelled of leather, a book about how to begin the Christian life, and a pamphlet called *The Romans Road*. Aha. He'd start there.

A brief introduction told Brady that this was a way of explaining salvation using verses from the book of Romans. He wondered why Chaplain Carey had not included the book of Romans with what he sent until the New Testament's table of contents page told him that Romans was part of the Bible. According to the pamphlet, he had everything he needed to learn about salvation: why he needed it, how God provided it, how to receive it, and what it all meant.

As Brady quickly scanned the pamphlet and started looking up the verses in his New Testament, he realized the chaplain had already hinted at much of this. So this was where he got it.

Brady started by finding the first verse on the Romans Road, Romans 3:23—"For everyone has sinned; we all fall short of God's glorious standard."

He didn't have any quarrel with that. In fact, it was interesting to consider that he wasn't the only wicked person. And he and other murderers weren't the only ones either. Brady knew he should look up only the verses cited in the pamphlet so he could follow the flow and get the point, but he was curious. While he was in Romans 3, he kept reading:

"Yet God, with undeserved kindness, declares that

we are righteous. He did this through Christ Jesus when He freed us from the penalty for our sins. For God presented Jesus as the sacrifice for sin. People are made right with God when they believe that Jesus sacrificed His life, shedding His blood."

To be made "right with God"—oh, if he could only believe this! Could it be true?

The booklet said that earlier in that same third chapter of Romans there was a description of how sin manifested itself. Brady was sure he had the gist of that, but since he was already there, he looked at verses 10 through 18 and realized that the chaplain had already quoted the first three verses to him about no one being good, not even one.

The passage continued: "Their talk is foul, like the stench from an open grave. Their tongues are filled with lies."

He could sure identify with that.

"Snake venom drips from their lips.

"Their mouths are full of cursing and bitterness.

"They rush to commit murder.

"Destruction and misery always follow them.

"They don't know where to find peace.

"They have no fear of God at all."

This was like reading Brady's own biography.

The next verse on the road, Romans 6:23, said: "For the wages of sin is death, but the free gift of God is eternal life through Christ Jesus our Lord."

Eternal life. That sounded a lot better than hell.

Then he was led back to Romans 5:8: "But God

showed His great love for us by sending Christ to die for us while we were still sinners."

Surprisingly, this was starting to make sense. That chaplain really knew his stuff.

Next came Romans 10:9-11: "If you confess with your mouth that Jesus is Lord and believe in your heart that God raised Him from the dead, you will be saved. For it is by believing in your heart that you are made right with God, and it is by confessing with your mouth that you are saved. As the Scriptures tell us, 'Anyone who trusts in Him will never be disgraced.'"

Was it really possible that salvation and the forgiveness of sins were available to anyone who just believed? It seemed too good to be true.

Romans 5:1-2 read, "Therefore, since we have been made right in God's sight by faith, we have peace with God because of what Jesus Christ our Lord has done for us. Because of our faith, Christ has brought us into this place of undeserved privilege where we now stand, and we confidently and joyfully look forward to sharing God's glory."

Romans 8:1 said, "So now there is no condemnation for those who belong to Christ Jesus."

And finally, Romans 8:38-39: "And I am convinced that nothing can ever separate us from God's love. Neither death nor life, neither angels nor demons, neither our fears for today nor our worries about tomorrow—not even the powers of hell can separate us from God's love. No power in the sky above or in the earth below—indeed, nothing in all creation will ever be able to separate us from the love of God that is revealed in Christ Jesus our Lord."

For some reason, when Brady came to the end of the pamphlet and saw a challenge in the form of a question, asking if he was ready to pray a simple prayer of salvation, it petrified him. He quickly closed the booklet and lay on his bed, staring at the ceiling, fingers interlaced behind his head.

He scolded himself. What was he afraid of? He didn't have to commit to anything. He was just looking into it, wasn't he? Words couldn't hurt him. Brady rolled over and reached for the pamphlet, hands shaking, and turned to the back.

The writer suggested this prayer:

God, I know I am a sinner and deserve punishment. But Jesus took my punishment so that through Him I can be forgiven. I trust You for salvation. Thank You for Your love and forgiveness and for eternal life.

Brady shut the pamphlet again and set it aside, rolling onto his stomach and hiding his face. He got it. He understood the basics. He just didn't understand *why* God would do any of this. And in spite of all the time he had spent in church whenever he and Petey visited their aunt Lois and uncle Carl, Brady didn't feel like he had ever really had a handle on who Jesus was.

As he lay there thinking, wondering, agonizing, the

dark thoughts of the murder sneaked up on him only a few times, way fewer than normal. He let the television blare, vaguely aware that the dinner count officers were coming soon, then the meal itself, then the long evening and night.

When Brady heard the banging and announcing of the stand-up count, he rose and nodded at the officers. His dinner did not appeal, but knowing that he had some serious thinking to do, he forced himself to eat a little more than usual.

Finally he settled in to watch a movie, a different one from what the rest of the pod had tacitly agreed upon. He still had not engaged in conversation with any of the other prisoners. They treated him like scum, and while he knew it was just their way of hazing and initiating him, he didn't want to blend into the nightly banter. The talk always wound up vile and profane, and while Brady had never been prudish, he found it better to just tune it out.

But now even his old movie didn't grab him. He switched channels for a while and found nothing, so he left the set tuned to a cable news network and grabbed the New Testament.

Brady had never read the Bible before. He'd pretended to follow along as a kid at Aunt Lois's church now and then, but all the *thee*s and *thou*s and *begat*s lost him along the way.

This New Testament, though, Chaplain Carey had described as easy to read. And the few verses he had looked up while reading the Romans Road pamphlet read simply enough. Brady turned to the very front and found an introductory paragraph that said the first four books were called the Gospels and contained the story of Jesus' birth, life, death, burial, and resurrection.

Well, if that wouldn't help him get to know who Jesus was, nothing would.

"Got a visual on Heiress Boy!" someone shouted. "He's readin' a Bible! Chaplain musta got to him!"

"Oh, glory! Here we go!"

"Come to Jesus, boy! You once was lost but now you found!"

61

Adamsville

Thomas tossed and turned until Grace asked what was the matter. He told her he couldn't sleep and was going to read for a while.

The truth was, he could not get Brady Darby off his mind. This was clearly the most crucial time in the young man's life, and if he was going to move from seeker to follower, it would likely happen soon. If he was to decide against Christ, that would happen soon too.

Thomas knelt by the couch in the living room. "God, as usual, I don't know how to pray for Brady, such a sad, lost, desperate man. I know Your will is that he come to You, and so that is all I ask."

Soon Thomas crept back to bed and slept soundly. In the morning he awoke with an idea. "Grace, would you record some hymns for me to share with Brady?"

"Oh, Thomas, I can barely draw enough breath to talk, let alone sing. And people his age don't appreciate hymns, do they? Has he even heard them before?"

"Yes, as a child. But I don't think he ever really listened. Maybe you could change some of the words, make them sound like plain English. I even have an idea which ones might best speak to him. I'll leave a list."

Death Row

For his station in life, Brady had always been a surprisingly fast and facile reader, and while he had no idea what to expect from the Bible—even a modern version—one thing he hadn't anticipated was that it would keep him up all night. Whatever he had thought the person of Jesus would look like in this history of the first century, he now realized he hadn't had a clue.

This man didn't act like a religious leader, a missionary, or a preacher, although He certainly preached. He spoke in riddles only those with true spiritual insight seemed to be able to understand, performed all kinds of miracles, and wound up dying and rising again, just as He said he would.

586

Brady found himself flying through the four Gospels, finding similar stories told in slightly different ways, then moved right into the amazing stories of the early church. Why hadn't someone told him about this before? Maybe they had. Surely his aunt Lois had. But back then he wouldn't have been listening.

Well, he was listening now. Brady simply could not get enough of this. He broke for the morning count, for breakfast, and for lunch, but otherwise, he just kept reading and reading and reading. He kept wondering whether the things he had read in the Romans Road booklet might actually be true. Was it possible that he could come to know and trust this same Jesus for his own salvation? Coming across those salvation passages from Romans again as he read the New Testament through helped him put them into context, and they thrilled him all the more.

Brady recognized a verse or two from childhood, something that had stuck, or almost stuck, as it flew by in a Sunday school class or a vacation Bible school. One, he realized suddenly, he had once actually memorized and then never considered again until now. John 3:16—"For God loved the world so much that He gave His one and only Son, so that everyone who believes in Him will not perish but have eternal life."

If Brady had ever heard what followed those familiar words, he didn't recall it. Yet now, in light of everything else, it all seemed part of the same package.

"God sent His Son into the world not to judge the world, but to save the world through Him. There is no judgment against anyone who believes in Him."

All through the rest of his reading, Brady kept turning back to that verse and reading it over and over. His emptiness, the despair that had gripped him since the night he had ended Katie's life and his as well, was being slowly replaced by something. What? Hope? If only it were possible to "trust Him" and avoid the coming judgment.

Brady knew that meant spiritual judgment, the fate of his soul. His flesh, his body, had been condemned to death, and nothing would or should change that.

And then he was thrilled to come across the verse in Hebrews that the chaplain had repeated so many times:

"I will never again remember their sins and lawless deeds."

If that was true, it might be the greatest miracle of all. For Brady knew he himself would never forget his sinful, lawless deed. Maybe he could one day get over all the stuff he had done that was so much like what so many others had done. But there weren't enough years left on earth for him to even come close to erasing from his mind the worst night of his life.

At the predinner standing count, Brady noticed a surprised look on the officer's face. This was a fleshy, rosy-cheeked man whose name plate read "Rudy Harrington."

"What're you up to in there, Darby?"

"Sorry?"

"Don't play coy with me. What've you got? What are you reading? You got an adult magazine? You look as excited as I've ever seen you."

"You wouldn't believe me."

"Try me. And make it quick; I gotta keep moving."

Brady held up the New Testament. "I'm reading the Bible."

Harrington looked crestfallen. "Bah! I shoulda known. You Row guys always get religion before long. Unbelievable. Hey, guys, get this—Heiress Boy is Dead Man Squawking!"

And here came the wave of chicken clucking sounds.

"We know! We been watchin'!"

"Gettin' saved in there, are ya, pretty boy?"

"Think the appeals court will buy this?"

Everybody laughed at that one, and Brady was as tempted as he had ever been to set them all straight. He wanted to demand to know if any of them had ever actually read the Bible. But then, he didn't care what they thought. They were gearing up for everybody to watch the same TV show, and that would give him plenty of time to keep reading. Every time he started, he found something new, even when he was reading the same passages again and again.

For the first time since his incarceration, Brady ate every bite of his dinner, using all the salt, all the pepper, and drinking all the juice and coffee and tea.

It didn't taste any different, but his nausea was gone, and he felt the need for fuel.

When Harrington picked up his tray, he said, "Back on your feed, I see."

"Yep."

"Have a good one, Darby."

That caused Brady to shoot him a double take. "You too, man."

Finally, late that night when the rest were engrossed in their show, Brady was reading yet again when he realized he had been putting off something scary. It wasn't that he was ready to pray the prayer of salvation as outlined in the Romans Road booklet. No, he wanted to be dead sure before he seriously considered that. But he did want to try praying.

What troubled him was the memory of his aunt Lois telling him once when he was a youngster that God might not hear the prayers of unbelievers, unless they were praying to become Christians. She had said something about having to pray in the name of Jesus and having to already be a believer to do that.

Brady hadn't found that in any of his reading so far, and he figured maybe Aunt Lois was sincere but not entirely right.

It was time to try this.

"God," he said, "in the name of Jesus, would You reveal Yourself to me? Somehow just tell me whether this is all true? Thanks."

Brady opened his eyes and remembered that he had prayed before and more than once. He had prayed almost every time he had ever been arrested or even interrogated. He had made bargains with God, promised he would go straight if the Lord would just get him out of whatever mess he had gotten himself into.

But this was an altogether different type of prayer. It was a genuine request, and if Chaplain Carey could be trusted, God had to answer a prayer like that. But what did answers to prayer feel like? Would God speak to his heart the way Reverend Carey said He had spoken to him?

How would he know?

62

Adamsville

Thomas had to smile when he listened to Grace's tape. He had always loved her sweet voice, but now, with her age and her illness, it had faded to a weak instrument, though she retained the ability to stay right on key. And her sincerity came through. Thomas's smile came also from imagining the men in the cellblock overhearing it. Poor Brady would never hear the end of it. There could not have been a sound similar to it in that place—ever.

"It would have been better if you'd sung along with me, Thomas," Grace said.

"No, no. It's perfect. The lyrics are paramount. I think Brady will enjoy it. I just hope it helps."

Brady was startled awake by the officers clanging on the cell doors for the morning count and realized he'd slept through the night for the first time since coming here. He had to shake his head and remind himself of when he'd fallen asleep.

He wasn't surprised at his exhaustion, after having read around the clock, including all night the night before. Last night he had finally dozed off late, just before TVs had to go off, and he recalled rousing in time to hit the switch on his. Soon after that, the blackness invaded, and Brady had braced for the ugliness of the ghastly images of the murder taking over his mind. He always knew when these were coming because something, anything, might remind him of the temperature, the light, the smell, the sound . . . and off his memory would go, unharnessed.

But he woke up before the murder played itself out. And it was predawn. And the guards were making the rounds, conducting the first count.

Brady had never before been able to sleep through the horror of his memories. But this time he had prayed. That was it! When it had all begun again, Brady had desperately pleaded with God for relief from the dreadfulness just one time.

"I know I don't deserve it," he recalled saying. "I know it's part of the price. But, please . . ."

And God had answered! Was it possible? That had been Brady's second prayer since reading the New

Testament and the booklet the chaplain had given him. Maybe Aunt Lois *had* been wrong that God heard only the prayers of true believers. Could it be that the answer to the second prayer was also an answer to the first?

Brady had asked God to reveal Himself, and then it seemed God had honored his request to be spared the horror just once. And Brady had slept. Maybe no one else would make much of it, but Brady couldn't deny it. He believed he had communicated with God, and way better than that, God had communicated with him.

"You know you don't need to stand for morning count," an officer said.

"I know," Brady said, sitting quickly on his cot. "Sorry. Good morning."

"You say what?"

"Good morning."

"Yeah, sure."

As soon as the officers had moved on, Brady prayed silently once again. *God, when You let me sleep, was that You revealing Yourself to me?*

He wasn't getting any audible response—nor did he expect any—but as Brady searched his heart, he believed that if God was impressing anything on him, it was something strange. It was as if God was making him think that the relief from the memories was simply what it was—an answer to a plea from a desperate man. The revealing of Himself to Brady, however, was something altogether different.

Brady's eyes fell on the Bible and the book and the

pamphlet. *That's it!* If it was true that the Bible was God's Word and His letter to mankind, as the chaplain had said, *that* was how He had revealed Himself to Brady.

Brady opened the Bible and *The Romans Road* and spread them out on his table. The other book, the one about how to begin the Christian life . . . well, Brady was going to be needing that one soon too.

He didn't want to be in the middle of reading when breakfast was delivered, so he just waited. He'd already seen men panic when meals were late. Their minds got the better of them. They thought they'd been forgotten or abandoned or that the end of the world had come and they would starve to death in their cages. Brady just wanted breakfast to come so he could be done with it and get back to his reading.

When it did arrive, he found himself uncharacteristically polite to the officers again and again noticed their surprise. He ate everything, as he had the night before, and while he would never be able to say it was good, for some reason Brady found the fare less repulsive than before.

He replaced his tray in the meal slot and hurried back to his reading. He read faster and faster, poring over texts that were quickly becoming familiar favorites.

When Brady came again to Romans 10:8-11, it seemed everything around him faded. Nothing existed but the text as he slowed to a crawl and memorized, burning every word onto his brain.

In fact, it says, "The message is very close at hand; it is on your lips and in your heart." And that message is the very message about faith that we preach:

If you confess with your mouth that Jesus is Lord and believe in your heart that God raised him from the dead, you will be saved. For it is by believing in your heart that you are made right with God, and it is by confessing with your mouth that you are saved.

As the Scriptures tell us, "Anyone who trusts in him will never be disgraced."

Brady had no idea if some special feeling was supposed to come over him or what was to happen, but as he read and reread the part that promised "by believing in your heart" that God raised Jesus from the dead "you are made right with God," he realized simply that he did—he did believe in his heart.

How much faith was required to believe the rest of it—that he was now right with God? As Chaplain Carey had said, some things were God's responsibility. All Brady could do was believe. But he didn't *feel* right with God. Would that feeling ever come?

He didn't expect to be happy, to be joyful, to smile, to jump and shout and sing. Brady felt that even if he could get his mind around the idea that he had been "made right" with God, that would never take away the ultimate ugliness of the sin he had committed. He might even be able to accept that God would never again remember it, but he could not believe that he himself would ever forget.

Nor should he. Even if he was right with God and would escape eternal spiritual punishment, Brady knew full well that he had not settled his score for murder—at least in this life. He was grateful, of course, that his soul might be saved, but there was still this human price, and he was willing to pay it.

He could do nothing more than believe; the rest of this being made right with God was God's work. But the verses went on to say that "it is by confessing with your mouth that you are saved."

Confessing what? He was no intellectual, but this seemed clear. He had to tell somebody that Jesus was Lord and that God had raised Him from the dead.

Brady leaped to his feet and began to pace. It was true and he believed it; now who could he tell? He was tempted to just shout it out, but what would it mean to all the other cons on the Row? It would become nothing but ammunition for them. "Officer?" he called out.

From the intercom came the voice of a supervisor in the observatory. "What's your problem, Darby?"

"No problem, sir. Is Officer Harrington around?"

Suddenly the place was alive, and Brady quickly realized why. Nobody on death row had ever heard him speak above a whisper.

"Lover boy has woke up!"

"You like Harrington, do you, sweetheart?"

"Forget about your Heiress already?"

With all the racket, the observing officer sent someone from the booth directly to Brady's cell. "What do you need?"

"I want to see the chaplain right away."

"You know the procedure."

"Yeah, but it's sort of an emergency, and I was hoping maybe Officer Harrington could get word to him."

"What're you, about to kill yourself or something?"

"No, nothing like that. I just really need to see him."

"Harrington can't shortcut the system any better'n anybody else. I'll get you a form."

"That could take days. I need to see him right away."

"You want the form or not? 'Cause it doesn't make any difference to me either way."

"Okay."

Under "Reason for Requested Meeting," Brady wrote, "Counseling. I need to confess with my mouth." Chaplain Carey would know what he was getting at.

About twenty minutes after Brady filled out the form, Rudy Harrington came by. "You looking for me, Darby? We're not friends, you know."

"I know, but I need a favor."

"So do I, but you've got nothing I want."

"Listen, I was just wondering if you could call the chaplain and tell him I need to see him right away."

"Why? You seen the light, wanna give your life to God now?"

"Maybe. Just . . . would you?"

"You fill out the form?"

"Yeah, but you know how long—"

"Give it to me. If I can get to him, I will. Now how are you going to repay me?"

"I don't know. Like you said, I've got nothing."

"I'll think of a way."

"Thanks, man."

Harrington leaned close to the door and whispered, "One thing I don't need is you gettin' chummy, understand? We keep our distance."

"Got it."

Administrative Wing

It was rare but not unheard of for Thomas to take a call from a corrections officer, but this was the first time he had ever spoken with Rudy Harrington. The man sounded cordial enough—more than Thomas could say about many of the officers.

"I appreciate your letting me know, officer. I'll need that form in order to expedite—"

"I got no time to be ferrying paperwork all over the place. I mean no disrespect, but how about you come find me and I'll have the form for you?"

That was reasonable enough, but Thomas found himself excited. Knowing what this could mean, he didn't want to waste any time. He stopped in Frank LeRoy's office on his way out.

". . . so if the form is asking for a visit and I deem it legitimate, can I just head directly to his cell?"

"Yeah, no. See, you're circumventing protocol here, and I think—"

"Frank, sir, now please. Nobody but you is going to know if something happens a little out of the ordinary here. I'm supposed to look after the spiritual well-being of these men, and frankly, I'm making some progress with this one."

"That's all we need, a high-profile con getting religion. You keep this under wraps, whatever it is, you hear?"

"I will, Frank. Now can I see him if—"

"Yes, yes. See him. Just don't make it obvious anything's out of the ordinary."

"I should tell you that Officer Harrington is aware that a form is in the works."

"Rudy? He's all right. Stellar record. You don't have to worry about him."

Thomas rushed back to his office for his Bible and for Grace's tape. As he swept past Gladys's cubicle, she called out, "Hey there, Reverend! Where's the fire?"

He peeked over the partition. "Pray for Brady Darby. And please call Grace and ask her to do the same."

She gave him a thumbs-up and he was off again, but as Thomas began the laborious process of getting all the way to the death row pod, something dark and depressing came over him. With every step, every procedure, and past every block of cells, he was reminded how difficult the work here had been for so many years and how many cons had tried to con him.

Thomas wanted to believe that Brady Darby was different, that he was sincere, but how could he know? He reminded himself that God had put Brady on his heart from the moment he saw him, that Thomas believed God had even told him to tell Brady that He loved him. More people were praying for this man than for anyone Thomas had tried to reach since Henry Trenton.

Ugh! Why did he have to come to mind? Thomas didn't think he could endure another case like that. Whatever he did, he was going to make sure Darby was for real.

It took more than five minutes for Thomas to locate Rudy Harrington. The officer appeared in a hurry as he thrust the request form into Thomas's hands.

"I appreciate this," Thomas said, "and I trust you and I can keep it quiet."

"Keep what quiet, sir? I didn't read it, if that's what you're wondering."

"Oh, very good, then. Say, this is a copy. I'll need the original."

"Oh yeah. We copy all that stuff, you know. The original must still be in the machine. I'll find it and send it to your office, okay?"

"You copy these?"

"Yep. Just protocol."

63

Death Row

Thomas remained out of sight of Brady's cell as he hesitated at the end of a pod and stole a glance at the visitation request form. *Oh, God,* he breathed silently, *let this be for real.*

The prisoner looked stunned when Thomas appeared before his house. He stood quickly. "Thanks for coming."

"I came as soon as I got word. You can thank Officer Harrington."

"I will. So, you saw what I wrote."

"I did, and I must tell you something, Brady. I want you to look directly into my eyes."

"What? Are you two dating now?" someone shouted, and the cackling and hollering began.

"Ignore them," Thomas said. "Don't worry about anybody else. Before you tell me whatever it is you need to tell me, hear me out. This may go without saying, but I need to be crystal clear. I take spiritual matters deadly seriously. I want you to think carefully before you speak and then mean every syllable. I will not be conned; I will not be manipulated. I have been in the saddle here long enough to know when someone is simply trying to use the things of God for their own gain. You understand me?"

"Yes, sir. And I want you to believe me."

"For right now, Brady, I owe you the benefit of the doubt."

Brady looked down and nodded.

Thomas feared he had scared the man off. "Now, I'm listening."

"So is everyone else."

"They're too loud to hear you, and even if they do, that's their problem, not ours, isn't it?"

"I guess."

Thomas just stood staring, inches from Brady's face, only interlaced steel between them. He tried to hide that his heart was sprinting. *God, please.*

Brady Darby spoke just above a whisper, lips pale, his voice breaking. "Jesus is Lord," he said. "And I believe God raised Him from the dead."

"What does that mean?" Thomas said.

"That means I'm right with God and that I'm saved."

"What does it mean that Jesus is Lord?"

"Just what it sounds like. That He's the boss. He's the one in charge."

"And what does it mean for you that you are right with God and saved?"

Brady said, "I'm a child of God."

"How do you know?"

To Thomas's wonderment, this pathetic young man, whose life had appeared worthless just the last time they had seen each other, began quoting Scriptures from memory.

" 'To all who believed and accepted Him,' " Brady

said, " 'He gave the right to become children of God. They are reborn—not with a physical birth resulting from human passion or plan, but a birth that comes from God.' "

"What did you do to earn this?"

"Nothing," Brady said. " 'God saved you by his grace when you believed. And you can't take credit for this; it is a gift from God. Salvation is not a reward for the good things we have done, so none of us can boast about it. For we are God's masterpiece. He has created us anew in Christ Jesus, so we can do the good things he planned for us long ago.' "

Thomas had to grimace to keep his lips from quivering. He poked his fingers through one of the square openings, and Brady pressed his hand against them. "If you're sincere, Brady, we're brothers in Christ."

"You need to do me a favor, Reverend, and stop saying 'if' about this. Sounds like you're doubting me."

"I apologize."

"Don't judge me by how everybody else acts in here. There's nothing in this for me in this life. I'll still be locked in here and will still get put to death, and I don't guess I'd want it any other way. That's justice."

"But you've taken care of eternity, and that's no small thing."

"The way I see it, I didn't have a whole lot to do with it. I just believe, that's all."

"Brady, I need to get going so we don't abuse this privilege and lose it. But let me just tell you: one of the things I've seen here over all these years is men who have not figured out how to redeem their time. The future holds nothing for them, so they either get themselves in all sorts of trouble or they just zone out and sit staring, watching TV, doing nothing. I don't know how they keep from going crazy. Your earthly future hasn't changed, but think what you can do with your time now. You can really get to know God."

"By reading the Bible."

"Exactly. And memorizing. And who knows? Maybe God will allow you to share this with someone else."

"These guys? I doubt it."

"Like I said, you never know. Sure, they'll doubt you and mock you, but you may be able to reach inmates who would never listen to me."

"I'll read that book you gave me."

"Good, and I have many, many more. Let me know every time you finish one, and I'll bring you another. And meanwhile, my wife has a gift for you."

"Your wife?"

"You didn't think I was married?"

"I never thought about it."

"I'll tell you about her sometime. Meanwhile, maybe you will enjoy this."

But of course it wouldn't fit through the openings.

"What're you doing there, Reverend?" came the guard over the intercom.

"Just trying to give him a tape."

"I'll have to see it first."

"Hey!" someone yelled. "Give *me* a tape!"

"If you like what you hear," Thomas hollered back, "I'll bring you one too."

"That'll be the day!"

Thomas moved into the observatory and showed the cassette to the supervisor.

"What is this?"

Thomas told him.

"Sorry, Reverend. This could be broken and made into a weapon."

"I'll take full responsibility."

"Yeah, that'll do a lot of good when he's lying there bleeding out, or one of my guys is stabbed trying to get him to the shower. I'm going to have to say no."

Thomas sighed. He couldn't have been happier about what had happened to Brady, but clearly, in trying to work with him, he was going to face obstacles every step of the way.

Thomas stopped by Brady's cell on his way out and told him to request a private meeting. "I'll play this for you over the phone in the isolation room. How are you feeling, by the way?"

"That's something I want to talk to you about. How am I supposed to feel? It's like I'm relieved, but I still feel unworthy, like I don't deserve it. I am what I am, and I can't be happy because of the people I've hurt."

"You feel unworthy because you *are* unworthy, Brady. Relieved is the right way to feel. And that may be as good as it gets. I need to warn you though: this voyage is not going to be all clear sailing."

"What do you mean?"

"You want to get to know God, right? to get to know Jesus by reading the Bible and the other stuff I'll get to you?"

"Sure. 'Course."

"As you start to grow and understand and get a picture of what God is really like, you're going to start seeing yourself in light of Him. If you're like me, you may have some real trouble with what you see in the mirror."

Brady snorted. "If I was like you, I'd have an easier time looking in the mirror. I already know I'm scum."

"I'm just telling you, the closer you get to Jesus, the harder it is sometimes."

Administrative Wing

Thomas went directly back to Warden LeRoy's office. "Frank, I'm going to be needing to see this inmate on a regular basis."

"Yeah, no. That's going to be hard to pull off without everybody else knowing he's getting special privileges."

"No special privileges. I'll change the rules for my office. Any inmate demonstrating a sincere belief and wishing to be discipled or mentored in his effort to become more spiritually mature shall not be restricted in his requests for personal time with the chaplain. How's that sound?"

"Like you rehearsed it. But I'd have to say that just might work, within reason."

Thomas was so stunned that Yanno would even consider this, he hardly knew how to respond. "Well, sure, within reason, Frank. He has to be in his cell for counts, meals, and to be taken to his shower and exercise. And the meetings would naturally have time limits."

"This would put extra burden on officers who have to transfer him back and forth."

"C'mon, chief. What else are these guys doing all day? What's another trip to isolation?"

"Put it in writing for the review board. I'll run it up the proverbial flagpole."

Thomas would do better than put it in writing. He would enlist Ravinia's help in crafting a document that would stand up legally—no holes, no exceptions, no soft underbelly. He left a message for her, then called Grace with the news. In the middle of telling her, Thomas began to sob and couldn't speak.

"I'm so thrilled," she said. "So thrilled. I can only imagine how you feel."

"Actually you can't," Thomas managed. "It's been so long."

"I'll let the people at church know."

"Tell them to keep praying. This has only just begun."

Thomas carefully studied his library, looking for just the right progression of titles to try to slowly but surely bring Brady along in his fledgling faith. When he thought he had it figured out, he put Grace's tape in his player and sat weeping as he listened.

I hear the Savior say,
"Your strength indeed is small!
Child of weakness, watch and pray,
Find in Me your all in all."

When from my dying bed
My ransomed soul shall rise,
"Jesus died my soul to save,"
Shall rend the vaulted skies.

Jesus paid it all,
All to Him I owe;
Sin had left a crimson stain—
He washed it white as snow.

"So you snagged a live one, eh?" his daughter said
when she called back at the end of the day. "Good for
you."

"I know you mean that," he said, smiling.

"Well, a little faith can't hurt these lost souls. I
mean, what else does Darby have to look forward to?
He still dies in less than three years, right?"

"Right."

"He understands that, I hope. He's not hoping for
some break because of this . . . ?"

Thomas assured her he believed Brady Darby was
genuine and sincere.

"How long has it been?" she said.

"Sorry?"

"How long since someone really changed under

your influence—and you don't have to remind me that it's God, not you."

She had hit him right where he lived, and he had been thinking that very thing all afternoon. It had been a lot of years and a lot of churches ago.

His silence must have unnerved his daughter. "I didn't mean to bother you, Dad. I was just wondering. Just saying way to go. You know we don't agree on all this, but if there's one thing I know, it's that you mean it. So this has to feel good."

Death Row

Brady didn't know if it was because Chaplain Carey had planted the idea in his mind or if the man had simply been right, but what he had predicted came true. The more Brady read and the more he learned, the more he was overwhelmed by the love of God and His perfection, His power, His might.

Brady was still relieved, and nothing made his new faith waver, but he began to feel so low, so worthless, so puny that he could barely stand himself. And then came the memories: not as ghastly as the scenes of the murder, but somehow someone or something was bringing to his mind every last thing he had done wrong his whole life.

Brady could not even begin to count the lies, the people he had swindled, the trouble he had caused, the damage he had done. He started a list, but it went on for pages. The induction material said that prisoners were not allowed to write letters to their victims or their families or try to make amends without approval from the warden's office.

What could be wrong with apologizing and trying to make things right? He wouldn't dare try to do that in the case of Katie and her family, because he knew how that would look. But what about how he had treated his aunt and uncle, his mother, his employers, Agatha, his teachers, everyone? The list seemed endless.

He submitted his request to see the chaplain in private again as soon as possible. Brady had so many questions, so many concerns, he was unsure where he should even begin. He sure hoped he didn't bug this poor guy to death. It was just that there was so much to take in, to understand, to deal with.

His life had changed; Brady could already feel it. But like the chaplain had said, it was not going to be easy. Verses he had already read several times hit him anew. And when he came across John 10:10 again, quoting Jesus Himself, it made Brady wonder.

The thief's purpose is to steal and kill and destroy. My purpose is to give them a rich and satisfying life.

How full could Brady's life be on death row at Adamsville State Penitentiary?

64

Adamsville

The Carey house was too full. The whole family was there, and the news was so good on the one hand and so melancholy on the other that Thomas didn't know how to feel.

He was always ebullient when Summer was around, finding himself with more energy than he knew he had. Thomas chased her and let her ride on his back as he scooted through the house on all fours. She squealed with delight.

He reminded her to be quiet when they got to Grandma's room. Remission was but a memory now, and Grace was again bedridden.

The glad news was that Dirk had come along, and he and Ravinia had announced to Thomas and Grace that they were going to give it another go. Dirk was subletting his apartment and moving back home. Thomas was pleased, but he could tell Grace was worried. She wanted them back together, of course, but she had told Thomas privately that she hadn't heard enough sound reasoning yet.

"I wanted to hear that they had a handle on what went wrong, that they had forgiven each other, and that they knew how to try to fix things. Short of that, I'm just not sure."

She was right, naturally. She usually was. But

Thomas believed they stood the best chance of surviving if they were together to try to work things out, and this had to be best for Summer. It had to be awful to be shuttled back and forth between estranged parents.

The next week in his office, Ravinia made one of her customary visits, and Thomas was able to bring her up to date on Brady Darby. He told her of meeting with him privately and playing Grace's hymns for him.

"If he can stand that, he may be for real after all," Ravinia said, laughing.

"He enjoyed it. Wants to hear it enough to memorize the words. I couldn't get him to sing along, but I know he was moved. He's reading the Bible and other Christian books, praying, memorizing. He's even eating better and actually exercising."

"Praise be."

Thomas chuckled. "It proves to me he's coming around mentally. A man doesn't eat right and work out when he's depressed. You still look dubious."

"Well," she said, "is he going to become like a monk, totally one-dimensional? I mean, it's bad enough he's a forced recluse like everyone else in here, but . . ."

"Oh no. He still reads his entertainment and movie magazines. I don't see the appeal, but it's a lifetime interest for him. But you know what he needs, Rav? A lawyer."

"Please. You know he's got Jackie Kent, the contract guy. Jackie's jumping through all the mandatory appeals hoops, which are just formalities. Everybody knows nothing is going to happen there, especially with Darby continuing to insist that he doesn't want his sentence overturned. Oh no—don't tell me he's changed his mind on that. I thought you were under the impression that this conversion—if that's what it is—was not a deathbed type of thing. Is he planning to use this now? Because there are rumors."

"First of all, to my knowledge, he has not changed his mind about that. In fact, he's so frustrated with Kent that that's why I think he needs you."

"Me? You didn't say me, you said 'a lawyer.'"

"Well, you're the best one I know. But what did you mean about rumors? What kind of rumors?"

"Hold on. He seriously wants to dump Jackie and seek new representation?"

"Yes. He's confused. He understands there are mandatory appeals at all these different levels, but he doesn't understand why his own counsel fights him at every turn. Rav, you have been bending my ear for ages now, decrying that these men seem to have lost every civil right and privilege."

"And they have. And I know in most cases they have brought that on themselves, but they should still be entitled to competent counsel and have their legal rights protected—those few they have left."

"Okay, then tell me why a man who simply wants to waive his right to appeal his own death sentence should not be able to do that. I can't make it make sense to him."

Rav looked away, and Thomas got the impression he was getting to her. "How deeply does he feel about this?" she said.

"Even with his immersion in spiritual things, this consumes him. I wish you'd talk to him."

"I'd have to talk with Jackie first."

"You'd actually consider it?"

"For you? Sure."

"Now these rumors . . . ?"

"Yeah, well, we're hearing that someone inside is leaking stuff to the press about Darby."

"Such as?"

"Would you believe none of what you've told me has been a surprise? Even down to him listening to hymns in private meetings with the chaplain?"

"Oh no."

"Who knows all this, Dad?"

"One too many, apparently. Why hasn't anyone run with it? I haven't seen anything on the news."

"It won't be long," she said. "I think the source is shopping what he's got. Or what she's got. Some think it's actually coming from someone on the warden's staff."

Thomas shook his head. "Heads would roll so fast in here if anyone was even suspected. I can't imagine it."

Ravinia shrugged. "You know best. Listen, get me something in writing saying Darby wants a meeting, and I'll clear it with Kent."

• • •

Even before the meeting between Rav and Brady could be arranged, Thomas suffered two setbacks that—combined with Grace's regression—made him wonder if this new season of encouragement was over.

First Ravinia broke the news to him that the return to normalcy by having Dirk move back home had ended in chaos and set them back further than they had been before. They had apparently engaged in heated arguments, including one overheard by Summer, and Dirk was already living by himself again.

Ravinia tried to convince her father that, ironically, even after all that, neither believed the marriage was over. Yet.

"We're going to try to cool down, reassure Summer, keep sharing custody, and take another run at this when we both feel up to it."

So Grace had been right. It had been too soon, and they had really not had anything solid to build on.

The second trauma was that Ravinia had been right too. The *Adamsville Tribune* had apparently won the bidding war for inside information from one Rudy Harrington, who made enough from the sale that he was able to quit his job before being fired by Frank LeRoy.

The papers had been on the street for less than an hour before every other news agency in town and around the state, and soon the country, was running with the story. While Harrington had most of the details right, the pundits decided what it all meant, and by that evening the story hit all the tabloid news shows on TV.

Everybody from paid commentators to the man on the street had opinions about the Heiress Murderer and his finding that old-time religion.

Most called it an obvious attempt to sway the appellate court to stay his execution.

Hardly anyone believed it was sincere.

Many people of faith said they hoped it was real and that people should take a wait-and-see attitude.

It was the topic of radio and TV programs for days, though Frank LeRoy had taken action immediately. He announced that the state would file suit against former corrections officer Harrington for violating his sworn duty. He further stated that any leak traced to any current employee would result in immediate termination. And he decreed that no one within the state penitentiary besides himself and the chaplain would be available for comment on Brady Darby.

The warden's comment:

> "It does not fall to me to judge the veracity of a man's personal beliefs. My job is to ensure that convicted criminals serve their sentences. Mr. Darby has been sentenced to death in this facility in less than two and a half years. Unless I hear otherwise from the legal system, our plan is to carry out that sentence."

Thomas's comment:

"No one knows the genuineness of a man's heart except God and that man himself. I do know, however, that despite Mr. Darby's profession of faith in Christ for salvation, he remains adamant that he will not seek any reduction, mitigation, or stay of his sentence. He insists, as he has all along, that he is guilty of the crime with which he was charged and will not cooperate with any attempts to appeal his fate.

"Based on such assurances from him, I believe his spiritual transformation is real and that he does not intend to benefit from this in any legal sense."

Warden Frank LeRoy did not have jurisdiction over Jordan North, who was eager to add his two cents' worth:

"Two and a half years is not soon enough to see the end of the monster who murdered our daughter. He can make any claim or profession he wants, but if there's a God and He doesn't send Brady Wayne Darby straight to hell, they deserve each other."

The press rode the story for as long as it could, but with LeRoy having effectively shut down the information coming from inside the prison and the news-hounds' inability to dredge up any evidence that

Brady had changed his mind about his death penalty, the din finally faded.

Isolation Room

When Ravinia Carey-Blanc, acting under the authority of an official request on the part of her new pro bono client, met with contract attorney Jackie Kent, he proved more than relieved to be out from under the Darby appeals. She told Brady, "We're still required by law to file these appeals, but you finally have counsel who takes into consideration your personal wishes, unconventional as they may be. The necessary documents will be filed with each appellate board at the last minute on the days they're due, and we will do nothing to encourage the court to act on them. When asked, if I understand you correctly, I will remind them that you wish each appeal to be summarily denied and the sentence expedited with dispatch."

Brady peered at his new lawyer through the Plexiglas and cocked his head. "If what you just said means I want to lose and lose fast, you got it."

"Anything else?" she said.

"Like what?"

"You being treated okay? Not every inmate still has a lawyer. You might as well take advantage of it. Is anyone treating you poorly? denying you anything? humiliating you? harassing you? making you wait egregiously?"

"No, I'm good."

"You have rights, Brady. That's all I'm telling you. Not many, of course. Neither of us should be naive about this. Nearly everything normal has been stripped from you, but it is not legal for you to be treated less than humanely, especially when it is clear you are not high maintenance. You'll let me know, won't you?"

He nodded.

"Now," she added, standing, "I want to remind you one more time: I am honoring your request to get these appeals denied, but just like your previous counsel, this flies in the face of everything I believe and everything I was taught. It's never too late to change your mind. I mean, you aren't likely to win after all the fighting you've done to lose, but all you have to do is say the word, and I can put on the brakes. I can probably buy you another year or two. Execution after just three years' incarceration is almost unheard of."

"But you promised to work for me, not against me."

"By all means. This is totally your call. Just know that I stand ready to serve you, regardless whether your decision changes."

"You know you look like your dad?"

Brady thought she blushed.

"People say that, but I think I look like my mother."

"I don't guess I'll ever meet her."

"Probably not. I'll bring a picture sometime."

"That'd be nice. I sure love her singing."

"I'll tell her you said that."

"Tell her I want some more."

"I'm not sure she'll be up to that. You know she's not well."

Brady shook his head. "Reverend Carey never said that. What's wrong with her?"

"Leukemia." Ravinia told Brady how it had manifested itself. "Maybe my dad didn't think you needed to know."

"That makes me sad. I'll pray for her. Will you tell her that? But don't say anything about me wanting more music."

Later, as Thomas met with Ravinia, he was surprised at her tone.

"There is something about that young man, Dad. A sadness. Grief maybe. But despite his obvious lack of education, he's got some sort of depth. I might just enjoy helping him."

65

Death Row

The tumult may have ended in the press and among the public, but the cons on the Row were not letting it go. They yammered incessantly, and Brady was convinced they were trying to drive him insane.

It wasn't working. While he could rarely bring himself to even smile, he did enjoy a deep sense of contentment and satisfaction as he continued to read the New Testament and all the other material he could get from Reverend Carey.

When the chaplain discussed Brady's maturing in the faith, he quoted Romans 10:17 from his own Bible: " 'Faith comes from hearing, that is, hearing the Good News about Christ.' In other words, Brady, the more you read the Word, the more faith you'll have."

Brady told the chaplain that he felt mixed up all the time. "I have what I've always wanted—forgiveness and knowing that I'll go to heaven when I die. But I can't quit thinking about what I did. I think God has somehow kept me from the worst of the daydreams and nightmares, but it doesn't feel right to even try to put it behind me, even though I know God promises to never remember it."

"I don't claim to speak for God on this," Reverend Carey said, "but I'm not sure you should try to forget it, unless it keeps you from pursuing Him. Sin has consequences. Sin leaves scars. Your crime left a shattered family. I'm sure you feel that if you simply tried to push that out of your mind, you would be doing Katie's memory and her family a disservice."

"Exactly. How can God forget it?"

"Because He's God and He chooses to and promises to. If you thought God was thinking of it every time He thought of you, how would you feel?"

Brady nodded. "I guess remembering just makes it more amazing what God has done for me."

"You look good, Brady," the chaplain said. "Still eating better and working out?"

"I'm actually running a little in the exercise kennel. Makes a big difference."

"And how goes the memorizing?"

"Good. I don't have much else to do. Besides all the stuff you send me, I only read a couple of movie magazines. I sure miss the movies."

Gradually Brady began noticing that the guards were nicer to him, less cold, more cordial. They even looked away when he showered or was strip-searched. He still knew enough not to trust anyone and had not gotten over how Rudy Harrington had betrayed him. Brady guessed they were more than even as far as favors went. He heard on the news that the state dropped the lawsuit against Officer Harrington. Brady worried that that might encourage other officers to trade their futures for payoffs.

Administrative Wing

Thomas found himself overwhelmed with gratitude to God for allowing him some role in Brady Darby's life. Thomas still had heartache. Dirk and Ravinia seemed stalemated. And he could see the pain in Summer's eyes. Plus Grace was getting only worse.

But of all things, business was picking up for Thomas, if he could phrase it that way. It wasn't that other inmates seemed impressed with what was happening with Brady. They heard it only secondhand, and no one knew too much about it because the work was done privately by Brady in his cell and by the two of them in an isolation unit. Everyone knew Brady claimed to have found God, but most on the inside were as skeptical as those on the outside.

And yet Thomas had been reinvigorated, and something in his earnestness or aggressiveness or urgency had made him a bolder witness. When a man asked to see him about some trivial matter or something only slightly related to Christianity, Thomas never missed an opportunity to contend for the faith. In season and out of season, as the apostle Paul taught, Thomas reminded himself.

And while no one else had come to faith or even claimed to, Thomas believed it was only a matter of time. He actually looked forward to coming to work these days.

One afternoon in the isolation room, it was clear to Thomas that Brady had something on his mind.

"I've been wondering about something. Do you think people understand what Jesus did for us? On the cross, I mean?"

"Well, not enough of them, obviously," Thomas said. "You mean taking our punishment?"

"Actually more than that. Tell you the truth, I'm getting tired of just reading the New Testament all the way through over and over, great as it is. I'm starting to skip Revelation. I don't get that at all. But I'm trying to do something when I read the Gospels. I keep flipping back and forth between them and seeing how each of them tell the same stories, you know?"

Thomas chuckled. "Theologians have been doing that forever."

"Well, I've been looking at when Jesus died on the cross. And it's just so different, really reading how it looked to them."

"Different from what?"

"Different from what I remember. Whenever I heard about Jesus dying on the cross for our sins, I saw pictures of Him hanging there like some angel. It was sort of heroic, I guess. I mean, it *was* heroic, but those pictures made it look all saintly. Then there are the paintings of His friends taking Him down. And of course Him rising from the dead. In a way I suppose I knew that it had to hurt. There was talk of agony and pain and thirst.

"But, you know, now that I'm reading it straight out of the Bible and really studying it . . ." Brady had a faraway look.

"I see," Thomas said. "It isn't so pretty, is it?"

"No, and I wonder how many people are so used to hearing about it and seeing it in paintings and movies that they think they know what it must have been like. It makes me wonder if people really understand. I mean, okay, Jesus died for our sins and we're all happy about that. But I think we say it too lightly. It was an awful, horrible death. To me, that makes it mean so much more."

Thomas could only nod. What a joy to see this

young man grow. The change from the wasted, lonely, broken boy to this vibrant young man astounded him. Brady's eyes seemed alive, and while there was—as he himself had described—a deep sadness over what he had done, Thomas was certain that what he detected in the man was hope.

Later that afternoon, Thomas caught himself rhapsodizing while recounting his conversation to Ravinia.

"The son you never had, huh?" she said. "And he's become what you always wanted me to become."

"I'm sorry, Rav. I'm just trying to encourage you about your client. Nothing and no one can ever rival your place in my heart."

She looked at him as if trying to formulate a response. "Well, anyway . . . ," she said. "It appears I'm in trouble with the federal appeals court. They assigned an independent auditor of sorts who informs me I'm suspect because I don't appear to be performing to the best of my ability for Mr. Darby. He accused me of being late on filing appeals, which we weren't, but also sketchy and seemingly not interested in the process, both of which are true."

"No such quarrel from the state?"

"Are you kidding? We have a hanging judge for a governor, more so than any since Andreason. The state review board is quicker to dismiss these appeals the more you push them. I gave them no reason to give it a second look, but they didn't even give it a first. This federal thing is the last hurdle, and then Mr. Darby gets his fondest wish."

"His fondest wish is that he could change history, take it back, make it so it didn't happen."

"Yeah, okay, and short of that he'll take death because he now has fire insurance."

"Brady insisted on death long before he came to faith."

"Fair enough," Ravinia said. "This guy is deeper than what meets the eye."

"So what are you going to do about this challenge to your work ethic?"

"Take it to the Honorable Jonathan Allard, I think. Once the governor gets wind of what Washington is trying to do to one of his state's inmates, it'll be newsworthy and could be noisy. All I need is Darby's permission."

Thomas shook his head. "I don't know, Rav. I mean, I'll let Brady speak for himself, but I don't think all this publicity is good for him. It frustrates him that he's not free to speak for himself. He wants everybody to know his motives now and to assure them that he's seeking no favors, no privileges because of what's happened to him."

"Then this will be exactly what he wants. No, he won't likely be quoted. But Governor Allard can speak for him. Believe me, he'll be saying virtually the same thing."

Thomas stood and wished he had a window to look out. "No, he won't. Allard would use Brady as a political football, making it look like he wants to give nothing to a condemned man. If you could be guaranteed that it would be clear that Allard wants the feds to butt out and so does Brady, that's one thing. But if it can appear that Allard is personally putting the kibosh on Brady's appeal, that's the way the governor would want it to appear."

"I'm resigned to acceding to his wishes. . . ."

"He admires you a great deal. He worries about you though."

"Brady Darby worries about me? Whatever for? Oh, Dad! You haven't revealed any personal information about me, have you? I don't need him knowing about—no, wait, you didn't even tell him about Mom. Surely you've said nothing about Dirk and me."

"Of course not. He just senses a sadness in you. That's all."

Ravinia squinted at him. "Really? Well, he can ask me if I'm all right if he'd like. Meanwhile, feel free to assure him I'll survive."

66

Adamsville

Thomas sat next to Grace's bed, helping her eat as they watched the evening news. Governor Allard feigned anger and waxed eloquent as he stood on the steps of the state capitol building and railed against Washington.

"We take care of our own state business," he said. "We caught Brady Wayne Darby, we sentenced him to death, and by heaven, we're going to carry it out. Delaying his fate even one more day would put an unnecessary financial burden on our taxpayers. The federal appellate court can stew over this as long as they want, but we have an execution date, and all the other mandatory appeals have failed. The condemned man himself, I remind my respected colleagues, pleaded guilty and has insisted all along that he will in no way cooperate with any attempt to overturn his sentence."

"That's the part Ravinia made him put in there," Thomas said. "She had counsel from her learned father on that."

Grace smiled. "She told me. Said you were afraid the governor would try to make it look like Brady was pushing the appeal."

"This will put an end to it," Thomas said. "The protesters will always be there, and I admire their devotion and tenacity, I really do. But any delay in this would be the most unpopular political move anyone could make."

"Brady will get what he wants," Grace said quietly. "It saddens me, but I know it's the right thing."

"Interesting," Thomas said. "Brady said your illness made him sad."

"Bless his heart. I wish I could record more music for him, but I just can't."

"He asks for the first one every time we meet. He's

got some of the songs down. You should hear him sing."

Grace seemed to study Thomas. "You light up when you talk about him. You love that young man, don't you?"

"Oh, I don't know. I care for him a great deal. He's such a sad case."

"But he's also your spiritual stepchild. You've invested yourself in him."

"It's not just him. I've wanted to do this with any of the men all through the years. He's just the first who's seemed genuine. Did I tell you he'd like a picture of you and wondered if you'd mind if he taped it on his wall?"

"Sure, but not a recent picture. I don't suppose they'd let you shoot a picture of him for me."

"No, but there have been plenty in the papers."

"He looked so forlorn in those."

The phone rang. It was Ravinia. "Anything wrong?" Thomas said. "Summer okay?"

"We're fine, Dad. I've asked Dirk if I can drop her off. I need to talk with you."

"Urgent?"

"Sort of, but nothing personal, so nothing to worry about. I'll be there within the hour."

Death Row

Brady sat trying to memorize some verses from Matthew while letting one of Mrs. Carey's songs echo in his mind. But he found it hard to sit still. He had spent much of the previous night penning a letter to his aunt Lois that began, "You're going to find this hard to believe, but some of what you tried to teach me about God must have stuck, enough to make me worry what was going to happen to me when I die. . . ."

She would be disappointed to hear that he had not become a true believer until recently, but she would also be overjoyed to be sure about him now. Aunt Lois would insist on coming to see him. And finally, he would be more than ready.

That morning Brady was struck by an idea so bizarre that he began to believe it could have come only from God. He paced. He sat. He stood. He turned it over in his mind. Impossible. Could it work? He couldn't wait to bounce it off someone. But he didn't dare even suggest it to Chaplain Carey yet, not until he found out if it could even be done.

At his end-of-the-day meeting with his lawyer in the isolation unit, Brady gushed his idea.

Mrs. Carey-Blanc just sat there shaking her head and telling him all the reasons why it would never fly. Rules, regulations, protocol, procedure, no exceptions, and the list went on and on.

He just smiled at her.

"I'm not going to pursue this for you, Brady."

"Yes, you are. I can tell."

"You can't tell it by me. Have you been listening? It's impossible."

"Nothing is impossible. 'I can do everything through Christ, who gives me strength.' That's from Philippians."

"Yeah, I know. Chapter 4, verse 13. Don't forget, I grew up with your spiritual adviser. I don't mean to be flippant, Brady, but not even Christ can help you with this one. Simply not going to happen."

"But you'll try."

Ravinia rolled her eyes. "I wouldn't even know where to start."

"Sure you would. You know everything, and you've been working inside the system a long time."

"I'd be laughed out of here," she said.

"Just tell me you'll try."

"Brady, really, be serious. Think this through. Can you imagine the warden going for this? Uh-uh. No way."

"I like your idea of starting with the warden," he said.

"I said no such thing."

"Start at the top; go right to the man."

"You know what his nickname is?"

Brady shook his head.

"It's Yanno." She told him why.

"That's funny."

"Neither of us will find it funny when he throws in a few expletives."

"But you'll try?"

"Brady, don't ask me to do this."

"I'm asking."

She sighed. "And you'll take *no* for an answer?"

"Not from you."

"From the warden?"

"Yeah, no."

"Very funny. But seriously, Brady, if he says no, it's over, right?"

"Okay, listen, ma'am, I know I'm new at this, and I'm not saying God spoke to me like He did to your dad, but I feel like He gave me this idea. If He did, no one can stand in the way of it, right?"

"Well, first of all, if you ever call me ma'am again, I'll drop you as a client."

"No you won't. You like me."

"I'm not even ten years older than you, so don't be using matronly names for me. And the sad answer is, yes, even if God gave you the idea, someone can stand in the way of it. Not everybody here acknowledges God, you know."

"And how about you?"

"Sorry?"

"You, Mrs. Carey-Blanc?"

"That's personal, and I'd appreciate it if we kept our relationship on a professional—"

"Sorry. I mean, I just, you know, wondered if you still believe in Jesus or—"

"If you must know, I have not entirely thrown the baby out with the bathwater, as the saying goes. But God and I have not been on speaking terms for a long time."

"The baby with the bathwater. I like that."

"Never heard that before?"

"Oh, sure. But I figure you mean the baby Jesus."

That stopped her somehow, left her silent. Finally she spoke, trying, he thought, to lighten the mood. "I'll tell you what: if we get anywhere with the warden on this, it'll be a miracle."

"Then maybe you and God will be on speaking terms again."

"That just might do it, but don't press your luck. And I'm serious—I do not want to discuss my personal life with you."

Adamsville

Thomas sat in his living room staring at his daughter. "That is so wrong on so many levels. You sure he was serious?"

She nodded. "He's earnest, I'll give him that."

"Earnest is one thing," Thomas said. "Insane is another. What an ugly idea. Well, I just hope his faith isn't shattered when it gets shot down."

"I'm already having second thoughts about even agreeing to pursue this," Ravinia said. "If Brady just went through normal channels, it would never see the light of day. But now Yanno will have to take this seriously because a lawyer is involved."

"That won't worry him," Thomas said. "He has every policy and procedure in the book backing him, and security overrides everything."

"Still, I'm obligated to represent my client. I suppose I could be less than enthusiastic or even confide in the warden that I know it's not going to fly but that I'm going through the motions."

"That doesn't sound ethical, Rav."

"That's why I'm here. Would you go with me when I talk with LeRoy?"

"Not if you want me as an ally. The whole thing hits me as grotesque. What was Brady thinking?"

"I figured you would *like* to see this happen, if there was any chance."

"You know as well as I do that there is no chance. But even if there were, why would I like it?"

"Because his motives are pure, and think of the impact. Even I can see that. But I have to get the warden on board. And having another interested party along can only help."

"So I'd be there to help intimidate Frank? Not sure I'm comfortable with that."

"You'd be there for me, Dad. If I'm to act in the best interest of my client, I need accountability. I hate to admit it, but alone I might cave and feel obligated to tell the warden I know it's a long shot and blah, blah, blah. I mean, I agree with you that this has zero chance, but I told Brady I'd try."

"I'm willing to go, but I prefer not to say anything unless asked."

"He may ask about how Brady is doing. You know that better than anyone."

"Sure, I can speak to that. But otherwise, I'm just there as moral support. Now you'd better check in on your mother, and feel free to wake her. She'll be disappointed if she misses you."

When Ravinia tiptoed into the bedroom, Thomas stood looking out the living room window, praying silently. What a cockamamy idea Brady had. It would make for an interesting meeting with the warden. Thomas could hardly wait to see the look on Yanno's face.

When Rav emerged, she whispered, "She's getting worse, isn't she?"

Thomas nodded. "The doctor says she'll slip a little further back after each remission, but that she has a few more remissions to enjoy too, if his guess is correct."

"I wouldn't count on it, Dad. I would love to see it, but I just don't know."

"Me either. Listen, I've got an idea about our meeting with the warden, but it may seem duplicitous."

"How delicious. I'm not above duplicity."

"Well, call it more manipulation."

"Even better, Dad. What?"

"I was just thinking that if you preceded laying out the idea to the warden with the fact that you expect a huge fight from the feds over this and so you wanted to come to him first, he'd have his back up right away. Nothing motivates him more than people who try to tell him what to do."

"Sort of like me, eh?"

"I wasn't going to say that."

67

Frank LeRoy looked wary as Thomas Carey and Ravinia Carey-Blanc sat directly across the desk from him in faded plastic chairs.

"Give me the shock of my life and tell me this is not about Brady Wayne Darby."

Thomas and Ravinia smiled at each other, and the warden said, "Yeah, no, that's what I thought. What now?"

"I'm just tired of Washington, aren't you, sir?" Ravinia said.

"I was until the governor gave 'em what for. You heard the federal appeals board finally caved and that's all over now."

"I informed you, sir."

"That you did. That you did. So, anyway, I think that takes the heat off, don't you?"

"Unless they try to tell you what you can and can't do with a prisoner who's going to die in a little over two years regardless."

"The governor made Director Andreason and me proud, ma'am. The feds have no say when it comes to Darby. We'd have sued their pants off if they'd ruled the other way on the mandatory appeal, but that wasn't necessary, and now they're completely out of it."

"No matter what you decide about Darby?"

"There's nothing more to decide. He's proved a model citizen. I wouldn't want to be quoted outside this office, but the reverend here has me convinced the guy's for real. Not sure I agree he's going to get into heaven after what he did, but that's just doctrine between your dad and me. But Darby serves out his time and keeps behaving, we do the deed on time, end of story."

"I'll bet you'd have Washington on your doorstep again if you do anything out of the ordinary with him."

"They wouldn't get past the guardhouse. And we don't plan on anything out of the ordinary."

"Want to put them to the test?"

Yanno leaned back in his chair with his hands behind his head. "How did I know this was coming? You know this guy already has more visitation privileges and time with you and the chaplain than anybody ever has here."

"And he's proven worthy of that trust," Ravinia said.

"Can't deny that."

"Okay, can I ask you to keep an open mind? I just want to make sure we're all on the same page if this bothers the press, the public, the victim's family, or Washington."

"Whatever it is, young lady, you don't have to sell anybody but me. I don't give a baboon's hairdo what anyone else thinks about it."

"That's the way you've always run this place."

"It's the way I do business, and it always will be."

Ravinia pulled out her notes. "Okay, so Darby is in his cell yesterday morning, minding his own business. As you know, he spends most of every day reading his Bible and memorizing it."

"So?"

"So he got an idea. It's . . . unconventional, but I think you might like it."

"Do tell."

"Actually, sir, he wants to tell you himself."

"Do I need to remind you two that Brady Darby is not my only inmate?"

"For right now he is," Ravinia said. "He's waiting in the isolation unit."

LeRoy slowly shook his head and rose. "I swear this is the last time."

Isolation Unit

Frank LeRoy said, "I've got about five minutes, so let's dispense with pleasantries. What's up?"

"If I may, Warden," Ravinia said, facing Brady, "we're heading into uncharted seas, no man's land, or whatever cliché you want to use."

"Just somebody tell me already, would you?" LeRoy said.

Brady was plainly hesitating. "All right, here's the thing. 'Keep on asking, and you will receive what you ask for. Keep on seeking, and you will find. Keep on

638

knocking, and the door will be opened to you. For everyone who asks, receives. Everyone who seeks, finds. And to everyone who knocks, the door will be opened.' "

Yanno squinted. "Okay, all right, then. You're quoting the Bible. If I were you, I wouldn't be doing that in front of your cellblock mates, if you get my drift. And there aren't any doors in here that just pop open when you knock. So what's this all about?"

"I'm ready to choose my form of execution, sir."

"There's a form for that. We're the easiest facility in the country on that score. As you know, you get to choose, and nobody can make the decision for you."

"Good."

"Yeah, it's good, but you didn't need me here for that."

Ravinia held up a booklet, which Thomas recognized as the induction pamphlet for death row. "Says right here that the decision is entirely under the inmate's purview."

Warden LeRoy extended his hands wide, as if pleading with everyone. "Could I have been more clear? Now you've got it from my very mouth *and* from our printed material. So can I please get back to my office?"

"As long as we're clear," Ravinia said. "Mr. Darby would like to inform you officially of his decision."

"That's unnecessary, but fine! Fine! Tell me, please!"

68

Brady leaned toward the glass. "I want to be crucified. Hung on a cross, spikes through the wrists and feet, thorns piercing my skull, side riven with a spear after I'm dead."

Frank LeRoy sat blinking. "You want your execution to be by crucifixion."

"Yes, sir."

"Yeah, no. That's pure megalomania. You've gone past identifying with Jesus to where you think you're Him now. That's insane."

"No, not at all. I—"

"C'mon, this is nuts. Now, see, what you've got to do is choose between our four options."

"Where does it say that, sir?" Ravinia said. "I've read and reread this, and not only does it not say that here, but this is also the first time you've said it."

"Yeah, but—"

"Yeah, but nothing, Warden. All due respect, but is it not true that one of the first executions conducted at this facility was not carried out by any of these four methods?"

The warden pressed his lips together, leaned back, and looked at the ceiling. "We did have a guy who wanted the firing squad," he said. "So we put him in the electric chair, set up bullet catchers behind him, and that was that."

"So despite that precedent, you're planning to discriminate against my client's final wish, violating his last remaining civil right? What do you care how he dies?"

"Oh, man, ma'am! Can you imagine the media circus? And think of the logistics! Whoever does the actual killing would have to be a bonded and registered and licensed executioner."

"I guess so," Ravinia said.

"Yeah, no."

"So this is *not* your call? You're worried the federal government will step in and put a stop to it as soon as the plan leaks to the press?"

"I'd like to see 'em try."

"Me too. Nobody tells you what to do."

"This is crazy," Yanno said. "You know that."

"Of course we know that," Ravinia said. "But I intend to vigorously defend my client's rights, and I believe that your own words—and your own publication—grant him the opportunity to choose his method of death, provided it is guaranteed successful and carried out no later than the date of his execution as prescribed by the court. Further, I find nothing to preclude this in the laws of the state, no precedent that would countermand your judgment, should you choose to comply with my client's legal wishes."

Thomas had seen Ravinia get her back up, but never like this. She had gone from doing her father a favor by looking out for Brady Darby to now seeming to own this fight.

"Sir," she said, "you don't want to face a legal challenge that might come from Mr. Darby if his wish, far-fetched as it is, is denied."

Frank LeRoy seemed to freeze. "You come to me with this craziness and now you're threatening me?"

"No, sir. I'm trying to help you. All we're asking for is permission, and to my eyes, you just have to decide whether you want to face a lawsuit on this."

"From Darby, you mean."

"Of course. I'm not worried about outside agitators, because you've already proven you know how to deal with them and are on record that this is not their decision."

LeRoy heaved a huge sigh. "I got to ask you a question, Darby. Why do you want to do this—this way, I mean? What's the point? You think you're dying for your crime, makin' some kinda atonement?"

"That's a really good question," Brady said.

"Thanks. I've been known to come up with one every once in a while."

"No. I can't atone for my own sin. That's already been done. I have just one reason, and that's so people can see what crucifixion really was. It was one of the worst ways a person could die, but I don't think we understand that anymore. If just one person finally gets what it meant for Jesus to be humiliated like that, beaten and broken and bleeding for them, it will be worth it. I'm going to die anyway, sir. Let me do it this way."

"And how are people supposed to see this? I'm not letting the press in here for that."

"Just one camera," Ravinia said.

642

LeRoy stood slowly and thrust his hands deep into his pockets. "Never a dull moment with you, is there, Darby? If it's not one thing, it's another. Well, no promises, because as much as your attorney wants to badger me into making this decision on my own by accusing me of kowtowing to the feds, truth is, I can't do this without Andreason and the governor. So all I can say right now is, I'll let you know. If someone with a camera wants to pursue this, given all the restrictions I'm gonna put on 'em, they'll have to sell me on how it would work. Bringing equipment onto this property and keeping it from being a distraction or threatening our security? I can't imagine."

"Thank you, sir," Ravinia said.

Thomas nodded his thanks.

"Humph. You're all nuts. And believe it or not, I'm not big on watching people die, even if I am a proponent of capital punishment."

"I would want you to watch, Warden," Brady said. "I want everybody to see it, not because of me, but like I said, so they know what it was really like."

"An awful lot of stuff is going to have to come together before this gets that far, son. I may need a pit bull like your attorney here in *my* corner before it's all said and done."

"You want my card?" Ravinia said.

Thomas and Ravinia went all the way back to the administrative wing with the warden without saying a word until they stopped before Yanno's office.

"Got to tell you," the warden said, "I've been through all kinds of stuff on this job, but this is a first. Has to be the craziest mixed-up deal I've ever heard. Ma'am, I expect we'll be seeing a lot of each other for a while. You realize this thing is just insane enough to happen."

It was all Thomas could do to keep from shaking his head until Ravinia had followed him into his office and the door was shut.

"I can't believe what I just heard, Rav. You played him like a fiddle."

Ravinia kicked off her heels and propped her feet on the edge of his desk. "I've never even considered writing a memoir," she said. "But this would be chapter one."

Thomas studied her. "This whole idea has captured you, hasn't it?"

Ravinia lowered her feet to the floor and looked away.

"What is it, sweetheart?" Thomas said.

She shook her head. "I told Brady it would take a miracle to make this happen."

69

Adamsville

Gladys's husband, Xavier, was a tall, knuckly man whose arms glistened black in the autumn Saturday sun. He labored over the charcoal grill in Thomas's backyard as Dirk cavorted with Summer. Ravinia sat with her mother, who—despite the Indian summer day—sat in a chaise longue bundled in a blanket to her neck.

Grace would tell Thomas later that the highlight of the day for her was discovering that Gladys shared her love of the old hymns and getting the chance to sing the melody on some of her favorites, countered by Gladys's bluesy alto.

After the little impromptu concert, Thomas and Gladys watched Xavier work from a respectable distance. "I'm glad you let him do this," Gladys whispered. "He won't admit it, but I think you offended him by implying he cooks for a living. You know he owns the place and just supervises now, only cooks in a pinch. He's loving this."

Thomas worried where everyone would sit at the picnic table, what with Dirk and Ravinia still living apart and enduring this only for the sake of their daughter. He decided to just sit next to Grace and let the others sit where they wanted.

"C'mere a minute, Rev," Gladys said, moving into the shade. "You got to tell me what's going on at work. I promise not to say a word, but what in the world is it with all the meetings with Andreason and even the governor? They gonna shut us down?"

"Shut us down? Really, Gladys. What would they do with all the inmates?"

"I don't know, but it has to be about money. It always is. I mean, this state is proud of all of its prisons, but the budget is in deep trouble."

"That's nothing new," Thomas said. "You think it's worse than it's been?"

"I'm not blind," Gladys said. "Something is going on."

Thomas was debating how much to tell her when Summer squealed that she wanted to see Grandpa, and his son-in-law brought her over. "Anything new with Darby's scheme?" Dirk said as Summer climbed onto Thomas's back.

"Darby's what?" Gladys said.

"Nothing," Dirk said, looking sheepish. "You heard nothing from me."

"Me either," Thomas said.

"All right," Gladys said. "I told you about the budget; you tell me what else is going on."

Dirk looked stricken and apologetic. "Goodness, Dad, I thought sure *she'd* know."

By the time they sat to eat Xavier's award-winning barbecue spare ribs and chicken, everyone was talking about Brady Darby's bizarre idea.

"No specifics in front of little ears," Ravinia said, dabbing her mouth. "And needless to say, none of this can go farther than this yard."

Two weeks later, the incendiary news engulfed the world. No one knew how the information had leaked from the prison to the International Cable Network (ICN), and it didn't matter anymore. Somehow the whole freakish plan had reached just the right person. All that mattered now was that the prison's money woes were over, and Brady Wayne Darby was the most famous man in the world for reasons far beyond his having been the Heiress Murderer.

Chaplain Thomas Carey was slowly coming to think Brady's idea might have some merit after all. The way things were coming together, maybe God was behind it.

The press credited the almighty dollar.

The news bombshell hit the planet simultaneously, as choreographed by ICN. Moments after dawn in every time zone, everybody everywhere was aware of the facts and began spouting their opinions.

The International Cable Network had, for an undisclosed sum that most estimated in the high eight figures, secured all media rights—including Web, radio, TV, motion picture, book, and any subsidiary right anyone could imagine—to a singular event. They would film, with one stationary camera, the execution of Brady Wayne Darby by crucifixion.

ICN reserved the right to show the footage live on international television, and naturally that announcement alone resulted in unending public debate over the next two years.

Besides its enormous payment to the state, and specifically to the Department of Corrections and its crown-jewel supermax, Adamsville State Penitentiary, ICN committed itself to a laundry list of obligations.

These included guaranteeing the security of the facility and its inmates, covering all related costs, and scheduling a separate extensive documentary that would put ASP in the best light.

Of primary importance to the Department of Corrections was that Darby not have personal access to the media. He could not be interviewed. It was, Warden Frank LeRoy said, a policy for which he could not finagle an exception. Neither was Darby, nor anyone associated with him, to benefit financially from the project.

The only further concession to Brady was that ICN agreed to pay for a simple headstone and a tiny section of the prison grounds where he would be buried four days after his death.

The firestorm of vitriol that resulted included dire predictions from pundits that all manner of public agencies would begin parlaying their capital cases and, in essence, selling condemned inmates to the media to show public executions.

Cooler heads pointed out that this spectacle was Darby's own idea and that no man or woman without a specific agenda like his was likely to allow the broadcast rights to his or her execution to be sold for the benefit of the state.

Virtually every municipality in the world immediately acted to prevent similar eccentric displays, and the federal government filed suit against the state to preclude what it called "a fiasco with the potential for irreparable harm to the common good."

While the case dragged on—Governor Allard guaranteeing he would defend states' rights to the end—a cross was donated from a research facility in Israel that claimed the item was as close to the first-century Roman death contraption as it could be.

Adamsville State Penitentiary

Meanwhile, Brady devoted himself to becoming more than a curiosity. With the exuberant support of his aunt Lois (and, she assured him, her entire church), he was determined to get to know Jesus as well as he could in his time left on earth. He requested books from the chaplain's library and began memorizing Scripture and reciting it aloud in his cell, despite a constant barrage of abuse from every con within earshot.

The at-long-last meeting with his aunt had been a curious affair, the two of them with both hands pressed against the Plexiglas as they wept and talked and prayed and sang.

"Somehow I always knew God had something in mind for you, Brady," she said.

He had to smile. "You coulda fooled me. Thanks for never giving up on me."

Brady spent most of his time pacing, memorizing, and quietly reciting line after line of Jesus' words from the Bible. He spoke just above a whisper, but no one could have heard him if he had shouted, such was the clamor from within death row.

"Think you're Jesus now, Heiress Boy?"

"Whatcha think Katie North thinks of you now?"

"You gonna burn in hell no matter how you die!"

And on and on it went.

Ravinia finally secured permission for Brady to listen to tapes and CDs in his cell, and besides recordings of the Gospels, he got to enjoy Grace Carey's a cappella hymns, humming along and sometimes singing with her while glancing at her photograph on the wall.

He had finally got Thomas to tell him all about her and not just her illness. Brady felt he really knew her, at least from Thomas's perspective. He enjoyed their love story and the adventure of their early married life as they ventured out for God.

All Brady's studying and thinking had made him more introspective and curious, and his sensitive questions seemed to open the chaplain to revealing more of his own life. Brady suffered with him through the tales of disappointment, especially Grace's leukemia.

One thing the man would not reveal, however, was much about his daughter. Chaplain Carey would rhapsodize about his granddaughter, but perhaps because Mrs. Carey-Blanc was Brady's lawyer, her father did not feel free to reveal much. Brady was getting the picture, though.

Adamsville

Thomas was energized as never before to get to the prison every day, as he finally had a disciple—what else could he call a man so eager to learn the things of God? It was as if the Lord Himself was making up for all that had gone wrong in Thomas's life by allowing him this one amazing student.

Thomas was stunned at the growth and maturity he detected in Brady, despite all that swirled about him. The prison, specifically Frank LeRoy, worked hard at protecting the young man's privacy and followed through on the commitment to keep Brady from the media.

Satellite trucks from every major news outlet in the world—not to mention every state, county, and local TV station—rimmed the vast prison property as far as one could see. They were restricted by barriers and overrun with the largest contingent of anti–death penalty demonstrators ever assembled in one spot. Various such groups had banded together and set up tent villages as close to the prison property fences as they were allowed.

Thomas couldn't get over the boredom that had to attend the unfortunate reporters and technicians who manned the TV trucks that sat there twenty-four hours a day. Day after day all they seemed to put on the air were interviews with protesters saying the same things over and over and prison employees who said they didn't know much and wouldn't be at liberty to say anything if they did.

Naturally that didn't stop the controversy. Enough employees were speaking anonymously, and many were making up stories. The press ran with everything, plausible or not, and opinion polls about the phenomenon became a cottage industry.

The press even camped out at Thomas's house until they tired of getting absolutely nothing from him. They tried to interview the mailman, delivery people, you name it, but though they surrounded Thomas every time he came and went, he followed the advice of his daughter and quit saying even, "No comment."

Each time he emerged to get in his car, he said, "Hello. Good-bye." And each time he returned from work or an errand, he said the same. Regardless how many cameras and microphones were stuck in his face, Thomas kept moving.

He apologized to the neighbors at every opportunity.

Eventually the media pulled away from Thomas's street, and Thomas knew Grace, for one, was grateful.

The press did, however, ferret out Erlene Darby, now living alone over a hash house in rural northern Florida. She said she couldn't afford to visit her son but that she was "glad he finally came back to Jesus, the way I raised him."

Thomas was intrigued at Brady's reaction to seeing that on the news. Knowing the man's history, he expected anger. But Brady just seemed sad. When public outcry forced ICN to pony up and fly Mrs. Darby to Adamsville for a visit, Brady told Thomas he was tempted to leave her name off the approved list.

"You can't do that," Thomas said. "No one would understand."

"If they knew the truth, they would."

"And yet they can't know that either, can they?"

About six months into the circus, Erlene Darby became a media star for a few days, her every step from Florida to the gate at ASP chronicled for all to see. In her late forties, she looked closer to sixty, haggard and pale despite a valiant makeover attempt sponsored by a popular talk show host.

"Hey, Ma," Brady said, forcing a smile.

She sat staring, and then she swore. "So, you're gonna die like Jesus. Why?"

"Thing is, I want to live like Him."

"Well if you don't sound like your aunt Lois. She been to see you yet?"

He nodded. "Got to see her one day and Uncle Carl the next. They've been wonderful."

"Which I haven't, is what you're saying."

"Haven't heard from you till now."

"You either. Don't put it on me."

"Let's not fight, Ma. I appreciate you coming."

"Well, I couldn't have except for the TV people. They're gonna pay me for a 'sclusive interview after, too. I just can't talk to anybody else on the way out of here. You should talk to somebody, get 'em to give me more."

"You want more money?"

"'Course! I ought to get something out of this. Never had anything, you know."

Brady fought to hide his disgust. "It's not up to me, and I'm getting nothing."

"Nothing? You're on TV every day! I never even knew anybody famous. Saw Merle Haggard once, or at least I thought I did; but then I found out he was on tour somewhere else, so I don't know who it was. But now my own son's on TV every day."

"Look what I had to do to accomplish that, Ma."

"Yeah, but TV."

"You'd murder to be famous?"

"Just about."

I'll bet you would. "So, anyway, thanks for coming."

"That's it?"

"You wanted something else?"

"I guess not, if you can't put in a good word for me with those TV people."

Erlene was hounded every step of the way from the prison to the exclusive interview and finally back to her ramshackle home. Brady forced himself to watch, heartbroken that she was clearly under the influence on national TV, though she had been able to recite a line that had plainly been crafted for her by some writer.

When asked if she would watch when her son died, she said, "Probably. But it'll be sad. He's the only one I have left. It's—what do you call it?—ironic. He was the devil growing up, and now he thinks he's Jesus."

That same broadcast also featured Jordan North for what he himself guaranteed would be the last time. "You bet I'll be watching," he said. "And I'll be cheering. This is all one cruel joke, but at the end of it, Brady Wayne Darby will still be dead."

No matter what radio or TV station Thomas turned to or what newspaper he read or whom he happened to run into at church, in his neighborhood, or even at the grocer, it seemed all he heard was what people thought about the idea of a public execution.

If the pollsters could be believed, the vast majority of people all over the world considered the idea barbaric and swore they would boycott it. Psychologists, on the other hand, prognosticated that few would follow through on that pledge, and media experts predicted that the event would be the single most-watched television broadcast in history.

Many stations went on record that they would not show the thing live and perhaps never, but ICN was negotiating with Web sites and private television venues, all the while publicly pontificating on the sacred right of responsible adults to decide for themselves what they preferred to watch.

One talk-show pundit intoned, "Need I remind all the nattering naysayers and holier-than-thou viewers that this was Mr. Darby's idea from the start? He *wants* mature adults to see it."

Thomas was impressed when Brady had Ravinia draft a statement in response. It said, "Mr. Darby wishes to clarify that his original intention was that viewers who choose to witness his death learn from it the cruelty and brutality of the crucifixion process. He did not have in mind a live TV spectacle in which the event may not be framed within its proper historic context. That said, he further urges that, if the broadcast is in the end allowed, parents will keep children from seeing it, as well as others who might be traumatized."

"Your daughter sure has a way with words," Brady said at his next meeting with Thomas. "Did you think that statement sounded like me at all?"

Thomas smiled and shook his head. "I'm sure she meant it to cover all the bases legally. But you know what you're going to have to speak to next. The whole issue of motive. Everybody knows by now, I think, that you are not benefiting from this beyond the fame and attention—"

"Which would do me no good anyway."

"Well, you'll have trouble convincing people of that. They think most criminals want attention above all. But I'm sure you've seen and heard the same things I have with all the coverage: people have their own ideas of what you're trying to accomplish."

"I keep the TV and radio off most of the time."

"I don't blame you, but you can't have it on for five minutes without hearing some expert, or some nobody, say you're trying to get into heaven by doing this. Like the warden suggested from the first, that you're trying to die for your own sin."

Brady shook his head. "You know that's not true."

Thomas nodded. "And yet you can see why people get that impression. It's human nature to suspect the worst."

"I guess I'll have to have my lawyer write another statement. Have you heard about this group that wants to worship me? They say I'm really Jesus come back to earth and that I'll rise again after three days."

"Saw it," Thomas said. "That'll be easy enough to disprove four days later, won't it?"

"You think your daughter can keep them from burying me until then, just to make it clear? Seriously, I wouldn't mind if they had a team of doctors that people trust do an autopsy and swear it's me, DNA and all, before they put me in the ground. I don't want to be another Elvis, where people claim they see me at Burger King years later."

Thomas laughed. "At least not without an endorsement deal."

Even Brady had to smile. "That's awful. If I'm going to reappear anywhere, I owe it to Burger Boy to show up there, don't I?"

Thomas drove home that day sad to his core about the eventual loss of his friend. But deep in his heart was also a flicker of hope about his own daughter. Something about her was changing. Was it just the time he and she were spending together? Was she seeing that Thomas wasn't such a bad guy after all? She was as earnest and committed to a cause as he had ever seen her, and yet her edge, her cynicism, her anger had seemed to soften. Maybe Brady was becoming her friend too and she was ruing what was to become of him.

70

Death Row

A year into the maelstrom of activity surrounding what was sure to be the most monumental media event in history, Brady was astounded at how much had changed, especially in his own life, which had settled into a unique routine.

A major part of his life continued as it would for anyone on the Row. He was awakened before dawn for first count, had his breakfast delivered, and every three days was soon thereafter escorted to the shower. Despite his celebrity and new casual friendliness to the officers, he was granted no special privileges during those routines. He was still searched, cuffed, escorted, uncuffed, stripped, showered, cavity-searched, dressed, cuffed, escorted back, and uncuffed every time. And he endured the same routine for his daily hour in the exercise kennel.

Brady's extravagance was that he enjoyed more time out of his house than any other inmate. Since it was impossible for him and the chaplain to accomplish anything with all the noise on the Row, they met approximately every other day in an isolation unit. There they studied Scripture and talked and prayed. Brady came to cherish every minute he had with the kindly old chaplain, whose enthusiasm never seemed to flag. Brady could tell when the reverend was worn-out and tired and worried about either his ailing wife or his spiritually straying daughter, and they soon began praying about those things too.

The advantage to incarceration was that Brady had almost all day every day to read, and it wasn't long before he had most of all four Gospels memorized. He gilded that by studying everything Chaplain Carey gave him on the life of Christ, by talking it through during their meetings, and even by studying the prophecies from the Old Testament concerning the Messiah.

The constant racket of the Row became just a backdrop of indistinguishable sound as he paced and recited verses aloud from just after breakfast to around midnight.

But one day in the spring, with just two months to go before his execution, something changed. On one of Brady's shower days, he awoke to the racket for first count and prayed silently while waiting for his meal. He ate all of it, as he had been doing for months now, then quietly cooperated with the laborious routine of getting to and from the shower. Along the way on both ends, Brady was aware of shouting, swearing, banging, and even an extraction when a con refused to return his breakfast tray to the meal slot.

But for once none of the commotion seemed directed at him. That was a nice break. Was it possible his commitment to never, ever respond had finally wearied the men and stolen their fun? They had kept it up for a whole lot longer than he ever would have without enjoying any reaction.

When Brady was dressed and back in his cell, he walked back and forth in the tiny area between his TV and the front corner of his cell opposite the toilet, very quietly reciting the words of Jesus he had memorized from the Gospels.

That had always elicited shouts and whistles, but today, nothing. In the past he could speak aloud and no one could hear over the daily ruckus. Now he was aware of a few men who had their TVs tuned to a morning game show, but oddly there was no conversation, let alone the usual shouting and cursing and barbs.

Brady was concentrating on remembering passages from the first half of Matthew. He closed his eyes, able to navigate the small space by memory.

In a normal tone, Brady began.

"Do not judge others, and you will not be judged. For you will be treated as you treat others. The standard you use in judging is the standard by which you will be judged. And why worry about a speck in your friend's eye when you have a log in your own? How can you think of saying to your friend, 'Let me help you get rid of that speck in your eye,' when you can't see past the log in your own eye? Hypocrite! First get rid of the log in your own eye; then you will see well enough to deal with the speck in your friend's eye."

Suddenly Brady stopped. Was it possible? He thought he had heard first one, then another shush noisy inmates. A couple of TVs even went off. From distant parts of the cellblock he heard other cons making noise, but the Row was virtually quiet. How could this be?

Brady held his breath. Was he dreaming? Surely not. He heard a low rumble of thunder outside, and soon heavy rain, and yet the Row got even quieter.

He continued, speaking evenly.

"Anyone who listens to My teaching and follows it is wise, like a person who builds a house on solid rock. Though the rain comes in torrents and the flood-waters rise and the winds beat against that house, it won't collapse because it is built on bedrock. But anyone who hears My teaching and doesn't obey it is foolish, like a person who builds a house on sand. When the rains and floods come and the winds beat against that house, it will collapse with a mighty crash."

Someone called out something, and another quieted him with a curse. It sounded like maybe two TV sets still blared until their owners were told to stifle them too.

Were these men listening?

"Foxes have dens to live in, and birds have nests, but the Son of Man has no place even to lay His head."

Brady waited. This was like a dance. Could he lead? Or was he imagining this?

"More," someone said quietly. Then another said the same. Then someone shouted it.

"Healthy people don't need a doctor—sick people

661

do. . . . Now go and learn the meaning of this Scripture: 'I want you to show mercy, not offer sacrifices.' For I have come to call not those who think they are righteous, but those who know they are sinners."

Brady hesitated again. Not a sound. He glanced at the observatory. Three officers had gathered on the other side of the glass, peering out, clearly as puzzled as he. The supervisor shrugged at Brady, then nodded, as if he should continue.

"Don't be afraid of those who want to kill your body; they cannot touch your soul. Fear only God, who can destroy both soul and body in hell. What is the price of two sparrows—one copper coin? But not a single sparrow can fall to the ground without your Father knowing it. And the very hairs on your head are all numbered. So don't be afraid; you are more valuable to God than a whole flock of sparrows."

Now, each time Brady stopped to gather his thoughts, the men seemed to encourage him to continue by making little noises, something tapped against their doors or scraped on their walls. He silenced the knocks and clacking by continuing.

"Everyone who acknowledges Me publicly here on earth, I will also acknowledge before My Father in heaven. But everyone who denies Me here on earth, I will also deny before My Father in heaven."

Brady stopped only for head counts and meals or when someone was taken to the showers. It was as if the entire Row was of the same mind, and everybody realized that the recitations would continue when a man returned. Brady did not stop when someone was in the exercise kennel, because they could still hear.

When he was summoned to the isolation unit for his regular meeting with the chaplain, Brady asked the officer to let Reverend Carey know that he should instead come to the cellblock. And Brady continued:

"O Father, Lord of heaven and earth, thank You for hiding these things from those who think themselves wise and clever, and for revealing them to the child-like. Yes, Father, it pleased You to do it this way!

"My Father has entrusted everything to Me. No one truly knows the Son except the Father, and no one truly knows the Father except the Son and those to whom the Son chooses to reveal Him.

"Come to Me, all of you who are weary and carry heavy burdens, and I will give you rest. Take My yoke upon you. Let Me teach you, because I am humble and gentle at heart, and you will find rest for your souls. For My yoke is easy to bear, and the burden I give you is light."

Isolation Unit

Thomas was alarmed when word came that Brady wanted him on the Row. He rushed through the security checkpoints, aware of the storm outside and wondering what might be wrong inside. When he reached the cellblock, he was struck first by the silence.

What could it mean? Anything out of the ordinary

here always resulted in more, not less, noise. These men had even been known to cheer the loudest thunderclaps, but they were ignoring the current boomers. Thomas glanced questioningly at a few officers, who just raised their eyebrows and shook their heads as if they had no clue.

As he neared Brady's cell, he could actually hear him quietly reciting Scripture.

"A good person produces good things from the treasury of a good heart, and an evil person produces evil things from the treasury of an evil heart. And I tell you this, you must give an account on judgment day for every idle word you speak. The words you say will either acquit you or condemn you."

When Brady saw the chaplain, he stopped and beckoned him close, though this resulted in more banging and knocking.

"What's happening, Reverend?" he whispered, telling him what had gone on.

"The Bible says the Word will not return void," the chaplain said. "Past that, I have no idea. But you should continue, don't you think?"

When Brady started in again, Thomas lowered himself to the floor and sat with his back against the cell.

"You are permitted to understand the secrets of the Kingdom of Heaven, but others are not. To those who listen to My teaching, more understanding will be given, and they will have an abundance of knowledge. But for those who are not listening, even what little

664

understanding they have will be taken away from them. That is why I use these parables, for they look, but they don't really see. They hear, but they don't really listen or understand."

Thomas started when he thought he heard a sniffle and then another. No way. Not these men. Not aloud, in view of each other! Brady himself seemed to grow emotional, his voice cracking. When he stopped, unable to continue, Thomas rose and picked up where Brady left off.

"If any of you wants to be My follower, you must turn from your selfish ways, take up your cross, and follow Me. If you try to hang on to your life, you will lose it. But if you give up your life for My sake, you will save it. And what do you benefit if you gain the whole world but lose your own soul? Is anything worth more than your soul? For the Son of Man will come with His angels in the glory of His Father and will judge all people according to their deeds.

"I tell you the truth, unless you turn from your sins and become like little children, you will never get into the Kingdom of Heaven. So anyone who becomes as humble as this little child is the greatest in the Kingdom of Heaven.

"'You must love the Lord your God with all your heart, all your soul, and all your mind.' This is the first and greatest commandment. A second is equally important: 'Love your neighbor as yourself.' The entire law and all the demands of the prophets are based on these two commandments."

When Thomas fell silent, the noises came from the surrounding cells once more, and Brady took over again. They traded off, continuing for hours, interrupted only by a count, a couple of showers, and finally by dinner. Thomas told Brady he had to get home to Grace but that Brady should continue for as long as he could.

"This is exhausting," Brady whispered. "Memorizing is one thing, but reciting for an audience really takes it out of you."

"I suggest you just announce when you're finished for the day and tell them when you will start again tomorrow. Who knows how long they will be willing to listen?"

"Let's try something," Brady said. "Let's have our next meeting here and see if they'll listen in while you teach me and we pray."

"Now you're really pressing your luck."

Brady chuckled. "My mentor would scold me for calling this luck."

Adamsville

Grace wept when Thomas told her of the phenomenon. She insisted he get the recorder and enlisted his help on a duet. When it seemed she didn't have the breath for a phrase, he carried the melody. The next day he would deliver one new song to Brady Darby, and if the cellblock was still cooperating, maybe they'd hear it too.

The love of God is greater far
Than tongue or pen can ever tell,
It goes beyond the highest star
And reaches to the lowest hell;
The guilty pair, bowed down with care,
God gave His Son to win:
His erring child He reconciled
And pardoned from his sin.

Could we with ink the ocean fill
And were the skies of parchment made,
Were every stalk on earth a quill
And every man a scribe by trade,
To write the love of God above
Would drain the ocean dry,
Nor could the scroll contain the whole,
Though stretched from sky to sky.

Death Row

Brady finished with a brief passage from Luke.

"The Spirit of the Lord is upon Me, for he has anointed Me to bring Good News to the poor. He has sent Me to proclaim that captives will be released, that the blind will see, that the oppressed will be set free, and that the time of the Lord's favor has come."

When he stopped, the light clanging began again, and Brady noticed that no TVs or radios were on. "I'll begin after breakfast tomorrow morning. Good night, all."

"Good night, Brady."

" 'Night, bro."

"See you then."

Here and there conversations began, but in normal tones of voice. A few TVs came on as Brady stretched out on his cot. He found himself overcome with emotion, little surprise after what he considered a daylong privilege. How long would it last? And wouldn't the press have a field day with this?

Brady turned toward the wall and shut his eyes, realizing that these men, his prison mates, had called him by name for the first time.

71

Administrative Wing

"This I got to see to believe," the warden said the next morning as Thomas sat across from him. "Quiet, you say?"

"Like nothing I've ever experienced here, sir, especially on the Row."

Gladys knocked. "Okay, what in heaven's name is going on?" she said, her fist full of paper. "We got all these in this morning's interoffice mail."

She slapped them down in front of the warden, and he began to pick through them, finally lifting his eyes to Thomas. "You been complaining about too light a workload. Well, here you go, Mr. Gung Ho."

Nearly every man on the Row had requested a visit

from the chaplain, and not one of them in the isolation unit.

"This is as close as I'll ever get to having a group meeting here," Thomas said.

"You better just go slow, that's all I got to say," Gladys said. "Something doesn't smell right, and the review board is gonna be sus-pi-*cious*. These men are up to something."

"Let's go down there," the warden said. "Gladys, how long has it been since you've been on the floor?"

"Oh no you don't. More'n six years, and that's too recent. I was with you, and they still wouldn't leave me alone."

"These guys might behave this time," Thomas said. "They would have yesterday; I guarantee it."

"Well, maybe so, but lucky for me and you, not to mention them, I'm busy."

Death Row

The polite banging and scraping began just as breakfast was ending, and someone called out, "Brady! You talking again today?"

Brady quietly began with passages from the Gospel of John.

"I tell you the truth, unless you are born again, you cannot see the Kingdom of God. . . . I assure you, no one can enter the Kingdom of God without being born of water and the Spirit. Humans can reproduce only human life, but the Holy Spirit gives birth to spiritual life. So don't be surprised when I say, 'You must be born again.' The wind blows wherever it wants. Just as you can hear the wind but can't tell where it comes from or where it is going, so you can't explain how people are born of the Spirit."

Brady hesitated as officers arrived at a cell across the way. It was time for the man's shower, but he held up his index finger as if asking that they wait a moment, and to Brady's utter amazement, they turned and looked at him, as if giving him permission to continue.

"These are the words of Jesus," Brady said. "No one has ever gone to heaven and returned. But the Son of Man has come down from heaven. And as Moses lifted up the bronze snake on a pole in the wilderness, so the Son of Man must be lifted up, so that everyone who believes in Him will have eternal life.

"For God loved the world so much that He gave His one and only Son, so that everyone who believes in Him will not perish but have eternal life. God sent His Son into the world not to judge the world, but to save the world through Him."

The intercom crackled. "Keep moving, gentlemen. Darby isn't going anywhere."

The officers escorted the man away, and Brady continued, breaking only while the shower was running. And while he waited silently, so did everyone else.

Thomas and the warden had showed up just as Brady was interrupted by the supervisor from inside the observatory. They stood off to the side, and Thomas peeked at the boss.

LeRoy was wide-eyed. "Can't believe it," he said.

When the shower stopped and all that could be heard was the man dressing and being cuffed, Brady began again.

"There is no judgment against anyone who believes in Him. But anyone who does not believe in Him has already been judged for not believing in God's one and only Son. And the judgment is based on this fact: God's light came into the world, but people loved the darkness more than the light, for their actions were evil. All who do evil hate the light and refuse to go near it for fear their sins will be exposed. But those who do what is right come to the light so others can see that they are doing what God wants."

Brady stopped and nodded at Thomas, who looked over at the warden.

"What?" LeRoy said.

"He wants me to jump in. May I?"

"And what, quote some verses?"

The signals from the cells began. "They want more."

"Then by all means. You can stand on your head and spit wooden nickels if it keeps them quiet."

Thomas stepped in front of Brady's house and turned to face the rest of the block.

" 'I know the plans I have for you,' says the Lord. 'They are plans for good and not for disaster, to give you a future and a hope. In those days when you pray, I will listen. If you look for Me wholeheartedly, you will find Me.'

"How can you say the Lord does not see your troubles? How can you say God ignores your rights? Have you never heard? Have you never understood? The Lord is the everlasting God, the Creator of all the earth. He never grows weak or weary. No one can measure the depths of His understanding. He gives power to the weak and strength to the powerless. Even youths will become weak and tired, and young men will fall in exhaustion. But those who trust in the Lord will find new strength. They will soar high on wings like eagles. They will run and not grow weary. They will walk and not faint."

Suddenly the place erupted with applause and cheering. Thomas was overcome and looked to Brady in tears, then stepped away.

Brady said, "I am not ashamed of this Good News about Christ. It is the power of God at work, saving everyone who believes. . . . This Good News tells us how God makes us right in His sight. This is accomplished from start to finish by faith. As the Scriptures say, 'It is through faith that a righteous person has life.' "

Thomas quickly collected himself and stepped back in as if part of a tag team.

"It is this Good News that saves you if you continue to believe the message I told you—unless, of course, you believed something that was never true in the first place. I passed on to you what was most important and what had also been passed on to me. Christ died for our sins, just as the Scriptures said. He was buried, and he was raised from the dead on the third day."

There was another lull as another man was escorted to the shower. The warden said, "I'm getting Gladys down here to see this. These guys'll behave; I can just feel it."

He moved into the observatory, and Thomas saw him on the phone. A few minutes later Gladys arrived, accompanied by an officer. She looked shy and tentative, and while Thomas had heard some catcalling as she advanced through the other units, not a man on the Row said a word.

As soon as the inmate was out of the shower, the clicking and clacking began, and Brady started in.

"I tell you the truth, the Son can do nothing by Himself. He does only what He sees the Father doing. Whatever the Father does, the Son also does. For the Father loves the Son and shows Him everything He is doing. . . . You will truly be astonished. . . . Anyone who does not honor the Son is certainly not honoring the Father who sent Him."

Brady paused. Then, "Jesus said, 'I tell you the truth, those who listen to My message and believe in God who sent Me have eternal life. They will never be condemned for their sins, but they have already passed from death into life.'

"Anyone who is thirsty may come to Me! Anyone

who believes in Me may come and drink! For the Scriptures declare, 'Rivers of living water will flow from his heart.' "

Thomas was startled when Brady stopped and Gladys stepped forward. She kept her head down, staring at the floor, her hands clasped before her. Then, in her low voice, at once sweet and raspy and soulful, she softly sang.

Alas! and did my Savior bleed,
And did my Sovereign die?
Would He devote that sacred head
For such a worm as I?

Was it for crimes that I have done
He groaned upon the tree?
Amazing pity! grace unknown!
And love beyond degree!

Well might the sun in darkness hide
And shut its glories in,
When God, the mighty maker, died
For His own creature's sin.

Thus might I hide my blushing face
While His dear cross appears,
Dissolve my heart in thankfulness,
And melt my eyes to tears.

But drops of tears can ne'er repay
The debt of love I owe;
Here, Lord, I give myself away—
'Tis all that I can do.

To a smattering of polite applause, Gladys hurried away.

"Gentlemen," Warden LeRoy said, "I don't want to spoil the mood. You boys are having some kind of church in here, and that's all right with me. Several of you requested visits from the chaplain, and, well, here he is. I'm overruling the policy that says you got to wait until the review board approves it. He's gonna go right down the line and talk with each of you as long as you want. That all right with you?"

"Can that lady come back and sing for us again sometime?" someone said.

"I don't see why not, if she's willing and you all act respectful. You know there's no assembling here, but I don't guess it violates anything if we bring the meeting to you. Everybody has to agree to it, though. One of you holds out and we can't do it. Anybody?"

No one spoke up.

"No guarantees, no promises, and no second chances. One incident and this all goes away."

Revival in a prison—and not just any prison but a supermax? And not just in any cellblock but on death row? Thomas felt he could have left for heaven right then.

Frank LeRoy turned and gave him a long look

before departing, and Thomas read into it everything he thought was implied—that the warden was impressed, stunned though he was, and that Thomas should do whatever was necessary to ride this wave as long as it lasted.

Brady took a break while Thomas began his rounds of visiting the prisoners. Apparently none of them wanted to miss Brady's recitations, so no one complained.

Some of the men were more articulate than others, but all expressed some variation of not knowing what had come over them. Some admitted they were embarrassed, but all asked for Bibles. Thomas would have to check his inventory. Running out of New Testaments had never been an issue before.

When he finished with the last man, he addressed them all. "I'm going to ask the warden if I can schedule a brief meeting like we just had—with some Scripture, a prayer, and even Gladys singing—every Friday if the Row has no incidents during the week. Fair enough?"

There was clapping and rattling.

Someone said, "No offerings now, hear?"

It wasn't long before the Death Row Revival leaked—likely through a corrections officer—and the story rivaled time on the air for the coming unique execution.

The cons seemed to enjoy hearing about themselves on the news, and somehow they were able to uphold their end of the bargain. As for the warden, the question was barely out of Thomas's lips before he said, "Yeah," not even followed by a "no."

"Got to love the reward system, Reverend. You've learned a thing or two here, haven't you?"

"I have, but I wouldn't have predicted this in a million years."

"Me either, but it's got to be a God thing, don't you think?"

"That's your assessment, Warden? You're giving God the credit?"

"Well, I'd love to say it was your doing or Brady's. Truth is, *I'd* love to take credit for it, but it just happened. And you say nothing just happens, right?"

"You won't get an argument from me, Frank. I do need to requisition some more New Testaments."

"Right now you can have just about anything you want."

72

Adamsville

D-day was approaching too rapidly. Thomas had come to love Brady Wayne Darby as a son and was already grieving the coming loss. The transformation in the man was unlike anything Thomas had ever seen. And the resultant revival in the most unlikely corner on earth had spread to other pods and cellblocks and showed no signs of abating. In fact, Thomas was busier than ever.

He found it harder and harder to leave Grace every morning. Her nights were becoming more difficult, and the doctor had urged him to admit her to a hospital or at the very least to start looking into hospice care at home.

"But hospice sounds like the beginning of the end, Doctor," Thomas said.

"Reverend Carey, your wife has been adamant about no radiation, chemo, or heroic measures. Her headaches, weakness, blurred vision, and balance issues are symptoms of a spread of cancer cells to the brain, so I'm afraid it's time to be realistic."

But Grace insisted she wanted to die at home, cared for by her family and friends from church. "That's all I ask."

More women from the church were added to the rotation, and every few nights, one stayed through to allow Thomas to get some sleep. On the one hand, he felt he was running on empty. On the other, with everything going on at ASP, he was able to keep his mind occupied and off his two impending losses for much of the day.

Several men were reading their Bibles daily, and Thomas was also teaching them individually a couple of times a week. A few had prayed to receive Christ, and each day he was visiting more men for the first time.

For hours every day, most of the inmates within earshot left their TVs off and listened to Brady reciting. They asked questions and he answered almost entirely in the words of Jesus. Meanwhile, Thomas made the rounds, making no attempt to whisper unless a man requested that, so he was able to minister to several at once while ostensibly visiting one.

And the men seemed to so look forward to their Friday meeting—though, of course, each remained in his own cell—that incident reports on the Row virtually disappeared. Every Friday Thomas spoke, Gladys sang, Brady recited, and someone prayed. Everybody behaved. A couple of times, even inmates other than Brady led in prayer. Other pods asked for similar sessions, and while Brady was not allowed to leave the Row, Thomas took Gladys or sometimes a CD of his wife's singing and recited Scripture as part of the program.

Thomas often brought a visitor just to observe. The warden was a frequent attender, Ravinia got a taste of it, and even Dirk stood off to the side for one session.

Ravinia seemed dumbstruck but told her father later, "I remember that 'first love of Christ' the New Testament refers to. I can see it in some of those guys."

Thomas was so tempted to urge her to return to her first love. She was a smart, successful woman in her early forties now, with a seven-year-old daughter and an estranged husband. Something had to give.

At long last the courts ruled that the crucifixion would not be allowed to be broadcast live on public airwaves. All that served was to change the International Cable Network's strategy. They went from cashing in through sponsors to cashing in through pay-per-view. Within days of the announcement, the event became the most subscribed-to feature in the history of television by four times.

The sign-up broke records in every country. Even on continents where it might air live at three or four in the morning, there seemed no flagging of advance sales.

"Sometimes," Thomas told Grace, "when I listen to Brady, I can almost forget it's him. It's as if I'm hearing Jesus. I've studied the Gospels since childhood, but he really brings it to life for me."

One of the hulking old men on death row, a tall, broad guy with a black and gray beard who called himself Skeet, asked Thomas if he could talk about "a whole different subject" at the end of their one-on-one Bible study one day.

"Briefly," Thomas said, peeking at his watch. "A lot more guys to see."

"I was just wondering. The pen is getting all this money for this crucifixion deal from ICN, right?"

Thomas nodded. "That's what I hear."

"We've all become pretty fond of this kid," Skeet said.

"Brady's no kid anymore. He's thirty-three."

"I know. Just like Jesus was."

"Right."

"Well, we're all gonna see him die when the DVD

comes out. But we're his friends now, and I think he wants us to see it when it happens. Some guys might not want to, but I do. It's like I want to be standing with him, know what I mean? It shouldn't take much for them to pipe that broadcast in here, to our TVs. Can you ask about that?"

Thomas went to Yanno, Yanno to Andreason, Andreason to the governor, the governor to ICN, and almost like that, it was done.

With Ravinia working late, Dirk brought Summer to see her grandmother one evening. Thomas had hoped to talk with Dirk, but he seemed distracted, not his usual self. He clearly didn't want to talk about family issues.

"This Darby has turned into some kind of a guy, hasn't he?" Dirk said.

Thomas heard Summer singing Sunday school songs to Grace in the other room.

"Dirk, he's the most transformed man I've ever seen. Some still say it's all for attention, but he's for real if anyone ever has been."

"He must really believe, though, right, Dad? I mean, he can't just change himself like that."

"I've never seen anyone else do it. And I've never been able to change myself. Have you?"

Dirk looked away and shook his head.

"Only God can change someone from the inside out," Thomas said.

"I'd better check on Summer."

"She's fine," Thomas said, but Dirk rushed into the bedroom.

"Let's let Grandma rest awhile, honey," he was saying as Thomas followed him in.

Grace did look exhausted, and Thomas detected pain in her eyes.

"I need to take care of her," Summer said.

"You already have," Grace managed. "I feel much better. Ready for my nap."

"Nap? Naps are for afternoons. It's almost bedtime!"

"Ready for bed, then."

"Grandma, are you going to die?"

Dirk looked stricken and reached for Summer.

Thomas spoke quickly. "Grandma's got lots of time left to see you grow up and—"

Grace held up a hand. "Guys, this child needs the truth, and she's going to hear it from me. If you're not comfortable with it, you don't have to stay. Dirk, do I have your permission?"

Summer was wide-eyed.

Dirk said, "I trust you, Mom. Just remember, I'm going to have to tell Rav whatever you say here."

"Ravinia would tell her the same things I will, I daresay." Grace turned to her granddaughter. "Sweetheart, yes, Grandma's going to die and go to see Jesus. Now, don't cry. I know you're going to miss me, and I'm going to miss you too. But I'm ready. You know why?"

"I don't want you to go, but 'course I know why. When are you going to die?"

"I don't know. When it's my time. The doctor thinks it could be another whole year. I hope so, because that gives me more time with you. But I'm okay either way because God knows best. He'll decide."

"I'm going to be sad."

"Sure you will, just like I was when my grandparents and my parents died. But they're all in heaven waiting for me, which is where I will be, waiting for you."

"I hope I never get lookameany or whatever that is."

Grace chuckled despite a grimace. "I hope you don't either. It's no fun."

"Don't die tonight, okay?"

"I'll try not to."

"Okay, bye."

Adamsville State Penitentiary

The next time Thomas wandered to the Row to listen, he was sobered to hear one dramatic line delivered by Brady from the Gospel of Matthew, when Jesus was speaking to His disciples: "We're going up to Jerusalem, where the Son of Man will be betrayed to the leading priests and the teachers of religious law. They will sentence Him to die. Then they will hand Him over to the Romans to be mocked, flogged with a whip, and crucified. But on the third day He will be raised from the dead."

To Thomas Carey, that passage alone signaled the end was near, not only for the story, but for his dear friend as well.

"It's going to be hard, seeing this done to you," Thomas whispered.

"It's not going to be 'done to me,' Reverend. This is my choice."

"The beauty of it is that it was Jesus' choice too."

"In case you're wondering, I haven't been sleeping well lately."

"That makes two of us," Thomas said.

"But there's no turning back," Brady said.

"You know you could be given tranquilizers first."

Brady shook his head. "That would defeat the whole purpose. I want to experience it and let the viewer see what it really was. I didn't expect this to be easy."

Thomas shook his head.

"Will you be with me, Reverend?"

"I don't want to watch, but if that's what you want, that's what I'll do."

"I'd like for you to come with me from my house to the chamber."

"Done."

As soon as Thomas got back to his office, Gladys said, "Caregiver called and says you need to get home."

"Oh no. What'd Nellie say?"

"Grace is fine, Thomas. Fact is, she's a little feisty. Nellie says Grace is insisting she call and order the pay-per-view for tomorrow."

"That can't be. That's the last thing Grace would choose to see."

"I'm just telling you what was told me. You want me to call Nellie back, or—?"

"Tell her I'm on my way. No way that's going to happen."

As Thomas drove out the front gate, he carefully picked his way through a thousand protesters, who by now recognized him from the newspapers and TV. They shouted and banged on his car and pleaded with him to stop the barbarism.

He couldn't find a radio station that wasn't airing opinions on both sides of the issue. All Thomas could hope was that everything would work as Brady had envisioned from the beginning and that millions would see what he wanted them to see—what Jesus endured for their sins.

At home, the matronly Nellie, who had agreed to stay until dawn, threw her hands up. "Talk some sense into her, will ya? I mean, I'll be gone, but if I was here, I wouldn't let her near that TV."

Thomas asked Nellie to fix Grace a light supper, then went in to talk with his wife. He intended to let her know he was not going to allow this. But she had an impish look, and he had to smile.

"What in the world?" he said. "You're not serious about this."

"And you're not going to deny me a last wish, are you?"

"Don't talk like that."

"I'm not being morbid. I'm just saying that I'm

asking for only this one thing, and I promise not to cross you on anything else as long as I live."

"Gracie, you turn your head when I squash a bug. You can't look when I'm emptying a mousetrap. When everyone else is craning their necks at an accident, you cover your eyes. Now you're telling me you want to see a man die?"

"The last thing in the world I want is to see anyone die, Thomas."

"I know, so—"

"It's not what I want. It's what he wants. Brady could have just taken the lethal injection, and justice would have been served. But God put it in his heart to show us something, to teach us something. Well, I think I need to see that too. When he was quoted about all the pretty pictures of the crucifixion, I knew exactly what he was talking about. If this will give me a truer picture of what it was really all about, I owe it to myself to see it."

Where was the timid little thing Thomas married?

"Now, Thomas, the news says the phone lines are jammed with procrastinators who are just now trying to sign up for this thing. So it may take you a while. I'm a grown woman, and I've decided it's what I want. If you won't do it for me, bring me the phone."

"I'll do it," he muttered.

Thomas skulked out into the kitchen, where Nellie was cooking. He dug out his credit card and gave her a sheepish look as he grabbed the phone.

"Wimp," she said.

73

Death Row

"No TV tonight, brothers!" Skeet said. "Let the man think."

All the TVs went off. Brady heard quiet conversations but nothing else. "Thanks, Skeet," he whispered.

He lay on his back in the darkness, pleading with God to make this whole thing be about Jesus and not about himself. Brady found himself naturally petrified at the thought of dying. *Lord, don't let that get in the way.*

He knew he should sleep, but there was no way he would be able to do more than doze for a few minutes at a time. His mind raced. Occasionally he had to rise and pace.

About four in the morning, wide-awake, Brady suddenly found himself enveloped in an agonizing fear. He had been so immersed in all the memorizing and reciting that he had somehow shoved from his mind the stark reality of his fate. He was going to die and in one of the most horrible ways imaginable. He had no doubt he was right with God and that he would be with Jesus in heaven, but to be crucified . . . and he himself had insisted on this!

"God, give me peace!" he whispered, realizing when he heard sounds from nearby cells that he had awakened some of the others. He covered his mouth, but his chest was heavy, his throat full.

Could he really go through with this? It was coming too quickly; he had been rash. Everyone said so, even his lawyer. Could she be reached in time to slow this, even stop it? His point had been made, people had heard his message, knew what he was about, knew what Jesus had done for them. Sure, there would be those who would call him a charlatan, a coward, an attention seeker, but he didn't care anymore.

He rolled out of bed and onto his knees on the cold floor. "Oh, God!" he cried out, unable to stifle himself. Suddenly Brady understood why Jesus had pleaded with His father to let "this cup" pass from Him. But Jesus had also insisted that His Father's will, not His own, be done. Brady couldn't do that, couldn't say it, didn't want to.

"I want out!" Brady said, sobbing. "God, please!"

He fell silent when he heard others rising from their beds, and he knew they stood at the fronts of their houses, watching, listening.

"We're with you, man," someone whispered.

"Yeah, Brady. Hang tough, bro."

Then Skeet, voice coarse and diction poor: "If any of you wants to be My follower, you must turn from your selfish ways, take up your cross, and follow Me. If you try to hang on to your life, you will lose it. But if you give up your life for My sake, you will save it."

The others tapped and rattled stuff against their cages, and Brady was overcome. He wept bitterly, pleading with God to give him the willingness Christ had exhibited in His darkest hour.

After nearly an hour of mental anguish, as his neighbors gently encouraged him with comments, scraping, rattling, Scripture verses, and even singing, Brady managed to rasp, "Not my will but Yours be done."

As he collapsed back onto his cot, Brady realized he still had ninety minutes before first count and breakfast. He had been asked what he wanted for his last meal, and he had said he wanted what everyone else was having. The warden told him that was a first. Brady couldn't imagine caring about food when you were about to die.

He rose and sat at his tiny table, sliding from the envelope his latest letter from Aunt Lois.

Brady,

We love you and we're going to watch this thing only because you made us promise. I go back and forth between being mad because you made us say we would and knowing that we probably need to see it like everybody else.

Just know we'll be praying for you all day. Carl and I will be there for the burial, but we know you'll be in heaven. No word yet from your mama about whether she can make it. You never know.

We're so proud of you, Brady. Just think, you'll be with Petey soon. We'll miss you, but we know we'll see you again someday.

Love, Aunt Lois

With ten minutes to go before the officers came around for the count, Brady found himself jumpy. One knee was bouncing, and he just wanted to get on with this. He prayed he would be able to be like Jesus, who was at once submissive and authoritative, enduring what He had to endure, willing but not eager.

Brady slipped the latest tape from the chaplain's wife into his player. He was alarmed at how weak and frail she sounded. She took deep breaths between phrases and long pauses between verses, but to Brady that made it only that much more poignant. Someone called out for him to turn it up.

> King of my life, I crown You now,
> Yours shall the glory be;
> Lest I forget Your thorn-crowned brow,
> Lead me to Calvary.
>
> Show me the tomb where You were laid,
> Tenderly mourned and wept;
> Angels in robes of light arrayed,
> Guarded You while You slept.
>
> Let me, like Mary, through the gloom,
> Come with a gift to You;
> Show to me now the empty tomb,
> Lead me to Calvary.
>
> May I be willing, Lord, to bear
> Daily my cross for You;

Even Your cup of grief to share,
You have borne all for me.

Lest I forget Gethsemane;
Lest I forget Your agony;
Lest I forget Your love for me;
Lead me to Calvary.

As soon as Brady was aware of the officers approaching, he moved to sit on his cot, ready to rise. But today, unlike every other day, there was no shouting or banging. In conversational tones the officers merely announced the count and moved somberly from cell to cell, noting that each man was alive and well.

"Morning, Brady," one officer said, quickly looking away.

"How you doin' today, man?" another said.

"Good luck today, or, you know . . ."

Brady just nodded to them.

The same happened when breakfast was delivered. No barking about standing back, no yelling at anyone. Brady had the feeling that this was what it would be like in an old-age home, staff just quietly making the rounds, delivering trays. The officers even seemed to open and shut the meal slot doors quietly, no small feat.

Not surprisingly, Brady was not hungry, and the food did not appeal. But he forced himself to eat and drink everything, knowing how difficult the task ahead would be.

Thomas had barely slept, while Grace was so quiet all night that he had checked three times to be sure she was breathing. She was either at peace about all this— sad as it was—or failing. He tried not to think about that.

He rose before dawn, knowing the day would be a scorcher. It had to be ninety degrees already, and the sun was just a pink hint on the horizon. Thomas had dreaded this day for so long, he didn't know how he would get through it.

He began on his knees, then showered and shaved and dressed. Then he read his Bible and prayed again. Finally he went to tap on the den door, where Nellie was sleeping, but the door was open and the room empty. He heard her in the kitchen.

"Poached eggs and toast," she said. "And I'll stay till your daughter gets here."

"Thanks, Nellie."

"You sure you don't want any day shift here?"

"No, Ravinia will be able to handle things. She'll be here by eight or so. A woman from my office will be here by then too."

Thomas had hoped to have breakfast in the bedroom with Grace, but she was still sleeping.

"I'll keep hers warm," Nellie said.

Thomas thanked her and headed out to the car. There, parked at the curb in front, was Dirk's car, and he was asleep behind the wheel.

Thomas tapped lightly on the window, making Dirk jump.

"What're you doing here?" Thomas said. "Everything all right?"

"Yeah, I just got it in my head to take the morning off and watch this thing here, if that's okay."

"You know Rav is coming."

Dirk nodded. "It might be a little awkward, but this just seems like the kind of thing you do with people you care about, know what I mean?"

"She know you're coming?"

"I told her I probably would."

"Well, go ahead on in. Nellie will fix you something. And I'll see you later."

The streets were deserted until Thomas reached the road leading to the penitentiary. Police were already having to direct traffic there, with satellite trucks jockeying for position and protesters emerging from tents and huddling around campfires. Their signs read, "Shame! Travesty! Pardon Brady!"

At the guardhouse, the officer ignored Thomas's badge and merely patted him on the shoulder. "Parking lot's full," he said. "Anybody not sick or on vacation is on the job today. We left a cone in front of your spot. Just set it off to the side."

Thomas was not surprised to find Frank LeRoy already in his office. What was a surprise was that he was wearing a new suit and had his shirt buttoned all the way up, tie tight at the neck. He clearly expected to be on TV today. He merely nodded as Thomas greeted him on the way by.

Gladys startled him with a "Mornin', Rev." He'd never seen her in her cubicle this long before starting time. It was also the first time in seventeen years he had seen her in anything but bright colors. She wore a demure, dark suit. She stood and embraced him. That was something new too, and while any other day it would have made Thomas uncomfortable, today he appreciated it. "You're still planning—?"

"Yes, sir, I'm about to head over there and spend the rest of the day with Grace. Your daughter too, right?"

"And son-in-law."

She raised a brow. "Really?"

Thomas shrugged. "Go figure."

"Surely not Summer."

"Oh no. Vacation Bible school."

Thomas looked at his watch. Brady was scheduled to leave his cell in fifteen minutes, and Thomas had promised to accompany him. He made it through the security envelopes in record time, old friends just nodding soberly and waving him through. The place was full of officers, every shift represented, all in crisp, clean uniforms, shoes shining, brass polished.

Normally when Thomas happened to be on the Row this early in the morning, every cell TV was tuned to the *Today* show. But now the few sets already on showed a silent, still view of the crude cross lying on the floor of the gas chamber. It reminded Thomas of C-SPAN coverage when a camera was just set in place and left on for the duration of whatever they were covering. This was the feed that would encircle the globe for the next several hours.

Thomas found Brady putting the last of his personal effects into a cardboard box on his table. He looked preoccupied and yet relieved to see the chaplain.

"You ready?" Thomas said.

"Ready as I'll ever be. Doc's supposed to check me over in a couple of minutes; then it's the whole searching and cuffing thing, then heading out."

Thomas turned to peer into the observation booth. A supervisor nodded from the other side of the glass. "Can I see you?" Thomas mouthed.

The intercom crackled. "C'mon in, Reverend."

The door was open by the time he got there and Thomas stepped inside. "Tell me the procedure."

"Officers will strip-search him, then cuff and manacle him before the doc checks him over."

"All right, I want that not to happen."

"But we got to go by the book today, sir—"

"Don't strip-search this man today, and don't restrain him either. You know as well as I do he's no risk. I'll be right there the whole time, and you can blame it all on me."

"Reverend, I don't think you're authorized to override protocol—"

"I'm asking you man-to-man. And I want to be in his cell when the doctor is."

"I can't let—"

"Yes, you can. Now you've been here through all

this, and you know what Darby's meant to the Row. Throw him a bone, man."

The supervisor pressed his lips together and looked past Thomas to where the doctor had arrived, accompanied by an officer. "All right, go ahead."

"Thank you."

"Just hurry."

Thomas met the doctor in front of Brady's cell, and they shook hands.

Over the intercom, the supervisor said, "Darby, to your cot please. I'm tripping the release here, officers. Admit both the chaplain and the doctor. No search, no restrains, but secure the door."

The officers looked surprised and hesitant, but the order had been clear. Seconds later, the three men were locked in Brady's cell.

The doctor had Brady sit at his table while he checked his pulse and blood pressure. "Both elevated," he said softly, scribbling.

"So I should take it easy today?" Brady said.

The doctor looked like he didn't know how to react. "I'll see you in the chamber, son. This is an amazing thing you're doing."

The doctor was let out and the door thrice locked again. Thomas was aware that all the officers in the observation unit had emerged, and all but the two officers stationed at Brady's cell were moving down the corridor away from the pod. What was going on?

Brady stood awkwardly and reached for Thomas. They embraced, and the young man buried his face in the chaplain's shoulder. "Pray for me," he said.

Thomas found his voice quavery. "Lord, thank You for Your servant and for what You have prompted him to do. And thank You for the impact he's already had. We know justice will be served today, but we pray Your greater purpose will be served too and that many will come to know You in deeper ways because of what they see. And thank You for what Brady has meant to me. In Jesus' name."

"Guess you heard they denied my request for the crown of thorns and someone to pierce me with the spear."

"No. Really?"

"Just got word this morning."

"Believe me, son," Thomas said, "it will be easy enough for everyone to imagine."

"I just wish the warden would have allowed it," Brady said. "The thorns were as much a part of the crucifixion as anything else. They weakened Him, crippled Him. And the fact is, His side *was* riven."

Thomas nodded to the supervisor, who instructed the officers to unlock Brady's cell. "No search. No restraints."

As they were maneuvering Brady into the corridor, one of the officers said, "Reverend, you know there's a bunch of us officers who are believers and some who are real interested. You think you could meet with us sometime, off-hours?"

"Absolutely."

"Proceed" came over the intercom.

With one officer on each of Brady's arms and Thomas about six feet behind, they slowly began the walk through the cellblock. With Brady's first step, the men on the Row began a slow tapping on their cell doors, and this continued the whole way.

When the tiny procession reached the end of the pod, Thomas saw that the rest of the way through security and all the way to the exit, officers were lined up on either side, standing shoulder to shoulder, feet spread, hands clasped behind their backs, heads lowered. As Brady reached them, each raised his head, snapped to attention, arms at his sides, feet together.

Thomas could barely breathe.

74

Moved by the respect and reverence shown Brady as he was escorted to the chamber, still Thomas felt as if he himself were on his way to the gallows. He fought to not show weakness or grief before Brady now, but this was the longest, most difficult walk of his life.

"Just stay close," was all Brady asked.

The warden appeared behind them. "Time for your good-byes, gentlemen," he said.

It was too soon. Thomas sensed the clock speeding. When Frank LeRoy retreated and took other dignitaries with him, Thomas and Brady were left with just the officer who would lead them in.

"So," Thomas said, "I guess this is it. I love you, Brady."

Brady looked to the officer as if for permission, and when the man nodded, he embraced the chaplain and whispered, "Jesus said, 'Be sure of this: I am with you always, even to the end of the age.'"

"It's time," the officer said.

Thomas followed the officer and Brady into the chamber, which contained the single camera, four officers lining one wall, a cheap plastic chair for the chaplain, and a rangy man in shirt and tie who had draped his suit coat over the chair. He looked self-conscious standing next to a wood tray filled with spikes and a heavy wooden mallet.

"I've practiced this and will do my best is all I can promise," he said.

"Thank you," Brady said.

God, Brady prayed silently, *we both know who I am, but let me be Jesus for these people and everyone who ever sees this, just so they know what He went through.*

A technician, the laminated card clipped to his shirt identifying him as from ICN, slipped in and double-checked the camera. "Rolling," he said quietly, backing out. The door shut and the curtains were opened, revealing the most crowded viewing area Thomas had ever seen for an execution.

"Stand by!" the warden called out. "When you're ready."

Brady hung his head, eyes welling. He imagined himself mocked, jeered, beaten, spit upon. He removed his clothes and stood shivering in his underwear. He had studied this and wished he could also have been shoved up against a broad pole and suspended from the top by his bound hands and there whipped thirty-nine times by a cat-o'-nine-tails, leather strips embedded with bits of rock and iron that would lacerate his back from his shoulders to his waist and lay him open.

Experts claimed irreparable damage had been done to Jesus' body and that parts of His spine and even internal organs would have been exposed. Each new stroke had dug deeper until Jesus had finally been released to crumble to His knees.

I'm getting off easy, Brady thought. If he could just force himself to go through with this.

"Lie down across the planks," the executioner said kindly.

Sickened, Thomas stole a glance at the TV monitor to see what was being broadcast. All Thomas could think of was whether Grace yet regretted her decision to watch.

Brady was shuddering, and Thomas leaned forward. "You all right?" he said.

"Fine, Reverend. Let me be."

"Let me get you a bottle of water," Thomas said, aching to cradle him.

"Please, no," Brady said, barely able to be heard. "This has to be authentic as we can make it."

"It's too close."

"Then we're doing it right. Please. I know you mean well."

Thomas sat back, gripping both sides of his chair and wishing he could be anywhere else, yet not willing to abandon his friend.

"Final check of vitals," Frank LeRoy called out, and the doctor stepped in, kneeling next to Brady.

Brady dreaded being nailed to the cross more than he dreaded the end. The state executioner was the only man there licensed to inflict upon Brady intentionally lethal injuries. He alone would drive spikes through Brady's wrists and feet, and at Brady's insistence, it would be done precisely so as to remain as close as possible to the scriptural account that none of Jesus' bones had been broken.

There were few angles and spots where the spikes could be driven to achieve that accuracy, and the man had to be strong enough to strike cleanly and quickly. The spikes had to hold Brady's weight when the cross was raised by the officers into specially designed supports. Brady knew his pinning to the cross and its being raised alone could kill him if the men weren't careful.

Was Brady's own mother watching? He knew Aunt Lois and Uncle Carl were. And Mrs. Carey. And Mrs. Carey-Blanc. And her husband. The guys inside. And much of the world.

God, don't let this be in vain. Let them see what You want them to see. Your will be done.

The executioner advanced.

When the man grabbed Brady's arm and stretched it out on the crossbeam, it was all Brady could do to keep from pulling away. He closed his eyes and gritted his teeth. One of the officers straddled his hand and placed one knee in his palm and the other near Brady's elbow. His flesh dug into the wood.

The executioner deftly lined up the spike just below the heel of Brady's hand, and Brady could feel the cold steel and the shift in the man's weight as he raised the thick wood mallet.

With a loud thunk the hammer drove the spike clean through Brady's wrist and into the crossbeam.

Brady cried out as blinding pain shot through him. All else was forgotten as flesh and tendon and sinew gave way and nerves fired messages of agony to his brain. With another quick blow, the spike was driven deep into the wood and Brady's wrist further severed.

He writhed and moaned and cried, his legs spasming as the men shifted to the other arm and repeated the ritual. Brady closed his eyes as everything around him spun madly. He could not imagine worse pain.

When the process was repeated to pin his feet to the vertical beam, he thrashed and pulled, heart thundering and breath coming in great gusts through clenched teeth.

Brady knew he was in danger of going into shock. He fought to stay conscious, determined to see this through. Chaplain Carey looked deeply pained. Brady only hoped his friend and mentor could imagine Jesus Himself enduring this for him.

Deep in another part of his consciousness, a hidden chamber he was surprised even existed, Brady was aware that many people who loved him and cared for him were weeping and saying their good-byes. Such a difference from those who jeered Jesus and called out to Him, demanding to know how He could save others and not Himself.

Even in the midst of His agony, Jesus had not forgotten His mission. "Father," He had said, His voice certainly as raspy and guttural as Brady's felt now, "forgive them, for they don't know what they are doing."

Brady came close to crying out for relief when the corrections officers gathered and used a rudimentary pulley to lift the cross upright. Everything in Brady cried out, even before they let it drop into the supports, and his whole weight pulled against the torn flesh around the spikes.

It was then that Brady fully understood what it was he was trying to get the world to see. Jesus had not just hung there in beautiful repose. He had to have done what Brady was forced to do now. Brady hung in a position that allowed him to draw breath, but to exhale he had to jerk and hunch himself up until his strength gave out and he slumped again, unable to exhale. He would die of asphyxiation if he didn't muster the strength to rise a few inches every several seconds. All this while his bloody, pierced body writhed, and every effort to rise and exhale put all his weight on the spike-torn wounds.

His head banged against the wood, and Brady felt himself slipping away. He closed his eyes against the pain and imagined he could hear the thieves hanging on either side of Jesus, one saying, "So You're the Messiah, are You? Prove it by saving Yourself—and us, too, while You're at it!"

But the other said, "Don't you fear God even when you have been sentenced to die? We deserve to die for our crimes, but this Man hasn't done anything wrong. Jesus, remember me when You come into Your Kingdom." And Jesus had responded, "I assure you, today you will be with Me in paradise."

Brady hunched again to exhale, knowing he was fighting the clock. His vision was going, his muscles cramping.

It was all he could do to breathe. Everything in his system fought for relief and labored to keep him alive, yet he was drifting, drifting. He had to exhale but didn't know if he had the strength.

For more than two of the worst hours of Thomas's life, he sat transfixed, tears streaming, as Brady continued to thrash just enough to exhale every few seconds. It seemed the young man would die any moment, and yet he lingered, writhing. Thomas was aware of spec-

tators who rose and left, clearly having not been prepared for such a lengthy ordeal.

God, please, Thomas said silently. *He's obeyed You.
Take him.*

Brady fought to pull himself up one last time, and as
he exhaled, he forced himself to speak once more the
words of Jesus.

"Father, I entrust my spirit into Your hands!"

Thomas stood as Brady's chest heaved, his limbs
twitched, and suddenly he was still.

"Doc!" the executioner called out.

The doctor slipped in and slid Thomas's chair to the
foot of the cross, mounted it, and pressed his stethoscope to Brady's chest. He pronounced him dead,
marking the time.

Thomas had seen enough. He had honored Brady's
request and learned the hardest way possible what
Jesus had endured on his behalf.

Thomas hurried away, out of the chamber, down the
long corridors, through the security envelopes, past
the cellblocks and pods. All were as silent as he had
ever heard them.

In every cell, at every security checkpoint, and even
in every office in the administration wing, TVs
showed the closed-circuit feed to sober, somber eyes.
No one spoke or even acknowledged Thomas as he
gathered up his stuff and headed out to his car.

The officer at the guardhouse waved him through,

and he drove past the media and the protesters—now on their knees, cupping candles incongruously flickering in the midday sun.

Fortunately for Thomas, hardly any other cars were on the road. At home he found Gladys sitting next to Grace's bed, holding his wife's hand as they silently watched the wrap-up of the televised coverage.

Dirk and Ravinia sat on Thomas's bed, ashen faced.

Thomas sat next to his daughter and draped an arm around her shoulder. She was shivering. Suddenly she let her head fall to her father's chest and buried her face in him as she sobbed.

After several minutes she pulled away, wiping her face. "I'm going to go," she managed. "I need to be with Summer."

"I need to be with you both," Dirk said softly.

"Well, come on, then," she said.

They each embraced Grace, and Thomas followed them to the front door and watched as they walked to their respective cars. Dirk put a tentative hand on Rav's shoulder. She slipped a hand around his waist.

Before they parted, they stopped and held each other.

EPILOGUE

Not since 9/11 had churches been so full, and this time the phenomenon circled the globe. Every ministry Thomas knew of reported record inquiries and changed lives. Thomas himself had been busy since the little revival started on death row months before, but even that was nothing compared to now. He even had to talk with Warden LeRoy about hiring help. Requests for visits and New Testaments and books poured into his office.

Four days after Brady Wayne Darby was crucified, his autopsy became part of the public record, and he was buried in a quickly fashioned one-grave cemetery at Adamsville State Penitentiary, per the agreement with ICN. No press was allowed.

Thomas officiated the brief, very private ceremony, attended by fewer than twenty people. Besides a few state officials, the group consisted of the warden, the warden's secretary and her husband, Brady's aunt and uncle, his mother, his lawyer, her husband, and the chaplain's wife.

Grace was bundled head to toe despite the heat and sat in a wheelchair. Thomas knew it was likely her last venture outside their home. But she had insisted on attending, and he would not deny her.

After Thomas spoke and the casket was lowered, Gladys sang "Rock of Ages," which had been Grace's suggestion. Most hummed along, but

Thomas noticed that Ravinia joined in, full voice.

As they were leaving, Brady's aunt Lois confided to Thomas that Erlene Darby had agreed to move in with her and Carl, "just for a few months until she can get back on her feet. We're going to get her to church somehow."

Dirk and Ravinia were back in counseling and talking about his moving back home again.

Four months later, many of the same contingent joined the congregation at Village Church for Grace Carey's funeral. And, acceding to his beloved's last request, Thomas asked Gladys to sing the same hymn again.

> Rock of ages, cleft for me,
> Let me hide myself in Thee;
> Let the water and the blood,
> From Thy riven side which flowed,
> Be of sin the double cure,
> Save from wrath and make me pure.
>
> Not the labors of my hands
> Can fulfill Thy law's demands;
> Could my zeal no respite know,
> Could my tears forever flow,
> All for sin could not atone;
> Thou must save, and Thou alone.
>
> Nothing in my hand I bring.
> Simply to Thy cross I cling;

Naked, come to Thee for dress;
Helpless, look to Thee for grace;
Foul, I to the fountain fly;
Wash me, Savior, or I die.

While I draw this fleeting breath,
When my eyelids close in death,
When I soar to worlds unknown,
See Thee on Thy judgment throne,
Rock of Ages, cleft for me,
Let me hide myself in Thee.

Again Ravinia joined in the singing, and as she and Dirk and Summer rode with Thomas to the cemetery, she reached for her father's hand.

"I want to come home," she said.

"Oh, I'll be fine," he said.

"No, I mean home to church. Will you save me a seat?"

CHRIST
Yesterday, Today, Forever

Center Point Publishing
600 Brooks Road ● PO Box 1
Thorndike ME 04986-0001 USA

(207) 568-3717

US & Canada:
1 800 929-9108
www.centerpointlargeprint.com